Pippa Roscoe lives in Norfolk, near her family, and makes daily promises to herself that this is the day she'll leave her computer to take a long walk in the countryside. She can't remember a time when she wasn't dreaming about handsome heroes and innocent heroines. Totally her mother's fault, of course—she gave Pippa her first romance to read at the age of seven! She is inconceivably happy that she gets to share those daydreams with you. Follow her on Twitter @PippaRoscoe.

Canadian **Dani Collins** knew in high school that she wanted to write romance for a living. Twenty-five years later, after marrying her high school sweetheart, having two kids with him, working at several generic office jobs and submitting countless manuscripts, she got The Call. Her first Mills & Boon novel won the Reviewers' Choice Award for Best First in Series from *RT Book Reviews*. She now works in her own office, writing romance.

T0337246

NAUGHTY OR NICE?

PIPPA ROSCOE

DANI COLLINS

MILLS & BOON

First published in Great Britain 2024
by Mills & Boon, an imprint of HarperCollins*Publishers* Ltd,
1 London Bridge Street, London, SE1 9GF

www.harpercollins.co.uk

HarperCollins*Publishers*, Macken House, 39/40 Mayor Street Upper,
Dublin 1, D01 C9W8, Ireland

Naughty or Nice? © 2024 Harlequin Enterprises ULC

Forbidden Until Midnight © 2024 Pippa Roscoe

Husband for the Holidays © 2024 Dani Collins

ISBN: 978-0-263-32029-9

10/24

This book contains FSC™ certified paper
and other controlled sources to ensure responsible forest management.

For more information visit www.harpercollins.co.uk/green.

Printed and Bound in the UK using 100% Renewable Electricity
at CPI Group (UK) Ltd, Croydon, CR0 4YY

FORBIDDEN UNTIL MIDNIGHT

PIPPA ROSCOE

MILLS & BOON

For Annie West.

Thank you so much for your time,
your thoughts, your walks, your book recommendations
and your company!

A delight and a true joy.

xx

CHAPTER ONE

New Year's Eve nine years ago, Munich

SANTO SABATINI GAZED about him with such open disdain and barely suppressed irritation that the guests attending the Albrechts' party were giving him at least a three-foot-wide berth. He scowled again, shrugging into the black tuxedo jacket he disliked intensely. Supposedly the mark of money, Santo only associated the formal attire with the sneering superiority that disguised the kind of wilful ignorance and laziness that turned his stomach.

He would have turned his back on the whole sorry affair, but for one reason. Six years ago he'd made an unbreakable promise, a vow, and nothing and no one would stop him from fulfilling it.

Pietro had been more like a father to him than the bastard that had given him blood, genes and the eyes that stared back at Santo in the mirror every day. The only other thing he'd inherited from his father, after his death, was the Sabatini Group.

'I don't want it.'

'You don't have a choice, mio figlio,' his mother had said, tears streaming down a cheek still bruised from his father's fist.

'Careful,' a feline voice warned from behind him. 'The glass you're holding so tightly could snap.'

And just like that, Santo released the white-knuckled grip memories had tightened around the champagne flute's thin stem. The alcohol handed to him upon arrival now at an unappealing room temperature, he paused a passing waiter and swapped the champagne for whisky. Wiping any trace of his thoughts from his features, he turned back to see Marie-Laure taking in the impressive display of opulent Renaissance architecture of the Munich Residenz's Hall of Antiquities.

'The Albrechts have outdone themselves this year,' Marie-Laure observed, unable to hide the lascivious greed in her tone.

Santo took in the changes since he'd first met her five years ago, the year he'd gained entry to the most exclusive event of the financial year that neither Wall Street nor the FTSE had heard of. The year she'd seduced him, aged eighteen, in a baroque bathroom in Dubrovnik. A memorable event he almost wished he could forget. *Almost*.

Her dyed red hair had taken on more of a brittle aspect but, no matter how she behaved, it was undeniable that Marie-Laure Gerber was a startlingly beautiful woman who wore her sensuality like both a weapon and a shield. And while it hadn't been his first sexual experience, it had been ironically his most honest. Proved perfectly by the way she had ruthlessly ignored him the following year.

But it would be wrong to mistake Marie-Laure as simply the lonely widow of one of Switzerland's richest financiers. There was a reason the blundering, bulbous man had reached such dizzying heights before his death; his wife was sharper than honed steel and just as dangerous.

'Tell me, *tesorina*, what has your claws out so early this evening?' Santo asked.

The delighted peal of her laugh was as fake as his term of endearment had been.

'Rumour has it that Edward Carson's precious princess of a daughter is making her first appearance.'

Santo's gut clenched instinctively, but only bland indifference marked his features. 'Is she?'

Marie-Laure cut a side glance at him, her eyebrow raised. 'They say she is absolutely exquisite.'

Santo gave a shrug of his shoulder. 'Not my type,' he dismissed.

'They all say that. *At first*.' Marie-Laure's tone took on a diamond-hard edge, before she turned to look out across the hall. 'The children have been talking of nothing else all evening.'

Santo looked over to where the progeny of the twelve families in attendance had gathered. Or, more accurately, eleven families. He was the last and only descendant of the Sabatinis. And it would remain that way too, he swore.

The group of young twenty-somethings were the heirs of the elite. They would grow up to become the wealth of Europe, the decision-makers of millions. And each and every one of them was a spoilt brat with absolutely no idea of what hard work was.

'You think I pay even the slightest bit of notice to what they say?' he asked.

'No,' she said, turning back to Santo fully. 'You don't. It's why I like you so much.'

'You only like cold, sharp, shiny things,' he dismissed.

'Exactly,' she said, patting his chest just above his heart, and left him to stand staring at the group of young men and women whispering and gossiping, a few daring to send a glance his way once in a while.

With barely veiled scorn, he turned back to the gold-embossed display of Renaissance architecture and artwork covering every inch of the large hall. It was gaudy, it was impressive, awesome in the traditional sense of the word and, as much as he disliked every single bit of it, he respected the history of it, he respected *history*. He had to, in order not to repeat it.

Munich was as beautiful as Helsinki had been the year before and Stockholm had been the year before that. Each New Year's Eve celebration was held in a different European city, by a different family. But Marie-Laure was right; the Albrechts *had* outdone themselves this year.

No one outside of the twelve families knew of, or even heard of, what happened here. And not because it was some bacchanalian event shrouded in generations of inherited wealth, hidden behind secret handshakes or cult-like devotion. Even though, deep down, Santo had expected as much the first time he'd attended the event.

No, what happened every year on the thirty-first of December, in a different European city, hosted by each different family, was simply this: the exchange and investment of money for *more* money.

In essence it was a financial cabal and he hated every single person here. Because they would do anything in order to protect their own financial security, including turning a blind eye to violence and abuse. The exclusivity of this group of people ensured the containment of inconceivable wealth. And it wasn't lost on him that while Pietro was one of the best men he'd ever met, as the son of an ex-Mafia enforcer he would never be allowed within these hallowed halls, despite the fact that the people here were probably even bigger criminals. No, what mattered nearly as much as the zeros in your bank account to these people was genetics. And those two things made nearly every single person here almost pathologically selfish. And Santo Sabatini knew first-hand just how dangerous that could be.

He swallowed a mouthful of his whisky as the hum of whispers grew louder.

'*She's here,*' he was just able to make out from the buzz.

Refusing to turn, to succumb to the desire to see her finally, in the flesh, take her place as Edward Carson's heir, Santo instead remembered the words his mentor had said to him.

'*It's not easy what I'm asking you. It's the longest game you'll ever play,*' Pietro had warned. '*It may even take years. What I'm asking you is a lifelong commitment, so think carefully before you agree.*'

Santo hadn't needed time. He didn't doubt what the older man was saying. He understood what he was being asked. He understood that it was a secret that must be kept from everyone. Because it could dramatically change the course of a young woman's life. But the answer was easy, all the same. After everything Pietro had done for his mother, for *him*, Santo would give his all to whatever was asked. Even if that meant maintaining his connection to this hideous group of people.

So now, as Eleanor Carson finally emerged into the Hall of Antiquities of the Munich Residenz on New

Year's Eve, the day after her eighteenth birthday, Santo Sabatini prepared to make good on that promise.

'Look after her, Santo. Protect *her.'*

'I will.'

Eleanor Carson gasped the moment she entered the grand hall. She had *never* seen anything more beautiful in her entire life. Her heart beat so strongly it pressed her chest against the tight bustline of her gold dress.

She had waited years for this moment. *Years.*

And now she thought she might actually explode with happiness. Eleanor looked at her father, the sparkle in his eyes, the joy on his beloved features, and knew that he was as happy for her as she was. She reached for his hand and squeezed, as he nodded for her to go to join her friends. Throughout all the beautiful and gorgeous celebrations that she'd had yesterday, *this* had been her real birthday present. She cast a glance back at her mother, something in her gaze catching Eleanor just a little strangely, before it was masked with a smile.

'Go on,' her mother said with a kind laugh, and that was all the permission Eleanor needed before she searched out Dilly from amongst the crowd of familiar faces. Friends of the family, school friends from a few years above, the circles she moved in had been tight knit but, now she was eighteen years old, finally, she got to join them *here.*

Until this moment, the New Year's Eve parties were known only to Eleanor through rumours and whispers. No one dared speak of what happened here, but the vague details and hints only increased her curiosity to fever pitch. In her mind it had become a fairy tale ball fit for a princess, and looking around the Hall of Antiquities, it was beyond her wildest imagination.

Gold, pale blue, dusky pink and alabaster filled the periphery of her vision, the gentle hum of chatter overlaying the pretty strains from a live orchestra hidden from view. Shivers of absolute joy rippled across her skin and her chest felt as full as if she'd held her breath for an eternity just to be here.

'Lee!' she heard Dilly cry from part way across the room and couldn't help but laugh at the friend she hadn't seen since she'd graduated a year earlier than Eleanor, last July.

'Oh, I am *so* glad to see you,' Eleanor said, allowing herself to be swept up in Dilly's warm embrace.

'Me too! It has been positively *dull* here without you,' Dilly confided. 'You look absolutely delicious—all the boys are having *conniptions*.'

Eleanor batted at her friend's arm. 'Don't be silly.'

'I'm not!' Dilly cried, before tucking her hand into the curve of her arm. 'Come, let me give you the tour,' she said, pulling Eleanor towards the far end of the hall. 'The Albrechts are hosting this year. Next year, it's going to be the Pichlers in Vienna, which will be equally, if not *more,* impressive than this,' Dilly confided.

Eleanor didn't think it could get even better than this, but kept that to herself.

'And how are the family? Mater and Pater?'

'They're good,' Eleanor said with a smile, and remembered her younger brother's sulking frown as they'd left him in the hotel before his bedtime.

'But I want to come with you.'

'Not until you're eighteen, like Ellie,' her father had said.

'I'll say. Your father's just done a spectacular deal with the Müllers, he should be on cloud nine,' exclaimed Dilly.

'They celebrated all last night,' Eleanor confirmed, with a secret thread of pride. She'd spent weeks listening to her father negotiate the deal, her nails almost bitten to the quick, because she had suggested the deal. Oh, she wasn't naïve, she knew that her father would never do anything he didn't want to do, but she *had* suggested it. And he had thought it was a good idea. And secretly she hoped that would help him begin to see that she really did want to study business at university. That she wanted to follow in his footsteps one day. Oh, the business would be passed to Freddie, she knew that. But…she might be able to be a part of that business too.

They came to the far end of the incredible hall and turned, so that the entire room was on display.

'Okay,' Dilly announced. 'As you know, no one from outside the families are allowed. It's the one night of the year where everyone can just be themselves without worrying about political enemies or financial repercussions.'

Eleanor nodded. The impossible exclusivity and secrecy surrounding the New Year's Eve gatherings had always been what had made her want to attend so much.

'Now, over by the tables, you should probably be able to recognise some familiar faces.'

Eleanor's gaze found a pair of deep brown eyes joining with hers, under a mop of rich blond hair and lips that had curved into a smile. Her heart beat just a little quicker, recognising Antony Fairchild.

'Of course, you know Tony already.'

'I wouldn't say I *know* him,' Eleanor confessed.

'Looks like he knows you though,' Dilly teased with a nudge of her shoulder.

Eleanor felt her cheeks pink under the older boy's perusal. He'd been a few years ahead of her at Sandrilling—the boarding school on the outskirts of London that many of the children of the families gathered here had attended. She'd not thought that he'd even known her name, but the way he was still looking at her made her heart trip over itself.

Unable to stop an answering smile from curving her own mouth, she allowed Dilly to pull her attention back with a roll of her eyes.

'Smitten already?' Dilly asked.

'I have no idea what you're talking about,' she replied, a wry smile on her lips.

Eleanor looked across the hall and from amongst the nearly two hundred people gathered in the glorious hall found her parents talking to the Fairchilds, her mother looking a little distracted. Unease twisted in Eleanor's gut. Her mother hadn't wanted her to come tonight, but Eleanor didn't know why. For years, all Eleanor had wanted was to be a part of this. To be part of the world her parents kept hidden from her. The glamour, the exclusivity, the *secrecy*... Being here meant they trusted her with that and it was as much a signifier of adulthood as her eighteenth birthday. Now her life could *really* begin.

Dilly was distracted by something over Eleanor's shoulder. 'Give me two secs? I'll be right back.'

Eleanor didn't mind one bit. She'd actually been hoping for a moment to herself, just to take it all in. It was so much *more* than she'd expected. The noise was quite something from a crowd of nearly two hundred or so guests. A couple passed in front of her, forcing her to take a step back out of the way and to bump up against something hard.

Someone.

'I'm so sorry,' she said, turning to see who she'd crashed into.

Horror filled her as she took in the sight of a dark-haired man staring down at the amber stain soaking into his white shirt.

'Oh, no, I'm so sorry!' she exclaimed, reaching quickly for some napkins on the side table beside them and pressing them against the spilled alcohol in the hope of limiting the damage.

The moment that her hand met his chest the man moved back, his arms raised, as if to avoid any possible contact with her. But no matter the distance, the simmering anger in the man's gaze was palpable.

She bit her lips together and raised her eyes from the man's chest to his face and then stopped. Everything stopped. The brief flick of the man's gaze to hers and then back to his shirt was all it had taken to strike her still.

Rich, dark, sumptuous curling hair covered a head that was bent to stare down at his now ruined shirt. But even then, she could tell that he was nearly a foot taller than her in her heels. The sharp lines of his cheekbones and patrician nose led her gaze down to near cruelly sensual lips that sent a shiver down her spine. A delicious one.

But it was the bright aquamarine of his eyes that struck her hardest. They were unexpected, against the clear Mediterranean stamp of his heritage. Greece maybe, Italy more likely. She was caught staring when he looked up and held her gaze when most would have looked away.

She should have looked away. She would have, but for the moment when she thought that she saw something other than disdain in his gaze, but then he snatched the napkins from the hand that had dropped to her side and dabbed ineffectually at his ruined shirt.

'I really am—'

'Sorry, yes. I heard you the first time. And the second.'

Shame and embarrassment coloured her cheeks a hot pink. She felt gauche, foolish and a little childish next to this man.

But that was no excuse for bad manners. Shaking herself out of it, she put on her best smile and held out her hand.

'Eleanor Carson,' she said by way of introduction.

Santo hadn't intended to actually have to speak to her. He'd thought, naïvely perhaps, that he might be able to keep watch over her from afar. So this awkward exchange had certainly not been a part of his plans.

As she stared up at him, her face strangely determined, he took a moment to take in the 'exquisite' Eleanor Carson. Oh, he could understand what had got the younger generation's knickers in a twist. Eleanor Carson would grow up to be quite a beautiful young woman, he was sure. Dark hair swept back stylishly from skin as pale as milk. Her eyes, a deep brown, were almost infuriatingly innocent. An innocence he'd never had the luxury of.

Her dress made the most of it, of course. Never one to be particularly interested in women's fashion, other than when he was taking it off his chosen companion, he supposed it suited her. Little puff sleeves capped her shoulders…his eyes skimming over a simple neckline and a corseted top…before flaring out into wide skirts, the entire thing made of a golden material that made him think of long-forgotten fairy tales.

But he had stared too long and just as he held out his hand, hers dropped away. He bit his teeth together, intensely disliking the awkwardness of the entire encounter, and waited. Belatedly recovering herself, she met his hand with her fingers, which left him fairly sure that the Carson girl was disappointingly insipid.

'Isn't it just incredible?' she asked, full of a wholly unwarranted exuberance.

He stared at her blankly, her observation only more evidence against her.

'It's my first time here,' she confided, pressing on despite his clear disinclination to pursue this conversation. He wondered absently what other inane observation she might be capable of, and looked away when she blushed beneath his scrutiny.

'Would never have known,' he uttered beneath his breath, snagging a fresh glass of whisky from a passing waiter, more than a little frustrated that he would spend the rest of the night smelling like a distillery.

Before the waiter could disappear, Eleanor beckoned him over and whispered something in the young man's ear. The eagerness of the boy—probably the same age as her—was almost pitiful. He nodded and rushed off.

She'd probably ordered some frothy cocktail that disguised any offending taste of alcohol.

He opened his mouth to make an excuse to leave, but Eleanor pushed on determinedly.

'I've not been to Munich before. I'm hoping that there will be some time to see it before we leave, the day after tomorrow. Have you? Are there any attractions you could suggest?'

He turned back to face her full on, with a raised eyebrow that was *sure* to convey his disbelief that she would actually be asking him for tourist spot recommendations.

Once again, he attempted to excuse himself.

'Because, honestly,' she pressed on, not giving him the chance, 'I quite like looking around cities when they're quiet. It's as if you get to see something that no one else does. And tomorrow, I'd imagine most people will be still in bed, or nursing a hangover so...'

She trailed off, having seen something while Santo was still trying to make sense of the image he now had of Eleanor wandering along isolated streets just before sunrise.

'Oh, thank you,' she said to the waiter, who had returned and passed her a bag before leaving.

Eleanor turned back to Santo. 'This is for you. It should fit. It obviously won't be as nice as the one I ruined, but at least it won't be stained. Or smell,' she added with a smile that was near delightful. She bobbed her head, wished him a good rest of the evening and disappeared, leaving him holding a bag with a cellophane-wrapped white shirt, quite unsure as to what had just happened.

'Wait,' he called before he could stop himself.

She turned back, just a few feet from where he stood, a small smile on her face. It was a Mona Lisa smile—not fake or forced, but as if she knew she'd surprised him. Because he hadn't thought her capable of the kind of awareness that was required not only to recompense him for the damage to his shirt, but more than that, to do it in such a way that it had been subtle, seamless. Anyone else here would have simply shrugged it off and left him to it.

'Santo Sabatini,' he offered.

'Nice to meet you, Mr Sabatini,' she said, a broad, almost beautiful, smile stretching across her features, before disappearing into the crowd, leaving a feeling turning in his chest that lasted for much longer than Santo was comfortable with.

As Eleanor made her way back to Dilly and the group she was with, she couldn't help but feel a fizz of excitement humming through her veins. She cast a quick glance over her shoulder to where Santo Sabatini—Italian, most definitely—was *still* staring after her. Her heart fluttered a little. It had hardly been anything, but something about surprising him had pleased her.

She risked another glance, but this time he was gone, and that pleasure dimmed just a bit. Dilly welcomed her back into the group and pulled her to her side, next to Tony Fairchild. Eleanor smiled shyly at him when he turned to make room for her.

He caught her up on the conversation, an argument about whether one of the boys in the group should invest with another. Eleanor let the conversation flow around them until there was a lull.

'Dilly, what do you know about Santo Sabatini?'

She wrinkled her nose. 'Best to stay away from him. His father died about six years ago and the ugly rumours are that Santo was *there*.'

The way that Dilly said 'there' seemed to imply *involved* rather than *present*, and Eleanor found herself frowning at the thought. Had she got it so wrong? Was Santo Sabatini actually dangerous? She didn't think she'd felt that he was.

'But he inherited the Sabatini Group—the biggest privately held company in Italy—at just eighteen and even though some of the families tried to group together to buy it from him, he refused.'

'He's a pompous git,' Tony added. Eleanor started just a little, not aware he'd been listening to their conversation. But he caught her gaze and rolled his eyes in a joking way, becoming the handsome, charming rake she remembered from school. He closed the distance between them to say, 'But don't mind him. He doesn't usually bother us much.'

Eleanor nodded eagerly as he took her arm and pulled her to his side, and when he smiled at her she felt a little flutter and thought that she was the luckiest girl here.

And by the time the clock struck midnight she'd forgotten all thoughts of the tall, brooding Italian and believed that perhaps, just like the fairy tales she'd loved so much, she had met her very own Prince Charming in Antony Fairchild. And the way that his eyes sparkled at her, she began to hope that it was more than just a fantasy.

CHAPTER TWO

New Year's Eve eight years ago, Vienna

WHAT A DIFFERENCE a year made, Eleanor thought as she emerged into the air-controlled environment of the Pichlers' wine cellars with a diamond ring on her finger and a fiancé on her arm.

Antony smiled at her, the not-so-subtle heat in his gaze making her heart flutter in excitement. Any hesitation she might have had about the fast-paced progression of their relationship had disintegrated beneath her father's exuberant encouragement three months ago.

The proposal had been nothing short of extravagant, Tony whisking her away for a few nights in a luxurious cabin in the Lyngen Alps, north of the Arctic Circle in Norway. Before the Northern lights, he'd told her that she was more beautiful to him, more precious, and he could never want or think of anyone else ever again.

She wasn't as naïve as some people thought. She *did* understand that her relationship with Tony benefited both businesses and families. Her knowledge of her father's company was enough to make that painstakingly clear, and if it hadn't been already then the whispers that such a connection in the group had never happened before would have made it doubly so.

But life had been a whirlwind ever since the last New Year's Eve party. They'd been almost inseparable since that night. Bouquets of red roses and white lilies had arrived the following day and within weeks she had been whisked away on a romantic trip to Paris. Date by date, each one increasingly extravagant, Tony had teased from her the future that she wanted—a family, just like her own, the importance of the family business, the tenets by which she had been raised, that she wanted to continue. And she'd been thrilled to discover that he wanted the same.

Impassioned declarations of love had made her feel special—desired and loved in equal measure. And if her mother had urged caution then her father's eager acceptance had swept any concerns aside and Eleanor had fallen head over heels for Tony's charm and his easy-going nature. She could see it, the lives they would make, familiar and comfortable, solid and successful. It would make her father so happy.

'I'm going to get us a drink,' Tony whispered in her ear, pressing a light kiss to the sensitive flesh just beneath, sending a shiver of delight across her body.

She'd been worried about asking him to *wait* until they were married, wanting her first time to be special, with the person she loved and trusted most in this world. But he had assured her that he wanted her only to be comfortable and happy. But recently she'd been regretting that decision. Maybe she didn't need to wait until she was married, she thought as he disappeared into the crowd filling the space under the low arched brick walls and ceilings of the Pichlers' underground wine cellars.

She'd been wrong to think that they would be dark and grimy, because the cellars were actually beautifully lit with carefully controlled temperatures. Racks of wine bottles were displayed behind gleaming glass and she felt as if she were in a gallery. The large wine cabinets created little nooks and corners that were already filling with people dressed in jewels and silks, all glittering in the festive atmosphere.

'Nineteen years old and engaged to one of England's finest bachelors—who would have thought it?' Dilly mused as she pulled Eleanor into a warm embrace and out of her thoughts.

'Yes, congratulations,' added Ekaterina Kivi, who had attended Sandrilling in the year ahead of her.

Eleanor smiled happily at the redhead. 'Thank you,' she said sincerely. 'I honestly never thought I could be this happy,' she confessed as she caught her father's proud eye from across the room.

'I bet Daddy is happy,' Dilly said, leaning into her shoulder. 'Barely a year out of school and you're already set for life.'

Eleanor's smile dimmed a little at the way Dilly made it sound as if her life was over. As if there was nothing else to achieve now that she had a fiancé.

Yes, Tony had talked her into taking another year off from university to help host several incredibly important dinners, as he tried to cement his place in his father's investment company. But she had enjoyed doing it, and doing it well. She hadn't found it difficult at all, following her mother's lead after so many years.

And no, she might not have liked keeping her opinions on their conversations about business to herself after Tony had laughed, excusing her enthusiasm, when she'd disagreed with one of his guests. But she knew what kind of pressure he was under. She'd seen that too, from her father. And she'd always wanted what her parents had. The perfect marriage, the love and the security. It had been what she'd wanted as a child and it was what she wanted now.

So she would happily accept the little adjustments to her life until they settled down and she could return her focus to her studies. Because she *did* have dreams for herself. Even if they were going to have to wait a little while.

'Well, I'm sure that you will be blissfully happy together,' Dilly said, pulling her into a hug. 'But remember, I want to use your business acumen for my fashion brand,' she said, releasing Eleanor long enough to point a finger in her direction. 'Together, we'll take the fashion world by storm!'

'Who's taking the world by storm?' Antony asked, returning from the bar.

'We are!' cried Dilly, her arms slinging across both Eleanor and Antony's backs, and she guided them onto the dance floor.

Barely an hour later and the crush of bodies was making Eleanor feel a little claustrophobic. Waving her hand at her damp neck wasn't even taking the edge off. Antony was busy shouting, slightly drunkenly, into the ear of his best friend and Dilly was nowhere to be seen.

She tugged at Antony's jacket, but he waved her off. She just needed to get somewhere where she could breathe a little easier. Making her way towards the edge of the low domed hall where racks of wine bottles created little nooks, she ducked into one and welcomed the cooler air away from the press of bodies in the centre.

Her head fell back and she took a deep breath of much needed air. She'd not had a lot to drink, but more than she did usually and was hoping that she could avoid the nauseous way it made her feel sometimes.

She opened her eyes, startled to find herself almost toe to toe with Santo Sabatini. There he was, leaning insolently against the back wall, drink hanging lazily from the tips of long fingers, bow tie loose around his neck, looking more handsome than she cared to admit, glaring at her.

And, just like that, her moment of calm was snatched from her grasp. Instinctively, she leaned back, but too far and too quickly, and she was about to fall when his arm reached out and latched securely around her wrist.

Flames licked at her pulse point and connected to places around her body she'd not experienced before. He held her there, the taut lines of his arms connecting them as she read both surprise and confusion in his gaze, before he eventually tugged her forward to regain her balance and she felt foolish all over again. He removed his hand from her but she felt indelibly marked by his touch.

A derisive smirk pulled at a mouth she couldn't look away from, even as she burned from the impact. His lips were different to Tony's. The bow of his upper lip curved in a subtle way, pressing sensually against the firmer, more angular shape of the one beneath it. Fascinated beyond rational thought, she took in the rest of his features, just like the year before. Having kept all thoughts of the powerful Italian carefully behind a locked door, her curiosity was let loose as her gaze raked over the hard angle of his jaw and across the firm lines of his mouth. Above those aquamarine eyes were dark brows, one of which was bisected near its end by a scar.

It made him seem so much *more* than Tony and his friends. Older, experienced...*knowing*.

That was what she saw in his eyes. *Knowing*.

'Had your fill, Princess?' he asked, not bothering to hide the humour he found in her fascination.

His derision was enough to cut through the heat that had begun to build deep within her, and straight to the heart of the shame she felt at finding anyone other than her fiancé remotely interesting.

She chose to ignore the taunt, for surely that was all it was. A cruel tease at her expense.

'You startled me, that's all.'

'I was here first, so that makes it *you* who startled *me*,' he said.

'You don't look startled. You look...angry,' she replied truthfully.

Something flashed in his eyes and the muscle at his jaw clenched reflexively. 'I get that a lot,' he said in a tone she couldn't quite decipher.

He raised his glass and took a mouthful of amber liquid without taking his gaze from her face. So why had she suddenly become incredibly conscious of herself? As if she thought he was trying to avoid looking at any other part of her.

'If you're expecting my congratulations, you'll be waiting some time,' he informed her in a bland tone.

The about-turn of their conversation pulled her focus back to Tony, or perhaps it wasn't an about-turn. Was he angry that she was engaged? She dismissed the thought as ludicrous.

But clearly whatever moment they had shared last year, whatever intimacy she had imagined might have formed between them, was gone. And in its place rose a defensiveness Eleanor wasn't used to.

'I suppose common decency would be too much to hope for,' she bit back.

'And there I was on my best behaviour,' he replied.

'Formality is not civility,' she reprimanded.

Something like surprise passed across his gaze before it was quickly masked, and somewhere deep inside her she preened at the realisation that she had caught him off-guard. Before his next words landed with all the weight of a prize punch.

'Civility?' he repeated with a laugh. 'You're marrying Antony Fairchild. The boy is rash and callow at best. Spoilt and mean at worst. You have only my commiserations,' he said with a wave of his glass.

'Are you drunk?' Eleanor demanded, shocked by his rudeness.

'Sadly, not enough,' he replied as if genuinely upset by the thought.

'Antony is not like that,' Eleanor said, ignoring his response.

And as if her words had sprung him to life, Santo closed the distance between them, peering down at her from nearly a foot of height above, and said, 'Illuminate me, Princess. Just how is it that your fiancé is none of those things?'

Her heart trembled in her ribcage, the scent of whisky, the woodsy trace of his aftershave, the heat of his body pressed close to hers, and everything in her felt…electrified. Something forbidden and dark shivered deliciously across her skin and made her squirm deep inside.

Santo looked at her again as if sensing the warring within her, as if knowing what was happening to her when she didn't even know herself. His gaze flickered between her eyes and her lips and for a heart-stopping moment she thought, *hoped*, that he might actually kiss her.

With a self-control he wasn't used to exercising, Santo stepped back from Eleanor and the moment. It would have been so easy. So easy to take what she didn't know she was offering, to give what she didn't know she needed. But to do so when she was so young, so innocent still, engaged or not…that would be unconscionable. He didn't play with girls who didn't know what they wanted, nor women who wanted more from him than he was willing to give.

He'd not been surprised by the news that she had become engaged, but the disappointment he'd felt was that it was Antony Fairchild of all people. He hadn't been lashing out at Eleanor when he'd called the Fairchild brat those things—Antony really was that and more. But Pietro had only asked that he make sure that Eleanor was safe, not to guard her from her own terrible choices. But was it really her choice, when Edward Carson would use Eleanor to make a financial match that would suit him and his business? Whether she knew it or not, if it hadn't been Fairchild it would have been someone else.

His chain of thought led him to the argument he'd had with his mother. One that still rang in his ears.

'Find a good girl, Santo... Settle down, Santo... Make me grandbabies, Santo...'

It amazed him that she couldn't understand why he had absolutely no intention of doing such a thing.

Eleanor looked at him, hurt still shimmering in her eyes from his callous words, and shame rose, strong enough to make him regret them.

'I apologise.'

She nodded in a way that told him he wasn't forgiven in the least.

'Truly,' he added sincerely, which seemed to soften her slightly.

He was in a foul mood. Between his mother and the demands of the Sabatini Group, he was having a rough year. The wildfires had come again and the Sabatini olive groves were suffering, along with a large section of Southern Italy and other parts of Europe. But no one seemed to want to invest in the kind of infrastructure that would actually tackle an immediate, on the ground response to the climate emergency that had near global reach.

He rubbed at his temple with the thumb of the hand that held the glass of nearly finished whisky and Eleanor seemed to look a little more closely at him this time.

'Are you okay?' she asked.

'Just a headache.'

'Yes, I've heard that whisky is the best cure for that,' Eleanor said tartly, and he couldn't help it. He threw his head back and laughed.

She might be an innocent, and impossibly young, but that made it all the more delightful when she surprised him with her wry sense of humour. The slight curve to her tightly pressed lips was a sucker punch he wasn't expecting though.

She rolled her eyes and looked away. And the moment she did, his gaze hungrily consumed her. The panels of the teal-coloured silk of her sleeveless dress clung to her body in a way that showed both her youth and her vitality as well as a promise of the woman to come. It was a heady combination for any man to see and she had no idea of the impact she made. None at all.

He pulled himself back from the brink of something monumentally stupid just as she returned her attention to him, castigating himself silently.

'Is it about the olive groves? Were they badly damaged by the fires?' Eleanor asked, wiping all trace of his immediate thoughts from his mind.

She knew about his business? He bit back his shock. All this time he'd been secretly keeping tabs on her it had not crossed his mind once that she might do the same to him.

'A little,' he admitted. 'But we'll survive.'

'We?' she asked, confused.

'Yes, me. My staff. *We*,' he clarified, and this time she seemed surprised. Knowing Carson, she'd probably only heard business discussed as to how it affected the singular, with no thought to the staff or the wider impact.

He watched her thoughts pass over her features, their expressiveness almost a wonder to see.

'Do you want some?' he asked, when he was able to regain his composure. 'I'll let you have some if you promise not to spill it over me,' he teased gently, knowing that he should never have asked.

She looked over her shoulder and back at the crowds.

Go, the angel on his shoulder urged. *While you still can.*

While I'll still let you, the devil whispered. A devil he ruthlessly pushed back to hell.

'Will you stop being such an arse if I do?' she asked, looking back at him.

'Probably not,' he replied, hiding the grin that tugged at his lips as he reached for the bottle on the floor beside him.

He stood up, surprised to hear a 'Yes,' come from where Eleanor had been standing.

'We'll have to share,' he said of the glass he waved between them. 'Still staying?'

She nodded, dropping her gaze, before closing the distance between them. For a moment he couldn't work out her intention, his pulse reacting to the sudden new proximity to her. Until she came to stand beside him against the brick wall.

'Wait—' He stopped her before she could lean back as he had been doing. Shrugging off his jacket, he slipped it around her shoulders. The dust on the wall would have ruined her dress, but it also would have given her hiding place away. He'd witnessed the telltale signs of one not-so-secret assignation already and he had absolutely no intention of letting unfounded rumours damage Eleanor's reputation.

She shrugged into it, the tuxedo jacket drowning her petite frame, and had to look away. Who would have thought the mere sight of her in an item of his clothing would make such an impact on him?

Bracing his body to ward off the unwanted arousal threatening to make itself known, he reached for the bottle of whisky and poured the sixteen-year-old Lagavulin Special Release into the glass before passing it to Eleanor.

'So, what are you hiding from?' he asked, genuinely curious.

'It just got a little hot out there in the press of people,' she said before taking a sip.

He wondered if that was all it had been, but had no intention of pressing further. His purpose here was to make sure she was safe, not monitor her for truths and falsehoods.

'What's your excuse?' she asked, passing him the glass back.

He took a mouthful and relished the peat on his tongue and the burn on his throat, the way the alcohol filled the cave of his mouth, and as he looked at Eleanor he noticed that her cheeks had flushed from her own mouthful.

'I was looking for some peace and quiet.'

'Well, you came to the wrong party,' she observed, as if uncomfortable with the noise and press of bodies out there in the larger area of the wine cellars.

'That I did,' he agreed, swirling the amber liquid around the glass in his hand.

There was a pause.

He opened his mouth to speak when a noise near the wine stacks stopped him.

'Here…in here.'

They both heard her fiancé's voice at the same time. Santo looked to Eleanor, whose eyes had widened in panic, presumably not wanting to be found in a dark corner with Santo. A mean part of him almost wanted it, wanted to see what that boy would do, but just when he expected that confrontation, he realised that no one was there.

He stepped forward just as a feminine giggle could be heard from over the wine stacks.

'Shh, you have to be quiet,' Tony could be heard saying.

'You told me you'd get away,' a whining voice replied.

'What did you want me to do? She hasn't left my side all evening.'

Santo turned to Eleanor just in time to see her realise what was going on, her eyes wide, skin pale, her lips opening to speak. He placed a firm hand over her mouth before she could. She wrestled against the arm he wrapped around her to stop her from rushing out to confront her cheating fiancé. She clearly couldn't see the situation she was in.

The entire group of families had talked of nothing else than their engagement from the moment it had happened. The joining of two dynasties had always been a long-held dream and, whether she knew it or not, Edward Carson wouldn't let go of it easily.

'Wait,' Santo whispered in her ear. 'Just wait.'

He looked her dead in the eye and waited until she registered his words, anger and confusion as easy to read as words on a page until she blinked them away and he saw sense return.

Her eyes narrowed and slowly she nodded.

'Oh, God, you don't know what you do to me,' the woman's voice moaned. 'I need you, Tony. *Now.*'

Santo didn't recognise the woman's voice, but from the sudden spark in Eleanor's eyes it was clear that she had. Tears began to gather in the corners of her eyes and it was the one thing, the only thing, that Santo had never been able to stomach.

'Stop,' he whispered harshly. 'Don't even think about shedding a tear over that bastard or whoever he is with. You *have* to be stronger than that.'

She blinked slowly, a tear escaping over her cheek. He swept it away with the pad of his thumb, but more tears seeped into the fingers still across her lips.

His gut clenched to see them. Anger, swift, sure and poker-hot, turned his gaze red. Helplessly, Eleanor looked up at him, begging him to take this away, to make it not be happening. And, just like that, he was back home with his mother and his father. And, just like then, there was nothing he could do to make it go away.

He closed his eyes, needing to take a moment, needing to push back the anger that combined a devastating past with the dangerous present. By the time he had regained control, Eleanor was looking at him with concern. He took his hand away from her mouth.

'Where is your phone?' he whispered.

'In my bag,' she said, offering up the small clutch that hung on a strap from her wrist. He grabbed it and pulled out the slim mobile.

'The PIN,' he demanded, showing her the screen.

With shaking fingers, she typed in the four-digit code that unlocked her phone. He found the app he wanted and turned on his heel.

Eleanor stood there shaking, unable to move. Unable to follow Santo around to the other side of the wine stack to where she knew what she would find.

Tony, her fiancé, and Dilly, her supposed best friend, having sex.

She couldn't believe it. She wanted to howl until she

couldn't hear those noises any more. The betrayal coursing through her made her feel utterly wretched. How had she missed it? How had she been such a fool?

Too many thoughts, too many questions crowded her mind. If she'd slept with Tony, would this be happening? Was it her own fault? Had she somehow brought this on herself? Or had this been going on before their engagement? How could they do this?

The dizziness caused by all the questions made her sway and she was beginning to slide to the ground when Santo came back around the corner. He reached for her and pulled her against him. And for just a moment she sank into him. Into his strength, into the protection he offered her, the strength of him.

He gave her that one moment before drawing her away from what Tony and Dilly were doing. She let herself be tugged along by the sheer power and determination of Santo, despite wanting to do nothing more than sink to the floor and cry.

'What did you do with my phone?' she asked with numb lips.

'Pictures.'

'You took pictures?' she demanded, outraged. 'Of *that*? Of *them*? Why would you—'

'Keep your voice down,' he all but growled, casting looks about them to see if she had drawn any attention to them.

When he had taken her as far away from her fiancé as he was apparently comfortable with, he pushed her gently back into another recess on the opposite side of the wine cellar.

Eleanor hastily wiped at the tears that had fallen on

the way, scrubbing at her cheeks as she wanted to scrub at her eyes, her ears and her heart.

Oh, God.

'Listen, Eleanor—'

She started to shake her head. She didn't want to listen to anything. Tony had cheated on her.

'Eleanor,' he said, taking her shoulders and shaking her a little. 'You have to listen to me.'

Eleanor clenched her teeth together. 'Okay,' she said, even though all she could hear was Dilly's moans of pleasure, turning her stomach.

'They're going to tell you that it wasn't as bad as you think. They're going to tell you that it was just a mistake, that he loves you and that it's not worth throwing your future away for,' Santo said, his tone dark, his voice full of gravel.

Eleanor bit her lip, the tears building and acid scratching at the back of her throat, wanting to get out.

'Eleanor, are you listening to me?'

She wasn't, but she nodded, looking up to find Santo staring at her with an intensity that surprised her.

'Don't let them convince you it was nothing. If you feel yourself wavering, if you feel yourself thinking that they might be right, look at the photos. Don't let them force you into a marriage you don't want,' he commanded.

A low moan came from deep within her.

'Eleanor, this is important,' he said, shaking her by the shoulders a little.

'My father wouldn't do that,' Eleanor insisted, trying to pull out of his hold. 'When he finds out about this, he'll go mad. There's no way he'll let Tony get away with this.'

Santo looked back at her with pity in his eyes. As if she were being naïve. As if she didn't know her own father.

'He won't!' Eleanor cried out, pushing back against Santo. 'Why would you say that?' she demanded. 'Why would you even think that?'

Santo stilled, something dark filling his intent gaze. He opened his mouth to answer, but her mother's concerned voice came from over Santo's shoulder.

'Eleanor, are you okay?'

Eleanor pushed Santo aside and, shrugging off his jacket, she ran into her mother's arms.

With her head buried against her mother's chest and her eyes filled with tears, she didn't see the look that passed between Santo and her mother, Analise, and, even if she had, Eleanor wouldn't have cared. Her heart was breaking in two and she thought she'd never recover.

CHAPTER THREE

New Year's Eve seven years ago, Oxford

SANTO COULDN'T HELP HIMSELF. He didn't know whether
to be impressed or outraged by Edward Carson's arro-
gance. Supposedly on the back foot after one of the most
shocking scandals ever seen by the group of twelve families that met each New Year's Eve, the man was hosting
this year—at his own home—as if it were equal, nay,
even superior, to the exquisite locations of previous years.

It irritated Santo that this was, in fact, the case. It
might have been called Roughbridge House, but the damn
thing was a castle. It hadn't escaped Santo's notice that
the greater the wealth, the greater the likelihood that they
would downplay it. As if calling a sprawling Jacobean
estate of nearly one hundred acres a 'house' was a private joke amongst the higher echelons.

Guests were welcomed into the large entrance hall,
squarely positioned beneath more rows of mullioned
windows than Santo had ever seen before. Staff dressed
in black and white uniforms led those invited through
to various exquisitely decorated rooms with names like
'the salon' or 'the drawing room', quaint references to
rooms with much less grandeur than the Carsons had on

full display that evening. Santo scanned the faces of the guests, acknowledging and ignoring whoever he chose, but in truth he sought only one person.

Although Pietro had not expected him to keep tabs on Eleanor beyond these annual events, knowing that it would be too much of a risk to draw attention to himself in that way, it would have been nearly impossible to miss the headline news of the ending of her engagement. And once again Eleanor had surprised him, because seeing the way she'd run back to her mother last New Year's Eve, he'd thought she'd buckle, just like his mother had. But she hadn't. And while there had been much speculation on the reason behind the split, both camps were insistent that it was mutual and amicable.

Of course, behind the scenes it was a completely different story. The stock market changes read like a roadmap of retribution. Things had been quiet for the first few months, presumably while Eleanor was being convinced to maintain the engagement. And presumably, Eleanor proving immovable on the matter, Carson had gone on the offensive before the Fairchilds could do so. All of this was conjecture, of course. However, the jagged, angry slashes across shareholder prices and through the ownership signatures of both families' companies looked like a bloodbath. Rumour had it that the other families had been forced to intervene, bringing Edward and Archibald Fairchild to the table for peace talks.

Santo retrieved a glass of whisky from a passing waiter as he moved slowly from room to room. Antony's betrayal of Eleanor Carson had cost the Fairchilds billions. But what had it cost Eleanor?

She had interrupted his thoughts more than he liked

over the course of the year. The way she'd looked up at him, so shocked and hurt.

'My father wouldn't do that.'

Santo shook his head. *Cristo*, he wondered what lessons she'd learned this year.

As he looked around the impeccably decorated ballroom, there was a heady sense of expectation amongst the gathering. It reminded him of some spectator event, as if it were the Colosseum, and the audience were waiting to be entertained. They were practically baying for blood.

He peered into the crowd, seeing the way that certain groups had gathered together. It seemed that in the aftermath of Eleanor's broken engagement, lines had been drawn and sides taken.

He caught sight of Antony Fairchild, his ruddy health only slightly dimmed by the events of the past year. Of Dilly Allencourt, Eleanor's so-called friend, there was no sign at all. Her father was here and her grandmother, but only those two. They had positioned themselves as far away from both the Carsons and the Fairchilds in the ballroom. He doubted they'd stay for more than an hour.

He was reluctantly impressed. Eleanor had singlehandedly achieved what no other person had done in the near five-hundred-year history of these gatherings; she had created divisions. And a ruthless person, a truly calculating one, could use that to their advantage.

If it had been any other year she might have got away with not attending, but as it was Edward's turn to host it would be painfully obvious if she were absent. He thought of the girl he'd first met two years before and wondered if she had the strength to stand up to the scrutiny she was sure to be under. And for just a moment, he found himself wishing it could have been different for her.

'It's really quite something, don't you think?'

He turned to find Eleanor standing beside him on the fringe of the crowd.

'All these people, all this power. Money,' she clarified.

Santo nodded, something in his chest turning over at the realisation that she was finally beginning to see the truth about the people around her. And when he looked at her he could see the lines of maturity marked in her face. Slightly thinner cheeks, a knowing glint in her eyes, slightly harder than the sparkle that had been there in previous years.

'You survived,' he observed, relieved in a way he didn't want to examine.

Something passed quickly across her eyes. 'Just about,' Eleanor replied. A thin smile pulled at lips that deserved better. 'Can I borrow you for a moment?' she asked hesitantly.

He shouldn't, not really. There were too many eyes on her, but a connection had been formed between them. A connection that would only help him achieve the promise he'd made to Pietro. Severing it now could make it much harder for him in the future. And Santo would do nothing to jeopardise his vow to Pietro.

Santo nodded slowly and gestured for her to lead the way. Relief flooded through Eleanor, a strange and unfamiliar feeling these days, and she began to weave through the crowd towards the part of the house that was off-limits to the guests.

It had cost her more than she would ever admit to hold

to what Santo had told her the year before. It had taken some of her innocence, a lot of her naivety and more strength than she'd thought herself capable of.

But finally, Santo was here. This was what she'd wanted, what she'd waited for. Through all the months following the awful argument that had broken out between her, Tony and her father, shortly after New Year. Through all the horrible predictions that Santo had made coming true, she'd clung to one single thought: that at least she'd see him again.

She wasn't quite sure how, but he had become the point on her map that was fixed, allowing her to find her North Star. She had told herself that if she could just get here, just see him again, that maybe things would be okay. Because somehow last year he had become her armour. Her protection. She'd reminded herself of his words and had clung to them with a ferocity that had surprised both Tony and her father. It had surprised even herself.

A familiar laugh resounded from the living room, casting a shiver across her skin. It was edged with cruelty—Tony, as if he were taking pleasure in the fact that he was here, in her home, despite all that had passed between them. The last time she had seen him had been horrible for her. The things that were said, the anger she had seen in him had shocked her terribly.

She had believed that this was someone she loved, someone she would spend the rest of her life with. It was unimaginable to her now. So much so that sometimes she wondered if she'd gone a little mad.

But she hadn't. Nor had she forgotten what Santo had said. Without that, Eleanor honestly thought that she might have actually taken him back. Tony and her father had persisted in their near constant attempts at persuasion for months, until Eleanor had sent the photographs to Tony's father, informing him that if he didn't take his son in hand, the images would appear on the front cover of several internationally respected newspapers.

The fallout had been devastating. Not because Tony's father had ignored her, because he hadn't. It was *her* father who had been the cause of her greatest hurt. She had never disappointed him before, and the sharp sting of it had been brutal. As if she'd lost the warmth of the sun from her life, the coldness harsh and visceral.

She turned back to the party to make sure they weren't spotted, before leading him up the back stairway to the library on the second floor. She could have laughed at herself, feeling as if she were sneaking around her own home. But these days she felt like a stranger here. Uncomfortable. Aware of everything. Trying not to put a toe out of line, when she wasn't the one who had done something wrong.

Behind her, Santo's presence felt solid, constant. He wasn't tiptoeing around, yet moving through the house as if it were more natural to him than her. His confidence… it was something she yearned for. Admired.

She reached the door to the library that had become her refuge in the last months. Her father was rarely home these days, and her mother let her have the space Eleanor had desperately needed. She hovered on the threshold, aware of how…*intimate* it felt to have Santo, a near perfect stranger who had changed her life so dramatically, in her personal space.

She opened the door and stood back to let Santo in, following him with her eyes as he walked to the middle of the room, lit solely by the gentle flames in the open fireplace. Shelves of books framed an old writing desk in front of a large bay window that, during the day, looked out over the manicured garden and the hedgerow maze. But now deep green, thick velvet curtains were closed against the wintry night. Santo scanned the photographs on the desk, one of her and her brother, one of her and her parents. The one of her and her father there to remind herself of the hope that things would return to the way they had been before.

'That's Freddie. My brother,' she said, coming to stand beside him, a smile on her lips as she looked at her little brother staring up at her with nothing but love. 'He's a terror. He's ten and thinks he knows everything.'

'I'm sure you have absolutely no idea what that feels like,' Santo observed wryly.

'He's the best thing in my life,' she replied with all the love she felt. 'Do you have siblings?' she asked, the smile on her lips dissolving as the air between them cooled, remembering too late the scant bits and pieces of his life she'd managed to find out online.

'No,' he said, the absence of inflection more damning and powerful than any emotional declaration could have been. And somehow she instinctively knew that whatever kind of relationship she had, or would have, with this man, it would never be one for small talk.

He took one glance back at the photographs, pausing on the one of her parents before turning to lean back against the table, his arms crossed as if impatiently waiting. He probably wanted to get back to the party. She should just say what she wanted to say and let him leave.

'I wanted to thank you,' she said, forcing herself to meet his gaze.

'For?' he asked, the Italian inflection in his clipped words harsher than she remembered.

'For what you did for me last year. I… My entire life would be vastly different if you hadn't said what you did.'

'You don't regret it?' he asked. She felt the impact of his observation, the touch of his gaze as soft as feathers, as if he were looking for signs of dishonesty.

'No,' she said, allowing him to read the truth in her face. 'But… I was ashamed that you were right,' she said, looking down at the floor. 'About everything.' She'd been so sure that he was wrong that night—the warnings he'd given her—but he hadn't been.

'I hated you for that at the beginning,' she admitted, thinking of those first few months when everything was still so raw. 'A part of me wanted it to just go away. To pretend it hadn't happened. But I couldn't. Because of the pictures.'

Santo's gaze never left her once, his expression unreadable in the dim light cast by the fire.

She bit her lip. 'I didn't know my father could be like that,' she confessed.

Her sigh shuddered out from her chest and Santo felt it deep in his soul. It was a strange thing to hear because Santo had always known. He'd grown up knowing, as if it were instinctive—as if it were an awareness that he'd opened his eyes to from the very beginning. It had made it almost impossible for him to believe that she couldn't see Edward Carson for what he truly was.

Yet in Eleanor he could still see the child that was

desperate for her father's love. Whether or not she could instinctively sense that love was conditional, he could hardly guess. But it wouldn't help her or him to burst that bubble—it was something that could only be discovered for herself.

But something had eased in his chest to hear her admit that she didn't regret her decision to end the engagement. A breath he hadn't realised he'd held almost through the entire year released, replaced by satisfaction that he had been right to do as he had done last year. Satisfaction that he had fulfilled something of his promise to Pietro, even if it had come much sooner than either of them had imagined. Santo didn't believe that his vow was fulfilled though. Eleanor was still very much influenced by the people under this roof and, as such, not entirely as safe as she believed. But it would do for now.

She was watching him closely and he was content to let her for the moment. What he had to hide from her was hidden too well for her to discern, and what he didn't, he was content for her to see. He nearly smiled at how easy it was for him to read her, seeing the expressions shifting across her pretty features—curiosity, hesitancy…something more that he didn't quite want to name. She would need to learn to hide her emotions much better.

'Spit it out,' he said, not unkindly, but he could feel delicate strands reaching out to bind them together and he couldn't afford it. And Eleanor, whether she knew it or not, most definitely couldn't afford it.

'How did you know?' she asked. 'How did you know that they would do what you said they would?'

If Santo was honest with himself, he'd known that she would ask it eventually. The scales had fallen from her eyes over this last year and he could tell she wasn't the naïve girl he'd first met two years before.

'Because that's what they told my mother,' he replied on an exhale, turning away from Eleanor and stalking towards the fire, the crackle and pop of the wood at odds with the pull of memories tugging him back to dark places. 'When she was having last-minute doubts, they lied to her and told her that he would change once he was married. When he *settled down*. They lied, Eleanor, because her marriage benefitted them financially. They do it time and time again. Anything to make money. Anything to keep that money.'

He turned to take in the room. The money in here was hidden well, but still there. The carpet beneath his feet, handmade silk from some far-flung corner of the world, bought by some unknown ancestor long ago. The desk, deep, rich wood and hand-carved. It would have been considered exquisite by many, but Santo couldn't help but see it as something that his father would have lusted after. Gallo Sabatini had wanted nothing more than the legitimacy of Eleanor's world. He'd hated his own family because *'they came from nothing and they died as nothing'*, his father used to snarl—often as a warning to him and his mother. As if he could one day make sure that they suffered the same fate, should he want to.

Gallo had bullied, blackmailed, stolen, beaten and eventually married his way into his empire and had never been able to sand down the rough edges of that dirt. And the greatest pleasure Santo had ever had was burying the man beside a family he'd resented for being backward, illiterate and miserable.

'You hate them?'

'Yes, I do,' he replied truthfully.

'Then why are you here? Why do you still come to these parties?'

Words halted on his tongue, struck silent by the desire to answer her and the promise he'd made to the man who had protected his mother when he, himself, had not been able to.

'She can never know, Santo. It would change her life irrevocably. It would put her in too vulnerable a position.'

But it wasn't just his vow to Pietro that kept him bound to this group of people, that kept him bound to Eleanor.

'Because while I gained an empire on his death, I am also shackled to it.'

She stared back at him, thoughts crossing her features like the turning of pages.

'What was he like, your father?'

'Violent, ugly and mean,' he replied, refusing to sugarcoat it for her when clearly so much of her life had been cushioned and softened.

'Is that where you got the scar?' she asked, her hand lifting almost to touch the mark that cut through his eyebrow.

He leaned away from her touch, the sudden shocking memory of how it had happened taking him by surprise when his defences were down. He clenched his teeth together until his jaw ached.

'Yes,' he said, turning away from her, not wanting to see her reaction.

The puff of exhaled air was barely audible over the crackle of the fire taking hold, but he heard it.

'I… I'm sorry.'

He huffed out a bitter laugh. 'What for? The man was a bastard—that's not your fault.'

Her silence filled the small room, pressing against him in ways he'd not experienced before. Finally, he looked up, only for the sympathy in her gaze to cut him off at the knees.

'Your father shouldn't have done such a thing.'

Her words turned over something in his chest that he didn't want to see. He never talked to anyone about his father. Not his mother, not even Pietro. And yet here Eleanor was, smashing through all the barriers he tried to put around the subject.

'Fathers are just men, Eleanor, nothing more,' he said with a weight she wouldn't understand yet. 'Sometimes they make mistakes,' he said, thinking not of his own, but hers.

'Was that what your father did? Make a mistake?' she asked, taking a step forward.

'No. He knew what he was doing,' Santo said with an honesty that he'd never revealed to anyone other than Pietro.

Anger and tension swirled headily in his chest, reaching for the back of his neck in an aching hold. But Eleanor held his gaze and her nod to herself as much as him, her gentle acceptance of the violence that had shaped his life, rather than shock at it or refusal of it, calmed him in a way he'd not experienced before, in a way that shouldn't have been possible from the spoiled daughter of one of England's richest families.

All along she had been a contradiction. From managing to replace the shirt she'd spilled her drink on, so smoothly and seamlessly, to her ability to empathise so easily. Santo had written her off as a spoilt heiress, but she was steadily proving herself to be a puzzle. One he wanted to understand much more than he should.

'What will you do now?' he asked, moving the conversation onto the kind of small talk he usually loathed.

Eleanor smiled, recognising his diversionary tactic. But it was probably for the best. They had skated too close to topics that were intimate in a way she wasn't ready for. He made her feel things that were too familiar, yet utterly alien.

She knew enough to both recognise her attraction to him but to be wary of it too. It was probably some silly infatuation because he'd been there to rescue her when she'd needed it. And it was something she sensed he wouldn't welcome.

'I started my degree in September. I'll continue on with that,' she said, thinking of the arguments she'd had with her father, who had wanted her to stay here at the house, rather than move into the halls of residence at her university.

'What are you studying?'

'Business,' she replied, bracing herself against the derision he seemed to assume so quickly around her, but it never came.

'It's a good degree, with a lot of fundamentals that can be built on with experience. I found it useful.'

'You did a degree?' she asked, shocked.

His brow raised, eyes wry. 'That surprises you?'

'Yes,' she admitted. 'But only in so much as not knowing where you found the time for it.' She knew that he'd inherited the Sabatini Group upon his father's death, and that it had been held in trust for the sixteen months it took for him to reach eighteen. But she'd always assumed that he hadn't had time for something like a degree.

'I studied at night,' he admitted. 'But if you tell any-one, I'll deny it,' he vowed with mock seriousness.

His humour made her smile, but she recognised it as yet another diversionary tactic, keeping her at arm's length. Despite that, she could still recognise the sheer amount of work he must have done to not only maintain his father's business but grow it, all the while complet-ing a degree.

'Why did you do it?' she asked, unable to keep her curiosity at bay. Every little piece of information made her hungry for more.

His pause made her wonder if he was debating how honestly to reply.

'I wanted something that couldn't be taken away from me,' he said finally, the ring of truth in his words.

And there it was. The same desire she had. To have something fully for herself. Something that she would *always* have. After the shocking loss of the future she'd thought she'd have with Tony, her degree had become something that she'd clung to whenever she felt at sea. It was a need for something solid, something *hers*.

'Did it work? Did it give you what you needed?' she asked hopefully.

'Yes…and no,' he replied. Again, she appreciated his honesty, even as she found his answer disappoint-ing. She'd wanted reassurance, even if it were fake. The promise that things would all be okay. But she would never get that from Santo Sabatini and she didn't know whether that was a good thing or a bad thing.

The flames in the fireplace were beginning to die

down. It would be time to go back to the party soon. Eleanor knew she couldn't stay up here for ever. Certainly, she couldn't be caught up here with Santo. And her father would send someone looking for her eventually. But she didn't want to leave just yet.

Santo was watching her, as if reading her thoughts in her expressions. It wasn't intrusive in the way that she felt from many of the other guests, especially this evening. But it made her feel…lacking in some way. As if he were looking for something that wasn't there in her yet.

She'd heard the rumours about him and Marie-Laure. The widow was beautiful, clever, sophisticated, powerful in a way that intrigued her, whilst also making her strangely jealous. It was a confidence, a self-belief that was so strong it was almost alienating. And Eleanor wondered whether she would ever be anything like the other woman.

'I'm keeping you from the party,' she said eventually, acknowledging the silence in the room.

'Yes,' he said simply.

She nearly huffed out a laugh, whether he'd meant it to be funny or not. She would always get the truth from him and she was thankful for that.

'Well, Mr Sabatini,' she said, returning to formality as if she could undo the intimacy of their exchange as easily, 'thank you again.'

He nodded simply, the firelight taking slow, unfurling licks across his cheekbones, casting shadows across his powerful jaw line, across the hair curling ever so slightly at the collar of his shirt and jacket.

She held out her hand and in a flash she remembered their first handshake, the awkward mistiming of it, the trace of his hand at her fingertips. There was none of that this time. He took her hand in his, again, his gaze searching for something in her that she couldn't help him find. His palm against hers was slightly rough but warm, his grip firm, but held just a second too long. Because in that time she yearned for something more. For something she didn't dare name. For in her wildest dreams she couldn't imagine this man wanting from her what she wanted from him.

'Happy New Year,' he said, taking his hand back and leaving the room without a backward glance.

'See you next…' The door closed on her words. 'Year,' she finished to herself.

Things would be different, she promised herself. People would have got over the gossip about her and Tony and would have found something else to talk about. Next year, she wouldn't be defined by anything other than herself, she promised herself, hoping that perhaps then Santo would see in her what he'd been looking for.

CHAPTER FOUR

New Year's Eve six years ago, Berlin

'AND THAT'S WHEN I took his entire company with an ace high,' Allencourt guffawed, as if swindling someone out of their company with the lowest hand of cards was something to be proud of.

Santo rolled his shoulders, trying to shake loose the tension that had taken up residence earlier that day.

'He never forgave you,' Aksel Rassmussen said, shaking his head.

'My conscience is clear,' Allencourt replied, and Santo nearly choked on his drink.

'More champagne, sir?' a waiter asked.

Santo shook his head. 'But I'll give you fifty euros for a glass of whisky.'

'It's a free bar,' whispered the waiter, leaning in.

'I know,' Santo whispered back drily, the poor kid not knowing what to say. Santo laughed, more at himself than the waiter, and waved the boy off.

There was something about humour that no amount of language lessons could teach. And that, he realised, was just another thing that set him apart from the people here. Or most of the people here, he thought as he caught sight of Mads making his way across the sprawling nave in the most beautiful church in Berlin's Kreuzberg district.

Santo felt rather dubious about celebrating the annual New Year's Eve event in a church. He might not have been particularly religious himself, but it still skated close to the line that apparently didn't worry the Müllers.

Gunter Pichler passed close by, glaring at him. Santo blanked the man completely, trying to keep the victorious smile he felt from escaping onto his features. Just that morning he'd received yet another begging email from Pichler, wanting to resume his investment in the Sabatini Group. Surprisingly, Santo had had a good year, better than some had expected—some, like the Pichlers, had chosen to cash in their shares and now bitterly regretted it. His lips curled into a bitter smile. *Good riddance.*

Unconsciously, he scanned the crowd, not quite sure what he was looking for. No matter the jewels displayed by the guests, it was the church's magnificence that truly shone. The high domed ceilings were nothing short of an architectural feat, even though the gentle neon blue and purple lighting felt out of place and strangely inappropriate.

The drawn lines from last year were nowhere in sight. He spotted Carson laughing with Dilly's grandfather, and Analise Carson talking to Archibold Fairchild. No matter how well Eleanor was doing, she couldn't have been happy with such a painfully obvious 'business as usual' message being conveyed by the families.

And he ruefully wondered what 'business as usual' would look like for his family, and bitterly regretted the harsh words he'd exchanged with his mother last week.

Santo had discovered that she had been visiting his father's grave in Puglia, maintaining it and keeping it clean. It had been their worst argument yet. There was simply too much between them to be able to speak clearly on it. Too much hurt, too much guilt.

But their raised voices had skated too close to the past. His mother's fearful retreat from him was too much to bear. Santo gritted his teeth against the wave of hot, sickly emotion that always came when he thought of such things. Guilt, hatred, fear.

He was distracted from his thoughts by the gentle probe of someone's gaze. Curious, he looked deeper into the crowd, searching for someone his mind hadn't quite caught up to. Because he recognised that feeling. The warmth, the heat that he tried to ignore. The spark that shouldn't be there.

But he couldn't ignore it because there she was.

Eleanor.

From across the room, she flashed him that little Mona Lisa smile that might just be for him alone, the thought touching him much deeper and stronger than he realised. She inclined her head, and he did the same in acknowledgement, and her smile kicked up just a little more.

She gave a slight frown, her gaze flickering between him and the company he was in—as if she were surprised—and he couldn't help but roll his eyes, their silent conversation communicating his boredom and frustration with the men bragging about destroying each other's businesses.

Whoever she was talking to called back her attention. Glimpses of her kaleidoscoped across his vision as other guests passed back and forth in between them, reminding him of the bits and pieces of information he'd picked up about her throughout the year.

She had proved a little more distracting this year, his curiosity such that he'd had to find a particularly unscrupulous individual working at the university offices where Eleanor studied to keep him updated on her progress, so as not to derail his working day. He'd been pleased, and not as surprised as he once might have been, to discover that she was excelling in her courses. The unique twist of something like pride overrode any concerns his conscience might have had—he was simply keeping his word to Pietro.

He was about to take a sip of his drink when the man obscuring his view of her moved and he was able to see her fully for the first time. His hand hovered in the air, paused, in the time it took to take her in. And while everything in him roared against the inappropriateness of noticing what he most definitely should *not* be noticing, he couldn't help himself.

She was beautiful.

He'd always known that, in some distant part of his mind. In fact, if he was honest with himself, it was what had driven him from her company last year. An awareness of her that felt so wrong next to an innocence that practically screamed in warning.

But he had overestimated his confidence in her youth as a barrier to his increasing interest, as the person talking to the red-haired daughter of Artur Kivi was clearly no longer an innocent adolescent. And so it was that, with a shock of realisation, Santo now recognised Eleanor as a young woman of twenty-one, only five years his junior.

Her hair, artfully piled on top of her head in a messy

bun, showed off the swanlike curve of her neck. The thick velvet sleeveless dress moulded to her torso and veed across her chest in straps that tied on top of her shoulders, leaving her toned arms and sternum completely bare. Skirts dropped in dramatic folds from her waist to hit her mid-calf, the shape of her legs turning into delicate ankles topped with indecently high heels.

Never before had anyone taken such a swift hold of his body and Eleanor Carson had done it effortlessly and unconsciously in the space of a heartbeat. Santo was about to turn away before he made a fool of himself in public, when she caught his eye once again and this time her smile was unrestrained.

And the slash of lightning that struck him stole his breath.

Eleanor tried to cover the word she'd stuttered over the moment she'd caught Santo Sabatini staring at her, and failed miserably. Because this time they weren't exchanging subtle, easy interactions across a crowded room. No, this time, she'd felt heat. Interest. Want. The very things that severed her thought processes enough for her to forget her words.

'I'm sorry, Kat, I completely forgot where I was for a moment,' she admitted helplessly.

Ekaterina smiled. 'That's okay. We were talking about Capri.'

'Oh, yes,' Eleanor remembered vaguely, and shook her head, trying to dislodge the impact Santo had made. 'How did you find it?' she asked. But, no matter how hard Eleanor tried, she couldn't quite focus on Kat's answer.

She flicked her gaze to where Santo had been, but he

was no longer there. Which was strange, because she could still feel the weight of his attention on her. She rolled her shoulders, enjoying the way that the thick black satin-lined velvet pressed against her skin.

Her father had barely spared her a glance, but Eleanor had loved the dress the moment she'd seen it. It made her feel like a *woman*. And she'd so desperately wanted to feel that way tonight. Not a naïve, foolish girl who'd become engaged too soon, or a silly young miss stumbling over thanks as she had been last year. She'd wanted to be someone who could command attention. Command *his* attention.

But the moment she'd felt it, it had almost completely overpowered her. That full force impact had stolen her breath and her chain of thought, so much so that she could still feel the ripples of it now in the goosebumps across her skin.

'Oh, here he comes,' Ekaterina squealed. 'Please don't say anything,' she followed in a whisper.

Ekaterina's crush on Mads Rassmussen had been all her friend could talk about all evening, and Eleanor felt only a moment's jealousy. She knew that feeling, that sense of thrill as if glitter fizzed in one's veins and invisible fingers traced down one's spine.

Because it was how she felt about Santo—not that she'd ever dare say. There was something about their interactions that was private. Secret. And she wanted to keep it that way, especially after the painfully public fallout from her broken engagement.

Eleanor smiled at Mads as he joined them, but was distracted once again by the feeling of someone watching her. She told herself she was being fanciful, but she *knew* it was Santo. She knew it in a way that felt...*fated*.

'Don't you think so, Elle?'

Kat looked at her expectantly, and Eleanor nodded quickly.

'Absolutely,' she hedged, hoping it was the right thing to say, breathing out a sigh of relief when Kat smiled.

Mads looked at them both in mock horror. 'No, not me. I'd never do something like that,' he affirmed, and Kat playfully slapped him on the arm with a little too much strength.

Eleanor bit the inside of her cheek to stop herself from laughing. Kat would never be as subtle as she thought she was being, but it felt nice. Nice to be talking about unimportant things and enjoying someone else's happiness after the last two years' tumult.

'Ah, there you are, Santo, stop skulking and come and join us,' Mads called over Eleanor's shoulder.

Her breath caught and the ripples across her skin turned to shivers.

Santo came to stand beside her and she smiled and looked away, not quite prepared for the stark impact of him yet. There was a sense that they were both battling to maintain a distance that had already been thoroughly destroyed, but it was almost part of the unconscious game they seemed to be playing.

'Have you two met?' Ekaterina asked, blissfully ignorant of the currents passing back and forth between them.

Eleanor panicked. What was she supposed to say? Nerves made words dry in her throat.

'Once, I believe,' Santo said for her.

'Yes,' she said, finally turning to him with a smile. 'It's nice to see you again.'

Santo tipped his head in acknowledgement, but the glint in his eye—the one just for her—teased and taunted in a way that thrilled her.

'Likewise,' he said.

Oh, God, he looked incredible.

All year she'd been thinking about him. Her starved imagination had forced her to search him online, although 'search' was a polite term for what many others would call stalking. But the sheer impact of his presence was something else entirely. She almost didn't know where to look first.

Dark hair, lazily curling, was shorter this year than it had been. The hollows of his cheeks were ever so slightly more pronounced, made so by a close-cropped beard punctuated by the slight cleft in his chin. But there was something in his eyes—so light they were nearly aquamarine—that meant she could hardly bear to hold his gaze. It was as if they refracted all that she was feeling and threw it back at her in glittering fragments, making her unsure what he felt or thought at all.

'Oh, I love this song,' Ekaterina cried, and Eleanor looked down at the ground with a smile of affection at the transparency of her friend's motives.

Santo glanced between Mads and Kat and raised an eyebrow.

'Would you...?' Mads started to ask.

'Oh, yes—yes, please. Let's dance,' Kat said, before practically dragging the poor man off to where a few of the others had begun to dance.

Eleanor looked back to Santo's carefully blank expression and smiled.

'What?' he asked, without looking her way.

Eleanor bit back her smile, enjoying her observation of him. 'I don't think you're as indifferent as you pretend to be.'

'I assure you I am,' he insisted as if offended, and this time she couldn't help it. She let the smile break out because their interactions made her feel as if she saw something that few people did. As if he gave her something of himself that no one else saw.

A waiter paused beside her and she took a glass, turning to Santo to make a toast.

'To the New Year,' she said.

'To the New Year,' he repeated, the clink punctuating their toast before they each took a sip.

'I hear congratulations are in order,' Eleanor offered.

'For me?' he asked as if surprised.

She huffed out a gentle laugh. 'Yes, for you. The Sabatini Group's turnover was nothing short of miraculous this year. And I heard you managed to rid yourself of one of your investors. That is no mean feat,' she added conspiratorially.

He frowned at her as if confused by her knowledge of his business. She frowned back exaggeratedly, receiving a begrudging smile in response—just as she'd hoped.

'Business degree, remember?' she reminded him.

'I do,' he confirmed, and those words meant more to her than he would ever imagine. It was like a present she'd been hoping for all year long.

Eleanor took a deep breath. It continued to be a bone of contention between her and her father. It was as if everything she did to please him took her further and further away from what she had meant to him before. Before she'd broken her engagement, before she'd ever started to attend these things.

Instinctively, she sought out her father in the crowd and noticed that he was looking their way. And suddenly she didn't want to be caught by her father with Santo, she didn't want to be out here where people could see them. She noticed more and more people looking their way.

'What's wrong?' Santo asked, feeling the change in her demeanour like a cloud passing over the sun. The smile that pulled up the corners of her lips became tighter.

'People are staring.'

She was right, of course. For himself, Santo had got quite used to the feeling, but it clearly upset her.

'Want to see something spectacular?' Santo whispered in her ear. She looked up at him, the gratitude in her eyes louder than a cry as she nodded, taking what he was offering with both hands.

Santo drew Eleanor away from the crowds and up the staircase at the back of the nave to a second floor. A narrow walkway took them beyond the pews that looked down onto the altar, to behind the focal point of the church.

He was aware of her with every step he took. It was madness to be alone with her, especially as he wrestled with the effect she was having on him, but the unwanted attention she was receiving had taken away that sense of confidence that had lit Eleanor from deep within and that was unacceptable.

He held his hand out to her as he guided her up the last

few steps towards his destination. And when she placed her hand in his he tried to ignore the sparks that fizzled and hissed between their touch.

If he'd expected Eleanor to ask where they were going, he'd been mistaken. She appeared utterly at ease with wherever he was taking her. Perhaps she hadn't learned enough from the past few years then. She should be on her guard. Especially around him.

He headed for the large ornately designed window with slashes of stained glass segmented by thick dark metal bleeding into the night, making it appear almost magical. Next to the series of crossing steps, the entire area reminded him of an Escher painting, making him wonder how different things could have been for him. For her. For *them*.

Just as they reached the window a firework scattering yellow and pink bursts into the night sky exploded and Santo heard a soft gasp of surprise fall from Eleanor's lips. And with just that Santo battled with a surprisingly fierce wave of arousal that shivered through his body.

He barely dared look at her. Up close, he could see that Eleanor's dress was made of a thick black velvet, studded with absolutely minuscule studs of gold that made it look as if she shimmered like the night sky on the other side of the window. The paleness of her skin, rather than seeming diminished, glowed within the material. And he was struck that the regality that she wore like a cloak across her shoulders had turned a princess into a queen. Something that made her feel so very far beyond his reach.

Another firework exploded and he watched the flares glitter in her eyes, the slight flush of pleasure on her cheeks, and indignation that he hadn't put it there himself was enough of a warning for him to step back. Only he couldn't seem to bring himself to do it.

But he really should. He was there to protect her, for Pietro, and that most certainly included protecting her from himself. The things he'd seen, the things he knew… they were too much for an innocent like Eleanor.

She closed her eyes and lost the sparkle of the night, as if somehow intuiting his attempt to withdraw from her.

'Your mother isn't here?' Eleanor observed without looking at him.

He was surprised, the turn in conversation yanking him out of his thoughts, and forced himself to answer the question. He supposed it was understandable, though. For a gathering supposedly of families, his was noticeably absent, even considering Gallo's death.

'*I* represent the family,' he stated grimly, finding it uncomfortable that perhaps he couldn't read her thoughts as much as he'd believed.

'Does she not like all this?'

'No. She never did,' he said, wishing that they had more than these silly glasses of champagne. He took a mouthful of the bubbly alcohol anyway, the taste of nothing but regret on his tongue. He looked down, knowing that he could change the topic of conversation. Knowing that she would accept it if he did, but for the first time he found himself wanting her to know. About him. About his childhood.

'She was an only child and her father was old when she was born. He was desperate to marry her off, and my father was desperate enough to take her name.'

Santo thought about how cruelly his mother had been used by the men in her life, how awful it must have been not to have anyone on her side. He wondered if that was why he was drawn to Eleanor, to the similarities between them as much as the differences.

'I didn't realise. I thought your connection here was through your father,' Eleanor said.

'He was happy to make it seem like that, and after the money he made for many of the families here they were happy to go along with it.'

He looked at Eleanor, staring up at him with those wide eyes. He could see her hovering on the edge of innocence. Yes, she'd had her fingers burnt by Tony, by Edward Carson's response to her broken engagement, but it was just the tip of an iceberg he wasn't sure that she would ever be ready to face.

'I'm sorry. This is a heavy conversation to have when everyone around us is celebrating,' Eleanor said, recognising that Santo was close to shutting down, when all she wanted to do was open him up. She'd thought so much of him over the last twelve months, but knew almost nothing about him—other than what was mentioned in the business pages. But perhaps there was a different way, a *lighter* way?

'Would you like to play a game?' she asked, forcing a playfulness into her tone.

For a moment, she wondered whether he'd take her up on her offer.

'That depends on the game,' he said, something glinting in his eyes that pulled at her body.

'Truth or dare,' she replied.

He frowned, those dark brows closing down over the incredible aquamarine of his gaze.

'Have you not played truth or dare before?' she asked with a laugh.

'I have heard of it, but never played it.'

Reading between the lines, his childhood sounded dark, hard and painful, and she suddenly wondered just how much Santo had been able to play as a young boy. She was about to retract the offer when he asked, 'Who goes first?'

'I will,' she said before he could change his mind. 'Truth or dare?'

He huffed out a cautious laugh. 'Do I not get to know the question first?'

She shook her head slowly, a smile curving her lips.

He nodded once, and seemed to lean closer in, their bodies speaking their own language to each other.

'Truth,' he said then.

'Okay, but it's a hard one, so think carefully,' she warned. 'What is…your favourite food?'

Santo barked out a laugh and it warmed her then. She'd seen him cynical, bitter, hard, disdainful, but this was something she only occasionally saw when it was just the two of them alone and that made her feel…thrilled. Excited. As if perhaps there could be something here between them. Something more than just a passing fancy.

'It is a cliché but tiramisu. I could eat a whole bowlful every day,' he admitted, leaning against the wall beside the large, beautiful round window. 'Your turn,' he announced.

'Truth,' she said, answering his unspoken question.

His inhale and narrowed eyes were playful, but still she found herself unaccountably nervous, until his gaze raked her body from top to toe, making her feel something else entirely.

'Where are you ticklish?' he demanded.

She blinked. 'What makes you think I'm ticklish?'

'You're avoiding the answer,' he teased.

Eleanor huffed, trying hard not to let a smile escape onto her lips. 'My feet,' she replied mock resentfully.

He nodded to himself as if he'd thought as much.

'Truth or dare,' she challenged.

'Truth.'

'Who was your first kiss?' she asked, pressing her lips together the moment the words were out of her mouth, the fizzle and crackle no longer outside in the night sky but hurtling through her veins beneath her skin.

A gleam of surprise flashed in his gaze just as another round of fireworks exploded over the Brandenburg Gate.

'Sofia Barone,' he replied with a slow smile as if remembering. 'We were fourteen years old, and were supposed to be playing hide and seek with her brother. He didn't find us,' he replied, clearly proud of his achievement.

She doubted he knew it, but his entire expression had changed. His face had relaxed, for once losing some of the intensity that marked him as different to almost everyone else here. And it was as if the shadows that haunted his gaze had lifted for a moment. Before he shook his head, his eyes clearing from the memory and focusing on her.

She could see it. The temptation to ask her the same question, the debate, the war in him.

'Truth or dare?' he asked slowly.

'Truth.'

She wanted him to ask her about her first kiss. She

wanted him to open the door, even just a little, to where she wanted to go. To what she wanted to do. The sensual pull she'd denied the year before had become insistent as she skated the edges of whatever this was between them. She wanted it to be something more. She needed it to be tangible.

'Did you sleep with Fairchild?'

Instantly her cheeks flushed. The raw gravel tone of his voice scratched over every sensitive part of her body. She should have been surprised by the question, but she wasn't. It had been there, simmering between them. She'd wanted it, Santo just had the confidence to dig that deep. Her heart thundered in one powerful pump, rushing blood through her body and making her skin tingle so much that she felt the echoes of it reverberating around her heart while she held her breath. She bit her lip, knowing that this was a line she couldn't come back from. That the door she had opened a little was about to be pushed further.

'No,' she said, holding his intent gaze. She wanted him to see the truth. To know it. 'Truth or dare?' she asked before she could chicken out.

'Dare,' he replied, sending sparks down into her core.

She closed the step between them, her heart in her throat, her pulse beating at a furious rate.

'I dare you to kiss—'

'Eleanor?'

Shocked, Eleanor spun round to come face to face with her father.

Edward Carson glared between her and Santo, and she took a step back just as Santo took a step forward, drawing her father's attention. Whether consciously or unconsciously, he had put himself between her and her father.

'Sabatini.'

'Carson,' Santo replied likewise.

Eleanor could feel the hostility between the two men, which seemed excessive for the context of the situation. She had never asked whether her father had investments in the Sabatini Group, or whether Santo had investments in her father's businesses, but it was clear, whatever the case was, there was contention between the two.

'Come. We're leaving,' Edward announced, not even holding out his hand for her as he might once have done.

'I—'

'Do not try me, Eleanor,' her father warned.

Everything that had just been within her reach was slipping through her fingers like sand. She bowed her head, giving up the fight, and followed in her father's footsteps. Just before the last step took her away from Santo she looked up to find something like regret in his gaze, before it was quickly blinked away.

It gave her hope. It made her think that perhaps next year things might be different.

And Eleanor was right. Things *would* be different next year, but not in a way that she'd ever imagine.

CHAPTER FIVE

New Year's Eve five years ago, Paris

'OF COURSE THE Dubois wouldn't be so crass as to arrange their event at the Eiffel. It's been done to *death*.'

'Naturally. But this is…*acceptable*.'

'Quite,' came the insincere response.

Santo ground his teeth together and checked his watch. He was late and impatient. His eagerness to see Eleanor had grown into almost monstrous proportions now that he was actually here. The two elderly ladies, a Müller and an Allencourt, conversing in English, hovered by the entrance, in the way. One of them peered meanly over her shoulder at him, disdain evident the moment she recognised him.

Those of her generation had been less inclined to accept his father's marriage to his mother and, as such, less inclined to accept *him*. However, as he made them and their children obscene amounts of money they tended to consider him a necessary evil.

He flashed his most charming smile, with just enough wickedness to melt the ice in her gaze, before her friend pulled her through the entrance to the Pavillon Dauphine. The grand building, situated at the bottom of the Avenue de l'Impératrice, was over a century old and every inch of its grandeur was marked in classic lines of beauty throughout. But at that moment Santo Sabatini couldn't have given a damn for any of it.

He had one goal and intended to find her as fast as humanly possible. For almost the entire year he'd thought of little else. She had occupied his waking thoughts and tormented his sleep. The innocence of her request, the clear intention behind it, had driven him near wild with want. He'd almost begun to regret keeping tabs on her university career, the updates keeping him tied to her in a way he both wanted and loathed.

But then, a few months ago, something had changed. Her online presence had dropped away to nothing, with no mention of her or—more surprisingly—Edward Carson or his business. For a man who craved attention it was a little unusual. Then, a month ago, Santo had discovered that she had stopped attending class, making both him and Pietro deeply concerned. But no amount of digging had uncovered anything.

Santo stalked through the grand entrance and into the large sprawling conservatory, where a long dining table was overburdened with a spectacular feast, but the smell of the rich food only turned his stomach. Scanning the faces of those seated, he knew she wasn't there. He couldn't feel her presence.

He reached the lavish ballroom, one wall covered in large mirrors encased in ornate mouldings, honey-coloured wooden floors gleaming beneath the gentle lighting, and still there was no sign of her. Ignoring the way that the pace of his pulse had picked up in concern, he swept into the next room and the next, until he'd covered all the rooms bar the ladies' toilets.

Then, through the window, he saw that there were people gathered outside, beneath the warm glow of heaters. An outside bar had been set up, and smaller seating areas attracted the few that were braving the cold in their furs and finery.

Ignoring his usual distaste for such things, he approached the patio doors that would have taken him out onto the area gently illuminated by strings of fairy lights, searching for a single face from amongst the crowd.

Already he felt a twisting deep in his gut. The only people outside were from Fairchild's group. And with a blinding sense of betrayal, he knew she was there amongst them.

He hung back in a darkened corner of the room until he spotted her, laughing at something someone had said in a gauche way he had never before associated with her. The rage that he felt in that moment, the pure fury that she had gone back to the very people who would have used her, who had abused her, was a red haze that he could barely breathe through. His heartbeat pounded in his ears like a war drum and it took nearly everything in him to wrestle himself under control.

The realisation drained the blood from his head so quickly he became lightheaded. Because in that moment he'd felt a violence he'd only ever witnessed in his father. Instinctively and unconsciously, his hand went to his eyebrow, fingers pressed against the scar as a cold sweat lay in a fine sheen across his skin beneath the shirt and tuxedo he wore tonight.

He braced his palm against the wall, holding himself

back, holding him *up*, knuckles gleaming white under the force of it.

How could she?

Past hurts mixed nauseatingly with the present as he almost violently forced himself back in line.

What had happened to him?

Behaving like some jealous schoolboy with his first crush. As if she had ever been anything more to him than a promise he'd made to an old man to whom he owed a debt.

In his mind, he wrote over the memories of their interactions, editing out the impact and the intimacy as if he could undo every effect Eleanor Carson had ever had on him. As if he could backpedal his feelings and shove them far back behind a line he had never crossed, and would never again.

He was done. He would fulfil his promise and no more.

Every single part of Eleanor was in agony. Her body, her soul, all buckling under the weight of the trauma that had taken everything she'd thought she knew about herself and those in her life and slashed a line through it all.

She laughed at something Ekaterina had said and it sounded as hollow and false as she felt. Resentment seethed beneath the surface as she reached for a glass of something she barely even tasted as she downed the alcohol, the faint buzz touching her senses but still not enough to take away the pain that cut at her lungs every time she took a breath.

She shivered, even though the heat from the outside lamps was such that many around her were without shawls or coats.

Tony slid a glance her way. Suspicion and anger mixed with that sense of snide superiority he could no longer hide from her. Because something had happened since she'd discovered the truth back in November, since her family had become something alien and unknowable to her. It was as if she could see through it all. The lies, the secrets, the bullshit.

She laughed to herself this time, uncaring of the concern in Ekaterina's face. For all Eleanor knew, that was as fake as the rest of them. She'd seen Dilly earlier in the evening, her one-time best friend giving her a wide berth. And suddenly the tears she'd been holding at bay pressed terrifyingly close to the corners of her eyes.

She bit her lip, hoping that the sharp sting would work to pull her out of that moment. The moment when she'd thought of how much she wished there was someone to confide in. Someone to seek help from. Support. *Love*. But all of that was gone.

She was on her own now in a way that had truly shocked her to her core. Because eight months ago she'd discovered that Edward Carson was not her father. And overnight he had become a complete stranger to her.

'Who is my father?' she'd cried, begged, pleading with her mother, whose own shock had been worn clearly on her ghostly white features, contrasting with the fierce red fury of her father's.

Eleanor looked around hazily at the sea of faces, wondering who—if anyone—knew. Or whether they could somehow tell that she wasn't Edward Carson's daughter. Were they all laughing at her behind her back? Had they always been?

No one can know. No one can ever know.

Little Freddie's blood drive to help the friend from school who'd been diagnosed with leukaemia had irrevocably changed the trajectory of her life. He'd happily gathered their donor cards together, ticking off each one of their blood types, blissfully unaware of the sudden, devastating change in room temperature. That evening, Freddie had been sent to his room without explanation and little drama because somehow, without explanation, he'd realised that something was terribly wrong.

The single slap across her mother's face delivered cruelly by the man she'd thought of as her father had broken something deep within her. But no matter how many times he'd asked, yelled or shouted, demeaned or bullied, her mother had refused to name her father. She had simply said, *'I don't know,'* over and over again, in the hope that either her daughter or husband might eventually believe her.

And then Edward Carson had turned on her.

'You listen to me, and you listen good. If you want to have even the smallest chance of maintaining any kind of relationship with your brother, not a word of this gets out. Ever,' he'd warned darkly. *'You'll go back to your friends, you might even find another fiancé. I don't care. All that matters is that none of this gets out.'*

As the words ran through her mind like a film reel, she knew that the worst was yet to come.

'I will not have it known that I let a bastard into my family and treated her like my own.'

A waiter passed with another tray of drinks and she took the glass of whisky, swallowing the tears that had gathered in her throat along with the peaty alcohol.

Everything felt wrong. Her skin crawled as if some

dark nightmare had slipped over her and she couldn't escape it.

The man she had thought was her father, the man she had loved, the man for whom she had worked hard to become someone he could be proud of, had turned into a vicious monster. He had all but cast out her mother, allowing her to remain in the house only to save face.

And her brother—poor little Freddie who, having turned twelve over the summer, knew that something was wrong—had begun to retreat into himself, as if pole-axed by the secrets in the family. Yes, Eleanor could leave. But she didn't doubt for one minute that her father would prevent her from returning or seeing her brother while he remained under his roof. And what would happen to Freddie without her mother or her around to protect him?

She didn't think her father would do anything to him, other than mould his young, barely formed personality into whatever he wanted. And that, she was beginning to realise, was the most terrifying thing about the whole situation.

That her brother would lose his innocence. That he would be twisted and warped into her father's image. That Freddie would become like these young men in the garden, laughing at whatever cruelty had taken their fancy.

Because that was what they did. They found something or someone and made them the butt of their jokes, casting them as an outsider to torment for their own amusement. And she didn't want Freddie anywhere near these people. Fighting back the cramp fisting her stomach, she threw back another mouthful of whisky, a drink she'd acquired a taste for two years earlier, with Santo.

Santo.

She knew he'd be here this evening. She thought that perhaps he might have come here with expectations. Expectations that she'd encouraged last year, back when she'd thought she'd survived the worst that life could throw at her.

A bubble of almost hysterical cynicism rose from deep within her.

Naïve. Foolish.

She knew that Santo had believed her to be both of those things. And he'd been right. All along, she had been incomparably naïve and utterly foolish. And now it seemed as if broken shards of rose-coloured glass lay at her bare feet, ready to cut her if she moved even an inch.

'Eleanor, are you sure you're okay?' Ekaterina asked, and she was about to reply when she felt it. When she felt *him*.

She swallowed, capable only of nodding her reassurance. Because if she opened her lips the only thing that would emerge was a miserable sob.

The hairs stood up at the back of her neck, goosebumps shivering over her skin. The weight of his attention was an icy finger trail across her shoulder blades, poking and prodding an accusation of betrayal and disappointment.

She could only imagine his shock at seeing her back here amongst the very people who epitomised everything he seemed to hate about this event. The very people she had turned her back on three years before. The very people that her father had blackmailed her into joining again.

'If anyone finds out, you'll never see Frederick ever again.'

And Santo would. He would find out, he would cut to

the heart of her secret so effortlessly, and she couldn't allow him to do that. She couldn't risk it. So, with that threat ringing in her ears, she turned her back to where she felt Santo's presence and said to Ekaterina, 'Let's dance.'

'And that's when I told him that he could invest whatever he wanted, but that I was having nothing to do with it.'

'Quite right. So have you considered…'

Santo tuned out from the banal conversation of the men and women around him. It was always the same: who had the most money, where could that money be put to use, what could they get? This constant grab, grab, grab.

His gaze scanned the room, refusing to settle on Eleanor, but always keeping her within his line of sight. He clenched his jaw as, from the corner of his eye, he saw her wobble awkwardly on her heels. He hadn't been counting, but he could tell that she had already had more to drink that evening than all of the previous New Year's Eve parties put together.

Something was wrong.

And she hadn't come to him.

Old insecurities rose to the surface. Memories of being unable to do anything to protect his mother, of being helpless against his father. And then, just when he'd got big enough to fight back, his father had used her against him. The threat against her was the only leash that Gallo Sabatini had needed against Santo, and he'd used it well.

Until that last day. He'd heard the argument from outside the house. The screams that had caused the blood to freeze in his veins. Santo had rushed through the doors of the villa just outside Rome and found his mother crouched over his father's broken body lying at the bottom of the curved staircase.

With shaking hands, she'd pulled her mobile from her pocket. He'd honestly thought she'd been calling the police until he'd heard her begging Pietro to come. When his mother had looked up and found him standing there...

He'd never forget the look on her face.

The shock, the guilt, the shame...the *fear*. His mother had been frightened. Of *him*. Of what he might have seen, or heard. And in his entire life he never wanted to see someone look at him with that same fear.

Pietro had arrived and quietly dismissed all the staff. He'd taken his mother into another room and spoken to her for nearly half an hour before he came out. He'd told Santo that he'd called the police and would speak to them himself, that Santo didn't have to worry about anything.

Santo had watched as Pietro managed the entire situation while he'd been unable to take his gaze away from the dead stare of his father's eyes. In the weeks and months that had followed, Pietro was the only person who could get his mother to leave her bed. It hadn't mattered how much he'd begged or pleaded, only Pietro could help.

At sixteen, it hadn't even crossed Santo's mind to be jealous of Pietro. He'd just been unspeakably thankful that there was someone in his mother's life who made her return to even the smallest semblance of the mother he'd once had.

Pietro had tried to explain to him that it had been an accident. That they'd been arguing and that his mother had acted in self-defence. But the older man didn't seem to understand that it didn't matter to Santo. Truly. Self-defence or otherwise. If it hadn't happened like that, it could have been his mother lying at the bottom of the stairs. It was that simple.

But of all the people in his parents' lives, of all the people *here*, it was only an outsider like Pietro who had ever cared about them beyond his father. Pietro, a man who had been born on the wrong side of the tracks and, no matter how much money he'd amassed, would never have gained entry into a society like this. Pedigree. That was what mattered to the people here.

And it turned his stomach.

Someone barged into his shoulder as they passed, Santo's head snapping to follow the blond head back towards the dance area, where various people were gathered. The head turned enough for him to recognise Antony Fairchild's sneer, the foolish boy believing himself to have scored a point on whatever childish game he played in his head.

'He still hasn't forgiven you for snubbing him last year, I see,' commented the richly accented Marie-Laure.

'But have you?' Santo asked in response, without taking his eyes off the boy until he disappeared into the middle of the throng. Santo knew that she was still displeased with him for turning down her advances. And the woman certainly knew how to hold a grudge.

Marie-Laure waited until she had his attention before answering. And he respected that. Whatever could be said about her indiscretions, or her political power plays, Santo always knew where he stood with her. There was artifice about everyone else, but at least with her he knew where he stood.

'That depends.'

'On?' he said, turning his full attention on her. He was standing close enough to see the way her body responded to him instinctively, the widening of her pupils, the almost imperceptible hitch in her breathing.

'How you're planning to make it up to me,' she teased. He smirked.

This was easy. *This* was what he wanted from life. He'd paid his dues with complexities and lies. He didn't need Eleanor or anyone like her. *This* was all he needed.

He bent his lips to her ears. 'Long,' he whispered. 'And slow.' He dipped his head lower. 'And hard,' he promised.

As Eleanor paused on the dance floor the room continued to spin. Frowning, she put her hand to her head, but that didn't help. But what did a little spinning matter when her entire life was spinning out of her control?

She shrugged and smiled at Ekaterina, who had at least stopped asking her if she was okay. She saw Dilly pass by at the edge of the crowd and growled in her mind. Or at least she thought it had been in her mind, but the way people had turned to look at her made her question whether it might have slipped out.

She lurched towards a passing waiter, who looked worried as she went to grab for another shot glass of sambuca.

She *loved* sambuca. She had decided that it was her very favourite drink. It was sweet and thick and after downing it she didn't care as much. Santo could keep his stinking whisky. She would now only drink sambuca for ever.

But as she put the empty glass back on the waiter's tray she caught Santo standing with Marie-Laure from the corner of her eye. Her stomach clenched involuntarily as she saw Marie-Laure gazing at Santo in a way that left absolutely no doubt as to what she wanted from him.

And that wouldn't have been so bad, had Santo not been leaning into her ear with wicked intent as he looked down at her. It was so markedly different to how he'd looked at her at the end of last year.

This was older, darker, *sexier*.

Burned by the shocking twist of jealousy that pierced her breast at the sight of the naked want in the older woman's gaze, Eleanor averted her eyes. It clearly didn't matter to Marie-Laure that he was twenty years her junior, and it clearly didn't matter to Santo who saw them.

She forced down her jealousy just as someone grabbed her around the waist and pulled her back against him.

'Dance with me,' a familiar voice urged in her ear, pulling her against his crotch as irritation and recognition flashed through her body all at once.

'Get off, Tony,' she said, pushing at his hands. But he didn't let go.

'Come on, Lore, you used to love dancing with me,' Tony insisted, his hands leaving her waist to press against her body in places she didn't want him anywhere near.

'Let me go,' she spat.

'You're just playing hard to get,' he accused, his breath hot against her already feverish skin.

Eleanor twisted in his embrace and slapped him hard, and for a second what she saw in his eyes made her blood freeze. And then, before she could feel scared, she was hit by a wave of nausea and she retched. Tony's expression turned from fury to disgust as he pushed her away and all Eleanor could think was that she needed to get to the bathroom before she threw up.

She pushed people out of the way as she lurched awkwardly away from the ballroom and towards the bathrooms she had seen in the corridor. Shoving open the door, she went straight to the sink and ran the cold water tap. Drinking straight from the stream of water, she swallowed, hoping that it would soothe her churning stomach.

After an eternity the feeling passed and she thrust her hand in the water before pressing the cool dampness against her face and skin, no longer caring about her make-up or anything other than making it stop.

She just wanted it all to stop.

Struck by a wave of loneliness, she sobbed and careened into the cubicle, flicking the lock on the door and sinking to the cool tiles of the thankfully clean floor.

'You're just playing hard to get.'

'No one can know.'

'I let a bastard into my family.'

'You'll never see Frederick ever again.'

Round and round the words went, spinning in waves of nausea and the sickly-sweet concoction of alcohol in her stomach. She just wanted to go to sleep. Perhaps then she might never wake up.

Santo stalked towards the bathroom.

'She's fine, Santo. Leave her.'

Santo didn't spare Marie-Laure a backward glance. Anyone in their right mind would have been able to see that Eleanor Carson was as far from fine as was humanly possible.

He'd let his own ego get in the way of what he was supposed to do, which was to keep an eye on her. Self-recrimination was a familiar stick to beat himself with, but he'd never thought he'd have to feel it with regard to her.

He went to knock on the door when a woman emerged from the bathrooms, just able to stop herself in time before she'd walked smack-bang into him.

'Is there anyone other than Eleanor Carson in there?' he demanded.

The woman shook her head quickly and ducked away from him to scurry off down the corridor.

Santo pushed the door open and found the bathroom empty. Decked out in the style of the late eighteen-hundreds, five sinks in front of five mirrors lined one side of the room and five bathroom stalls the other. Powder pink, pastel blue and gold mouldings around the room suited the pavilion's overall design but did nothing but irritate Santo's alert senses.

'Eleanor,' he growled.

No response.

'I know you're in here, I saw you come in.'

Still no response.

'If you don't let me know that you're okay I'll have to assume that you've drunk yourself into such a stupor, you've passed out and I will start kicking down doors,' he warned.

'*Gowwaay...*' finally came a rather slurred reply.

'No can do, Princess.'

'*Jussst leave me alooone...*'

Merda. How could her friends let her get like this? And then he remembered what kind of friends they were and felt the resentment build in him again.

'Open the door, Eleanor,' he commanded. 'Now,' he warned, pulse pounding until he heard the click of the lock.

He pulled the door open and looked down to find her crumpled on the floor.

His heart yanked, hard.

Pitiable. That was what she looked like, and from the flush of shame on her cheeks she knew it too. Anger began to dissolve as he crouched down to her level.

Questions filled his mind and throat.

'Are you okay?'

'Whassit matter?'

He frowned, struggling to interpret her slurred English. 'Eleanor—'

'Doesn't matter. Not any more.'

And, to his horror, she started to cry.

'I want to go home,' she whimpered.

'Okay. I'll get you home,' he said, pulling her gently into his arms.

'But I can't,' she confessed, tucking her head into his chest as if she could hide from the world.

'Of course you can. I'll take you,' he insisted.

'Don't have a home. Don't have a father. Not any more,' she said, before closing her eyes and seemingly passing out.

'Eleanor—' He shook her gently in his arms, but she didn't rouse.

Alarm spread through Santo's entire being.

'Don't have a father.'

Did she know? Did Edward Carson know? *Cristo*, that changed everything.

Santo was halfway out of the door when he came face to face with her mother, Analise. She took one look at Eleanor in his arms and gestured for him to follow her.

They drew several curious glances as she led Santo towards the back exit.

'Edward's waiting,' Analise warned and Santo nodded to acknowledge he'd heard.

'He knows?' Santo asked Analise.

'Yes. Since November.'

'Are you okay?'

'No. Not at all.'

'What about Eleanor?' he demanded.

'She'll be okay, if she plays along,' her mother confirmed.

Santo gritted his teeth together and unconsciously tightened his hold on her.

'What do you want me to tell Pietro?' he asked.

There was an almost imperceptible hitch in her stride before the words, 'Tell him whatever you want,' were tossed over her shoulder.

As they came out into the slap of cold night air, Eleanor stirred in his arms. He followed Analise Carson to where a black limousine waited, with Edward Carson glaring angrily at him and his wife, yet not even bothering to spare his daughter a glance.

'If you've touched her, I don't want her,' Carson stated.

The accusation hit Santo low and hard, everything primal in him rising against delivering Eleanor back into the man's care.

'If I'd touched her she wouldn't be coming back to you,' Santo growled and he knew in that moment it was the truth. If Eleanor ever came to him she would never need anything from Edward Carson again. He would give her whatever she needed for however long she needed it.

'Put her in the car,' Carson ordered and he looked to

Eleanor's mother for permission. All she had to do was
say no and he would take her away.

He could see the warring in her gaze and he knew
what was holding both women back. Frederick. Eleanor's brother.

Fighting every instinct he had, Santo put Eleanor gently into the car and watched as Carson slammed the door
and went round to the other side of the limousine, not taking his eyes off Santo until the last second.

As Santo watched the car disappear into the night he
retrieved his phone and found Pietro's name.

'Carson knows,' Santo said the moment the call clicked
through. 'As does Eleanor.'

The silence on the end of the phone was deafening.

The rules of the game had now changed.

CHAPTER SIX

New Year's Eve four years ago, Prague

FIREWORKS EXPLODED ACROSS Prague's Old Town Square. In the distance, the fourteenth century church stared down at the hundreds of thousands of people cramming themselves onto its streets, each as eager as the next to count down the New Year by one of the oldest medieval astronomical clocks in the world.

The mishmash of old architectural styles, statues and memorials stood firm against wave after wave of tourists and locals alike, each entertained by the ferocious fireworks that exploded nearly at eye level, causing fear and delight in worryingly equal measure. Santo looked out upon them all, separated by a pane of thick glass, wondering what he would do with this one night a year if he had the freedom to choose for himself.

'I wasn't sure you'd come this year,' said Mads Rassmussen.

Santo gave him a death stare. For nearly twelve months, rather than the literal fires he had fought in previous years across his olive groves in Puglia, he had been defending himself against financial attack from not just one but two different sides, Edward Carson on one and Marie-Laure on the other.

Mads laughed. 'You have nothing to fear from me, Sabatini. And besides, I've enough on my hands with Rassmuss Technologies to worry about olive groves. But I did hear a rumour that you might be interested in renewable—'

'No idea what you're talking about,' Santo replied, cutting off the young Scandinavian before he could finish his sentence. A flash of concern rushed painfully through his body. The number of people who knew about his business interest in renewable energies could be counted on less than one hand. It was certainly something he didn't want anyone here to know about.

'Relax. When you're ready, let me know and I promise it will go no further,' Mads said, a business card palmed into Santo's hand with a shake.

Santo waited until the other man had joined his father and some others before looking at the handwritten mobile number on the blank card with the initials MR embossed in the corner. He barely restrained himself from laughing at this silly game of cloak and dagger but, after the year he'd had, he understood the need for it—and appreciated Rassmussen's understanding of that more than he'd care to admit.

Santo had expected Carson's underhand tactics, Pietro and he had all but prepared for it, but when Marie-Laure had decided to use her investments to take out her frustration and resentment at his abandonment of her last year, it had forced him to split his focus and his business had suffered.

It had suffered because of Eleanor.

But that wasn't why he was ignoring her increasingly desperate attempts to snare his attention from across the room. Steeling himself, he turned in the opposite direction, making his way to the bar of the old banquet hall acquired by the Svobodas for the evening. They must have booked it several years in advance; every window along the entire length of the hall had a view of the clock tower. But, no matter how much he tried to shake her off, she consumed his thoughts entirely.

Resentment and frustration reinforced his determination to keep her at arm's length. He had never argued with Pietro before this year. Not once had they exchanged anything more than support and encouragement. But Santo's feelings for Eleanor had become much more complex than simple attraction, and he'd struggled with Pietro's decision to maintain the fragile status quo. Their heated exchange had made Santo feel as if he were both disappointing Pietro and himself at the same time. As if neither could win because neither was wrong. But with the disconcerting feeling that neither was right either.

Santo might have disagreed with Pietro's decision, but he respected the man completely. And what was the alternative? Eleanor would hardly come to him, leaving her brother and her mother behind under Edward's control. The helplessness of the situation ate at him and his sense of control in a way he disliked intensely.

And the difficulty he had in leashing his wants beneath the yoke of his word was enough to warn him of just how dangerous she had become to him. Almost as dangerous as he was to her. But his decision to keep distance between them seemed to make her only more desperate to seek him out.

Santo was no stranger to the feeling that eyes were on him. Edward had thrown a few daggers his way upon entry, which was only to be expected. That Santo had managed to slip out from the financial chokehold Edward had tried to get him in was a source of great amusement to some, and consternation to Carson and his supporters. Edward had moved too fast and too hard and had lost himself, and them, a significant chunk of money. But it had cost Santo personally. He'd had to pull his funding from the project he'd been working on in secret to do so and set himself back maybe three or so years. And that hurt.

As Santo moved through the various groups discussing their business interests, he kept his gaze purposely away from the Carsons. The less they interacted, the better for everyone concerned. But he could almost feel Edward's attention being turned to him by his daughter's behaviour.

Cristo. Hadn't she learned anything from last year? he thought angrily, reluctantly realising that there was only one way that this would end, as he turned on his heel and stalked from the room.

He barely saw any of the grandeur of the old banquet hall as he entered the hallway, from which various private rooms led. And while there were nearly two hundred people in attendance that evening, he was painfully aware that only one tailed him down that corridor. Barely restraining a growl, he shoved open a door and shut it behind him, hoping that Eleanor Carson wasn't so stupid as to follow him in here.

Eleanor wanted to know why he was ignoring her. Needed it like a feral thing in her blood.

All evening she'd hoped to snare his attention but had

failed, again and again. At first, she'd simply wanted to thank him for last year. Again. Over the year, she'd come to think of him as her knight in matt black armour. Santo certainly had none of the shine and pomp of fairy tale heroes. But what use did she have for them? No, she needed the brutal honesty he offered.

But when she'd realised that he was ignoring her on purpose she'd been devastated…until that had turned to anger. She had been shocked by the fury that had whipped through her like wildfire. She'd almost had to physically hold herself back from going up to him and demanding why.

She knew it was dangerous to speak to him, it would draw her fa—*Edward's* ire. More of it, anyway. She clenched her jaw, hoping that the tension would hold her still enough to stop her from looking his way. She knew they were by the bar set up along the back wall of the hall, speaking to the Müllers.

Her mother would be standing beside him, Eleanor imagined, wondering if anyone would notice the paleness of her skin beneath the make-up, or the brittle way she held herself. Fragile, breakable, fractured—most definitely—but not yet broken, Eleanor thought of her mother.

But the lies that lay between the three of them were like splinters stuck under the skin, festering, infected, untreated.

She'd thought that the worst thing had happened to her when she'd discovered that Edward wasn't her father. But when she'd finally emerged from her room after the drunken disaster of last New Year's Eve she'd found out the true extent of her situation.

Her grades at university had slipped under the strain

of her personal life and Edward had decided that funding any future studies was a waste of his finances, so he had cancelled them. He had put a block on her cards and her account and finally she had realised how much of her life was under his control. Any attempt to circumvent his authority was met with the reminder that he would take Freddie and leave. Her mother's desperate urging for her to do as he said only damaged what was left of her soul that bit more.

And standing in the grand banquet hall overlooking the cobbled streets of this beautiful, ancient European city, she'd just wanted someone who wouldn't make her feel like a stranger in her own body. She'd wanted Santo. But he had cut her dead. It was the final straw and she barely cared whether Edward saw or not, as she followed him out of the hall and into the corridor.

With all the hurts and denigrations and misery she'd had to suffer this last year riding her hard, at that point it wouldn't have even mattered if he'd gone straight to the men's toilets, she would have followed him. A red haze had descended and even if distantly she could see that she was skirting the edge of hysteria…it didn't matter. It was too late.

She turned the handle on the door she'd seen Santo disappear behind and pushed.

Barely half a step across the threshold and a hand snatched around her wrist and she was dragged into the room, the door slammed behind her, and she found herself pushed up against it, staring into the furious depths of Santo Sabatini's unfathomable gaze.

'Who do you think you are playing with?' he demanded.

'Wh-wh-what?' she asked, everything in her—all the

anger, the edge of hysteria, the determination—retreating under the sheer force of *him*. He crowded her, the press of his body oddly delicious to her near delirious state, his piercing aquamarine gaze flashing shards of ice that burned where they fell as he took in her every response.

Life. Her body had come to life for the first time that entire year.

She was touch-starved, and her body responded to his as if it were food. She wanted to gorge on him. Worse. She wanted him to gorge on *her*. To feast on her. To take everything that remained of her and leave nothing behind.

'Little girl, do not mess with me,' he warned, his voice a growl that sent shivers down her body to parts of her she'd been utterly unaware of until that moment. It called to her in a deep, primal way—the challenge, the dare, the taunt from him.

She had been dismissed, rejected, cast aside by almost everyone. Even him, and she was so damn tired of it.

'Then stop messing with *me*,' she stressed, pushing herself away from the door and walking him back further into the room. 'Why are you ignoring me?' she demanded.

'Why are you looking for me?' he retaliated, his question, his tone throwing her off-course.

She clenched her teeth together. 'I was looking for you because I thought you were different,' she accused.

'Don't you dare compare me to them,' he threw back at her almost before the words had left her lips. The slash of his hand through the air punctuated his response, his fury feeding her own.

'Why not? You're here every year, just like them. Your business is financed through investments in their companies and they invest in yours. You keep yourself pleasured with their wives,' she lashed out, her eyes narrow and the seething anger that she wasn't able to unleash *anywhere* else, here suddenly free to roam. It rose within her like a fire-breathing monster, consuming everything in its path.

'Jealousy? It doesn't suit you, *cara*,' he all but snarled at her.

'I'm not jealous of a widow nearly twice my age,' she lied. Because she was. Because Santo had looked at Marie-Laure in a way that he'd never looked at her. And she wanted that. She wanted something, anything other than the near violent fury that threatened to tear her sanity from her.

He frowned, just for a moment, as if he'd read her thoughts. As if she'd let them slip from the locked box she kept them in all year round.

'You should go before someone finds you in here,' he said, turning his back on her and once again dismissing her from his company.

Go here. Stay there. Don't do that. Do this.

He was just like Edward. Ordering her around as if what she wanted, what she felt, had absolutely no importance to them.

'No,' she replied stubbornly. 'I won't.'

'Fine. If you insist on behaving like a child, *I'll* go.'

'Don't you dare,' she warned, moving to stand in his way.

Santo barked out a mean laugh. 'Why? What are you going to do? Stop me?' he demanded and made to push past her, but she moved to block his path.

Muscle clenching at his jaw, Santo could feel the anger

in her pulsing from her in waves. But it was more complex than pure anger—something he was intimately familiar with. He could sense her helpless frustration, confusion, hurt… Arousal.

Cristo, she didn't know what she was doing to him, he thought as he looked away.

She didn't know how much *he* felt, as he wrestled with his own frustration and anger, his own confusion. They were both breathing hard, as if they were fighting battles and demons that demanded their all.

'What do you *want*, Eleanor?' he growled, hoping to scare her off, hoping to send her running back to the safety of the party. Back to someone else.

'I want you to kiss me,' she said. 'Like you kiss *her*.'

A ripcord was wrenched within him, suspending him in mid-air on a piece of string tied right to her.

'What?' he asked, half convinced he'd imagined her words.

'I want you to kiss me like you kiss her,' Eleanor repeated, the dark gleam in her eyes swallowing the innocence whole.

Her tone left no doubt about whom she was speaking. Eleanor must have seen them last year. *Merda*, she didn't even realise that she was the reason that nothing had happened between him and Marie-Laure. And that nothing would ever happen again.

And here Eleanor was, with that awful question on her lips. Couldn't she tell how different they were? Couldn't she see?

'No,' he bit out through clenched teeth. 'I can't do that.'

'Then what use are you to me?' she said, shoving back at him.

The taunt, the accusation, cut too close to the bone after years of stepping back and forth up to this line—the line that he couldn't, shouldn't, cross. Ever.

'You want to use me?' he demanded, stepping closer to her, crowding her a little more, letting just a little of his own anger loose.

'No, I want you to use *me*,' she cried, stepping forward, closing the distance between them until they were head to head, more like enemies than potential lovers.

'You want me to be just like all the other men in your life, do you?' he demanded, sick to his stomach.

'No, I want you to do what I want, on my terms,' she cried. 'Because I *want* this. I want to feel anything other than abandoned, rejected, unworthy, unloved and unknown.' Each of these descriptions of herself twisted the knife in his chest. But then her eyes darkened.

'And if you're not going to help me, then I'll find someone who will,' she threatened, turning on her heel as if to leave.

His hand snaked out and slipped around her waist, pulling her back against his chest with gentle force. Fast breaths expanded her ribcage, flexing against his arm, tension holding her stiff in his arms as if she wasn't sure whether she wanted to move or not, the scent of her rising from the curve of her neck and striking him deeply. Irrevocably.

He could lie to himself and dress it up a million different ways. But what really hid beneath the layers of protest and objection—towards her, the situation, the consequences that Eleanor Carson seemed wholly ignorant of—was that he had never, not once, been able to stop thinking about her...about the way she had looked up at him that night in Berlin. The way she had dared him to kiss her.

The way he'd wanted to, like nothing he'd ever experienced before in his life. The way he'd been tempted to throw away his promise to Pietro. The way he'd wanted to throw away everything he knew about himself and how devastatingly close he could be to his father sometimes and take what he wanted. It had nearly broken him and she'd had no idea. And here she was, threatening to find someone else to satisfy the same craving that coursed through his veins like a curse. And as she arched into his hold, her hands wrapping around the arms that held her tight, her backside restlessly pressing against his crotch, the last fragile tie to his sanity broke.

He spun her in his arms and her eager mouth met his in an almost violent confrontation. Tongues teased, teeth clashed, but it was her half-cried moan of sheer arousal that cut him off at the knees.

Santo pulled her tight against the length of his body, the hard ridge of his need for her pressing against her core. Unable to restrain himself, he felt feral, animalistic, primal and raw, in a way he'd *never* experienced before in his life. It was as if all their anger, all their frustration, all their hopelessness was bleeding out into their passion and he could only hope that it would run dry and leave him spent enough to let her go when it was done.

Eleanor pulled him against her by the lapels of his jacket, and he let himself be led straight into the drug that was Eleanor Carson. The boldness of her tongue had taken him by surprise and he was insatiable, addicted, unable to stop himself from going back for more... Dammit, for everything and anything he could get.

His pulse raged beyond his control, need a stronger impulse than his desire to breathe. She was pushing him closer and closer to the same hot-headed insanity of his father…and that alone was enough to make him sever the kiss.

He pulled back, breathing as if he'd run a marathon, the struggle to get himself back under control alarmingly close to a limit he rarely tested.

'Why are you doing this?' he demanded on a shaky inhale, his forehead pressed against hers, his eyes closed, half-hopeful and half-fearful of what he might see in the espresso rich depths of her eyes.

'Because I have nothing left to lose,' she whispered against his lips as if it were some great confession.

Santo hadn't realised he'd been holding his breath until it whooshed, hot and hard and heavy—and devastated.

Her words had broken something inside him and he let her go from where he'd been holding her with numb fingers and turned, his back to her, while he gathered himself.

He shook his head. He should have known better. He should have realised. Oh, she probably hadn't meant to be so cruel. But her words still cut him like a knife. She was only here, only asking that of him because she had reached the bottom of the barrel. She was only here be-cause it was about *her*.

Had she still been the darling daughter of Edward Carson there was no way she'd have been standing here, beg-ging him to kiss her. She'd have got as close to the flame as she could before running back to her friends with a near-scandal she could titillate and delight them with, without ever once having got her hands dirty. Because that was what she saw him as—playing in the dirt. She could walk away from him and wash her hands clean.

Oh, he had sympathy with her plight. But only to an extent. Because when *his* world had fallen apart he'd not had the luxury of buckling. He'd not had the opportunity to be self-indulgent and drink himself into a stupor, or act out like a child. No, he'd had to assume control of the Sabatini Group, and within months of his father's death he was standing head-to-head with some of the men in this room who would have taken his company from him. Almost every day for nearly three years he'd had eye-watering, heart-stopping buyout packages. The kind that would have erased an entire country's debt. And what was Eleanor doing? Dropping out of university and trying to lose herself in mindless hookups.

'You don't get it, do you?' he sneered, returning to her words. Her self-pity, her self-absorption, burying the sharp sting of hurt beneath frustration and anger.

She looked back at him, wide-eyed and confused.

'You're such a child,' he continued remorselessly. 'You *always* have more to lose. If you have no care for yourself, then what about your mother? What about your brother? Or has it not even occurred to you that Edward could be using you against *them*?'

'Y-you know?' Eleanor reeled back in shock as if she'd been slapped.

But she hadn't. She'd just been told the truth, Santo thought grimly as he followed her back into the room. Something that had clearly been denied her far too long. And it had done her absolutely no good whatsoever.

'Yes, I know,' he confessed. 'You said as much last year before I returned you to your mother.'

'You can't tell anyone,' she begged.

A single bitter laugh burst from him. 'Do you not think I would have done so by now, were I going to? Oh, not for you. And not because Carson hasn't been trying to tank my business for the last twelve months. Your mother deserves *none* of this.'

Eleanor shook her pretty head, as if to try and both deny and assimilate what he was saying at the same time. Santo bit back a curse at the way she had paled.

'Sit down, before you fall down,' he ordered, ushering her towards a chair, before walking over to a glass-fronted drinks cabinet.

He reached for the whisky and retrieved two glasses from the backlit glass shelf. This was clearly some kind of after-dinner retirement room and had everything one would need. The décor was rich forest greens and golds and burgundy reds, so dark and so different from his own taste. And suddenly he just wanted to be home in his villa in Puglia, nestled in the olive groves beneath the heat of the sun and the simplicity of the landscape around him.

He was damn tired of all the politics and manipulation, the bribery and secrets and retaliations for perceived or real slights. He wanted to be away from it all. Including *her*.

He turned back to find Eleanor staring ahead as if in shock.

'I hadn't...' She paused, cleared her throat and tried again. 'I hadn't thought of it like that,' she confessed, as if ashamed.

He went to where she sat in the chair and passed her the glass, before going to stand by the window as far away from her as he could get.

'Every single thing I thought I knew about my life was untrue,' she said, as if putting her thoughts into words for the first time. 'And I don't know what that makes me,' she said sadly. 'I don't know who I am.'

And wasn't that the difference between them? Santo had never had the luxury of the lie—he had always known the terror and fear of his father, the false smiles of people who would never help his mother or him, but only profit from their silence. He had always known who he was: the son of a violent, selfish bastard. Santo had inherited his genes, his blood, and always had to be watchful for when those characteristics would appear, when that anger would finally take hold and he would break the things most precious to him. Like father, like son. And the only way to ensure that he didn't inflict that kind of hurt on the people he loved was simple. Don't love.

Eleanor's fingers gripped the seat of the chair as her head spun. A distant part of her thought she should be used to this by now. But she wasn't.

Santo's kiss had been one thing—spectacular. A short-lived moment of ecstasy she could never have imagined. That rush of all that she had felt had thrust her to the very brink of what she'd thought she'd always wanted. Before she had dashed them both on the rocks with her thoughtless words.

She had realised her mistake almost the moment the words were out of her mouth. Guilt coloured her cheeks. She had asked him to use her, but she was the one using him. Tonight. Maybe last year and the year before that too. Shame coursed through her blood, thick, heavy and hot, and she deserved every minute of discomfort it brought her.

'I'm sorry, you didn't deserve—'

'What I deserve or don't deserve is nothing to do with you. You asked for a kiss. You got what you asked for.'

Eleanor paled beneath the realisation of the truth of his accusation. She *had* been behaving like a child, thinking only of how the situation had affected her.

She nodded and, leaving the glass of whisky he had offered her untouched, stood.

Her head swam a little and she wanted air. Fresh air. She needed to think. She couldn't afford to be so selfish. She couldn't afford to behave like a child. She couldn't afford to keep hurting the people around her: her mother, her brother... *Santo*.

Raising a shaking hand to her lips, she knew that no matter who she kissed, or how many people, none would stand up to what she had felt with Santo.

'I—'

'You should leave. Now,' he commanded, deliberately turning his back to her, and she knew that it was the end of the discussion. It hurt, but she'd done it to herself and it was time that she owned that.

But as she left the room she could only wish that her selfishness hadn't cost her *him*.

CHAPTER SEVEN

New Year's Eve three years ago, Barcelona

ELEANOR LOOKED OUT beyond the bustling lights glowing from the Port of Barcelona, even on this night, to the dark blank space of the Balearic Sea, wondering if she could count the ways that her life had changed again.

Santo wouldn't know it, but what had passed between them last year had altered her fundamentally. In rare moments she thought that he might have said what he did because she'd hurt him. But then she came to her senses, refusing to overestimate her importance to him. Whatever had caused them, his words had been blunt and forceful to the point of bruising, but she had desperately needed to hear them.

And from the moment that she'd returned home she'd known that she needed to make serious changes in both her behaviour and her mindset. Shame and embarrassment at how selfish she had been were only useful if they drove her to do better. So that was what she'd made them do. Drive her forward.

At home, when Freddie was back from boarding school she had spent as much time with him as she could. She had soaked in all that he was, hoping that he would some day realise how much she loved him, and how much she'd tried to protect him from Edward—who was unable to separate them without making an unnecessary scene.

And with her mother, Eleanor had tried her hardest to make peace with what little relationship they had under Edward's watchful eye. Although it seemed paranoid, she couldn't help but feel that the staff had been instructed to report back any conversations she shared with her mother, and the newly increased number of them meant that there was very little time for them to be alone.

She'd reached out to her university professor and had arranged to repeat the last year through remote learning. She'd been able to take out a personal loan to cover the tuition fees, whilst also securing a job at Mads Rassmussen's London office.

Edward hadn't liked that one little bit, but she'd sold it to him that it would enable her to keep an ear to the ground about the financial goings-on of one of the families. She doubted that Edward believed a word she'd said, but he'd surprisingly let it go.

But between the full-time job, her studies and trying to keep a fragile peace at home, Eleanor was feeling the strain. Strain that she pushed down hard. Other people had been through worse. She'd had twenty years of privileged pampering. She would certainly survive the next few years. All she had to do was wait until Freddie was eighteen, and the three of them could leave. Until then, Eleanor would do everything she could to ensure that they had somewhere to go and some money to take with them. They didn't even need that much. Just enough. Enough *never* to be dependent on someone else ever again.

'Ah, here she is, my latest employee,' announced Mads with Ekaterina on his arm.

Eleanor smiled warmly at the couple. While she worked hard to keep her guard up around them, about what she said of herself and her family, she liked them. And God knew, she would have been nowhere without Mads taking a risk on a woman with no work history, no experience and no degree to her name.

'How is it, working for Mads? Is he a mean boss?' Kat asked, poking her fiancé teasingly.

'Terrible,' Eleanor replied with mock horror. 'He even makes me work on Fridays,' she replied.

'You can't make her do that.' Kat turned to him, outraged.

'My love, *most* people who are employed have to work on Fridays,' he chided.

A part of Eleanor was amazed at how clueless Ekaterina was, but the other part was sympathetic. Just remembering the sheer basic day-to-day things that she hadn't known when she'd first started work filled Eleanor with deep embarrassment.

It had been hard to win over her fellow staff members, all of whom—understandably—thought she was only 'playing' at having a job. The first few months as a personal assistant had been truly awful for her. But every day she went back, every time she worked a little longer, a little harder, she won another inch of their respect. Eventually she'd picked up the basic skills that she lacked and was able to add that to the foundation from her university degree and she had finally found her feet.

Eleanor gritted her teeth as Dilly passed by, her slow head-to-toe perusal making it clear that her one-time

friend had recognised the dress that Eleanor had worn
before at a previous event. The mean tittering from Dilly
and another girl told her that it wouldn't be long before
whatever rumour the other woman had spun it into would
be around the room in no time.

Well, let them. Eleanor no longer had the luxury of
wasting money on brand-new gowns. And while the income she had saved that year was almost embarrassingly
low, in some ways it was more than she could ever have
imagined. It was *hers*. She'd earnt it. Herself. It hadn't
been given to her and couldn't be taken away. And that
made her feel like it was millions.

'Well, Thompson has been saying how good you've
been getting on in the last few months, so keep it up!'
Mads said, with a little fist pump that made her smile.

When she'd first approached him she knew that he
had been both suspicious and surprised. She'd told him
only as much as she'd dared. He'd taken such a chance
on her, and she'd never forget it.

'Uh-oh,' Kat said, leaning in to whisper. 'Grumpy is
here. And it seems he's not alone,' she added.

Eleanor frowned and turned to see who had just entered the room.

She masked her expression the moment she saw him,
not wanting a single reflection of the impact he made
on her to show. Not wanting anyone to guess that the
moment she'd seen him it had felt as if the air had been
sucked from her lungs. As if time had stopped the beat
of her heart.

Standing nearly a foot taller than almost everyone else,
he insolently surveyed the room. Thick, dark hair, effortlessly styled; his hands had run through the wet strands,

with maybe the slightest slick of gel, she imagined. A rich olive tan graced his skin, presumably from his time outside amongst the olive groves.

Eleanor's cheeks flushed. In the brief moments she had to herself, away from work or studies, she had pored over any news about him she could find.

From where she stood, his face side on to her, she couldn't see, but could well remember, the scar he'd confessed was inflicted by his father. And yet she couldn't help but wonder at the invisible ones he bore, where no one could see them, or reach them to heal.

Santo turned to the doorway and smiled, the expression completely changing his face. The stern lines that defined him eased and he looked a little younger, he looked softer, without undermining the powerful impact he made. He reached out his hand and Eleanor followed the line of his arm to see a young woman emerge from the doorway.

She pressed her lips together to stop the gasp of hurt from escaping. Because the way that Santo looked at the young, dark-haired woman was nothing she'd ever seen from him before.

Just as he returned his gaze to the room, Eleanor shifted so that her back was to them, desperately hoping that Santo hadn't caught her staring. After what had passed between them last year, she wanted to avoid him at all costs.

Santo held his arm out to Amita. The new stepdaughter of one of the few men here he could almost bring himself to respect, Santo had promised to accompany her to her first New Year's Eve party. Karl Ivanov's investments in the Sabatini Group were largely silent, making him one of the easier investors to deal with. But also Santo appreciated that the man didn't get into any of the backbiting and backstabbing that most of the others seemed to delight in.

Amita was a nice girl, but timid. Her stepfather was right to be worried. Originally from Jaipur, her whole sheltered world had been uprooted dramatically and Karl was incredibly concerned about her.

Despite the clear and very platonic understanding between him and Amita, she'd clung to him like a limpet from the moment they'd entered the room. He could feel the curious gazes they'd attracted and when Karl and Amita's mother, Aditi, joined them the whispers grew to an almost audible level.

'They're going to think we're together,' whispered Amita for his ears only.

'Let them. It doesn't matter,' he replied sincerely.

In fact, after the last few years, it was probably a good thing that people here thought that he was 'off the market'. Carson's blows had lessened, having presumably found bigger fish to fry, and Marie-Laure had found herself a new plaything. He was hardly surprised that the rumour mill had named Antony Fairchild as her new lover.

Poor bastard didn't know what he was in for.

As Santo led her towards their table in the Casa Llotja de Mar, he was impressed by the space. White and black squares covered the floor like a chequerboard, but it was the huge stone arches that drew the gaze to the dizzying height of the ceiling. A first-floor balcony wrapped around the magnificent room, and a smile caught his lips when he heard Amita gasp.

'It's so beautiful.'

'Mmm,' he replied noncommittally.

The white-clothed, perfectly dressed tables waiting for the promised eight-course meal that evening hugged the edges of the space, leaving the centre of the room free for those standing and chatting or even dancing a little.

As he took his seat, he kept his gaze firmly on his companions and away from where he knew Eleanor Carson would be found. He had absolutely no intention of running into her tonight.

He was here, keeping his promise, he just didn't have to interact with her personally.

Which was precisely why he'd asked Mads Rassmussen to dangle himself enticingly as a prospective boss for her. Santo had killed two birds with the same stone—created a way to keep an eye on Eleanor without getting directly involved, in exchange for working with Rassmussen on the side project he'd resumed after rectifying the damage done the year before.

Pietro hadn't been overjoyed by the news of what she was doing, but his hands were still firmly tied. Watching the old man's helplessness had been…difficult for Santo. He'd been a mentor, a father figure, representing authority and security. But Eleanor was making the man weak, making him vulnerable, and Santo didn't like that one bit.

She was a thorn in both their sides and he wanted her gone.

But, no matter what he wanted, his body had different ideas. Torturing him with erotic images at night, with memories during the day, with awareness of her right here, right now. Fingers tripped across his skin, beneath his shirt, gripping him in places that made him damn thankful he was sitting down at the table.

'Do you two want to go and mingle before we eat?' Aditi asked, her accent inflecting her words in a pleasant way.

Amita shook her head, and Santo nodded that it was fine to stay at the table. Aditi's smile was enough to tell him how important this was to her. He should tell Karl to get them both away from here and never come back. But Karl had enough of both clout and charm to make himself unthreatening to others, so Santo was sure that they would be fine.

As the waiter passed, he and Karl removed the bottles of wine from the table.

'You can drink,' Amita assured him.

'That's okay, I'm happy not to,' he explained, the gratefulness in her answering gaze more than he deserved. He'd already decided that he was done drinking around this lot.

He had warned Eleanor last year about growing up and taking things seriously. It was time that he did the same.

As Karl, Amita and Aditi fell into easy conversation, Santo's mind was elsewhere. One of the largest neighbouring competitors for olive oil in Puglia had approached him last week, needing to sell the company. The man's brother-in-law had got into gambling debt with some very dangerous people and he needed capital fast. Others had come sniffing around, but the man wanted to sell to Santo because he respected the land and the local community.

Santo knew that everyone here thought he'd made his millions by being ruthless. Not a single one of them would have considered that one could make money and still keep one's morals. The work he'd done in the past years to create a community response to the fires that had ravaged Puglia and, in all likelihood would continue to do so in the future, had garnered respect. And that had paid dividends.

His phone rang and, excusing himself from the table, he left to find a quiet place to take the call.

He followed the staircase behind him up to the second-floor balcony, the lighting dim and the noise much quieter up here. It was a quick call, barely a few words, and just like that, Santo had nearly doubled the size of his estate.

Pocketing his phone, he braced his elbows on the railing and surveyed the scene below. People were chatting, dancing, laughing and drinking and all he could think was that a man's entire career, his life, had just been surrendered.

A movement further along the balcony caught his eye and he'd barely turned when recognition struck him hard. *Of course* it would be her. *Of course* they would have somehow found each other amongst the two hundred guests that evening.

Eleanor wanted to hide but she knew he'd seen her. He hadn't at first, not when he'd been on the phone, but in trying to leave she'd made herself known.

'I'm sorry, I didn't mean to interrupt.'

She felt the pause between her statement and his response like an eternity.

'Nothing to interrupt.' The clipped words dropped to the floor between them like a stone.

She nodded, deeply uncomfortable with the seething

twist of self-pity and jealousy coursing through her veins. It shouldn't matter. She could be happy for him. Because, truly, he deserved to be happy.

'I...' She let the sentence trail off as she saw he'd turned away, but the word stopped him.

Eventually he looked back at her. *'Sì?'*

'It's okay,' she said, gesturing for him to leave.

Santo bit out an irritable sigh. 'What is it, Eleanor?'

She swallowed. 'I just wanted you to know that I heard what you said last year,' she explained, staring at the floor, cursing herself for being so weak. He'd told her to be strong. To be stronger. And she wanted to show him that she *was*. 'I...have made some changes this year and I...just wanted you to know that,' she said, raising her eyes to his face before the overwhelming urge to turn back into the shadows and disappear crashed over her.

He stared back at her, the blankness painful, but nothing more than she deserved. She had used him last year. And instinctively she knew that few people did that and survived unscathed.

'Did you want an award? A round of applause, perhaps?'

'No, I just wanted you to know,' she said, holding fast against the disdain she saw in his gaze. But disdain was better than what had been there before, which was nothing less than a brutal indifference. 'I have a job now. And I'm finishing my degree. I have a plan,' she said, determined for the first time that evening. To prove herself to him, to herself even.

He frowned for the first time, the tiny movement showing that he wasn't just a statue.

'What plan?' he asked.

She shook her head. 'It's not important,' she said, suddenly feeling the urge to run. She went to push past him on the shallow balcony, but he caught her upper arm in his hand.

'What plan, Eleanor?' he asked again, more forcefully.

'It's nothing,' she dismissed. 'Certainly nothing to do with you,' she said, confused by the sudden whiplash of his interest.

'Carson is not a man to mess with,' Santo warned.

Eleanor let out a surprised laugh. 'You think I don't know that?'

'Whatever you're thinking—'

'Is none of your business, as I've said,' she stressed, getting annoyed. Yes, he'd helped her see what a mess she'd been making of things, but that didn't mean he got to treat her like a child.

She pulled her arm back and, as if only because he didn't want to make a scene, he released her.

'Don't do anything stupid, Eleanor,' he commanded.

She wanted to rail against the accusation, but the problem was, she had earned it. He had seen her passed out drunk. He had experienced her misguided attempts to lose herself in *him*. He had every right to believe that she would do something stupid.

And, just like that, any anger or indignation at his tone evaporated.

'I won't,' she replied sincerely. If she had learned anything about Edward it was that the man was fiercely intelligent. And she would have to be more so.

'But I really don't want any bad blood between us,' she admitted, seeking for a sense of the control and calm that she had heavily relied on throughout this year. 'I sincerely apologise for any offence I caused last year. I wasn't…' I wasn't *okay*, she wanted to confess. The last time she'd seen him, she'd been so very bleak. 'I wasn't quite myself,' was all she could admit to.

She swallowed, looking once again at the floor, unable—no, *unwilling*—to meet his gaze.

There was a pause.

'And you are now?' came the enquiry.

She bit the inside of her cheek. In truth, probably not completely, but he didn't need to know that. She nodded instead, not wanting to lie to him.

Santo peered at her through the gentle downlighting of the balcony. He wasn't sure he believed her. In fact, when he'd first taken a look at her—a proper look—he'd been surprised, and not in a good way.

She had lost weight since last year. Quite a bit, and she hadn't had all that much to lose in the first place. There was a dark smudge beneath each eye that was still visible through her make-up. And he recalled earlier having heard some mean gossip about her wearing a dress she'd been seen in before.

The grey dress served only to make her look even more pale than usual, he thought. He cursed himself for being mean. She was clearly suffering in one way or another.

Some protector he was, he thought, viciously chastising himself.

'If there's something I can do,' he offered lamely, knowing with absolute conviction that she would never turn to him for help. No. Her pride—which he respected—wouldn't allow that.

She dismissed his offer with a wave of her hand, just

as he'd expected, surprised to find that it stung as sharply as a slap.

'Not at all. Things are actually going really well,' she said gamely, her eyes bright. *Too* bright.

Cristo. He had let his ego override the promise he'd made to Pietro, but also what was staring him right in the face. Yes, she might have behaved selfishly, but what should he have expected? She'd grown up pampered, indulged and spoilt. It was a miracle she'd lasted a week at Rassmuss Technologies, let alone eleven months.

He didn't think for a moment that any of her contemporaries would have had even half the fortitude she must have had to still be standing, once Edward had turned against her. How had he not seen that? How had he not recognised that?

Because you let your attraction towards her mess with your mind, his inner voice said.

'If you need anything…' he tried again, but once again she shook him off.

'I'd rather not, actually,' she said, her smile a little more brittle this time. 'I…want to do this on my own.' She nodded, as if to herself. 'It feels good,' she admitted. 'The things I've earned. I've enjoyed it.'

Truth rang loudly in her words and he instinctively knew that this time it wasn't false bravado. She meant what she said.

'I'm pleased,' he replied honestly.

'Actually,' she said, frowning, half hesitant, 'there is one thing you could do for me.' Her hands were twisting in front of her.

Anything, he nearly replied and, not trusting himself to speak, he simply nodded for her to continue.

She bit her lip. 'Could I ask you for a promise?'

The confusion must have shown on his face, because she smiled.

'Don't worry, it shouldn't cost you anything.'

'Money would probably be easier,' he replied without thinking and where once she might have laughed, now she only smiled awkwardly.

Oh, yes, it was safe to say that Eleanor Carson had very much learned the value of money in the last year.

'Could I ask you to promise never to lie to me?'

He blinked, closing his mouth before it dropped open more than the few millimetres it already had in shock.

Money most definitely *would* have been easier.

How could he make that promise to her? He was already lying to her. Had lied to her every single time they had met. Their entire interactions were coloured by that lie.

But how could he not, when she stared up at him with something in her eyes that he couldn't shatter? So much had been taken from her, could he really afford to take this from her too?

But agreeing to her request would cross a line that he would be unable to reinstate. And a perverse part of him almost welcomed that knowledge. Welcomed the fact that what she was asking from him guaranteed a future in which he would disappoint her. One way or another, it would be a certainty if he gave her his word.

He took a breath, and ignored the way it shuddered in his lungs as he did so.

'Yes, I can promise that,' he said, wondering if by not saying the words it made his crime any less.

The smile that lit her features this time was genuine

and warm. She bounced a little on the balls of her feet and he wished it didn't make him want to smile in response.

'Thank you. I wanted at least one person here who won't lie to me,' she said and, before he could react, she leant forward and reached up to kiss his cheek, his stomach flipping into his throat and his soul going straight to hell.

By the time he had regained control of himself, she had disappeared back down the stairs and off somewhere he couldn't follow. Slowly, step by step, he returned to his place at the table with Karl, Aditi and Amita.

'Is everything okay?' Amita asked.

He forced a smile to his face. 'Yes, in fact I've just acquired a new business.'

'On New Year's Eve?' asked Karl, impressed.

'Yes. A neighbour. I've nearly doubled my land.'

'Now, that really is a reason to celebrate,' Aditi exclaimed.

He nodded, and let them raise their glasses, even though there was no alcohol on the table. And no matter how self-righteous he'd been about the need to keep his head that evening, he would have given his neighbour's business back for a bottle of whisky in that moment.

'Who was that woman?' Amita asked quietly, looking back up to the empty balcony.

'No one important,' he lied for the second time that night.

CHAPTER EIGHT

New Year's Eve two years ago, Amsterdam

THE SOUND OF laughter was painful to Santo's ears. He'd flown in from a meeting in Helsinki with Mads in his private jet and not bothered to stop at his hotel room first.

He felt...angry, disappointed. Frustrated and just damn tired of playing this game.

'She's not a game, Santo.'

'Then tell her the truth yourself and leave me out of it.'

'If you want to stop...'

'No.'

No. Santo didn't want to stop. He wouldn't break his promise to Pietro. The old man—who was *really* beginning to look every day of his sixty-two years—had made the visit out to Puglia especially.

They'd spent hours talking about it. About how Pietro had been reaching out to Analise Carson in secret. How he'd never stopped loving the woman he'd spent only a few short months with when she was travelling around Europe on her own.

Pietro had been devastated when she'd returned to England, believing that her family would never agree to let her be with someone like him, so he'd acted rashly and become engaged to a family friend from Naples. It hadn't taken long for the news to get back to Analise, who had found herself rebounding into the arms of Edward Carson. And when she'd discovered she was pregnant, it was too late. Edward had believed the child was his and proposed. It had all spun so out of her control that she'd been unable to stop it.

When Pietro had finally found out he'd broken the engagement amicably with his fiancée and tried to win Analise back, but they'd discovered just how dangerous Edward Carson could be. He might not have got his own hands dirty, but the 'mugging' which had broken Pietro's leg, collarbone and several ribs, as well as fracturing an eye socket had left him with all the money in his wallet. The message to Analise's 'ex' couldn't have been clearer. But that didn't stop Carson from going after Pietro financially for years. Every now and then Carson still poked and prodded, believing, like most, that Pietro's finances were simply the middle of the range business acquisitions that appeared on paper. But he hadn't been born the son of an ex-Mafia enforcer for nothing.

'We just have to keep playing the long game, Santo.'

The past and the present swam in his mind like flotsam, catching and snaring on thoughts and holding for a moment before slipping out of reach. Like mother, like daughter, Santo thought as he saw Eleanor talking to Kat and another member of the group that failed to draw any of his attention. He saw a glint and wondered whether it was fancy, or whether he'd seen the glitter of Eleanor's new engagement ring.

Someone passing gave him a strange look and he wondered whether the growl that had sat at the back of his throat had somehow drawn their gaze. It was possible. The control he usually had on his emotions was pushed to the limit this evening.

And he blamed it on her. Her and her absolute unwillingness to learn from her mistakes.

The announcement had been fairly quiet this time. Whether that was because of Edward's reluctance to acknowledge Eleanor any more or because of the insignificance of the man she had apparently *fallen in love* with, who could say.

Love.

Even the thought of the word turned his stomach and brought a sneer to his lips. He swallowed another mouthful of whisky and turned his back on her, telling himself that he didn't care what she did, as long as it kept her out of Edward's reach.

He spent some time catching up with Karl and Aditi, pleased to hear that Amita was getting on so well back in Jaipur at university. He could tell that Aditi missed her daughter, but they all agreed that she was better where she was. She'd found the gathering too intimidating last year, but her mother said she sent Santo her regards.

A little later he was cornered by Ivanov, who wanted to know when they could expect to see returns on the new expansion of the land in Puglia after the sale had gone through with Santo's neighbour. After that, Müller tried to get him to invest in his latest venture, and failed miserably.

All the while he sensed Eleanor on the outskirts of the crowd, being pushed closer and closer to where he stood, each footstep ratcheting up his pulse, pushing a little harder at the blood pounding through his veins. His irritation inching higher.

Unaccountably, he was absolutely convinced that she didn't want to be anywhere near him. And that, perversely, only pissed him off more. After their encounter last year, he'd thought, *hoped*, even, that she might have actually learned something. Might have grown up a little.

Her laugh, getting closer and closer, grated on already stretched nerves.

'How did he manage with Analise and Edward?' he heard someone ask.

'He…did well,' Eleanor replied, and Santo barely concealed his cough of disbelief. There wasn't even a chance that the hedge fund manager to whom she was presently engaged had even met Edward Carson. Not a single chance.

He could practically *feel* Eleanor bristling behind him.

'And how long until the wedding? Are you looking for a long engagement?'

'No, actually, we're hoping to marry in April.'

'So soon?'

'We're just so excited,' came the patently false reply from lips the flavour of which he could still taste on his tongue.

It was obscene. Her desperate plea for truth from him, and then *this*.

'Well, you and James have my congratulations,' insisted whoever it was Eleanor was speaking to.

Santo all but sneered, watching Eleanor smile and accept them graciously in the reflection of the large mirror on the opposite side of the wall.

Whoever it was made their excuses to leave, and he didn't have to turn around to hear the angrily delivered whisper from over his shoulder, aimed for his ears alone.

'Just stop it,' Eleanor bit out, glaring daggers at him in the mirror's image.

He clenched his jaw, intensely disliking that she thought she could have any say over his actions whatsoever. He glared back until she averted her gaze, smiling and waving at another guest.

Eleanor felt his gaze like a hand clasped loosely around her throat, a little like a leash with enough rope to run, but not get far. And that was the problem. It always had been. Her thoughts, her mind, her body's wants, always came back to him. Inescapably and inexorably. And she had realised this last year that if she had any hope of escaping this life, this world, she'd have to escape him too, wouldn't she?

He was just as much a part of this entire machinery as Edward Carson was. Even if he *did* want her in the same way that she wanted him—which she honestly didn't believe any more—there would always be *this*. There would always be one night a year spent amongst these people, the majority of whom made her skin crawl.

And even if there were times when she'd thought differently of him, when she'd thought she'd seen something else beneath the surface, she had been wrong, clearly. Because she'd seen the financials, read the reports in the newspapers, lauding the joint venture between the Sabatini Group and Ivanov Industries. Not to mention the supposedly secret project between Mads and Santo. No, the Italian was as deeply intertwined with this group of people as the rest of them. He might despise them as much as she did, but that wasn't stopping him from being here, year after year. And that was why she'd agreed when James had invited her for dinner early last year, believing that the only way to get over Santo was to meet someone else.

No, James didn't have the same dramatic impact that Santo had on her. Eleanor wasn't naïve, she knew it was highly unlikely that anyone would. She was bound to Santo by a connection forged at a moment in her life when she'd been so utterly impressionable. When he'd protected her, even as he'd teased her and taunted her. He'd changed her and she would be thankful for the rest of her life. But a part of her felt as if she was always missing the one piece of information that would make sense of their interactions, and a small part of her wondered whether *that* was the reason for her infatuation with Santo.

But it had been so different with James. He'd been… calm. Considered. Attentive. Kind. He wasn't trying to score points in some powerplay. And he had absolutely no interest in her family name or investments. He was handsome and nice and hadn't baulked when she'd intimated as much as she could about her family. She'd forced herself to tell him the truth—that theirs wasn't, and quite possibly never would be, a love match—and James had understood. What she wanted from their marriage was safety and security for her mother and brother, and freedom for herself. And, in exchange, what he wanted seemed almost easy to give: companionship.

In the meantime, Edward's chokehold on their interactions lessening just enough, she had been able to carve out some time with her mother, who had revealed her father's name to her. *Pietro.* That was all she knew. The way that her mother had looked when she'd spoken of him…it nearly broke Eleanor's heart. She knew in that moment that her mother had loved Pietro and had never stopped loving him.

She'd wanted to ask more, she'd wanted to ask if he'd tried to find them, if her father had tried to come for her, but she couldn't afford to ask that question. Couldn't afford to be so reliant upon another man ever again. And at least she knew with startling clarity she would never have that with James.

Eleanor found herself unable to avoid the reflection in the mirror. Santo was *still* looking at her. A flush of angry heat painted her cheeks and she went to walk away, when suddenly Dilly appeared right before her, forcing Eleanor back a step and causing her to brush up against the wall of Santo's immovable back.

'Congratulations,' Dilly said with disdain.

'Thank you,' Eleanor replied, trying to find her equilibrium.

'Maybe this time it will stick?'

Eleanor felt as if she'd been slapped.

'I mean, it would look almost incompetent to lose two fiancés.' Dilly leaned in, as if confiding, in the way that she used to when they were friends. Before Eleanor had caught her with Tony.

Eleanor felt indignation at Dilly's words swimming in her blood, rushing to her head, urging her to say or do something rash. She was so bloody tired of being everyone's punching bag. But next year would be different. Next year she would be married, and could finally stop coming to these damn things.

'I don't have to listen to this,' she said, trying to sidestep her one-time friend.

'What are you going to do? Run back to Daddy?'

Eleanor spun round on the woman, fury sparking like electricity. Dilly couldn't have known the effect of her words, would never understand how much they had cut and sliced and twisted. But this woman, who had been so wrong to do what she'd done, had no right to be angry with her when she had done nothing wrong. She'd never done anything wrong.

'I don't have to run back to Daddy,' Eleanor said in a low voice, with more control than she felt at that moment. 'I have everything I need right here. I have an audience of nearly two hundred of your nearest and dearest,' Eleanor continued with a smile on her face, while Dilly began to lose hers. 'I could easily tell them what I overheard you and Tony doing, but I haven't. If people know, it is because Tony told them, not me.' Eleanor took a breath and looked, really looked, at her once best friend. 'I know what desperation looks like, Dilly,' she said not unkindly. 'And I can see it in you, coming out of every single pore.'

'You ruined me,' Dilly whisper-hissed in accusation.

'You ruined yourself,' Eleanor replied without missing a beat. 'So what are you going to do about it?'

'Do?' Dilly asked, as if genuinely confused.

'You got yourself into this mess. Stop blaming other people and do something about it.'

With that, Eleanor smiled, aware of the attention they had drawn, and placed a kiss on Dilly's cheek, hoping that she could wait until she'd left the room before wiping her mouth with the back of her hand.

Spinning on her heel, she exited the room, blind to the sea of faces swimming before her, driven forward by the building pressure in her chest. It was a sob, a cry, it was tears and oxygen, it was sadness, grief, loss wrapped in anger and frustration. But the one thing it wasn't was helplessness.

She just needed a moment to gather herself. Just one.

But then she felt him hot on her heels and her stomach flipped, her heart pulled on a string tied to him, yanked hard, and her body felt flushed for all the wrong reasons.

Oh, why wouldn't he just leave her alone?

She opened a door and slipped into the room, knowing that a closed door wouldn't keep him from coming after her. She backed into the room and was halfway across when Santo came in, closing the door behind him.

Battling hard against the realisation that she wasn't scared but thrilled, her breath punctuated the air between them. Why was he the man her body surrendered to? Why was he the man who made her pulse leap and her heart pound? Why was he the man who, no matter what she wanted, what she needed, she always came back to?

'I want you to leave,' she tried.

'No.'

'No?'

'No,' Santo repeated.

Every step he took into the room not only made her step back but also drew them closer and closer to that damn line that, once crossed, couldn't be taken back. But there was something primal in the air, working a magic that was unrecognisable to his brain, but known fully by his body.

It was the same alchemical reaction that always happened when they were near each other. As if they were magnets, unable to help the physics of their make-up. Drawn to each other, repelled from each other. It had worn him down to the last vestiges of his patience and it wouldn't take much for him to lose it altogether.

'You can't say no,' Eleanor accused, as if logic and etiquette had any place here.

'I just did,' he all but growled, hating that she had driven him to this, that he had become the very thing he'd never wanted to be. Completely driven by impulse and need. He clenched his teeth together, but one look at Eleanor and he could see that she was fighting this as much as he was.

'What is your problem?' she demanded.

'You, Princess. It's always you,' he said, closing the gap between them as she came up against the back wall of the room.

Cristo, she was exquisite. He wanted her. It was that simple and that undeniable. And how much of a bastard did it make him that he didn't even care that she wore another man's ring?

He peered down at her, aware that he was using his body to crowd her, relishing the way that their need for each other filled what little air there was between them.

'Why are you angry with me?' she asked, staring up at him, wide-eyed and begging for something she probably didn't have the courage to name.

'I'm not angry, I'm *furious*,' he clarified.

Only that wasn't quite true, not any more. Because the fury that had ridden him so hard only minutes ago had been replaced and he had to call it what it was. Desire. Need. Wrapped in a fist so tight that no one could prise it apart.

No one but her.

She continued to stare up at him, as if aware that his

arousal had stolen the heat from his anger. Did she feel it too? The swollen throb that poured through his body with every beat of his heart whenever she was near, the fist that gripped his lungs and made it impossible to breathe.

'Why?'

'Because you demand honesty from me, yet everything about you is a lie,' he said, the truth slipping out into the air between them, surprising them both. Just the acknowledgement, just the memory of the promise she'd forced him to make, the lie she'd forced him to tell, tapped back into that heat and once again the magnets flipped and he was repelled from her, taking a few steps back, sucking air into his lungs that wasn't tainted with the scent of her body.

Merda, he needed to get control over himself. He should never have come in here. But when he turned he found her right back there in front of him, having crossed the room with silent steps. This was madness.

'You think this guy will be able to give you what you want?' he couldn't stop himself from demanding.

'Yes,' she said defiantly, her eyes flashing with warning.

'He'll be able to keep you, your mum and Freddie safe?' he scoffed, incredulous—incredulous and more than just a little outraged. From the background check he'd authorised, the man was inconsequential at best. He didn't have the power or the reach to protect her.

'Yes. Yes, he can.'

'So, you'll marry and then what?'

Eleanor shrugged as if confused by the question, the elegant line of her shoulders drawn with tension beneath the dusky pink silk dress she wore.

'Are you planning to hide out in suburbia for the rest of your life?' he demanded, pushing her again, stepping closer, daring her almost to run from him. *Cristo*, why was it that just the thought turned his blood to molten lava in his veins?

'If that's what it takes,' she replied, refusing to back down, refusing to bow to his blatant display of power.

'You won't last a week,' he sneered.

'I've lasted six already,' she bit back.

Santo clenched his jaw, his whole body on fire with the tension it took to hold himself back.

'Tell me he's what you want,' he growled.

'He's what I need.'

And while everything in his entire being roared at the thought that another man could be that for her, could fulfil that role for her, instead he latched onto the most important thing.

'Eleanor. You are a strong, capable woman who can get what she needs for herself. Tell me he's what you *want*.'

For a moment he saw it. The impact the first part of his sentence made on her. As if it were a surprise to her that someone would see her that way.

Did she not know? Did she not realise how amazing she was?

'You are capable of so much more than being a house-wife,' he said. He knew that. He didn't even need to read Mads's updates to know that. Eleanor had become a highly valued member of his London office, having graduated with a first in her degree despite all the odds. She was wasting her potential and he couldn't stand it.

'There is nothing wrong with making a home,' she

cried, her own anger painting her cheeks pink, the flashes in her eyes now exploding like fireworks.

'Of course not,' he wholeheartedly agreed. 'But you don't want that. You want more.'

She spun away from him in frustration, her fists clenched and her growl of frustration audible.

He felt some sympathy. After all, this was exactly how she made him feel.

'Why is it always like this?' she asked, still facing away from him.

'Haven't you figured that out yet, Princess?' he said before he could stop himself.

She turned, looking up at him, hoping for an answer. He would probably come to regret it, but he just couldn't fight it any more.

'It's foreplay,' he explained.

'Don't be ridiculous,' she dismissed, but the blush on her cheeks told him she knew.

'Some people like sweet nothings and pretty gifts. It appears you like something altogether different,' he said, as if observing the weather, while his mind already imagined a future where he could finally get his hands on her, when all this frustration and need was spent and he was free.

'I'm leaving,' she said.

'You can try,' he offered, having already seen how this would go down. It was inevitable really. Almost as if it were too late.

'What's that supposed to mean? I can leave if I want.'

'You can, but you don't want to,' he said, leaning forward, his lips just above her ear. 'This is the most fun you've had all year.'

'Don't be stupid,' she replied, staring ahead at his chest, but making no attempt to move away from the press of his body.

'Sorry, sweetheart. You made me promise not to lie to you,' he taunted, half cruel, half driven out of his mind with lust.

Her swift inhale pushed her chest against the neckline, and pushed him even closer towards the precipice.

'Tell me you don't want this. Tell me I mean nothing to you. Tell me you haven't thought about this, like I have, every night for *years*.'

'I… I…' The word *'can't'* had barely left Eleanor's mouth when his lips crashed against hers.

The sudden shocking reality of what she had fantasised about for years stole her breath. He didn't wait, he wasn't patient, he just expected her to keep up—as if absolutely no time had passed between the kiss they'd shared two years before and now.

He walked them back to the far wall, her hands raising of their own volition to grab the lapels of his dinner jacket, her fingers slipping on the silk before fastening more securely around the material and, before she knew it, *she* had taken the lead, *she* was the one pulling him into her, *she* was the one drawing them further back until they couldn't go any further.

Her back slammed against the wall at the same time as Santo's hand swept to the back of her head, cushioning any possible blow. But then, sneakily, he used that same movement to his advantage and angled her to him so that he could tease her lips open.

To compare this to their earlier kiss was almost laughable. Oh, God, she all but *dissolved* into him. The heady moment his tongue met hers was enough to stop time and steal a heartbeat. He was a thief, taking what she didn't know she wanted to offer. Her heart thundered in her chest, and all she could think was that it wasn't enough. That it would never be enough.

He trailed his fingers down the arch of her neck to her collarbone, while his other hand fastened her to him at the waist. As he held, she pulled, and she wanted more. Her hands flew to thread through his hair, to encourage him to take more, to show her more, to give her more.

Breathless, heated, heart racing and aching in places and ways that could never be appeased by any other man, pleading, begging words fell from her lips, incomprehensible wants, pressed into his kiss. Each one met by an answering growl of agreement, or encouragement, she couldn't tell any more.

His hand moved torturously along the side of her body, down her ribcage, skirting around the edge of her breast, sending a shiver of goosebumps across her skin, dropping to her backside, making her gasp, and finally to her thigh, where he reached for her leg. Hooking it over his hip, he pressed against her body powerfully, once, twice and the third time she could no longer deny what he was doing.

The mimicry of what she wanted more desperately than her next breath clogged her throat, thickened her blood and made her nearly blind with want. Again and again, she felt the press of his erection through the impossible barrier of their clothes, the large, hot, insistent ridge of his arousal *finally* proving beyond all reasonable doubt that he wanted her as much as she wanted him.

Her hands grasped his waist, not to stop him but to

hold him, to delight in his need of her, to commit it to memory and to know what could have been. She teased herself with the feel of him, coming shockingly close to orgasm, which was enough to bring the sharp stab of sanity crashing down into her heart. She pulled back from the kiss, the breath panting in and out of her chest mixing with his hard inhalation and fast exhalation.

There was no touching moment like before, their foreheads pressed together, allowing the moment to sink in. No, instead, Santo glared at her, full of accusation, arousal, determination and resentment. In that moment she realised how truly he had proved his point. How James could never measure up to the wants and needs that Santo unleashed in her. Wants and needs deep within her, innate to her, part of her as much as her DNA.

She was devastated, he was victorious. But neither was happy.

He smoothed his shirt down over his torso, checked his belt and tugged on his cufflinks, all the while she was utterly incapable of speech.

He nodded to her once and then, with a, 'See you next year, Princess,' he left the room, the words less like a promise and so much more like a threat.

CHAPTER NINE

New Year's Eve last year, Venice

ELEANOR POSITIONED THE mask over her face, thankful that this year's hosts, the Capparellis, had decided on a masquerade ball. After the bad press over her second broken engagement, all she'd wanted to do was hide. She'd hoped that Edward would let her stay back at home in England, but it appeared he still planned to use her as bait to lure investors' attention with the hope of marrying her off to one of their sons.

Now twenty-six years old, Eleanor stood looking out over the Venetian canal, lit with strings of white lights, seeing couples being propelled along the night covered waterway in gondolas, sharing romance and love, all the things she began to fear that she might be now too damaged to experience.

This time last year she'd honestly not thought that she'd ever have to return to one of these events. She'd thought she'd be married, her first year away from Edward, away from here and away from *him*. But she had been so very wrong.

James had been almost alarmingly calm when she had broken their engagement. Inside, she'd been torn to pieces, chewed up with guilt, knowing what she'd shared with Santo, seeing the perfect, easy future she'd envisioned slipping through her fingers.

But, once again, Santo had been right. And she hated him for it. Hated that he got to stand there and pass judgement over her actions, when they were so limited in the first place. But she'd used that anger, honed it and let it fuel her.

The one advantage of being at home, under Edward's control, meant she'd had no bills. And she was putting the money she'd earned from her job with Mads, especially after her recent promotion, to good use. After paying off the loan she'd taken out to pay the last year of her university fees, and to cover the few expenses she did have, she'd opened a savings account. And last year she'd started to turn her hand to investments. Some low yield, long-term, but some the opposite. And those were the ones that had paid off. Big time.

Freddie, now sixteen years old, picking up on the increasingly difficult emotional undercurrents wrecking their small family, had started to avoid coming home. She'd spent as much time with him as she could, telling him as much as she dared, which wasn't enough but was still something. Her brother could see that her hands were tied, but he was also frustrated and upset about being kept in the dark about something he knew but didn't actually understand.

Which meant that Eleanor had a lot of free time in the evenings to spend online on the stock market. She was good enough at picking through a company's financials to see a little more behind the scenes than most, and the knowledge that she had picked up from the world Edward had drawn her into had given her a strong basis for her investments. She had begun to build a rather impressive portfolio and relished the security that gave her. Because everywhere else it felt as if she was losing.

In the first years that had followed the shocking discovery of her parentage, survival instinct had made her focus on what was in front of her. But she had acclimatised to the way her life was now, and it wasn't enough just to accept things the way they were. The need for more was urgent in her blood.

Edward's attention had begun to wander, and she'd been able to speak to her mother more and more. Did her father even know about her? If he did, why hadn't he tried to reach her? In even some small way at least. The thought that he hadn't was painful, so much so that she'd tried to put it out of her mind.

Just like she had tried to put other things out of her mind, but Santo was always there, waiting for her every night as she closed her eyes.

'See you next year, Princess.'

Even now, a shiver rippled across her skin. He had known. Just like he always had. What was it about him that he saw so much? That he knew so much about her, if not more than she knew herself? She felt as if she'd lived with him inside her skin all year. Every thought was tainted by him, by what he would think, by what he would say.

Each imagined response whispered in her ear as he—in her mind—loomed from behind. Teasing, taunting, promising. But it wasn't just words. Her fantasies had run rampant. Each time the sensual anticipation of what they could share became more vivid, more lurid—just *more*. And no matter what release she tried to find for herself, it wasn't enough. It wasn't him.

She shook her head at herself in disgust. She had turned into an obsessive.

'Something bothering you this evening, Eleanor?'

It was so close to her daydreams that she half expected it to have been a figment of her imagination. But the heat of his body, the scent pressed against her senses, the way that she responded to the impact of his voice...those made it real. *He* was real. The thrill that went through her, as if he had pulled on the invisible chain that bound them together.

'How did you recognise me?' she asked, her hand reaching up to adjust the mask again.

'I'd know you anywhere, Princess.'

It had shocked him, as much as it would anyone, to discover that the first kiss that he had shared with Eleanor had not been an anomaly. Because the second kiss only confirmed what Santo had thought for some time—that, no matter how much he fought, denied and refused to believe it, Eleanor was the one and only woman for him. As such, he'd been left with no other choice.

After he had left her last year—only because had he not, he would have taken her right there, in a room with no lock on the door, when anyone could have walked in on them, and honestly, he probably wouldn't have even cared—he had confronted the fact that he would do whatever it took to make her his.

No doubts, no more second-guessing, no prevarication.

She had broken her engagement because he'd been right. Because she could never hide in suburbia, she could never hide behind a man. She deserved more than being safe, because she was strong enough to survive it. She deserved more than being secure, because the risk was worth the reward. And the rewards for her would be more than she could ever imagine.

And since then he had spent every waking minute of every day making sure that everything was in place, so that when he made his move *nothing* would stand in his way. He had successfully managed to disentangle his business from Edward Carson. Yes, it had meant reinvesting with some of the other families—committing to business relationships that he didn't want—just so that Carson would have no ability to impact the Sabatini Group, and thus, by extension, both himself and Eleanor, ever again.

And while she didn't know it *yet*, he would make one hundred percent sure that she never had to worry about her mother, her brother or Edward Carson ever again. The only thing playing on his mind was that Pietro didn't know. That he wasn't sure that Pietro would approve. He certainly wouldn't approve of what Santo had been wanting to do to the man's daughter for nearly as long as he'd known her. It was the first time he'd ever withheld something from the man who had been more like a father to him than his own, and it was a twist of the knife in his conscience. But Pietro would have to wait.

Santo spotted Eleanor at the edge of the crowd, something easing in his chest for the first time since he'd left her the year before. No more would he allow so much time to stand between them. Tonight he would see to that, he was determined.

He stalked towards her slowly, guests moving from his path as he closed the distance between them, anticipation and expectation burning in his chest and scouring his veins.

He came to stand behind her, taking a moment to inhale the sweet scent of her. To know that he would wake up with it in the morning nearly unmanned him right then and there.

'Something bothering you this evening, Eleanor?' he asked softly.

She started, the hitch of her shoulders enough to tell him that he'd caught her by surprise.

'How did you recognise me?' she asked, fiddling with her mask.

'I'd know you anywhere, Princess,' he told her truthfully. He could be blind, deaf, his tongue could have been ripped out, but he'd know this woman until his last breath. She was as much a part of him as the beat of his heart.

'Dance with me?' he asked, his palm upturned, open to her.

Eleanor's head turned half towards him, the profile of her face and the gold feather detail of her mask beautiful.

'Here?' she asked, her gaze locking onto his.

'No, out in the canal,' he teased and the edge in her eyes softened and warmed.

'Are you sure?' she asked, as if worried that he wouldn't want to be seen with her here, amongst these people.

He leaned forward, holding her gaze with his. 'Absolutely.'

A large space in the exquisite ballroom had been created for dancing—the orchestra, also masked, filled the hall with the sound of perfectly played waltzes. One piece was drawing to an end as Eleanor placed her hand in his and he led her to the centre of the room. It fitted so perfectly in his palm he almost forgot himself.

He noted a few whispers, felt more than a few gazes across the back of his neck, and hated the way that Eleanor stiffened at the feel of them too.

'Ignore them. You are the only one that matters here tonight,' he said as he led her to face him in a waist-hold. They stood, waiting for the music to start, and he marvelled at how right it felt to have her in his arms.

'What is it, *cara*?' he asked, noticing her gaze downward.

'I'm not used to pretty words from you,' she admitted with a smile.

Regret shot through him. They had lost so much time over the years, but no more. He would not, could not, let her go this time.

More and more couples filled the dance floor, but still they drew the most attention.

'I might find such things difficult,' he admitted. 'But if you want them, you'll have them every single day,' he vowed.

She looked up at him in surprise, a flush coming to her cheeks, gold shards glittering in the deep brown of her gaze. If this was her reaction to a few pretty words, then he'd shower her with them every minute of the day.

Her gaze scoured his, as if searching his features for the truth, hoping to divine his thoughts.

'What would you say?' she asked as the music began and he swept them into a dance his mother had forced him to learn when he'd been barely twelve years old. And for the first time in his entire life, he was thankful for the lesson. Because Eleanor moved like a swan on a lake. Graceful, *beautiful*, poised, in all the ways that made him feel like a clumsy oaf beside her.

'That you are the most precious thing in the world to me,' he admitted. 'That my life doesn't make sense when you are not here. That I ache to see you every moment of every day that I do not. That I want to know what you think, how you think, why you think, so that maybe, just maybe, I might understand you just a little more. Because that has become my only worthy endeavour,' he said.

As they moved around the room and his words fell in their wake, not once did she take her eyes from him. The small smile that had curved her lips grew, millimetre by millimetre, until it was the most beautiful thing he'd ever seen.

Titters from the crowd began to intrude and he didn't want that. He wanted her all to himself, and he thought that maybe this time she was ready to come with him. Not because she was fleeing, or hiding, or drowning. But because she wanted to.

He drew to a halt, not caring or needing to wait any longer.

'Come with me?' he asked.

'Anywhere,' she replied, and for the first time ever in one of these horrible New Year's Eve events, Santo Sabatini felt joy.

Eleanor let him lead her away from the ballroom, down the stairs and out through doors, and she didn't care who saw them. As he led her out into the frigid winter's night air, she didn't feel the sudden sharp icy sting, she felt alive, her blood burning through her body, a heat that had nothing to do with temperature and everything to do with the slow burn that had taken her over the moment he'd whispered into her ear that night.

They slipped through the throng of tourists hoping to celebrate the New Year; blurred faces stared after the two beautifully dressed people in masks racing across the cobbled square. He drew her into the entrance of his hotel, his hand in hers all but dragging her over the threshold and up an exquisite wooden curved staircase, towards a door on the uppermost floor, only four storeys above the street level.

And all she could think was, *Now. Please, God, now.*

After all the times that things had got in their way, after mistakes and wrong choices, she suddenly feared so much that this too would slip through her fingers, so much so that she thought she felt tears press against the backs of her eyes.

His pace slowed as he drew her towards the door at the far end of the corridor. And this was it, she thought, panicked. He was going to change his mind, and her heart wrenched as if she had already lost him.

With his key card pressed against the scanner for the room, the door partially pressed open, Santo looked down at her, something like alarm passing across his features.

'What's wrong?' he asked, searching her eyes.

'I…' She bit her lip, worried about what she would say. 'I…' She shook her head and looked down.

He lifted her chin with his forefinger, forcing her eyes back to his.

'Please don't change your mind,' she whispered. She couldn't bear it if he turned her away now.

'Why would…' He trailed off, as if unable to finish the sentence, let alone the thought.

'Because you see me,' she whispered again. 'All of me, from the very beginning. You have seen *me*. Not Edward, not money, not access, not a prize. And now I want you to *know* me and…if you stop then I don't think that I could bear it.'

'Why would I stop?' he asked, confusion clouding his gaze.

'What if you don't like what you find? What if I'm not good enough for you?'

'*Cristo, amore mio,* that would never happen.'

'Even if I'm…' She could hardly bring herself to say it.

'Innocent?' he finished for her.

She clenched her teeth together and nodded, not ashamed but embarrassed. Because she wanted him to see her as a woman, not some silly naïve girl asking for more than she could handle.

'Does that change things for you?' she dared to ask.

'Not at all, Eleanor. The only thing that will stop me tonight is a word from you, *prometto cara.*'

His promise skated over her skin, leaving goosebumps in its wake. But all thought stopped the moment that his lips met hers to seal the vow.

He kicked the door open with the back of his heel and enticed her across the threshold with a kiss promising so much that it filled her heart and soul. And she knew in that moment that wherever he went, she would follow.

Her fingers reached up to wrap around his neck as, at the same time, his hands reached for her, lifting her from the floor effortlessly and into his hands. With one hand supporting beneath her, the other cradled her head, fisted in her hair, pulling just tightly enough to angle her head where he wanted her, where he could plunge his tongue into her mouth, where he could possess her wholly, fully, *completely*.

In the second it took her to process the power of his kiss she realised just how much he'd been holding back before. Whether it had been decorum or the risk of discovery, it didn't matter because, released from his restraint, he was so far beyond her wildest imaginings.

Overwhelmed by all the sensations flooding her system, her breath caught in her lungs and she forgot to breathe. Her pulse leapt and dipped when he plunged his tongue into her mouth, when he pulled her closer into his body, when his hands swept around her dress, as if trying to find a way beneath it to her skin, and she wanted that more than anything.

Holding her up above him, he walked further into the suite, not breaking the kiss until he put Eleanor down on the breakfast bar, where she was momentarily distracted by the most magnificent view. Not the nightscape across the Venice canals, but him. Staring at her as if he would never be able to tear himself away from her ever again.

He pushed at the thick skirts of her dress, closing his eyes as if in bliss when he finally found the sleek curve of her calf. Fascinated, she watched how young he suddenly appeared as he gently took her shoe in his hands, bending her leg a little between them so that he could dip his lips to the space just above, where her high heel was buckled.

It was perhaps the most erotic thing that had ever happened to her, her cheeks instantly flushing from the proximity of him, of his *mouth*, making her damp with want.

He looked up at her without bringing the kisses he pressed against her leg to an end, heat in his gaze, knowing…promise. He knew exactly what he was doing to her and he was watching her as intently as she was watching him, documenting each response, each reaction, the way that each touch thrilled, each kiss sent needles of sharp need into her lungs.

Panting now with desire for everything he could give her, her legs trembled beneath the weight of her want.

'I want to worship you,' Santo whispered honestly against her skin. 'I want you to know what that feels like.' And God, she wanted that too.

Santo wanted her to see what he saw. Her beauty, her strength, her power, her humour, her kindness and her confidence. He wanted her to know what he felt, but struggled to find the words that would make her understand how everything outside of them ceased to exist for him. Everything.

'I want you to feel nothing but pleasure,' he confessed.

Eleanor bit her lip as he trailed kisses up her calf, over her knee and across her thigh, the bare skin like silk. He wanted so much more for her than he'd ever had himself. He wanted to care for her throughout it, not steal it, bribe it or seduce it from her. He wanted her with him, in truth, in honesty and in pleasure.

'But if for one single minute you need me to stop, or to slow down—'

'Are you going to ask me for a safe word?' she said, trying to joke.

He stopped, his lips hovering barely an inch from her skin, and looked up at her, locking his gaze with hers. 'You are *always* safe with me.'

Her eyes glistened, emotion brimming to the edges,

and he knew that she understood what he meant. That promise went beyond this night, to all the nights. To for ever, no matter what happened between them. It was unbreakable, written in the marrow in his bones. He would care for her, love her, until his last breath on this planet.

Barely able to contain his own feelings, he pressed another kiss and another against the flesh of her inner thigh.

Her sigh turned into a gasp that fisted his erection as if she held him in the palm of her hand. Involuntarily, a growl escaped his lips and she shifted on the counter as if responses unfurled between them, back and forth on the tie that bound them together.

This was why it had always been inevitable. This was why she was the only woman for him now. Because his entire being depended on her, on what she felt, how she felt it, and how much better he could make it for her.

He gently parted her legs to make space for him fully, leaning forward to reach behind her to pull her closer to the edge, closer to him.

'I will stop if you want me to, but you have to tell me. So, I need you to talk to me.'

'You…you want me to talk to you?'

He leaned forward and kissed her, teasing her mouth open for him, one powerful thrust with his tongue against hers, before pulling back.

'I want you to tell me how it feels for you.'

He could see the flush on her cheeks deepen.

'What if I use the wrong words?' she asked, biting that lip of hers again.

'There are no wrong words here. There is nothing to fear, and nothing to be ashamed of, *cara*. I mean it,' he said, almost sternly.

Eleanor nodded, placing her trust in him, and he felt it like a gift. One that he was not worthy of in the least.

He kissed her again, swiftly, passionately, one hand pressing her into him, the other lifting her leg again behind her knee, over his hip, knowing that she could feel his need for her at the juncture of her thighs, knowing, as he ground against her, the moment he pressed against her clit because of the way her head fell back and the snap of pleasure rippled across her body.

He repeated the move again and she pressed, shaking, into him further.

'Words, *cara*,' he reminded her.

'Again,' she whispered.

'Why?' he asked, reaching the edge of his sanity.

'Because it feels good,' she said on panted breaths.

He slowly swept her skirt aside, lifting it over her knees, kissing each inch of flesh that was revealed across her thighs and higher, until finally he could see the dark, damp silk of her underwear, the musky scent of her driving him near feral with lust and want.

'May I?' he asked, with his thumb hooked into the waistband of her panties.

'Yes,' she said, her eyes so exquisitely full of desire, a strand of her hair falling loose as she nodded.

She raised her backside from the counter so that he could draw her underwear from beneath her and away from her body.

And then, with Eleanor open before him, the smile dropped from his mouth. Because she was incredible. Exquisite. She was it for him. There was no other option or possibility or future. It was all her.

There was nothing holding him back now. All he could

do was let the fire consume them both. And that was the last thought he had as he bent his head to the juncture of her thighs and pressed open-mouthed kisses to her core, the taste of heaven he had fantasised about for years entering his bloodstream like a drug he would never quit.

Eleanor fell back against the wall, her hands fisting the edge of the table, knuckles white, trying to hold on, while Santo thrust her into a pleasure so acute she thought she'd break apart if she took another breath.

Curses filled her mouth and she thought, impossibly, that she could tell Santo was smiling as he pressed yet another open-mouthed kiss against her. His hands pressed her thighs open to him, his thumbs massaging gentle circles as his tongue laved over her clit in lazy sweeps that sent shivers across her entire body.

Oxygen battled against pleasure in her lungs and if she could survive on bliss alone she would happily do so, but couldn't, so gasped for breath as he pushed her closer and closer to the edge.

She writhed against him and he growled against her delicate flesh, nearly splitting her apart with desire. He did it again, and she cried out from the sensation alone. He circled his finger around her entrance, the feeling exquisitely new, teasing, making her want him there more than she could have possibly imagined.

'Cara?'

'Yes, please. Please, Santo…'

The words tripped over themselves as they fell from her lips. She would beg if she had to, but he would never let her do that because he was already where she needed him and then he thrust into her with clever, knowing fingers that filled her, the palm of his hand pressing against the rest of her as his tongue teased her clitoris to the point of near madness.

'Oh, God,' she hissed out. 'Santo, I...'

'Breathe,' he whispered. 'Breathe into it, let it fill you,' he guided. 'Let yourself come.'

He didn't push her further than what she could handle but instead deepened her experience for her, letting it sweep at her feet like the tide rather than a tsunami, letting her sink into it rather than drown, as if it were something to luxuriate in.

Breath after breath, swallowing down pleasure in a way she'd never known, never experienced, as her orgasm built from the ground up, from where he pressed his tongue to her, from where he added a second finger to fill her, from where he held her so securely against him. Her orgasm was like Santo himself, slow, inexorable; it stalked her like prey, closing in on her with a fatefulness that she couldn't escape, that she didn't want to escape.

He whispered words of encouragement against her, unintelligible to her overstimulated mind, but known instinctively by her body. She unfurled for him, she opened to him, wanting more, like an insatiable being hunting her own pleasure even as it stalked her, until finally her body couldn't take it any more.

With one final sweep of his tongue she exploded like the fireworks filling the night sky.

CHAPTER TEN

.

New Year's Eve last year, Venice

IN HER MIND she was distantly aware that Santo had gathered her into his arms and gently pulled her from the countertop, carrying her over to the large, soft leather sofa that looked out at the Venetian night sky, where stars vied with fireworks above waterways that reflected it all over again on shifting silken waves.

He lay back against the head of the sofa, pulling her onto him, keeping her in his arms.

'Did we miss New Year?' she asked when she found her voice again. He shook his head, his lips resting against the top of her head, ruffling her hair a little, and she didn't mind it a single bit. 'We've never done that.'

'*That?* No, I'd most definitely remember if we'd done that before,' he insisted.

'No,' she said, laughing and slapping the hand that was secured around her waist as if he never wanted to let her go. 'Seen the New Year in together.'

They'd either been with other people or they'd been pulled apart by other people. Even this moment felt stolen. As if, at some point, reality would come crashing down to take it away from her, just like everything else she'd thought she'd had in her life.

Eleanor turned her head to burrow against his chest as if he could ward off her fears. Her hand slipped beneath his shirt, where it had come open at his neck, and relished the hot skin, the texture of the swirls of hair that dusted his chest. And just like that, her curiosity was ignited, desire curling up like a flame from the ashes. She twisted in his lap, unbuttoning his shirt with curious fingers, before his hand came down around them.

'*Cara,*' he said, shaking his head, 'we can stop here. We can take it as slow as you want or need.'

But they couldn't. She didn't know what it was, waiting there on the horizon, she didn't know how it would happen, but she felt that this was it for them. That they *didn't* have all the time in the world. Whether it was because of the past or because of how it always was between her and Santo, something would happen to take this from her, and she wouldn't waste a single moment she had with him.

'This is what I want, Santo,' she said and meant it truly. 'You. I want you so much that I...' She stopped herself, but saw the questions in his eyes. 'I can't explain it... words don't explain it...' She shrugged. So she crawled up to take his lips in hers and poured every inexplicable, complicated, messy, passionate, desperate feeling she had for him into her kiss.

She wound her fingers into his hair and rose onto her knees, straddling his hips, before pressing herself down into his lap. He lurched forward to meet her, feeding off her passion, increasing it, multiplying it exponentially, his arms around her waist, holding her in the way that only he ever had, as if she were both incredibly precious and strong enough to take it—to take *him*.

This was what had been missing from her life, this was

who she could love with unrestrained abandon, not without fear, and not without caution, but *with* those things, making it so much greater than anything she could have imagined. And it scared her witless.

He shifted her around him and she felt the hard length of him beneath her and she let the sensations draw her back into the sensual bliss he offered her.

His hands were full of her and it would still never be enough. Stomach muscles taut, he held himself and her upright as she pulled at the buttons on his shirt, shucking it from his shoulders, her palms smoothing over his skin as if learning the feel of it.

Cristo, her skin was like silk. Her tongue tangled with his as his hands swept across her body to find the fastening that held the dress together. As if sensing his impatience, she smiled against his lips and guided his hands to the buttons at her back, to tiny buttons that, when undone, unwrapped the dress like a present.

Before she could be revealed, his hands slipped beneath the gold layers of stiff silk and tugged the material from her body. And there she was, naked, and he nearly lost his mind.

Was this how it would be—that she would push him to the edge of his sanity? Was it something that someone like him could risk?

Her gaze beckoned him back to her, but a part of him edged away, inch by inch, seeking a self-protection that was never coming back. He was done for—a lost cause.

But that didn't mean he should stop protecting her.

'Santo?'

Like a siren song, she called and he went to her as if

she were his redemption rather than his damnation. He rocked beneath her and relished the shiver that ran up her body. Thrusting upward as she pressed down against him, goosebumps broke over his skin as she moaned in pleasure.

Unable to wait any longer, Eleanor's hands went to the fastening of his trousers, slipping the eye from the hook and releasing the zip. He couldn't take his eyes off her as she studied him, slowly pulling him free from his briefs, her hands around his length enough to make him come like some untried youth. He barely repressed the growl forming in the back of his throat but, from the knowing smile pulling at her lips, she'd heard him anyway. And liked it.

She looked up at him, the humour passing from her eyes. 'I don't want anything between us,' she said solemnly as she stroked the length of him again.

He bit his lip, trying not to be seduced by her desire.

'You should always use protection, *cara*,' he warned, aware of the irony of him lecturing her on protection when the thought of her being with anyone but him was untenable. 'For health, for contraception,' he bit out through the waves of pleasure her inexperienced hands teased from him. He was barely holding on and she was offering him everything he could ever want, whilst risking his worst nightmare—the continuation of his line. Of his genes. Of his *father's*.

He held his forehead against hers and tried to keep himself from thrusting into her caress.

'I'm on contraception.'

Her words pressed against his lips, and this time he was unable to hold back the groan that she swallowed as she opened her mouth to his in a kiss.

This woman was his undoing.

And then he cursed for a different reason.

'Bedroom,' he said against her mouth.

'No time,' Eleanor replied, pulling his waist between her legs.

'We will *make* time,' he commanded as he stepped back, plucked her from the sofa, hauled her into his arms, smiled when she squeaked, and stalked towards the bedroom. He was damned if he'd let her first time be some desperate scramble on a sofa.

He carried her down the corridor, almost disbelieving that he had her in his arms. That this time was theirs, finally. He toed the bedroom door open and, in the gentle upward lighting, made his way to place her gently on the bed.

She was utterly beautiful to him. It was a rush of knowledge, of blood, of conviction, of want, and he wasn't ashamed that he shook from the power of it. In that moment, he nearly turned back. He wasn't worthy of her, of this. There were things that Eleanor didn't know. But, just as his conscience began to stir, she sat forward, a frown between her eyes, a thread of concern that he never wanted to see passing across her exquisite features, and in his rush to reassure her, his thoughts fled.

He kneeled on the edge of the bed, coming for her, relishing the delight that now filled her gaze.

'You're wearing too many clothes,' she accused, as if in a sulk.

He cocked his head to the side, testing the game she wanted to play.

'What are you going to do about it, Princess?'

She rose to her knees, meeting him much closer on the bed than he'd expected. His entire body reacted, the hairs on his skin raising, the tightening of his muscles, ready for action, bound by restraint. A little smirk pulled at her lips and it was almost adorable. But the humour dropped beneath sharp need, when her hands went to the waistband of his trousers and pushed the material from his hips.

His jaw ached with the tension running through his body, holding him back, letting her explore as she wanted to. He pulled back enough to remove the loose trousers from his legs, to find her frowning at his briefs.

'Those too,' she commanded imperiously.

And he barked out a laugh. 'As you wish,' he said, his thumbs hooking into the band and drawing them slowly from his legs, delighting in Eleanor's fascination.

Her sharp inhale when she saw all of him pulled him back to her innocence, to why he hadn't just taken her up against the wall, as he'd wanted, the moment they'd crossed the threshold.

He was about to reassure her, remind her that they didn't have to do *anything* she didn't want, when she came to the edge of the bed, still on her knees, her cool little hands pressing into his body, his skin, his torso, around his hips and finally, exquisitely, around the length of him.

His head fell back as she explored him, as she felt her way around him, learning while she mystified him. But when he felt her mouth close around him, he nearly yelled out loud. He wanted to tell her she didn't have to, but he was drowning in a sea of such pure bliss it was near pain.

'Eleanor...' Her name was a plea and a prayer on his lips. *'Cristo.'*

Her response was a moan of delight around the hard length of him. Her tongue, the wet heat, the vibration of her pleasure was too much, and with a resolution that took more strength than he liked, he gently drew her away from him and pulled her up to face him.

'Did I do something wrong?' she asked, eyes wide, worried.

'Absolutely not,' he managed through the pounding in his chest. 'But if you want me capable of anything more we have to stop there. For now,' he said, more to reassure her than expecting more.

Realisation dawned in her gaze, a slight flush rose on her cheeks, and in that moment he thought that the crack in his heart began to close just a little. He kissed her then, covering the little fissures shifting like tectonic plates in his soul. He kissed her gently back against the bed, her arms sweeping up around his head, enfolding him, protecting their kiss against the outside world. He kissed the inside of her upper arm and just relished the heat of her body, the scent of her driving him wild. She opened for him, her legs gently wrapping around him, unconsciously guiding him to where they both wanted to be.

'Remember, *cara*, talk to me. Tell me what you feel, what makes you feel good, what doesn't, when you want me to stop,' he said in between kisses.

'If. *If* I want you to stop,' she insisted.

He smiled, but the seriousness remained in his gaze. 'It might hurt.'

She nodded, understanding and expectation serious in her eyes as he nudged himself at her entrance. The slick wet heat of her was urging him on, but he controlled himself with a ruthlessness that bordered on pain. Slowly, he leaned into her, inch by inch, filling her, joining with her, hating that the pure ecstasy of it for him caused her pain, the price she was paying indecent in that light. And in that moment he knew that nothing would ever be the same again.

The feeling of intrusion was almost overwhelming.

'Breathe, *cara*.'

Eleanor did as he asked, relaxing her body into it. Slowly, just like before, pleasure emerged from the pain, breath by breath, inch by inch, and her body, as if it knew him, as if it recognised him, began to unfurl for him.

As she adjusted to the size of him, she began to feel other things—the satisfaction of him inside her, the sense of completeness that began to fill her. The more she wanted him, the deeper she wanted him. The way that when he moved, he pressed against the bundle of nerves that snapped intense pleasure through her body.

A gasp fell from her lips and Santo responded by moving exactly the same way again.

'Good?'

'Amazing,' she hissed on an exhale.

'In what way?' he asked, and she could tell that he was struggling. Struggling to hold himself back, struggling to care for her, to protect this for her. To make it special for her.

'I never knew it could feel this way,' she admitted as he slowly filled her again, her head falling back on the pillow, her body rising to meet his. 'As if I had been empty until now,' she said as he drew back, the slide so delicious, and once again the gentle tide of her orgasm began to build. 'As if I had always missed you and never known it.'

He pushed into her slowly, deeply, as if he *was* that tide, gently covering her with a pleasure that was as

strong as a life force. Not terrifying, not plunging towards the edge of a cliff, but, once again, accepting that
inevitable conclusion where he would join her as they
willingly stepped into the abyss together.

She started to shiver under the weight of that pleasure.
'*Cara?*'

'It's so much, what you do to me. It's everything,' she
said in wonder as she breathed through a bigger wave of
pleasure, as if they were wading into deeper and deeper
waters.

Santo's head dropped to her chest, her hands coming to
wrap around him, holding him to her breast as he teased
her nipples. His movements became less smooth, and she
knew that he was as affected as she was. His skin, slick
with the same sweat as her own, the gentle slap of his
body against hers, the gasps and moans no longer distin-
guishable between them as they came closer and closer
towards this inescapable and undefinable *thing*.

Eleanor lost her breath, lost her sense of self, only
knowing him, only knowing this. Her orgasm swept over
her, over Santo, drawing him with her as they fell together…always together.

Eleanor woke, realising that the bed was empty. Smoothing circles on the cool sheets where Santo had been, she
shook away the heavy sleep she had fallen into and sat up
in the bed. Frowning, she pulled the silk throw from the
bed and, wrapping it around her, she went in search of him.

He wasn't in the en suite bathroom, so she passed
through the open bedroom door and, barefoot, made her
way back towards the main part of the suite.

'No, it's not like that,' Santo insisted, his voice low.

Eleanor hung back at the threshold of the sitting room, reluctant to intrude on something that was clearly deeply personal. Santo was on the phone, wearing nothing but his black trousers. For a moment, she allowed herself to indulge in the planes of his muscled torso, remembering the feel of his skin against her palm, her lips…and deep within her. She cast her gaze back to where he'd placed her on the countertop, a fierce blush rising to her cheeks, purely from the memory of the pleasure he'd brought her there.

'No, absolutely not,' Santo whisper-hissed again, drawing her attention back to him, his hand slashing through the air like punctuation.

Frowning, curiosity drew her a step forward into the room when his next words stopped her dead.

'She might be your daughter, Pietro, but you sent *me* to look after her,' he bit out angrily.

Pietro.

The name sounded like a bell in her mind, casting ripples across her thoughts, her memories… Pietro. The name of the man who was her father, her mother had confided. The father who she had put from her mind because he hadn't come for her. Because he hadn't wanted her.

'I don't care what you think, I'm going to—'

Eleanor's head snapped up as Santo's words cut off, to see him staring at her reflection in the window.

'I have to go,' Santo said, ending the call without taking his eyes off her.

Neither moved for what felt like an eternity. And then they both moved at once, Eleanor away from him and Santo towards her.

Nausea hit her so hard, so fast, she was nearly sick.
Pietro.

He knew her father.

He had lied to her.

He had *been* lying to her the whole time.

'You sent me to look after her.'

'What's going on?' she asked with numb lips, as a stranger stared back at her from the other side of the room.

'Eleanor, I…' Santo's mouth shut, opened and shut again.

Start, stop, start, stop—it had always been like that for them. So much so it made her dizzy.

'You know my…my father,' she said, her voice breaking on the last word.

'Yes.'

Her head swam and the sands shifted beneath her feet all over again.

'You *knew* he was my father the whole time,' she stated, trying to pull all the threads together.

'Yes,' Santo confirmed, the words like bullets getting closer and closer to their mark.

Her hand pressed against her lips to stop the shock from overwhelming her. From escaping. From betraying her. He knew her father, he'd known. He'd known when…

'I asked you not to lie to me,' she said, remembering that night, remembering the desperate need she'd felt then, and now, never to experience this kind of truly life-altering devastation. Her breath shuddered in her lungs.

'Eleanor, it's not what you think,' Santo said, a plea in his gaze as he approached her.

She threw up a hand to ward him off.

The buzzing that she heard in her ears grew louder and louder. 'You promised. You *promised* you wouldn't lie to me.'

Something happened to him then. She saw it distantly through the haze that was slowly wrapping itself around her.

'Yes, I did,' he said, pulling himself to his full height. As if he were shedding the person that she had known only moments ago, the person she had given herself to. 'I did, because I made a promise long before the one I made to you, and I believe that those two promises weren't mutually exclusive.'

'Mutually exclusive?' she just about managed to repeat. 'This is my *life*, Santo.'

'And it is mine. I owe a debt to your father.'

A knee-jerk reaction had her thinking of Edward, instead of the name of the man who Santo knew more than she did. Enough to make a promise, enough to pay a debt.

She shook her head as he made another step towards her.

'I meant everything that we shared tonight, Eleanor. Everything I said, everything I did.'

'You lied to me,' she cried, the outburst shocking them both. 'You lied to me, and that's not even the worst of it. Because what *is*, Santo, is that you knew *then*, when you made that promise, what it would do to me if I found out. You made that promise, knowing what breaking it would do to me.'

The betrayal was devastating. Her heart tore apart as she reimagined the last eight years under a new lens. One from Santo's perspective, of knowing more about her than she knew about her own life. Each successive New Year's Eve overlaying the next, seeing things differently, remembering little oddities—a vague recollection of Santo talking to her mother. Of Edward interrupting her and Santo.

'Does my mother know? That you know my father?'

The muscle in his jaw flexed. 'Yes.'

'Does Edward?'

'I think he may have suspected,' Santo admitted.

'What else did you lie to me about?'

Something flickered in his gaze. Not a lie as such, she was beginning to see, but something else. 'How else have you interfered with my life?' she demanded, thinking through all the possibilities. She came to the realisation almost as he opened his mouth to speak.

'I spoke to Mads before you...'

Eleanor's legs nearly gave way, the hand she thrust out to the wall the only thing keeping her up.

Her job. The one thing she'd had. The *one* thing she'd thought she'd achieved herself. And everything that had followed from that job, fruit of the poisoned tree. Lies.

Everything.

Could she even trust him? Could she trust anyone in her life? Every single person had lied to her, kept secrets from her. Everyone.

'I need you to leave,' she whispered, wrapping the last thread of determination she had left around her heart like a bandage. She didn't care that it was his hotel room. He could wait out in the hall naked for all she cared. But she needed to gather her things, *herself*, and she couldn't stand him watching her while she did.

'No, Eleanor. I'm not leaving until we talk this out.'

'There is nothing to talk about,' she spat.

Santo wrestled with control, anger, frustration, fear. She was slipping through his fingers, he could feel it, and it terrified him. But fear had never been a friend to him and it wasn't going to start now.

'Of course there is—this is worth fighting for, Eleanor.'

'Fighting for? Worth it?' she demanded, glaring at him from where she stood. 'You ruined this before it even had a chance, Santo. You knew what lying to me would do.'

'They were lies to keep you safe, Eleanor,' he ground out, frustration and fear pushing him to a point he knew was wrong. Pushing him into a corner that he knew he'd fight his way out of.

'Lying to yourself now? That must be a new experience for you,' she threw at him.

'Oh, don't be such a child, Eleanor. Things aren't so black and white,' he lashed out.

Fury whipped into her gaze. 'You don't get to accuse me of being a child, while saying all this was to protect me,' she bit back. 'You don't think that keeping these secrets has cost you too—kept you isolated, separate from forming proper relationships based on trust, on understanding?'

'Secrets have kept the people I love safe,' he growled, closing the distance between them, anger making them both rash.

'Now who's being the child?' she accused. 'Secrets kept me from making a choice, of doing things by myself, without you, without being dependent on you, on my mother, on whoever my father is. Secrets are just a way of manipulating people when you can't, or won't, trust the decisions they will make on their own. It's *your* way of manipulating people because you don't trust anyone enough to let them in.'

Injustice tore through him that she would so wilfully

refuse to see what he did for her, what it cost him to do for her.

'Me not letting anyone in? Me not trusting enough?' he demanded, his hurt running away with him. 'You wanted me to know you, all of you,' he said, using her words against her. 'But you don't want to know me. *All* of me. Once again, you're going to run away the very first chance you get. What is it going to take for you to stand your ground and fight for what you want, Eleanor? Because, apparently, it's damn well not me,' he finished, his words a devastating crack in the already fragile bond between them.

'You have *never* shown me all of you!' she cried out, the tears in her eyes dissolving his resolve like acid rain. 'Whether you're lying to me or lying to yourself, the man I thought…' she clamped her lips together and he could see her struggle to find a word that wouldn't betray them both '…the man I thought you were was a fabrication. You know everything about me, every single secret I have, but I only know what you let me know. I would have stood my ground for you if you had been willing to show me who you truly are,' she finished on a whisper, defeated.

He shook his head, her confession slipping through the cracks of his hurt, and leaving only what he had expected to see, what he needed to see. She didn't want *him*. He wasn't enough. For her. For his mother. He'd never been enough. His heart broke under the weight of her words.

'I don't believe you. You, me, this—' he gestured between them '—it was nothing more than a distraction for you. It was you wanting to play with a boy who Daddy didn't approve of. Because, deep down, Eleanor, no matter what happened between you, you're still that same little girl looking for Edward Carson's approval and I would certainly never meet that.'

'How can you say that?' she demanded, her cheeks suddenly pale, her deep brown eyes wounded.

'Because you're still there!' he yelled. 'You're still playing by his rules, you're still bowing to his commands.'

'He has my family,' she bit back.

'Your mother is an adult, and your brother is barely a year away from being one. They can make their own decisions, so why haven't you?' he demanded. 'Maybe you should ask yourself that as you sit in your ivory tower where you look down upon us mere mortals and cast your judgement,' he growled.

Cristo.

He shook his head, the crack in his heart widening with every beat. He had to get out of here. Distant thuds exploded beyond the window as the crowds in the Venetian streets shouted their countdown to midnight.

Ten, nine, eight...

He grabbed his keys, his phone and his shirt from the back of the sofa.

Seven, six, five...

The horrible words they'd hurled at each other echoed in his mind as he made his way to the door.

Four, three, two...

And as the silence rained down, more deafening than any explosion, he pulled the door to the suite open and didn't look back as he left.

One.

CHAPTER ELEVEN

New Year's Eve tonight, Brussels

ELEANOR CARSON APPROACHED the stone steps towards the gothic building that housed this evening's New Year's Eve party knowing that, one way or another, it would be the last time she would ever come to one of these events. And she was more than ready for that to happen.

It had been three hundred and sixty-five days since she'd last seen Santo Sabatini. Yet, despite that, she'd thought of him almost every single minute of every single day. She had been a wreck after last year. She had thought of him as her anchor, the North Star by which she navigated her life, her route through the madness of this place and these people.

But discovering that he'd lied, knowingly, willingly and continually, for their entire relationship had coloured everything. Every interaction, every exchange, look, word. All that time he had known who her real father was. And yes, she'd been devastated that he'd kept that from her, but what had been worse was that he'd kept *himself* from her.

Eleanor didn't like looking back at those first few weeks. She could barely remember them, but what she could recall wasn't pretty. She'd felt utterly empty, with nothing to numb the bone-deep ache that had settled beneath her skin and taken up residence.

Her mother had tried and cajoled but, being part of the chaos Eleanor was trying to find her way through, was unable to help. Freddie had wanted to delay his return to boarding school, but Edward refused to allow it. But her brother had sneaked back three days later, when Edward was away. At seventeen, bright blue eyes and blond hair, huge tears rolling down his cheeks, he'd begged and pleaded with her to tell him what was going on.

In that moment she'd realised that she was doing exactly what she had accused Santo of doing. She was keeping secrets from her brother in the hope that it would protect him from the fallout. From Edward. And, deep down, she was forced to face the fact that Santo had been right about that too. That what she had been *really* afraid of, why she hadn't left or fought back against Edward, was the terrifying thought that her brother and her mother would let her be exiled. That they would choose Edward over her. And that she would be left alone. Truly alone in this world.

She and Freddie had spent two days talking and crying and planning. Freddie had been so angry and hurt about the secrets they'd kept, and as she'd explained how terrified she'd been of losing him she'd begun to wonder if that was why Santo hadn't told her the truth, her mother too.

She'd returned Freddie to the boarding school and made up an excuse that wouldn't get back to Edward. In the Easter holidays Freddie had convinced Edward to let the two of them go to 'Europe', Edward naively believing that he had enough control over her to stop her from doing something 'stupid'.

Which was how it had come to pass that Freddie had accompanied her to meet her father, Pietro Moretti, in the late spring. It had been one of the scariest things she'd ever done, but that Freddie was with her meant the absolute world. She knew then that, no matter what happened, what Edward did or threatened, she would never be alone. She was loved and she loved. Greatly. And that was far more important than blood ties and truths.

Pietro Moretti was older than she'd imagined—that or time hadn't been kind. The poor man had been as nervous as she was, but beneath the cream awning of a café in Rome, conversation unfurled in a way that swept away hesitancy and heralded a tide of familiarity that struck her bone-deep. She hadn't expected it, but it was there. They shared mannerisms that were impossible but undeniable, and regrets that would never be healed but could be soothed.

She could tell that Pietro had been sad that Analise wasn't there with them, but it had been important to Eleanor for this to be just for herself. Analise had understood, and that was enough. Eleanor's feelings towards both her parents were complex. She couldn't deny that there was a deep sadness that her father hadn't been able to come for her and her mother hadn't been able to be truthful with her, but she could also recognise that, had they been different, she wouldn't have had Freddie in her life, and she wouldn't trade him for the world.

Eleanor walked up the red carpet covered steps, wondering how many of the guests would have noticed the slight fraying at the edge, or the smears of mud and wet gathered from rain-covered streets. Not many, she decided as she presented her invitation. Now the scales had fallen from her eyes, Eleanor could see the darkness that touched everything about these people and these events, because no amount of money could hide the gluttony, selfishness and greed that were at the heart of nearly everyone here.

She hadn't talked about Santo with Pietro. It had been too much of a sore subject for her to broach. But he had tried. Just before she'd left him that afternoon in Rome, he had told her how good a man Santo was. Tears had filled both their gazes and she'd left with a twist in her heart.

Freddie had flown back to London, but she'd decided to stay on in Italy for a while, seeing some of her father's country. It was hard to distinguish the hope for connection with her birthright and the feel of the country as a stranger, but she'd found her way down south to Puglia almost by accident. And once she had ensured that Santo was away in London on business, she couldn't stop herself from heading out to the olive groves where the owner of the Sabatini Group had his residence.

There had only been a few people on the public tour at the unseasonable time of year and the estate manager had proudly shown off the grand estate. Rows and rows of olive trees filled the groves, some only just planted and others established over years. There was something incredibly beautiful about the vegetation blooming beneath the spring sunshine.

The tour had passed by a villa that looked so homely and inviting she had nearly refused to believe it when the manager had told them proudly that it belonged to the owner of the Sabatini Group.

The manager had explained how Signor Sabatini spent

as much time amongst the olive groves as his staff, caring for the land far beyond what was expected for such a busy man. And it was evident, not just in the health of the land, but the happiness of his staff. And she'd realised then that the things Santo chose to keep secret, the things he kept to himself, was what he valued the most, so much that he couldn't risk any of the families seeing that and using it against him.

It was like seeing him for the first time, she'd felt, as if she'd seen him, untainted by vows and heated exchanges, untainted by *them*. Here, she could see the real Santo, in the soil, the work, the place that he had carved for himself in the world, and she liked that man, was impressed by him.

And it had given her hope. Hope that had led her all the way here tonight. To *him*.

Two suited men held the doors open for her to pass through and she entered the Black and White formal ball planned for that evening by the Fouriers. As she walked into the large ornate gothic hall, decorated in gold and cream on one side, and black and silver on the other, she squared her shoulders, a wry smile gently pulling at her lips at the gasps and whispers as she passed.

The crimson silk dress hugged every inch of her figure, and matched the slash of carnal red lipstick she wore on her lips. It was a silent battle cry, and she intended full well to wage war tonight.

She was done playing their games and by their rules.

With his back to the large entrance on the other side of the hall, Santo heard the ripple of consternation shiver out across the guests.

Only one woman could do that.

Eleanor.

He'd honestly thought that she wouldn't come tonight. He knew that she'd met with Pietro earlier in the year, had tried to ignore the rumours and gossip about what she was up to. He'd told Mads that he no longer wanted to know about what she was doing and how she was getting on, but he'd been like an addict, desperate for a fix, and his only solution had been to cut himself off from her completely.

For months following their night together he'd been utterly unbearable. To have gone from such incredible highs to such incredible lows in the space of what had felt like minutes had been utterly devastating. But the accuracy of Eleanor's accusations that night had been inescapable.

The dramatic contrast between what he'd thought they'd have together, the future he had constructed in his mind, and what she had shown him he had in fact offered her, had left him numb to almost everything around him. He'd let things go at the Sabatini Group, his panicked assistant and board desperately scrabbling to cover in his absence.

He'd blocked Pietro's calls and ignored his mother as he'd cut himself off from everyone and everything. And eventually he'd found himself at his father's grave for the first time since he'd been put in the ground.

He'd thought about bringing a bottle of whisky for the bastard who had shaped Santo's life with fists and fury, and then decided that he wasn't even worth it. For days he'd come back again and again, pacing and cursing him to hell and back and hating that what Eleanor had said was true; it *had* been safe for him to hide behind the lie.

He'd made that promise knowing as much and, coward that he was, he had hidden from the truth the last time they'd been together.

Because if he could get away with showing her only what he wanted her to see, if he could cast himself in the role of her protector, he might just be able to make up for what he had never been able to do for his mother.

And by the time his mother came to find him at Gallo's graveside, he'd realised that he would never have been able to use Eleanor to appease the hurt in his heart. Not while he was still lying to her and himself. And there, by his father's grave, in his mother's arms, he'd wept like the child he'd never been allowed to be. For the fears he'd never been allowed to express and the love he'd so desperately wanted, no matter how much he'd denied it.

Santo braced against the memory of it, forcing himself not to tense against it, not to push it away, but to welcome it in, to let it wash over him and accept his feelings about it. It was a hard thing to do, given that he'd spent so many years refusing to even acknowledge such a thing.

Mads and Kat glanced between him and over his shoulder, and the sympathy and concern that he saw in their gazes told him that she was getting closer. The fact that they were worried about him was enough to let him know just how awful he'd been since the last time he'd seen her.

Mads had been the first person Santo had turned to when he'd come away from his father's grave. He just hadn't realised, truly realised, how isolated he had kept himself, until Eleanor had accused him of it. How much he'd done that to *protect* himself. And the stark irony of discovering that he hadn't been protecting Eleanor but actually only protecting himself this entire time had nearly brought him to his knees.

So he had started with Mads, letting him in, bit by bit. And Mads had paid that back in kind, slowly opening up to Santo, enabling them to form a friendship that Santo knew would last, no matter what. He had also made his peace with Pietro, realising that the reason he had clung so staunchly to his vow to the man who had been like a father to him was because he'd been convinced that it was the only reason Pietro had stayed close by. Pietro had told him that he was like a son to him, had offered his love freely, and let loose something in Santo he hadn't realised he'd been hiding. And that had finally given him the courage to come here tonight, for the one and only thing that could make him whole.

Mads and Kat made to leave and Santo took a deep breath, slowly turning around to face the woman he loved beyond distraction.

Eleanor.

Her steps almost faltered when she saw him turn. Almost, but not quite. Because she knew. She knew that he was it for her. He was her family, her home, her heart, no matter how much distance between them, or how much time had passed. He had been that for her from the moment she'd first laid eyes on him, all those years ago.

She wasn't quite sure of the response she would get, but she knew her love for him, she knew her own heart and her own mind.

The guests parted before her, but she barely noticed. Her gaze was on Santo, only Santo. She crossed the entire length of the ballroom while whispers grew louder and, for the first time in her life, Eleanor truly didn't care that she was under the scrutiny of the near two hundred guests in attendance that evening—including Edward Carson.

The man she had finally released herself from the night before.

No, Freddie wasn't eighteen yet, and no, her mother couldn't leave Edward Carson until that happened, but Eleanor had finally stepped out from beneath his control and into her own light. A light that she desperately wanted to share with Santo.

She didn't have much to offer him. Although her investments were good and her turnover impressive, her bank balance was truly insignificant compared to the people in this room. But she had enough to gain her own independence. Enough to know that she could and would move forward with her life alone if she had to. And that knowledge, the knowledge that she could rely on herself to recover from whatever life threw at her, to get back up and stand on her own, had given her the confidence she'd needed to come here tonight and to confess her feelings for the man she loved.

'Santo,' she greeted him, her gaze hungrily consuming the sight of him.

He nodded, that muscle in his jaw flickering, warning her of his restraint. But she didn't want his restraint. She never had.

There was so much she wanted to tell him, so much that she could see in his eyes, but the most important of all was simply this.

'I love you,' she confessed with a shrug, as if she'd tried not to. As if she couldn't help it. As if she were sorry for herself, when she was none of those things.

'I…don't need you to love me back,' she said, her confidence wobbling, but not wavering. Because it was the truth. 'My love for you doesn't depend on a response. It's not a transaction, to be bought or sold, like so much here is. My love for you doesn't depend on what you choose to do or not do with it,' she confessed.

She'd learned that about herself and about what she wanted from life. That she had to be happy with her choices, her decisions, her feelings, first and foremost. And, no matter what happened, she needed Santo to know that she wasn't ashamed of her love for him and never would be.

She had been devastated that he had thought himself unworthy of her. She had heard that in his tone when he'd accused her of being with him just to disappoint Edward. Seen through his accusation to the hurt that lay beneath. And she couldn't understand how he was unable to see that he was the best of every single person in this room.

'I just wanted you to know that. There will never be anyone else for me. There never was. It was always you,' she ended on a whisper.

Eleanor desperately imprinted the image of him on her memory in case it was all she would have in the months and years to come. Thick waves of dark hair making those aquamarine eyes even more hypnotic, lips almost cruelly carnal. She couldn't linger too long on any one feature because it was nearly too much for her to bear.

The silence in the room was deafening, not even a pin drop, not even the sound of her own heartbeat. Pressing her lips together to hide the way that they wobbled, she was about to turn, when suddenly he moved. And suddenly he was there. Everywhere. All at once.

His arms wrapped around her in that way of his that made her feel worshipped and loved and precious all at the same time. His lips found hers, not even trying to prise or entice them open to him, just to press against hers as if that was all he would ever need. She felt it, the passion, the love, the sheer magnitude of what she felt herself, returned to her by him. Her heart just gave itself to him and he accepted it.

'I didn't believe it. I couldn't trust that this was real, that you were real,' he whispered into her ear, holding her to him as if she might be snatched away from him at any minute. She felt his heart racing in his chest against her own. She felt the panic, the fear, the excitement, knew those same feelings *as* her own.

For a moment she couldn't believe it either, questioning whether it was real, whether she actually got to keep him this time.

'Can you ever forgive me?' The question exhaled from him as if it had been lodged in his chest for the entire year that they'd been apart.

She closed her eyes as the tears built, threatening to escape even as she wished them back.

'Can you ever forgive me?' she asked, unable to believe that she might have earned the right, having made him feel unworthy of her love.

The whispers and tittering of the people in the crowd began to grow, even as she would have been content to simply stay there, held by him, *loved* by him.

He pulled back to gaze into her eyes. And, just like that, the heat that had been banked behind declarations and confessions simmered into being.

'*Cristo*, Eleanor, I love you so damn much,' he said

and she couldn't help the smile that split her heart apart and pulled it back together at exactly the same time— reformed by him, reformed *for* him. 'It's inconceivable to me that you don't already know. That you don't feel it. Because I can't feel anything else. At all. *All* I feel is my love for you. Nothing else matters. Not these people, not my company, not even the promise I made to Pietro. They are all insignificant in comparison to how much I love you.'

But before she could say anything he dropped to one knee as a gasp of shock echoed across the guests, filling the large ornate hall. Shivers racked her body as she realised that he was going to propose to her. It was more than she had dared let herself hope for in all the years she'd known that he was the one she wanted to spend her life with. And now that it was here her heart nearly exploded from the joy of it.

'Eleanor Carson—'

She shook her head so fast that it cut off his words. A second of doubt passed across his features before comprehension blocked it out completely. She hated that she'd put that there, but it was important to her that they got this right.

'It's Moretti,' she clarified, loudly and clearly. 'My name is Eleanor Moretti.'

Santo looked at Eleanor, the pride, the confidence shining from her as she declared herself Pietro's daughter. As she finally turned her back on the man who had caused more damage than any one man had a right to.

Things were falling into place in a way that he'd never dared hope for. He had asked for Pietro's approval just before flying out here, knowing that had Eleanor not come tonight, he would have searched the world for her.

And as she stood before him, beautiful beyond his comprehension, exquisite in scarlet, he held open his palm and lifted the lid on the box that his mother had given him. It wasn't her ring—that had been buried with the man who had never earned their love—but her mother's ring, his *nonna*'s.

The women of his family were some of the strongest people he knew, and Eleanor was no different. He loved her with a fierceness that would never weaken, and it was the bare minimum of what Eleanor deserved from her future.

From the corner of his eye, he saw Edward Carson throw back his drink and make a fuss leaving the room. He knew that Eleanor had seen it too, from the way that she stilled. Outwardly, no one would have seen her move, her gaze didn't falter from his, but Santo knew the courage that she'd needed to brave this and marvelled at how strong she had become.

'Eleanor Moretti,' he said loudly for the whole room to hear, 'would you do me the greatest honour of letting me love you, honour you and worship you for the rest of my days?'

'Only if you'll let me do the same,' she said with a smile that could have lit the world. The strength of her love felt like a wave of heat.

'Do you always have to argue with me?' he mock growled from the floor.

'I will be needing the last word in all arguments, yes,' she confirmed happily.

'Only if I get to kiss that word from your lips,' he replied, rising from his knee to his feet, his hands reaching for her as he drew to his full height, lifting her from the floor, her legs wrapping around him so that he could feel her all around him once again.

With his entire heart full, he leaned to whisper in her ear, 'Say yes. Please,' he all but begged. 'I just want to hear it.'

She turned her lips to his and replied, 'Yes. Yes, yes, yes, yes, yes,' she said, over and over again, and he would never tire of hearing it.

Mads and Kat led a round of applause that gained volume and strength throughout all the guests in attendance, aside from Tony Fairchild, who was as red as a beetroot, and Dilly Allencourt, who was practically green with envy.

Neither Santo nor Eleanor cared one bit. This would be the last time they ever attended a New Year's Eve event with these people, they knew it, and Santo marched from the grand ballroom with Eleanor still in his arms without a second look.

'Where are you taking me?' Eleanor asked him, laughter and happiness filling her in the way that only Santo could make it.

'Home,' Santo announced. He was taking her *home*.

EPILOGUE

New Year's Eve four years later, Puglia

SANTO WOULD NEVER grow tired of the sound of children's laughter. It pealed through the house and out on the wind, carried to him as he made his way home from the olive groves. There had been a time, in the not so distant past, when he would never have thought it possible to feel such a thing, knowing the promise he'd made to himself growing up with Gallo's fury. And now he was determined to fill his estate with as many different cries of joy, laughter and happiness as he could.

Since walking out of the Fouriers' party in Brussels four years ago, his life had changed considerably, and he didn't regret a single moment of it. Thankfully, the work he'd done to disengage himself from Edward Carson in the preceding years had significantly lessened the financial blows that fell.

But he was still hit hard. Some of the families had followed Carson's lead in wreaking their revenge, but a surprising number of them hadn't. And even more surprising was how quickly the group of twelve families had fractured and broken apart in the years following. Some of the younger generation had little inclination for the cut-throat backstabbing that their forefathers had gone in for, and there had been an exodus as they followed Santo's suit.

The Sabatini Group had been forced to trim down operations in the wake of existing stakeholders' internal fighting. However, the resulting loss of their income had forced them to cut their losses or sell out. All of which was more than fine with Santo. It had simply meant that he could focus his business life on his venture with Mads Rassmussen and his personal life on Eleanor, on his relationship with his mother, with Pietro...with himself.

Santo had started that process four years ago and it hadn't been easy to work to rebuild some of the damage his father had done in his early years. Becoming a father himself had been the most incredible moment of his life, but also one of the hardest as he'd struggled to understand his father's actions and his complex feelings about his mother.

Eleanor had been there to support him every step of the way, but the help he'd needed went beyond her abilities. He'd started to see a counsellor for himself, but also for his children, wanting to make sure that he didn't repeat the pain of his childhood on them. And while it was one of the hardest things he'd ever done, every single minute he spent with his children showed him how much it was worth it—to make sure that they grew up with the kind of emotional strength and stability that he'd never had.

Eleanor had borne his emotional storms with a love and patience that astounded him and no one had cheered him on more as he'd created a charity for victims of domestic violence here in Puglia. He'd wanted her to be a part of it, but she was right, again, in that it was something that should be his alone.

He looked up at the light in the children's window and saw Eleanor's outline in the gauzy curtains billowing in the cool dusk breeze. She was getting them ready for the New Year's party that evening. He checked his watch; if he didn't get a move on he'd be late.

Santo cut through the garden and came into the villa by the back door, taking the stairs up to the second floor at a jog, stopping the moment he heard that sound again.

A fit of near hysterical giggles.

Only one thing caused that sound. His wife tickling their oldest. Little Pietro had inherited his mother's skin and sensitivity, but his father's humour and cheek. It was a lethal combination.

Their daughter Lucia had his eyes and from the first moment he'd looked on them he'd felt the erasure of pain when seeing his own reflection. His eyes were his daughter's, not his father's, and that meant more than he could ever hope to put into words. She had a mop of adorable blonde curls, but his mother informed him that they would eventually darken over time, just like they had with him. Personality-wise, though, she took very much after her mother and he adored her.

'Santo?' Eleanor called and he smiled to himself. She always knew when he was near.

'Sì?'

'Can you please convince your son that he needs to wear trousers for this evening?'

Santo came down the corridor to the bedroom opposite his and his wife's, and peered in with a frown.

'I'm not sure I can do that,' he said with grave seriousness.

'Oh, really? And why would that be, husband?' Eleanor asked with a raised eyebrow, but the glint in her eye told him that she knew there was mischief afoot.

'Because I don't think he *should* wear trousers this evening.'

Pietro jumped up and down, celebrating exuberantly.

'And if he's not wearing trousers this evening, then I don't need to wear trousers either,' Santo announced with a flourish.

Pietro stopped in an instant. 'No, Papà. You have to wear trousers!'

'But I can't leave you to be the only person not wearing trousers. So I'll keep you company by not wearing trousers.'

His gorgeous little boy frowned, trying to work through the complex reasoning of his desire to not wear trousers and his intense dislike of his father not doing so. It looked almost painful, and Santo tried very hard not to laugh.

'Papà wear my dress?' two-and-a-half-year-old Lucia offered in broken English.

'Oh, can I?' Santo asked with absolute delight.

'I'm not sure you'll fit,' Eleanor mused.

'I absolutely *will* fit,' Santo replied dramatically. 'Here, I'll show you.'

And both of his children descended into even more laughter as he toed off his shoe and tried to put his foot in Lucia's dress.

Eleanor didn't think she could love her husband any more than she did in that moment. This was everything she had never dared to dream that she could have.

It seemed incredible that she even wanted to celebrate New Year's Eve after the awfulness of the ten occasions she'd spent in different cities around Europe. But Santo had done that for her—healed parts of her that she'd never even known were damaged.

She still felt raw that he had suffered so much after the broken ties with the twelve families. She had grown up in business, become an adult in business. She knew the impact of the devastating loss and betrayal from such a large number of investors in the Sabatini Group.

Santo had done everything he could to reassure her that he was fine with reducing the company in the way he had been forced to do, and she believed him. It didn't stop her being angry for him though. And there had been quite a lot of anger for her to deal with in the months that had followed their escape.

Because that was what she'd seen it as. An escape. She had been imprisoned by lies and manipulation, and freedom had been quite an adjustment. But Santo had loved her through it all. Reassured her, soothed her, accepted her in every possible way.

It would have been so easy for him to dominate the relationship she had with Pietro, but he had encouraged her to find her own way with her biological father and it had meant everything to her. That he accepted the complexity of her feelings towards both her parents was huge for her. Parents who would, for the first time, be together under this roof tonight.

Much had changed in her mother's life, and Freddie's too. Analise had stayed with Edward until Freddie was eighteen years old and then moved out into a little flat, cutting all ties with her husband apart from communication via her lawyers. Freddie had gone with her and together they had weathered the storm of Edward's wrath.

Eleanor had begged them to come and stay with her and Santo, who would have welcomed them with open arms, but Analise and Freddie insisted that they wanted to handle it their way and she'd respected that. Freddie had grown into a man in so many ways since then. He was now at university and seeing a girl he'd met there, both of whom would also be coming tonight.

Santo's mother would also be joining them and bringing her companion. It had taken a while for Santo to warm to Enrico but the man had earned his grudging respect for the way that he treated his mother and she could tell that there was a sense of peace about Santo now that his mother had eventually found her own happiness. It was a peace that soothed many old hurts for her husband and, for that, she would be thankful for ever to Enrico.

'Right, you terrors, I'm going to leave you in your father's capable hands while I get myself ready. In my *own* dress. One that actually fits!' she cried, giving them all a last final kiss before getting into the shower.

Washed, scrubbed, moisturised and bright pink from the heat of the water, Eleanor wiped the steam away from the mirror. Wrapped in a towel and nothing else, she thought she saw traces of the girl who had so optimistically entered the Hall of Antiquities in Munich thirteen years ago. There were laughter lines at her eyes now, knowing in her gaze, a few healed scars and a sense of self she'd never have had without the journey she had taken to be here.

And she'd change nothing. She loved the person she was, the man she'd married and the children she'd born with a passion and fervour she'd not known, let alone thought herself capable of. What she had achieved with Santo was a life, a home, a family that she was proud of.

Tears pressed against the backs of her eyes and she waved her hand at them to stop them from falling. She needed to put on her make-up and she couldn't get this emotional yet.

'*Il mio cuore*, what's wrong?' Santo asked, stepping into the bathroom behind her and wrapping her in his arms.

'Oh, it's nothing. I'm just being silly,' she dismissed, feeling the tears press even harder against her eyes. *Oh, stupid hormones!* They were going to give it all away. 'I'm just so thankful for all that we have,' she said, holding his gaze in the reflection of the mirror.

His heart was in his eyes. She saw it every time he looked at her, at their children. The love he gave them was incredible.

'I never thought that I would feel this much love in my life. You brought that to me, and there isn't a minute of a single day that I'm not thankful for it,' he said, pulling her gently back against his chest.

Eleanor sighed, a small smile playing at her lips. She was never any good at keeping secrets anyway.

'Do you think there might be room for a little more?'

'A little more what?' he asked.

'A little more love to give. Because I have some news,' she confessed, turning in his arms and whispering that she was pregnant into his ear.

This time it was Santo's joy and laughter that could be heard from outside the villa as the Sabatini family members gathered to celebrate the happy news on New Year's Eve.

* * * * *

HUSBAND FOR THE HOLIDAYS

DANI COLLINS

MILLS & BOON

For Doug, my husband, for holidays and
all the rest of the days in the last thirty-plus years.

Happy Anniversary!

PROLOGUE

Seven years ago...

THE DOOR CLOSED behind her brother and Eloise Martin was left alone with the enigmatic Konstantin Galanis.

Her seventeen-year-old heart began to pound. Not with fear. Not exactly. Ilias was only running to the corner for eggnog and would be back in five minutes, but she was still overcome by something between awe and dread, as though she'd been left alone with a tiger and the promise that *he doesn't bite*.

Like heck. From what she'd read of his business acumen, Konstantin picked his teeth with the bones of his enemies every morning.

He was king of the jungle magnificent, too. He wore a stylish knitted pullover in ivory with brown suede patches on the elbows and the tops of his shoulders. His jeans were black, matching his short boots. His hair was cut short around his ears and was rakishly windswept on top. Given it was late afternoon, a hint of shadow was coming in on his jaw, framing his somber mouth and accentuating the hollows in his cheeks. His brows were strong thick lines over eyes that were cast down to ignore her in favor of his phone.

This crush of hers was silly. Childish. She knew it was, but she'd never been able to shake it. While her friends swooned over a cute actor or a boy band star, she secretly took screenshots of Konstantin from news releases and imagined a world where she was part of his life.

It was so immature! Especially when she was looking at him now and all she felt was intimidated and mesmerized.

He must have sensed her staring. His spiky lashes lifted and his dark brown gaze snared hers. Her pupils dilated in reaction. The lights on the tree suddenly seemed to paint the whole room in psychedelic reds and blues and golds and greens.

Quit gawking, she ordered herself and shakily turned back to the tree she was supposed to be decorating.

She didn't allow herself to look over her shoulder. He'd probably gone back to reading his phone, but her acute awareness of him had her imagining she felt his gaze traveling down her back and bottom and legs. She grew clumsy as she took each ornament from its case and looped it onto a branch.

"Ilias said you came to New York to settle some business with him." Nerves made her voice off-key and sharp.

Silence, except for the music switching to "Santa Baby."

She looked over at him.

He *was* looking at her, which made her pulse hitch.

"Yes," he replied.

"I don't…" She cleared her throat, feeling extra awkward. "I know that Galanis is a freight and shipping enterprise, but I don't know what you do there." She had the impression it was more involved than managing an inherited fortune the way her brother did.

"I oversee it. We're expanding into media and tech so it's being rebranded as KGE."

"You run it by yourself?" She hung the next ornament and glanced over.

"I have employees."

He made her feel gauche, quirking his mouth in that ironic way.

"I meant that it sounds like a lot to shoulder for one person." He was twenty-five, same as Ilias, even though he projected an air that was light-years ahead of everyone on the planet in maturity and life experience. "I only wondered if you have brothers or sisters who help?" Ilias had never mentioned any siblings and gossip sites were distressingly vague when it came to Konstantin's personal life.

"No," Konstantin replied.

"Other family?" His grandfather had died a few years ago.

"No."

This was going well. "Pets?" she asked facetiously.

"No," he pronounced dryly. "What do you really want to know? How I came to live with my grandfather? I don't talk about it."

Well, that was clear enough, wasn't it?

"I wasn't trying to be nosy." She ignored the sting of his less than subtle rebuff and hung another ornament, this one shaped like an icicle. The heat in her cheeks should have caused it to melt into a puddle on the floor. "You and Ilias have been friends forever." Since their boarding school days in England. "But he's never told me much about you."

Ilias had rarely brought his friend around. Aside from early glimpses over the tablet, Eloise had only seen Konstantin in person a handful of times. This was the first time in well over five years that she'd spoken to him in person, but she'd been idolizing him from the first time she heard his voice.

"Good."

"What? I mean, pardon?" She had forgotten what they were talking about.

"I'm glad he doesn't gossip about me. I'm a private person."

Okay, then.

She stifled a sigh and looked toward the door. Was Ilias milking the cow and growing the nutmeg himself? What was taking him so long?

She moved to the dining table and started to carry one of the chairs toward the tree.

"What are you doing?" Konstantin was beside her in three long strides, sending a jolt of electricity through her blood.

"I'm a shortcake." She was pointing out the obvious. It was the bane of her existence that she was barely five feet tall, especially at times like this when she found herself staring into the middle of a man's chest, feeling at every disadvantage because of her size. "I can't reach the top branches."

"I'll do it. Show me what you want." He replaced the chair, body almost brushing hers, fritzing her brain cells.

He moved to the tree and waited with bored expectation.

"I'm not one of those people with a rigid set of rules around how the tree looks." She made herself move closer even though she was walking right up to the tiger with his razor-sharp claws and giant teeth. "I just pick something from the box and stick it in a bare spot."

It wasn't rocket science, but he took the frosted globe from her hand, held it near a top branch, then looked at her again.

"Sure." She shrugged.

A snowflake went next, then a snowman. Each time, he checked with her before he looped the string around the branch.

"Have you never decorated a tree before?" she asked with bemusement.

"No."

"I guess that shouldn't surprise me. Mom hasn't hung her own decorations in years. If I hadn't come to spend the holidays with Ilias, he probably wouldn't bother, either. I like doing it, though. Put this one here." She extended the reindeer as high as she could.

His fingers brushed hers as he took it.

They were standing really close. Close enough that she caught the faded scent of his aftershave and the traces of the rum he'd taken straight because they'd run out of eggnog.

The music switched to Mariah Carey crooning "All I Want for Christmas Is You."

As Eloise looked up at him, Konstantin looked down at her and their gazes tangled. The world tilted and Eloise fell into an abyss.

Oh. Something happened within her. She had always felt giddy and nervous around him. Awestruck. She thought he was beautiful and compelling and she had always longed for him to like her. To *notice* her.

She hadn't realized it would be like this, though. She was old enough that she garnered sexual attention. Sometimes it was flattering, other times unwelcome.

It had never felt reciprocal. Not until now. The sensation was like an implosion that compressed heat into her, then expanded in an all-over blush of pleasure.

Konstantin looked at her the way a man looked at a woman and whatever cocoon she'd been occupying was suddenly too confining. She wanted to break out and step out and open herself. She felt fragile as a butterfly, but weighted, too. As though her blood were made of molasses.

That's what his eyes were made of, she thought distantly: dark gold bittersweet molasses. And his mouth…

Her heart fluttered as she willed him to kiss her.

The keypad beeped and the lock hummed. Ilias called out, "They didn't have the good kind. We'll have to make do."

Konstantin moved to the table where he'd left his phone and pocketed it, then met Ilias in the foyer.

"I have to get back to Athens."

"What? Why?"

Ilias's shock echoed hers. She moved closer to eavesdrop, hearing the rustle of Konstantin's overcoat as he slipped it on. His voice lowered, but she heard his rumbled words.

"Your sister is cute, but I don't want to encourage her."

Oh, Gawd.

She covered her face, mortified that she'd misinterpreted that moment and made such a fool of herself that Konstantin couldn't even stick around to face her.

"I'd hoped she'd grown out of that." Ilias's voice held humor. "Thanks for not making me call you out for pistols at dawn. We'll talk soon."

The door closed and she wanted to run into her room and hide. She made herself go back to the tree and pretend she hadn't overheard anything.

"That looks good," Ilias said behind her. At least he was kind enough not to tease her.

"I think so," she lied, refusing to look at him. She hated this tree. The whole season was ruined. Based on how sick she felt, she doubted she would ever enjoy Christmas again.

CHAPTER ONE

Present day...

THE TWELVE DAYS of Christmas was turning into twelve
nights of acute anxiety.

Eloise glanced again to be sure she had the right name on
the present and knocked on the door of the Manhattan high-
rise apartment.

A woman in silk slacks and a cowl-neck sweater answered
the door. Her blond hair was in a ponytail, but the loose,
messy kind that had been teased to look casual. Her makeup
was fresh enough to signal she had plans for the evening.
She gave Eloise's elf costume a pithy once-over and sighed.

Eloise knew what an atrocity it was. Even the smallest
uniform had been too big for her and the fabric was so cheap
static made it cling in all the wrong places. Plaits of orange
yarn protruded from either side of her green bent cone hat
behind pointed ears. The whole thing was probably askew
because the yarn was itchy and she kept flicking it away from
her face. Fake fur trimmed the green vest she wore over a
long-sleeved turtleneck of red-and-white stripes. Her green
skirt fell to mid-thigh and ended in triangles adorned with
bells. Her legs were made to look like candy canes complete
with shoes that turned up at the toes.

She was a caricature looking at a version of the affluent
person she used to be.

"Good evening," she said with a polite smile. "I believe the doorman announced me? You ordered Twelve Days for Noah?"

"My sister-in-law did. She must be mad at me." The woman turned to call out, "Noah? There's someone here to see you."

"Again?" A four-year-old boy ran to the door in his pajamas.

"Hi, Noah!" Eloise crouched and dug deep for a voice that was playful and filled with the magic and wonder of the season. "I'm Merrilee. I think you met Rocket yesterday? I'm another one of Santa's helpers. He asked me to bring you this." She offered the gift.

"*Cool*!" He grabbed the gift. "Can I open it?" He was already retreating back into the apartment.

"Say thank you first," the woman said in a harried voice.

"Thank you," Noah called back, but he was gone.

"See you tomorrow," Eloise said as she stood, but the door was already shutting in her face. "Merry Christmas," she added, faint and facetious.

She might once have been as rich and well-dressed as that woman, but she had never been that awful to people who were just trying to make ends meet. She had definitely taken for granted living in places like this, though. And having plans on Tuesday night and being showered with gifts just because.

She dragged her oversized velvet sack full of gifts back to the elevator. It was affixed to a square of wood on casters and was worse than walking a dog, wandering every direction and clipping her heel when she least expected it.

Once in the elevator, she dug for the next parcel, checking the time and the address on her phone. The building was only a few blocks away, but dragging this cloth bag through the streets was a lot harder than it looked. Snow clogged up the casters and—

Wait. Were there two kids at this next address? She pawed

deeper into the bag, vaguely aware the elevator had halted and the doors opened to the lobby. This one? She turned the gift over inside the bag.

"Up or out?" a gruff male voice asked with tested patience. *That voice.*

She jerked her attention upward and recognition crashed over her along with a hormonal rush of yearning that nearly took out her knees.

Oh, my God.

Horror followed because she did not want Konstantin Galanis to see her like this.

He wasn't even looking at her. His profile was every bit as remote and compelling as she remembered, every bit as dismissive as he stood to the side, holding the open door to give her room to exit while he looked toward the front doors of the building.

He was as impossibly good-looking as she remembered, too, broodingly handsome with his black hair and stern brow and strong freshly shaved jaw. His overcoat hung open over a cranberry-colored jacket, a pleated shirt and tuxedo trousers.

Did he live in this building? Or—

He started to turn his head, probably wondering what was taking her so long. She ducked her head in panic, wanting to dive into this giant sack of hers and disappear. Hunching her chin into her chest, she scurried past him, sack veering uncontrollably behind her.

"Hey. How'd that go?" the overly friendly doorman asked her as he brought her coat and boots from his parcel shelf behind his desk.

"Fine." Horrible. Worst night ever and she had some doozies to compare to.

"Are you coming back tomorrow?" He was mid-twenties, same as her. His smile invited her to linger and chat, but she didn't have time. Or inclination.

"Depends on the schedule. I'm a spare, covering for who-ever calls in, but it's only Day Four. I'm sure I'll be back here at some point." As she spoke, she hurried to toe off her silly shoes and zipped into her knee-high boots, then shrugged on her coat, still feeling as though Konstantin were standing over there staring at her when he had definitely already for-gotten about her and was twenty stories up by now.

"Let me give you my number. Maybe we can have a drink—" The doorman's expression changed into one that was more professional. "I'm sorry, sir. Is there a problem with the elevator?"

Eloise glanced up from tucking her curly shoes into the sack, realizing that Konstantin was still here in the lobby, still holding the doors open while he stared at her with a thunderstruck look on his face.

No! Her stomach curdled. She ducked her head again, skipped the switch of hat and finding her gloves. She didn't even belt her coat before she yanked the sack toward the door, desperate to get away before—

"Eloise!"

No, no, no.

She pushed out the door, cringing more from hearing her name behind her than the slap in the face of a blustery win-ter evening in New York.

She kept walking, letting the door drop closed behind her. It was rude. So rude. But it had been bad enough that he'd seen her like this and *hadn't* recognized her. Why should he? It had been six years since her brother's funeral. Before that, it had been that awful Christmas when she had imprinted on him like a duckling on a drake.

"Eloise." He was right behind her, commanding her to stop.

"I'm on a tight schedule," she said, refusing to look at him. "Children are waiting."

It was true. The sort of indulgent parent who booked

twelve days of personal deliveries for their children were not the type to be inconvenienced. If they said the delivery should happen before little Sally went to bed at seven o'clock, then that was the time the knock should resound on the door.

And who had designed these stupid sacks? Satan? She felt as though she were pulling a fully loaded sled.

"You can spare me five minutes." Konstantin caught her arm.

Even through the layers of her coat and shirt, she felt the sizzle. She had managed to convince herself that weird moment seven years ago had been the product of a desperate, juvenile imagination. That she was over her crush and didn't expect any man to save her, least of all this one.

But, ugh. She immediately felt the pull. The draw.

She shook it and him off.

"I really can't." She pressed on to the end of the block, then had to stop to wait for the walk signal.

She couldn't resist glancing up to see that he'd stayed right beside her, though. Damn him for keeping up with his long legs and no effort. He looked perfect, of course, with snowflakes landing on his dark hair and the collar of his overcoat turned up like a secret agent from the cold war. His eyes were still that depthless dark brown, not that she could tell in the flash of headlights and the liminal glow off the snow. She only remembered the color because she had been so fascinated by his eyes those other times. She wished she understood how his bottomless, steady gaze could cause such a trembling sensation inside her. When he looked straight at her this way, she felt as though he were pulling her soul from the depths of her body.

People began crossing the street. She lurched to go with them, to escape.

He caught the edge of her sack, preventing it from leaving the curb.

"I don't want to get fired." She turned back and tried to yank the edge from his grip, but he closed his fist tighter.

"Why are you working at all? At *this*?" His disparaging tone told her exactly what he thought of her job, but it was honest work. It was better than the forced marriage her step-father had tried to sell her into.

That was the real humiliation. That her life had descended to this. Not just working to support herself. There was no shame in that. It was the part where she had failed to protect her mother and they were both victims of a con artist. It was the fact that she had allowed herself to live like a spoiled princess, never questioning where the money came from, so she'd been completely unequipped when the vault was slammed closed against her.

It was the fact that the one man her brother had looked up to was looking down on her.

Frustrated by all of that, she stepped around the sack so she was right beside him. She grabbed the velvet near where he held it and yanked it free of his grip, then turned to lurch across the street. But now the sack was in front of her, caus-ing her to trip forward onto it.

In the same millisecond, the light changed. A car acceler-ated to take the corner before the oncoming traffic crossed the intersection.

There was a honk and a flash of a headlight, a shout and a sensation of being snatched out of the air like a sparrow into the claws of a hawk. There was a horrible crunching noise that made her cringe into the wall of wool as she waited for whatever injury she'd sustained to explode with pain.

"Look before you cross the street!" Konstantin's harsh voice blasted against her ear. His arms were banded around her, squeezing the breath out of her. One hand was splayed on the back of her head, tucking her face into his overcoat.

She hadn't been hit. She had fistfuls of his sleeves in her

hands while her feet pedaled to find the sidewalk. Her heart was rattled and thumping, her ears ringing. The fragrance of aftershave filled her nostrils, going straight into her brain like a drug.

A wave of helplessness tried to engulf her, one that urged her to melt into his tempered strength and cry. She was cold and tired and hungry and scared. And there was also that older, ingrained and immature longing for exactly this: to be rescued and coddled and held by him.

She refused to buckle to any of that.

"Let me go," she muttered, struggling even as he loosened his hold and let her slide to the ground.

He had to steady her as her foot slid in the slush, then she was free of his touch and felt utterly bereft.

"I have to—oh, no!" The sack had spilled off the curb. Two gifts were half crushed by tire tracks while the limp velvet sat in an icy puddle, collecting a dusting of wet snow. "What am I supposed to do now?"

"That could have been you. Do you realize that?" He sounded livid, which stung because she had only ever wanted his approval.

She started to bend, wanting to see if there was anything to be salvaged.

"You're not crawling in the gutter after useless parcels." He caught her back, his clasp on her arm keeping her standing beside him. "The sanitation people will clean it up when they do their rounds."

"I have to deliver these toys. I'll lose my job if I don't." She waved her free hand at the disaster.

"What sort of foolish job is it?"

"It's called Twelve Days of Christmas. Parents sign up for twelve days of personal deliveries for their children. They're *expecting* me." She shook off his hold.

"They'll survive. You may not," he added scathingly. "Come." He tried to turn her back the way they'd come.

She dug her boots into the clumping snow. "I need my job if I want to eat." That had been a harsh lesson, but she'd sure learned it in the last eight months.

"I'll feed you." He looped his arm behind her in an arched cage that swept her along like a blade plowing snow. "While you eat, you can tell me what the hell has happened that you're resorting to this."

Her feet stumbled to keep up with him while her back absorbed his strength all the way into her blood cells.

"You're acting like I'm dealing drugs." She looked back at the carnage of her paycheck, losing any chance at keeping her job when a figure darted out of the shadows to claim the sack and what was left of the parcels. They dragged all of it around the corner.

She couldn't begrudge someone living on the street for seizing an opportunity. She had a better understanding of poverty these days. She was even a little glad that some poor soul would enjoy something like a Secret Santa windfall, but it only reinforced that she was *very* fired.

Konstantin cursed under his breath and dropped his arm from around her as they arrived under the awning of the building they'd just left.

A beautiful woman had just walked out and—

Wait. Was that Gemma Wilkinson, the actress? She was red carpet–ready in a pine green gown under a black wrap. Her hair was up, her ears adorned with diamonds and her smoky eyes were trained on them with appalled astonishment.

"I asked Giles what was keeping you and he said you walked out. I thought you were having a cigarette."

"Something has come up." Konstantin didn't introduce Eloise or even look at her, only told Gemma, "I can't take you to the party tonight."

Gemma's incredulous laughter was aimed directly at Eloise in her crooked ears and ugly hat.

Where were catastrophic events when you needed them? Or even just a clear path of escape? A dog walker was behind her, the mesh of leashes hemming her into this curbside carnival act.

"Konstantin," Gemma said in a purr of sensual warning. "If you don't take me to that party tonight, you won't take me anywhere. Ever."

"Fair." It was one of the most dispassionate responses Eloise had ever witnessed and she'd seen the complete lack of pity in the eyes of the landlord when he'd informed her and her roommate that rent would double on January first.

Konstantin withdrew his phone and brought it to his ear, saying to Gemma, "I need my car right now, but I can send it back for you if you like."

"Oh, don't bother," Gemma said with subdued fury and spun to reenter the building.

The dog walker and the doorman and two passersby were all witnessing this drama. Eloise wanted to die. She truly did.

While Konstantin was on the phone, however, she seized the chance to call her supervisor—who was not paid nearly enough to care about the details of what had happened.

"So you'll miss the last five deliveries?" she summed up briskly. "I'll contact the customers and reschedule. You know I can't use you again?"

"I know. I'll turn in my uniform tomorrow. Oh. Except I lost the shoes."

"I'll tell head office you were hit by the car. That way they won't take the cost of the gifts out of your pay."

Wow. The Christmas spirit was alive and well. "Thanks. Merry Christmas."

"You, too, hon."

As she pocketed her phone, a gleaming SUV pulled up to

the curb. Konstantin stepped forward to open the back door himself, waving her to climb inside.

"I think you've mistaken me for your date. I'll head to the subway—"

"Get in."

She curled her cold hands into fists, suspecting her gloves were in the lost sack since they weren't in her pockets.

"You want to know what happened to make me take a job like this? I refused to buckle to an overbearing man." *Take that*, she added with a lift of her chin that made the bell on her hat give a muted tinkle.

"How's that working out for you?"

Not great, obviously. That didn't mean she should buckle to him.

"Get in, Eloise. Or I'll put you in."

She held his I-mean-it stare and to her eternal shame, frissons of excitement curled through her abdomen. She wanted his hands on her. The sparks of attraction she'd always harbored for him continued to smolder inside her.

"Do I have to count to three?" His patronizing tone called her a child. It was the ultimate insult, considering the very adult things she'd had to deal with lately.

Somehow, she channeled the privileged socialite her mother had taught her to be.

"Since it's your fault I lost my job, you may buy me dinner." She held his gaze as she passed under his nose, then clambered into the vehicle with a musical rattle of the bells on her skirt.

CHAPTER TWO

KONSTANTIN WALKED AROUND to the door that his driver opened for him, taking these few seconds to shake off the last of the adrenaline that had punched through him when Eloise had almost stepped into traffic. That had been the most terrifying—

No. He never let emotions of any variety sweep over him. When things didn't go as planned, he took control of himself and the situation, made adjustments and carried on.

This was quite the unexpected detour, though. Not that he'd wanted to attend tonight's soiree. Gemma had insisted. Since he had invited her to accompany him to the Maldives, Konstantin had relented, but the party wasn't even raising money for a good cause. It was purely a see-and-be-seen thing, something he loathed and typically avoided.

He settled into the captain's chair behind the driver and looked across the console to Eloise in the other one, studying her as the glow on the overhead bulb faded and his driver pulled into traffic. Between the painted freckles and round pink circles adorning her cheeks, and the hat and yarn that hid her real hair, he had almost missed recognizing her.

His only thought while he'd waited for the elevator had been that he couldn't wait to leave New York. He could stand the bustle and honks, but the relentless assault of seasonal cheer, of carols and blinking lights and jangling bells, almost made him nostalgic for the deprivations of his childhood.

Winters back then had been damp and gray. He'd shivered so hard his teeth had hurt and the only escape had been the rocky slopes and barren vineyards of northeastern Greece, but at least it had been quiet.

When the elevator opened and yet another ludicrous manifestation of the season appeared before him—a young woman in an elf costume—he'd barely looked at her. He'd had the sense she was staring at him, but that was normal. Konstantin owned a conglomerate worth billions. He didn't seek the spotlight, but he often earned reactions of awe and deference.

While his front brain essentially ignored her the way he ignored any staff who were getting on with their work, some preternatural sense had prickled to life in him as she brushed past. Once she was out, he should have stepped into the empty elevator to get on with his life, but his inner beast had snatched a look at a retreating woman, gauging her to be *not* a teenager as he'd first assumed.

She was petite, yes, and her clothing was an eyesore, but the doorman was hitting on her, indicating she was old enough to drink.

Konstantin had been irritated by that other man's attention toward her, which had been irritating in itself. What the hell did he care? He wasn't the possessive type even when he was in a relationship. This stranger was nothing to him. She wasn't even the kind of woman who usually caught his eye. He preferred tall curvy blondes who looked him in the eye and radiated sexual confidence. He slept with women who knew their own worth and went after what they wanted, even if it was him and his fortune. At least he knew where he stood and that they were capable of looking after themselves.

Vulnerable waifs were a hard no.

But he'd lingered to watch the interplay and listen to her speak. Even as the neutral elocution that denoted a cultured education was hitting his ears and ringing bells, she shook out her coat.

It wasn't a remarkable coat. Konstantin had seen many like it on various women through the years. It was a classic trench-style lined with a signature plaid from a popular designer. It looked well-worn so maybe she'd picked it up from a thrift store because it seemed high-end for someone in her position.

Yet, it fit her perfectly.

And suddenly Konstantin had heard a voice from the grave.

I have to buy my sister a coat. Something warm. She's coming for Christmas and I don't want her to be cold.

The ground had shifted beneath him. A flare of something dangerous had whooshed alight inside him. It was a reaction he had deliberately distanced himself from the first time he'd felt it. And the second.

But as she flashed him a last persecuted glance, he finally *saw* her. It was a gut punch and a knee to the groin and an awakening of something primal in him that he didn't even know he possessed.

She ignored his call of her name, which propelled him outside after her. None of this made sense. What the *hell* was Ilias's little sister doing, trudging through a snowstorm in a Peter Pan costume, dragging a sack like she was moving a dead body in a cheap detective movie?

She was aggressively ignoring him. Still. As the vehicle moved forward in the heavy traffic, she kept her stiff profile turned to the busy sidewalk beyond her side window.

"I told you to contact me if you needed anything," he reminded her. "Why haven't you?"

She made a noise between a choke and a laugh. "That was six years ago. At a funeral. You were being polite."

To some extent, perhaps, but… "I always mean what I say."

No response.

"How is Lilja?" he asked of her mother.

"Fine."

"In the same way that you're fine?"

She drew a deep breath, as though ready to launch into a lengthy reply, then said a cryptic, "She remarried a few years ago." Her breath hissed out and her chin went down. Her fingers twined together in her lap. "They live in Nice."

"I heard about that." Distantly. He had had his assistant send an appropriate gift expressing his felicitations. "Are *you* married?" It was a jarring thought that had him recollecting her remark about not buckling to an overbearing man.

"No," she said pithily.

"Living with someone?" Who was looking after her? Because it wasn't herself.

"I have a roommate," she said, talking to the window again.

"Are you using drugs?"

"*No*," she cried. "Why would you think—" She clammed up.

Exactly. Given her upbringing, finding her like this defied logic.

They arrived outside Konstantin's building. Eloise leaned to peer upward.

"Is there a restaurant up there somewhere?"

"I'm not sitting in a restaurant with Santa's Little Helper."

"You're not kidnapping one, either. That sort of behavior puts you on the Naughty list."

"I've never been on the Nice one," he drawled as he stepped out into the gust of wind and peck of snow. He liked to believe he was civilized and fair, but nice? No. That skated too close to caring and sentiment. He wasn't one to be *moved*.

Eloise had left the SUV and was standing on the sidewalk under the awning when he got there, hugging her coat lapels tight under her throat.

"I'd rather go home. Which way is the subway?" She squinted into the wall of flakes falling on either side of the awning.

"You said I could buy you dinner. Oscar will pick up our meal." He nodded at his driver to leave and the car pulled away. "Come wash your face and tell me what's going on."

He started toward the entrance, but she stayed where she was.

"Really?" He stepped back to face her. "We've been alone before. Nothing happened." It was a lie. Something had happened to him the last two times he'd seen her, but he'd put the brakes on before he stepped over any lines.

At least, he believed that until her gaze flashed up. Her hazel eyes reflected the white lights roped around the potted trees that lined the carpet to the door. He caught a glimpse of something in her eyes that was so naked, he felt the jolt of it travel into his chest and zing into his gut and groin.

Her lashes swept down, breaking that connection, but the electrical lines inside him were still smoking and tingling.

That was what he had turned away from twice before. She sparked a sexual reaction in him that was not only inappropriate, it was as dangerous as a keg of dynamite. He had walked away those other times because she'd been too young. She'd been grieving. And she was his best friend's kid sister.

He could have done it again right now. She wanted to leave and he could let her. He wasn't stupid enough to bring explosives into his home and start playing with matches.

But he couldn't let her go, either. She wasn't even wearing gloves or a proper hat.

"If I wanted sex tonight, I would have gone on my date," he said tersely, hoping to alleviate that worry from her mind. "This outfit of yours is not as seductive as you think it is."

"Rude." She scowled at him, but she was shivering.

Ilias's voice was in his ear again. *I don't want her to be cold.*

"Come inside," Konstantin insisted. "Your brother would expect me to help you."

* * *

"That's emotional manipulation," Eloise accused with affront.

"It's the truth." He glowered at her.

Eloise rolled her lips together. A strange hotness had arrived behind her eyes and in the back of her throat. She missed Ilias *all the time*. The promise of talking to someone who remembered him, who had cared about him even a fraction as much as she had, was tempting enough to override all her reservations.

She wasn't really afraid of Konstantin, anyway. She was afraid of her outsized reaction to him. The tiniest little remark seemed to slide straight through her skin and leave a wide bruise.

But she was freezing and hungry and her brother would have at least expected her to give his best friend a few minutes of her time.

Also, *she* wanted to give Konstantin her time.

She sighed and walked to the door into the building, allowing him to reach past her and open it for her.

This high-rise was even nicer than the ones she'd been delivering gifts to. The elevator he guided her into read Private above the doors. Konstantin's fingerprint triggered the single button inside it and it shot skyward in silence.

Eloise wasn't a stranger to wealth. She'd grown up benefiting from the Drakos fortune, the one her mother had married into and her brother had inherited. She had attended a top boarding school and skied St. Moritz and shopped Paris and Milan every season.

Konstantin was way above that, though. Maybe if he had survived, Ilias would have kept up with Konstantin, but maybe not. Ilias had commented once that Konstantin was *driven in a way I never will be*. She had always wondered if that had anything to do with Konstantin being an orphan, but who knew with him. He was a private person, as he'd made clear more than once.

The doors opened into a two-story mansion that took up the entire top of the building.

"Let me take your coat."

She hadn't had anyone stand behind her and act so chivalrous in a long time. It gave her a shiver as his fingertips grazed her shoulders. She slipped off her boots and felt drawn to peer into his home.

A floating staircase rose on one side. The main floor was an open living space within an arced wall of windows that offered views of the Hudson River and New York Harbor. Comfortable furniture beckoned under gentle lighting and a central fireplace clicked on as she approached it.

"You don't have a tree," she noted.

"I'm leaving tomorrow." Konstantin had removed his overcoat, revealing his red jacket, crisp white shirt, bow tie and black trousers.

She swallowed, freshly accosted by his good looks, but also reminded that he'd been going on a date. A clench of envy squeezed her heart, one that had barbs of inadequacy attached to it. Her whole life, she'd wished to be taller and curvier and capable of exuding authority. Instead, she was "cute"—she loathed that descriptor—and funny and rarely taken seriously. She folded her arms, chilled despite the warmth coming off the flickering flames next to her.

"I can't take you seriously in that." He started up the stairs. "Come."

She cautiously followed him and halted at the double doors to his bedroom. It was expansive and luxurious, with a huge four-poster bed and a sitting area with a desk.

He sent her a pithy look as he peeled off his jacket. "You're my friend's baby sister. My designs on you are strictly platonic."

He disappeared into a walk-in closet, coming back with a pair of drawstring track pants, a blue T-shirt, a cable knit pullover and a fresh pair of white socks.

"Change in there. Help yourself to whatever you need." He nodded at where a pair of doors stood open, revealing a bathroom twice the size of the apartment she currently shared with a roommate and her roommate's on-again, off-again girlfriend.

Eloise gathered the clothes and inched into the showpiece of marble and gleaming gold taps. She took in the freestanding tub before the bank of windows, the massive sauna shower and—

"Why is the toilet behind a clear wall?" she called. "Is this a break glass in case of emergency situation or…?"

He walked in and touched a button that cast the cubicle in a gentle glow while darkening its clear walls to opaque.

"Oh. Fancy." She couldn't help glancing longingly at the tub. Her building hadn't had proper hot water in weeks. She'd been making do with birdbaths and heavy use of deodorant.

"Do you want a bath?" He pulled his shirt from his trousers.

Her whole body flushed in panicked confusion. He had *just* said—

"Alone," he said dryly, popping his cuffs.

She was starting to despise that patronizing look of his.

"Come downstairs whenever you're ready." He walked out, pulling the bathroom doors closed behind him.

CHAPTER THREE

ELOISE LATCHED THE DOORS, planning to change quickly, get through dinner, then get herself home where she could start searching for a job to replace the one she'd lost.

Temptation got the better of her. Maybe it was vanity. Or cowardice.

Facing Konstantin was becoming more daunting by the second, especially when she looked as bedraggled as she felt. She hated that he was seeing her at her very worst.

Not that she'd looked great at the funeral. No wonder he had pushed her away *again* that day.

She swept that awful memory from her mind and hurried to wash her face.

Somewhere between drying her face and getting undressed, however, she found herself starting the shower. She wanted a few minutes to pull herself together, and yes, wanted to feel the way she used to feel when her needs were abundantly met and her problems were mostly superficial.

Seconds later, she was under the soft rain of the warm water, almost moaning aloud. *This shampoo.* The lather was silky, the conditioner rich as melted butter. The body wash smelled of sage and agave and made her skin tingle with rejuvenation.

She could have stayed here all night, but made herself step out and bit back another groan when she realized the towels were heated. The robe she stole off the hook was luxuriously soft and smelled like the body wash, as though Konstantin had worn it against his own clean, naked skin earlier today.

Oh, why was she like this? She'd had years to find a man who interested her as much as Konstantin, but he had set an impossible bar. She kept looking for someone with his same balance of intellect, confidence, sophistication and wit coupled with raw, masculine sex appeal.

Me and every other woman on the planet, she thought dourly.

Konstantin didn't even see her as a woman, only as his friend's *baby* sister.

We've been alone before. Nothing happened.

She closed her eyes, trying to block out the memory of finding him in the garden of her mother's villa in Athens. The rest of the guests had gone home. She'd been tired, so tired, but the service was over, the house was empty and her mother had gone to bed.

"Thank you for everything you've done," she had said, hovering on the final step of the stairs to the lower terrace. "It means a lot."

Silently, she had begged him to open up in some way, to reveal he was as gutted as she was or hold her maybe, so she didn't have to be the strong one.

He turned and came toward her, but stopped in front of her without touching her.

"You'll call me if you need anything." His voice was raspy, but that was the sum total of emotion he revealed.

She didn't doubt that he was affected, though. He had to be. He had been in America when Ilias's small plane had gone down. He'd offered to identify him and had then made all the arrangements for Ilias to come back to Athens.

"I will," she agreed and hugged herself.

"You shouldn't be out here without a coat." He touched

her arm. It was only protected by the sheer black sleeve of her dress.

"I don't feel it," she said in a dull voice. "I'm so numb I can't even cry."

"Don't cry," he commanded gruffly and stepped closer, enfolding her.

She was still on the step so the top of her head was right under his chin. She leaned into him and the sweetness of being held by this man, whom she had been alternately yearning for and cursing since last Christmas, began to break through her shell.

He was warm and strong and seemed to care, really care.

Without any conscious thought to it, she let her folded arm slide upward to curl around his neck. She stood on her tiptoes on that step and turned her face into his neck, tilting her mouth up to brush his jaw.

There was a sharp inhale as he stiffened. He looked down at her and their mouths brushed. His hands hardened on her and his mouth opened across hers in a rough claim that dragged her from a yearning for comfort into a cyclone of twisted emotions: anger and sorrow, pain and assuagement. A spike of pure, carnal hunger that jolted like lightning into her belly.

Then he wrenched his head up with a curse and pressed her away from him.

"That's not—get inside. I'll see myself out." He had left her there, swaying and stunned.

The tears had finally come. She had collapsed on the concrete stairs and cried so hard she couldn't walk or speak. It had been pure hell, leaving her with a bruised heart and a terrible cold, but at least she'd been able to resent him and blame him after that. Her crush had been crushed. She hadn't seen him again until today.

But he insisted nothing had happened.

She cringed, hating that he still had this effect on her! And how was he supposed to see her as a grown-up if she was dressed in his giant-ass clothes? She held the track pants against herself, thinking they'd look as ludicrous as the elf costume.

She left the humid bathroom and brought the clothes back to the bedroom, planning to enter his walk-in closet to find something else, but she lost her nerve.

At least the robe was more of a one-size-fits-all. It probably only fell to his shins while hitting the floor on her. Same for the cuffs. They fell past her wrists, but the thick velour was warm and snuggly and very comforting.

She dropped his clothes on the foot of the bed and belted the robe tighter. Then she found a comb and worked on her hair. She hadn't had it cut in ages so the tangles fell past her shoulders, taking forever to work out.

Konstantin had left the bedside lamp burning. Otherwise, the room was quiet and dark, allowing her to move to the window where she admired the sparkle of city lights and the few boats moving across the iced waterways.

She sank onto the sofa, letting her arms take a rest in her lap, thinking…

She was too tired to think. Too tired to talk. What would she even say? Everything had become very difficult and grim. Unbearable.

She blocked it out by closing her eyes. She resented that he wanted her to face him and find the words to defend her choices. To explain…

She sighed. At least when she was running flat out, trying to stay afloat, she didn't have to dwell. She didn't have to feel. She didn't have to…

She yawned and let herself tip onto her side. She pulled a cushion under her cheek, needing to rest just for a minute…

* * *

Eloise hadn't come down by the time dinner arrived so Konstantin went back upstairs to find his room empty.

Even as alarm jolted through him, his gaze snagged on the green and striped clothing discarded on the bathroom floor. His own clothes were abandoned on the foot of his bed.

He strode toward the phone on the night table, planning to ask the doorman if a naked woman had walked through the lobby, when he spied the bottom of her bare foot resting on the arm of the love seat that faced the windows. He peered over the back and found her fast asleep, arm curled under the cushion she'd pulled under her ear.

She didn't look as young now that she was out of her costume and her clownish makeup was washed away. Her cheekbones were high and well-defined, her mouth relaxed and somber. Her skin was so smooth and fine-grained, he wanted to touch her cheek, but he was torn over whether to wake her.

Patience wasn't one of his virtues. Virtues weren't really among his virtues. He abided by the law and treated people with civility, but he wasn't trying to prove anything to anyone. He didn't believe in heaven so he didn't strive to get there.

But he didn't needlessly torture people when they were at the end of their rope, either. He wanted to know how she came to be working a dead-end job that left her so exhausted she passed out before dinner, but he let her sleep. And, not for the first time, wondered if she might be taking drugs.

He took the decorative throw off the back of the love seat and draped it over her, then went downstairs to shamelessly go through the pockets of her coat. He came up with a handful of loose change, a subway card, a lip balm, a broken candy cane and a set of two keys, likely for an apartment door and a mailbox.

He sat down to eat alone—which wasn't unusual for him.

It was, however, the first time in a long time that he wished he could call Ilias. Not that Konstantin had ever called him. No, Ilias had reached out so often Konstantin had rarely placed the call himself.

Ilias had been Konstantin's friend whether he had wanted one or not. He hadn't. Friendship had been an unfamiliar concept to him. Konstantin hadn't had siblings and had rarely seen children his own age before he'd been plucked from his father's remote farm and thrust into his grandfather's lavish world.

But Konstantin had no sooner got used to the cavernous mansion outside Athens when his grandfather had sent him to "get a proper education."

At ten years old, he had found himself in a rainy English autumn, unable to speak a word of the language, surrounded by boys who all seemed to know each other, or have common interests, or understand how things were done.

It had been a nightmare. Konstantin understood how to be alone and preferred it. He had tried to seek solitude at every opportunity, but Ilias had said, *We're the only two Greeks in our year. We have to stick together.*

Ilias already spoke English he'd learned from his mother. He was outgoing, quick-witted and so personable, even Konstantin couldn't hate him.

By contrast, one of the first words Konstantin had learned was *sullen*.

Why so sullen, Master Galanis? the teacher had mocked, making the entire room of boys laugh at him.

He'd been sullen because he'd been cold and miserable and bewildered. He'd never had proper schooling, only what his mother had managed to teach him. Even the basics of math and reading in Greek were difficult for him, but Ilias had sat with him for countless hours, teaching him to draw the letters, tutoring him and helping him finish his homework.

Half the time, Ilias would say, *Just copy mine so we can go play football.* But the end result was that Konstantin had kept up and passed all his exams. He had also learned there was at least one person in this world who had his back.

Aside from those first couple of years when they'd both been homesick for Greece, Konstantin had never understood what Ilias saw in him. Konstantin would sometimes kick a football or walk to the shops if it was only him and Ilias, but he had little desire to spend time with anyone else. The rest of the boys and their mindless pursuits were superficial and immature.

Ilias would seek him out, though, especially after talking to his mother. Ilias's father had died when he was six and his mother had only relinquished him to boarding school because it was the school Ilias's father had gone to. It had been his father's wish that his son attend it, too. His mother had seemed to need a lot of connection with her son, calling nearly daily from wherever she happened to be, needing advice and reassurance. Ilias was always patient with her, but after ending the call, he would seem quietly distressed.

Konstantin had never known what to do with that. He understood the pressure of responsibility if not the weight of emotion that Ilias seemed to carry. The other boys would cajole Ilias to "cheer up!" but he would dismiss them, then ask Konstantin if he wanted to study. Over time, Konstantin had concluded it was the very fact that he *didn't* ask anything of Ilias that made Ilias gravitate to him.

When their university years arrived, they took different directions. Konstantin went to Oxford while Ilias went to Harvard, then Konstantin had to cut his education short. His grandfather had become ill and left such a financial mess of the shipping business, Konstantin had had to step in to right it.

By then, Konstantin had lived half his life in poverty, and

the second half in luxury. He knew which lifestyle he preferred. He'd been prepared to grind himself to the bone to
keep the company afloat and keep himself in the comforts
of wealth.

To his shock, Ilias had not only learned what he was up
against, he had stepped in with a loan, completely unasked,
leveraging the trust fund he'd gained access to at twenty-
one. That had given Konstantin enough breathing room to
make swift, radical changes that had been risky, but had not
only saved his grandfather's company, but doubled its share
value within two years.

At that point, investors had lined up to throw money at
him. They liked having young ambitious blood at the helm.

Konstantin had been growing the company ever since, expanding into tech, commodities, green energy and anything
else he thought could turn a profit.

When he had repaid his loan to Ilias, with suitable interest, Konstantin had gone to the US to arrange it. By then,
Ilias had been finished at Harvard and was living in New
York, beginning his career as an architect. It had been December. The streets and pubs and shops had been bustling
with crowds, but Ilias had dragged Konstantin into all of
those places.

"Mother has a new boyfriend. She's spending Christmas
with him at his castle in Scotland. Eloise would rather come
here. You should stay and spend the holidays with us."

Konstantin had been introduced to Ilias's little sister
through toothless photos and clumsy drawings that had
arrived at school in the mail. Occasionally, he had eaves-
dropped on conversations over the tablet when she had
plonked her way through a piano lesson or complained about
something at school. She was eight years younger than they
were so she'd always been very much a child, especially

once he had left school to work and she was still wearing braces and pigtails.

He didn't dislike her, but the invitation reeked of sentimentality. He had never celebrated any winter holiday, not beyond a quiet meal with his grandfather who had been gone for three years by then.

Nevertheless, out of respect for his friend and the enormous financial favor Ilias had done him, Konstantin had stuck around.

He barely recognized Eloise when he saw her. She had never looked much like her brother. They had different fathers, but she was no longer a child. She was seventeen and looking chic in snug jeans and a turtleneck. Her hair had been cut as short as his own, revealing her ears and nape. Her green-gold eyes and wide mouth dominated her otherwise delicate face.

Konstantin hadn't known what to say to her, but the siblings had bantered enough that it wasn't noticed. As Ilias started to pour drinks, they had argued over who had finished the last of the eggnog and who would pick up more. Ilias refused to let her go.

"I'd like a rum and eggnog today, thank you. If you go, you'll be gone for hours, chatting with everyone in the store. I don't need to know the bodega operator's hobbies or how many kittens the neighbor's cat had. No. You asked for a tree. You stay here and decorate it." He pointed at the fragrant evergreen.

"This from the man who can't get a coffee without getting a number," she lobbed back.

"Good luck with this one." Ilias thumbed over his shoulder with mock disgust on his way out the door. "I may or may not come back."

Konstantin had tried to ignore Eloise, but she did like to chat. Before he'd known it, she had corralled him into helping decorate the tree. As they'd stood close and their fingers had brushed and she looked up at him, he'd been struck by the woman she was on her way to becoming. He'd *seen* her.

And he'd wanted her.

That sudden rush of masculine energy had been so far off-side he'd stepped *way* back. So far back he'd left the apartment and flown to Athens that night.

Ilias had been surprised by his abrupt departure and Konstantin had blamed Eloise's childhood case of hero worship, which had never actually bothered him, always seeming harmless. In those moments beside the tree, however, he'd seen her attraction to him. He wasn't flattering himself. He was a healthy, wealthy man. Women had been noticing him for years. He damned well knew what mutual attraction was and feeling it with her had sent him into a mental fishtail.

So he left, and Konstantin had never seen Ilias in person again. He hadn't seen Eloise until the news had reached him that Ilias had been killed in a small plane crash.

He never looked back if he could avoid it and didn't let himself dwell on those nightmarish days now. He had done what he could for Ilias and his family, but it had been pure hell. The funeral service, the eulogy, had been like driving his car into a brick wall at full speed. He had made himself do it, but the impact had nearly destroyed him. Especially when he looked at Eloise.

The agony in her eyes had nearly broken him in two. He hadn't known what to say, how to mitigate the vastness of loss she was experiencing. He would fall into it himself if he tried. He'd had a near irresistible urge to take her away from all of this. To somehow pull her behind the wall he used to buffer himself from pain.

Don't feel anything, he silently urged her. *Don't suffer.*

She had been glued to her mother's side, steel to Lilja's shattered glass. There had been people everywhere, all wanting to approach mother and sister, to condole with them. Ilias had always been popular.

It had been winter again. An Athens winter, but still cold. At the reception after the service, Konstantin had stood outside in the bite of weather, done with old faces from school who he'd never liked in the first place. Done with small talk. Done with the sheer brutality of life.

But he couldn't make himself leave.

Then, as the light faded, Eloise had found him in the garden. She'd been a shadow of herself. Her black dress had made her look shapeless and washed out. She'd struck him as translucent. Brittle as a sculpture made of ice.

He remembered wanting to warm her. *Needing* to hold her. Then, somehow, his mouth was on hers and light burst forth inside him, gusting into a furnace of heat. She had tasted like salvation. Like purpose and hope and the future.

She hadn't pushed him away. Her arm had curled tighter behind his neck.

That was small comfort. What kind of man *did* that to a grieving woman? Especially one who was still too young for him?

He had pushed her away and he pushed from the table now, stalking across the room to get away from a kiss that had only happened because his self-discipline had been smashed by loss. He'd been too disgusted with himself afterward to reach out to her.

He had told her to contact him if she needed anything, but he hadn't been surprised when she never did. She and her mother had been surrounded by support that day. That's how it had looked, anyway.

Now he had to wonder.

Everything in him was wondering about her. Wondering in that way that went well beyond polite interest in an old friend's kid sister.

She wasn't a kid any longer. She was at least twenty-four. Her blush of awareness when he had asked if she wanted a bath, and the way her lashes had flickered as her gaze swept over him, had signaled she was still attracted to him.

An answering interest was gripping him, sharp and barbed.

He tightened his hand around his glass, resisting this involuntary reaction. It was carnal and human, but still misplaced. She was Ilias's little sister. She was on her back foot and needed help.

She was still off-limits.

He tilted his glass to let scotch bite his tongue.

CHAPTER FOUR

ELOISE WOKE DISORIENTED, thinking she was still dreaming because she was flying through the snow falling over the city. No. Those buildings were real. She was—

She sat up with a startled gasp, catching at the blanket before it slipped to the floor, but it was only the robe falling open across her bare legs. Her head swam as she stood to retie the belt and get her head on straight.

Through the predawn light, she saw the shape of someone in the bed.

Oh, no.

Her insides writhed with discomfiture at falling asleep in the first place, then sharing the room all night with Konstantin. It felt intimate, but also provocative. Did he sleep naked?

Don't.

She had to leave.

She tiptoed to the bathroom, planning to dress and slip away, but he spoke in a graveled voice muffled by the pillow.

"We don't have to get up for another hour. Do you want to sleep in a real bed?"

"No." Her voice hit a note that should have shattered the windows.

"There's one down the hall," he clarified.

Oh. Of course, he wouldn't invite her into his. Thank goodness it was barely light, not that he was looking at her to see the stinging heat that rushed into her cheeks.

"I'm fine. Go back to sleep." She went into the bathroom and closed the door before she turned on the light. Her elf uniform wasn't here. Neither were the clothes he'd loaned her.

She cracked the door to whisper, "Where are my clothes?"

"I threw them out."

"*Why*?"

"We're doing this now, then?" The blankets rustled as he rolled over, then they fell down his chest as his bent arms came up and flexed.

Dangerous tendrils of intrigue curled through her belly. "Doing what?" Her voice was still too high.

"Getting up. Talking."

"No. I'm going home."

With an impatient sigh, Konstantin threw back the covers and rose.

The winter light cast his bare chest and muscled legs in shades of pewter. He wore boxer briefs in a slash of black across his hips, but a jolt still went through her as she confronted all that naked skin. His physique was lean and powerful enough to dry her mouth.

And was he—?

She yanked her gaze to the windows, trying to unsee the press of his morning wood against his underwear.

"Did you take something?" he asked briskly.

"What?" She glanced to see he was dressing in the clothes she'd left on the foot of the bed. He had the track pants over his hips and yanked the drawstring before he tied it off.

"Drugs. Is that why you passed out?"

"*No.* I already told you I don't take drugs."

"Are you ill? Pregnant?"

"What on earth do you think I'm doing with my life? No. I've been working two jobs. I was tired." She looked to the door, thinking she'd have to go home in just her coat. It would look like the ultimate walk of shame, which it kind of was, but it was hardly the worst outfit on the subway on a Wednesday morning.

"I found an all-night boutique and had them deliver something closer to your size." He bent and snagged a massive shopping bag from the floor. He plopped it on the bench at the foot of the bed.

"That—" She couldn't really claim it wasn't necessary, could she? "Thank you."

"Come downstairs when you're dressed." He walked out, pulling the T-shirt over his head as he went.

She wavered briefly, then carried the oversized bag into the bathroom where she sifted through her options.

Drugs? Really? She was too broke to be anything but stone-cold sober.

She shook out a pair of jeans and looked at the selection of tops. There were a couple of plain T-shirts, a waffle-knit sweatshirt and a fuzzy blue cardigan along with fresh undies and bright pink socks.

The jeans were loose and she had to turn up the cuffs, but they were better than wearing anything of his. The layered tops hugged her comfortingly and the fuzzy cardigan was almost as snuggly as the robe had been.

Her hair was a disaster, given she'd slept on it wet before fully combing it out. It was flattened to one side and the part felt wrong, but she mostly wore it in a ponytail or a bun these days. Did the man own anything resembling a hair tie, though? Of course not.

She dampened her hair, combed it, then tucked it behind her ears and turned away in disgust.

When she got downstairs, Konstantin was speaking to a middle-aged woman who was setting two places on the end of the long dining table. The T-shirt shifted and hugged his muscled shoulders as he poured himself a coffee. His biceps bulged below the short sleeves. His feet were bare.

Eloise faltered, trying not to be mesmerized. She had only come this far to say goodbye, but the aroma of waffles and bacon and fresh coffee hit her nostrils, making her stomach cramp with hunger.

She hadn't had a lot of time to sleep these days and even less for eating.

"You missed dinner. Sit," Konstantin said, then dismissed his housekeeper with the news that, "We'll be gone by nine. Come back then and close the apartment. I'll email in the New Year to let you know when I'll be back. Enjoy your vacation."

"Thank you." The woman nodded and sent a pleasant smile toward Eloise on her way through the door beside the pantry.

This was quite a feast to be thrown together at the last minute. His housekeeper must have known Konstantin was expecting company this morning.

Unjustified jealousy twinged through Eloise at the thought of him sharing his wide bed with Gemma Wilkinson, then coming down here to play footsie while they ate breakfast.

Konstantin held a chair to the right of his spot at the head of the table. "Tell me how you've come to this."

The meal was too tempting. She sank into the chair and spooned berries from the different dishes onto her waffle, topped it with a drizzle of strawberry syrup, then added a dollop of whipped cream.

Konstantin sat and leaned to fill her cup with coffee, extending his tanned arm across her line of vision. How could the sight of an arm cause sizzling heat to climb from the pit of her belly up her lower back, across her chest and into her neck? It was ridiculous!

She slid a crispy morsel of waffle into her mouth, putting off answering because she felt so stupid about being here like this.

"Mmm…" The sweet flavors exploded on her tongue along

with the burst of berries and the fluffy texture of the whipped cream. She closed her eyes to savor it.

When she opened her eyes, Konstantin was watching her intently. Her heart flip-flopped and a fresh blush flooded with a sting into her cheeks.

She forced herself to swallow, but where to start?

Maybe if she hadn't been so entitled in the first place, taking food like this for granted? Maybe if she'd taken better care of herself and not been so oblivious and selfish?

Her descent into this predicament was intensely painful to look at and admit to, but at least he would understand how it started.

"Things were difficult after Ilias." She cleared her throat with a sip of coffee. It was a dark roast, bitter and delicious and piping hot. "Mom has had a lot of loss in her life and losing people isn't something anyone could get used to. She's always been on the sensitive side, anyway. Emotionally, I mean. She feels things very deeply."

She glanced up, not wanting him to think she was bad-mouthing her mother or judging Lilja. Her mother's personality tended toward codependent. That was just reality.

He was listening intently. His condensed attention made her feel as though she had a lens on herself that amplified everything, making her ultra self-conscious.

"I was trying to be strong for her, the way Ilias had always been. I didn't realize how badly I was taking his being gone until I went back to university. Mom had started seeing someone so I thought I was ready to resume my life, too. I wound up staying in my room for an entire semester."

Konstantin's brows crashed together. "No one helped you? Schoolmates?"

"I didn't have any. I'd only been there for a couple of months when it happened, then I was gone for more than a year. The few friends I'd made were doing their own things."

Partying, studying, dating and traveling. "Eventually, I got myself back into the lecture halls, but my interest wasn't there. I was failing out of classes, couldn't settle on a major. Mom still needed a lot of support. She likes to have a man in her life and she loves to talk about it when she does." Eloise found a wry smile, but it slid straight off her mouth because she should have been paying closer attention during that time. "I've always found it better to distance myself when she's dating someone new so I stayed at uni, trying to find my way."

"Why is it better to distance yourself?" His eyes narrowed inquisitively.

Men were so naive sometimes. She hesitated, but the reason men were naive was because women hated talking about it.

"Growing up, there were times when the man she was dating viewed us as a two-for-one deal," she admitted flatly.

"Lilja put up with that?" His voice thickened with outrage.

"Of course not. She always got rid of them immediately."

"How did it happen more than once? Did Ilias know?" he demanded.

"Sometimes. Don't look at me like that," she said of his accusatory glower. "It was hard enough telling my mother that her beau had grabbed my butt or tried to kiss me on the lips. I didn't want to repeat it to my brother. She always dealt with it and I learned to keep out of the way."

"This is unbelievable." He scraped his chair back and rose to pace near the window.

"You think I'm *lying*?"

"No," he barked over his shoulder. "I'm reminded of the depths some of my sex will sink to and I'm sickened by it. I just can't believe…" He pinched the bridge of his nose.

"Don't judge Mom too harshly," she said into the silence. "Her happiest time in life was when she was married to Ilias's father. She's been looking for that ever since. It's not her fault that some of the men she kissed turned out to be toads. The fault is mine for letting her marry one. Although, I think one of the reasons she liked Antoine so much is that he's always taken this very paternal attitude toward me instead of, you know, being overly friendly."

Konstantin turned, arms folded across his powerful chest. "What's his last name again?"

"Rousseau?"

He shrugged. "It wasn't familiar to me when she married him, but… He's no good?"

She dipped a strawberry in whipped cream and ate it, trying to sweeten the bitterness that had landed on her tongue.

"At first, he seemed like the answer to my prayers. Mom had known him for years and she had always found him charming."

Konstantin's brows went up in speculation.

She nodded grimly. "Given what I know of him now, I can't help thinking he'd kept a hook baited for her. He gave her what she was looking for, though. He romanced her and he's very attentive, pampers her and placates her moods. Once she started seeing him, she called me less often. When I did talk to her, she sounded calmer and happier. You don't realize how badly you need a full night's sleep until you get one, you know? Kind of like today," she joked, glancing up again.

His expression remained stony. She looked back to her plate.

"Mom always said she wouldn't remarry unless she was in love so when they got engaged, I thought it was the real deal. She was excited for the wedding and the honeymoon. He was always a gentleman around me, even though he was always *there*."

"What do you mean?"

"At first, I thought he was just trying to, you know, bond

with his wife's daughter. But he made it impossible for me to get Mom alone for more than five minutes. He was constantly inserting himself, driving the conversation where he wanted it to go. Or didn't want it to go. Part of me thought, who cares? *I'm* not married to him. He makes her happy." She braced her elbows on the table and covered the shame that creased her face. "I hate myself so much for being *relieved* that she was leaning on him instead of me."

"She used to do that with Ilias."

"She did," she agreed, picking up her head. "I really took him for granted that way. I took a lot of things for granted," she muttered as she gathered her cutlery again, but her appetite was muted by remorse. "Anyway, having that breathing space gave me a chance see that I hadn't been taking care of myself. I finally began thinking about what I wanted to do with my life."

"That's when you began your excursion to the North Pole?"

"Ha-ha. No. Ilias had always told me I should work in music. I'm not orchestra-level talent, but I wound up talking to a grief counselor who used music therapy. I realized that was something that interested me. The problem was, I'd already failed out of two universities. None of those classes really transferred, anyway. I found a program here in New York that accepted me, but when it came time to pay tuition and look for an apartment, Antoine refused to pay for any of it."

"*Antoine* did." A deep note entered Konstantin's voice that was lethal enough to make her skin prickle.

"Yes. Mom had always used a trustee to manage her fortune. Cyrus. When he retired, Antoine took over. It's totally within Mom's right to let him. It's her money from her first husband."

"None came from your father?"

"No." A small pang of mixed feelings struck, those that reminded her she wasn't really a Drakos, merely a product of her mother's whimsical appreciation for a good-looking man. "My father was a professional surfer. He made enough to stay on the circuit, but he had a bohemian personality. He died when I was five. I don't really remember him."

"What did your mother say about Antoine cutting you off?"

"Nothing." She got another bite of waffle into her mouth and chewed, but all her enjoyment was gone. "Given the history between us when it came to men, I didn't want to get between her and her husband. And Antoine had a point. It had always been on Mom to support me. I'm an adult and she doesn't owe me a penny. She had already given me four years of university and I had nothing to show for it. I accept all of that, but…"

"Surely, Ilias made arrangements for you."

"He didn't expect to die before he was thirty, did he?"

"That shouldn't have happened," Konstantin said with muted fury, looking toward the window where snow swirled beyond the glass. "I ask myself daily if I should have talked him out of taking those lessons. He always seemed so competent."

"He was. And he had a qualified pilot with him." Bird strikes didn't always take down a plane, but in this case, it had. "We met with lawyers once the funeral was over, obviously, but all of that is a blur to me."

At the mention of the funeral, Konstantin flashed his attention back to her. His delving look caused that strange pull in her belly.

She looked down at her plate, not wanting him to know how many times she'd relived their kiss. How much it had confused her and left her incapable of fully tracking what had happened those immediate days after, when they'd been trying to chart the path forward.

She rubbed her brow.

"I remember Cyrus saying there were sufficient funds for my schooling, but I don't remember how much. Control of the Drakos fortune reverted to Mom and I'm almost certain they said I would become a cotrustee if something happened to her. At the time, she just handed everything back to Cyrus. He had managed it before Ilias was old enough to do it and when I emailed *him* to say I was ready to go back to school, he took care of all my bills. I'm embarrassed to say that's all that mattered to me at the time. Then Cyrus retired and Antoine got his tentacles in."

"You're still her daughter. Does she know you're living like this? Surely, she wants you to be safe?"

"Safely married," she said dryly. "Antoine is very persuasive. He's got her convinced that I should marry Edoardo Ricci. You might know the banking family?"

"He's too old for you." His words lashed like a whip across the room.

"He's thirty-three," she said with a snort. "One year older than you."

His cheek ticked, but he didn't insist *he* was too old for her.

"Do you want to marry him?" he asked gruffly instead.

"No. Otherwise, I'd be there, getting married, wouldn't I? Not that there's anything wrong with him." Beyond the fact he wasn't Konstantin. She looked into her coffee. "I think about giving in every day. I know it would ease Mom's mind if I was settled. She would love to plan a wedding," she said into her cup, sipping to wet her damp throat. "But I find Antoine so patronizing. He said there was no point in Mom paying for my education if I'm only going to be a wife and mother, anyway. He said I've been enough of a drain on her resources and it's time that I…" She looked to the ceiling, still galled. "That I *contribute to the family fortunes in a constructive manner.*"

"That implies *he* has contributed to her fortune in some way. Has he?"

"I don't know. He has money from a previous marriage, I think." She hated the sound of Antoine's voice so she rarely listened to it. "Anyway, I told him to get stuffed, that I was going to school and walked out. I admit I was behaving like a spoiled brat. I flew here to look for an apartment, thinking he would cool off and go back to paying my bills. I thought Mom would insist on it. I've *always* had an allowance."

She massaged the tension that invaded her brow again, unable to look at him because she was so embarrassed by that sense of entitlement.

"Maybe I deserved to be brought down a peg, but as soon as I landed, he cut off my credit cards and bricked my phone. I had to sell what jewelry I had on me to pay my hotel bill. When I finally got hold of Mom, Antoine was right there saying that if I wanted to come back and continue talking about Edoardo, he would send me a plane ticket. I said no thanks and hung up. I've been here, living on spite, ever since."

He didn't laugh. "When was this?"

"April."

"What does Lilja think you've been doing all this time?"

"Going to school. When I said it, I was planning to get a student loan, but it felt like too big a hole to dig myself into. I kept up the lie as an excuse for not going home. I don't want Antoine to know he has my back against a wall."

"And your only income is door-to-door sales?"

"It's not—no. I serve breakfast at a trattoria on Fifth Avenue." She'd been crying into her espresso when the server had mentioned they were looking for help. "I room with one of my coworkers. She gets the more lucrative dinner shifts, but even the tips from a coffee and croissant are good. So were the tips from the Twelve Days gig. One of the dads gave me fifty dollars the first night. I was like, dude. Pace yourself. There are eleven more deliveries to go." *So much for that cash cow*, she thought wistfully.

"This is not what Ilias would want for you."

"Neither is marriage to a stranger. He wouldn't want Mom at the mercy of someone like Antoine, either. I feel *horrible* for that." The guilt ate at her constantly.

"Antoine took advantage of both of you. I'll step in. Straighten things out."

"How?" Her heart nearly came out her throat. "No. Don't get involved." It killed her to say it but, "I'm finally connected to Mom again. It's only a few texts and Antoine listens to all our calls, but if you go stirring the pot, he'll cut me off again. *No.* Thank you," she added in a shaken voice. "Stay out of it."

"He has no right to prevent you from speaking to your mother."

His lash of cold temper was... She wasn't sure. He was outraged on her behalf, which was heartening, but it seemed deeper and broader and more personal than it warranted. She didn't know how to interpret the cold malevolence that seemed to radiate from him. It made her cautious as she tried to defend her position.

"She thinks she loves him. He seems to love her back. What are you going to do? Shatter her beliefs and force her to suffer yet another heartbreak? I've caused her to lose men before."

"Men who didn't deserve to be with her," he pointed out with a flash of temper.

"Sure, but it would still be my fault. Again." Eloise had been down that road. Maybe her mother wouldn't hold a grudge, but it would still be painful and awful. "No. I appreciate the sympathetic ear and the hot meal, but I have everything under control."

That was such a lie that she couldn't look at him as she said it.

His snort told her he didn't buy it, either.

She stabbed at her waffle, focusing on finishing her breakfast so he wouldn't see the shadows of hopelessness in her eyes.

Konstantin retook his seat, resuming his breakfast while he filtered through the various avenues of inquiry he would take to correct for his failure to ensure Eloise and her mother were properly taken care of after Ilias had passed.

How had he thought they would be okay? That had been so shortsighted on his part; he was beyond disgusted with himself.

"What sorts of things have you been up to since, um…" Eloise's voice broke into his concentration, but then she seemed to realize that "since I saw you last" was a reference to the funeral and their kiss. "Lately," she mumbled and closed her lips over her fork.

Why was she engaging in inane small talk?

"Is that too personal?" Wariness edged into her expression. "I was only trying to make conversation."

"My life never changes. Work keeps me busy. I like it that way."

"But you're seeing, um… She's the actress, right? I'm really sorry about your date last night. I feel like I should apologize to her."

She sounded like Ilias, voice soaked with empathy for a complete stranger, wanting everyone to get along and willing to pave the way with their own beating heart if necessary.

"That's over. Forget it." He shrugged it away.

"The relationship is over? Or…?" Eloise searched his eyes as though delving for truth. For *feelings*. "Or do you mean you've made up with her and it's all okay?"

"I'm not in the habit of discussing my personal life," he reminded her.

Her expression went blank, proving she was even more sensitive than Ilias had ever been because he'd hurt her feelings. It brought out an agitation in Konstantin that wanted to bark, *For God's sake, protect yourself.*

Especially from me, was the follow-up thought.

He'd been hardened off very early in life while she had been raised by a high-needs mother who had left her so emotionally drained she'd neglected herself after suffering a devastating blow. Now she was being put through the wringer by her stepfather.

Guilt twisted like a knife behind his navel. That was more his fault than hers. He knew it even if she didn't.

"The relationship wasn't serious. Now it's over," he clarified for no particular reason except that he wanted her to know it. He refused to pick apart why. His cup went into its saucer with a click. "I sent flowers and something she could exchange at Tiffany's."

Her faint nod frustrated him for some inexplicable reason. Because she was judging him? No, he decided. It was the situation that was eating at him.

"Ilias would have paid your tuition and supported you through your education—"

"Please don't." She put up a hand, sounding appalled. "I didn't come here expecting anything more than a friendly catch up."

"Why is that?"

"Because we're strangers," she stated. "You don't owe me anything."

Like hell. He rejected that remark at such a base level he was insulted she would even say it aloud.

"Ilias bailed out my grandfather's company when we were still at university. Did you know that?"

"No. I mean, I remember him saying you had to quit school early because your grandfather was ill. And I know that you came to New York that time because you were squaring up with him on some old business." A blush crept into her cheeks and her gaze skittered away from his as she referenced that day by the Christmas tree. "Ilias never implied it was a big deal, though."

"It was a very big deal." Konstantin tried to ignore the sexual awareness that ignited within him each time he saw her react to him. "My grandfather became ill and I wasn't fully prepared to take over. Things were a mess. Vultures were circling. If not for Ilias, I would have lost everything."

"I doubt that." A smile flickered across her lips. "He always spoke about you as being very intelligent and ambitious. He admired you."

Konstantin couldn't help a reflexive frown at that, not caring for the pitch of emotion it caused within him: pain, loss, *more* guilt that he had ignored his obligations to Ilias's family.

"The point I'm making is that I remain in his debt." He was embarrassed that he had allowed himself to believe that paying off the financial side of things had been enough.

Eloise regarded him solemnly. "Ilias was never one to keep a score sheet. You know that."

"But he had a strong sense of right and wrong. What is happening to you is wrong." It made him livid.

It didn't sound as though Antoine was violent, the way Konstantin's father had been, but his controlling, bullyish behavior was all too familiar. And Antoine's neglect of Eloise looked an awful lot like the way his own grandfather had ignored his daughter's plight, leaving her in the hands of a monster.

"If Ilias were alive today, you would be well taken care of." Konstantin had no doubt in that. "What if something happens to your mother? Who inherits the Drakos fortune? *Antoine*?"

"Probably." She sighed as though that were something she couldn't bear thinking about. Then she sent him a beseeching look. "This isn't about the money, though. I honestly don't care if I have to work grubby jobs and live with a roommate. I need my mother in my life. She's all I have. I don't want to hurt her, or see her hurt, or get hurt myself. And I don't see any way that I can intervene in her marriage without that happening."

"So you intend to continue tolerating this?"

"What are my options?" She threw up her hands. "Either she stays with a man who wants to push me to the periphery of her life, or I start a war with him that tears Mom and meI apart, anyway. How would I even go about extricating him? Claim that she wasn't competent when she put him in charge? He's her husband. Calling her state of mind into question would only bolster his position as custodian of her money. Even if I somehow pried him from her life, then what? I'm the one who broke up her relationships *again*. Believe me, I spend every day trying to find a good way out of this and there is none."

"I don't accept that." He understood that relationships could be complicated. It was another reason he avoided them, but it was very clear to him that he couldn't allow things to go on as they were. "I'll take you to Nice. I want to meet this man."

"Why? There's no point," she protested.

"There are many points. You want to see your mother, don't you? For Christmas?"

"That's so unfair, it's cruel," she said with a wounded pang in her voice. "Of course, I want to see her. But she already told me she's going away. Antoine booked it," she added sullenly. "I think he did it to keep me from asking to come home, but maybe I'm being paranoid."

"Where are they going?"

"Como, I think. It's a house party. They're leaving after their own party on Friday."

"Which means she's in Nice until Friday. Come with me or don't, but I intend to see for myself what kind of situation she's in."

"I can't—I have to work my shift." She sent an anxious look at the clock. "I can't leave town without covering my share of rent. My roommate will get kicked out and it will be my fault."

"Your sense of responsibility would be commendable, Eloise, if you weren't clinging to such a sinking ship. Please," he said with deep irony. "Since it's my fault you lost your job, allow me to cover your rent."

CHAPTER FIVE

By the time they were buckled into Konstantin's private jet, Eloise's roommate was sending her every Christmas emoji and a text.

Why did he send so much? Aren't you coming back?

Eloise had run into their apartment to grab her passport and a quick bag to travel, but her roommate hadn't been home. She'd been called to the trattoria to cover the shift Eloise was missing. Now she was fired from that job, too.

"How much did you send her?" Eloise asked Konstantin, looking up from her phone.

"A year's worth."

"Because it's Christmas?"

"Because you're not going back there. Even before I saw the building, I knew by the rent that those are squalid living conditions. Tell her to use it to find a better address along with a new roommate."

If they weren't already taxiing along the runway, Eloise might have staged more of a rebellion. As it was, she could only relay exactly what he had said, mostly because she didn't know how she would get back to New York, let alone pay rent again when she did.

She didn't know what would happen when she arrived in Nice. If it were up to her mother, Eloise would be invited to move back into the house, but Lilja had bought it with Antoine. He wasn't likely to allow Eloise to stay overnight, let alone through Christmas.

She glanced at Konstantin, so effortlessly sophisticated and compelling. He'd shaved and changed into a black turtleneck with a casual fawn-colored jacket. His dark brown trousers were tailored to graze perfectly across his polished ankle boots.

He looked up from his phone and caught her staring at him.

"Where…um…?" She cleared her throat. "Last night you said you were leaving town today. Where were you supposed to go?"

"The Maldives."

"Oh? Do you have property there?"

"No."

"Just vacation, then?"

"Yes."

"With…um…" She adjusted her blind as though there were something to see outside the window beyond a wall of white clouds.

"Yes," he said before she finished asking if he'd been planning to take Gemma.

Maybe it was better that he wasn't a talkative person.

"Have you told your mother that we're coming?" he asked.

"Not yet." She picked up her phone again.

"Don't mention me. I'd like the element of surprise."

She was still uneasy about all of this, worried about what he might say or do when he saw her mother again. She chewed her lip as she considered what to say, then spoke as she typed out her text.

"I'm arriving in Nice late tonight." She tried to go down a line and accidentally hit Send. "Argh, this phone. Let me know… Tsk… Give me a sec."

While she cleared the garbled letters, her mother's response came through.

"Where are you staying? With friends or at a hotel?" she read aloud. "That has to be Antoine replying."

"He takes her phone?"

"I think he must. And I think he deletes anything he doesn't want her to see. When I talk to her, she always asks when I'm coming to visit. Then one time I said why don't you come see me in New York and suddenly Antoine wanted to take her to Australia." She tried to keep the pain of rejection off her face, but Konstantin had to see it.

"Just say both," he instructed.

That she was staying with a friend at a hotel? She didn't want to be even more indebted to him, but had no choice. She stifled her protest and texted.

Both. Let me know when it would be convenient to drop in.

"I'm invited to lunch tomorrow," she conveyed a moment later, mollified as her mother's invitation came through.

See you then.

She typed her reply and touched it to Send. It didn't go, making her sigh. She rubbed the screen on her thigh before trying again. Finally, it whooshed.

"Honestly, half the reason I can't stay in touch with her is this stupid phone."

"What's wrong with it?" He frowned.

"It's just old. And the screen is cracked. I swapped my good one with my roommate for rent the first month. It works well enough for texting, which is really all I need. Definitely no photos, though. The poor thing goes into a sulk and I have to put it down for a nap before it will work again."

"Do you even have my number? Is that why you never called me?"

"I'm sure I do somewhere, but I wouldn't have called it." She tucked her phone away and turned her eyes to the window.

"Why not?" he asked in a dangerous growl.

"Because…" She winced, hating to offer up the last of her dignity, but his tone demanded an answer. "In those first weeks after arriving in New York, when I realized Antoine was playing hard ball, I reached out to some people I knew, friends who had apartments. One let me stay with her for a few days, but Antoine wasn't coming around and I was very broke. That stinks worse than old fish. I quickly got the message that if I wasn't able to drop everything to fly to Turks and Caicos, if I needed a *job,* then I didn't belong in their world. That stung enough that I didn't want to risk getting the same treatment from anyone else." Especially him.

"You presumed I'm as shallow as they are?"

"I didn't know how you would react. I barely know you." How were they still in the clouds and not above them?

"You keep saying that." He sounded aggravated.

"Because it's true," she said with an ironic quirk of her mouth. "You're a private person. Remember?" She was sorry she'd brought it up as soon as she said it. She hurried to add, "The fact is, Antoine had a point. I needed to grow up and quit expecting other people to take care of me." She made herself meet his gaze, even though it was hard to hold his flinty look. "I miss Mom and I *really* appreciate you taking me home to see her, but you honestly don't owe me anything. Carry on to your vacation tomorrow."

He narrowed his eyes and looked as though he were ready to say something, but the flight attendant came to ask if they wanted breakfast. They'd only eaten two hours ago so Eloise declined, but she asked the woman how she could watch a movie, purely to put an end to this charged conversation.

Konstantin spent the rest of the flight working while Eloise moved to the sofa and put on noise-canceling headphones to watch movies.

He shouldn't have been distracted by her. She sat quietly with a blanket across her lap, absorbed in Christmas-themed storylines with heavily decorated sets, women in garishly bedecked pullovers and handymen who held hammers but never swung them. Every time he looked up, there seemed to be an impromptu kiss in front of a glowing tree.

He rarely watched movies. Work relaxed him. There was something about making decisions and taking action that powered him up. A dopamine rush, he supposed. And the triumph in arriving at a peak that put him that much further from the rock bottom he'd been born into.

After a while, Eloise drifted off again. He wasn't surprised. The low stakes and cozy fires on the screen were enough to put him into a coma, but it reminded him how rundown she was.

He almost sent another email to his assistant, asking for a doctor to give her a medical checkup, but he had already overloaded the young man with research requests on Antoine.

He was actually leaning on his executive assistant's assistant. His EA was on vacation because Konstantin had expected to be on vacation himself. Everything slowed down at this time of year, forcing him to do the same, but Konstantin found vacation very boring. He usually continued working and the junior assistant stuck around the office to remotely pull reports or pass along messages.

It didn't take a psychologist to work out that Konstantin preferred to keep his brain busy so he could avoid his emotions, and that he was leaping on Eloise as a project so he could sidestep the more volatile guilt of letting down his friend and the shame of seeing his friend's sister through a carnal lens.

You don't owe me anything, she had claimed, but he damned well did.

He owed Ilias, but it went deeper than that. When Eloise had said that she hadn't wanted to risk Konstantin rejecting her request for help, he'd suffered a deep sting of culpability, as though he *had* rejected her.

Hadn't he, though? It was far too similar to the way his grandfather had stayed deliberately ignorant to what was happening to Konstantin and his mother. He could remember her pleading with the old man on the phone, after they'd walked all the way into the village.

Please, Baba. Please let me come home.

The old man had been unmoved by her regret in her marriage. She'd gone against his wishes and gotten herself pregnant, hadn't she? She would have to lie in the bed she'd made.

Konstantin couldn't help feeling he'd been just as heartless in not staying in touch. That infernal, misplaced kiss had stopped him. If he saw her again, he'd feared, he would pursue her. She'd been too young. Too vulnerable. But his excuses didn't matter.

He shouldn't have waited for her to ask. He should have *seen.* He should have been like Ilias and simply stepped in.

He was doing that now. And he wouldn't allow her pride get in his way.

CHAPTER SIX

RATHER THAN EAT dinner on the plane, Konstantin said they'd eat at the hotel, but it was already midnight, local time, when they landed.

"We're staying at Le Negresco?" Eloise blinked at the hundred-year-old icon of a building.

"Problem? I've never stayed in Nice, but my staff knows to get me the best," Konstantin said.

"They have. I've dined here with Mom. I doubt the kitchen will still be open, though."

"It's all arranged," Konstantin assured her.

It was. The concierge met them curbside with a bellman who took their luggage. As they were escorted to their room, they were treated to a brief history of the building, which had been designed to bring artists and royalty to the French Riviera. It was filled with authentic period furniture and an abundance of fine art.

The concierge then showed them into a sea-view suite decorated in shades of rose pink and sage green. The bed had an ornate headboard of brass and quilted silk. Sheer drapes framed the doors to the balcony and a sitting area held mahogany furniture upholstered in striped silk. A welcome basket of fruit and chocolate sat on the coffee table. An ice bucket held a bottle of wine.

"Room service will be up shortly with the meal that your

assistant requested," the concierge informed them with an obsequious smile.

"My room is through here?" Konstantin opened a door.

Eloise stepped forward to see through it, but it was only a bathroom.

They both looked for another door, but there was only the one from the hall, where the bellman was setting both of their bags.

"Pardon?" the concierge asked.

"*Où est l'autre chambre*?" Eloise tried in French.

"Ah." Understanding and apology flickered across the man's face. "There has been a misunderstanding. We were told two adults, not two rooms. At this time of year, we are fully booked. Tomorrow, perhaps, we could accommodate you in one of our larger suites. This is all we have for the moment."

"I thought this only happened to pregnant women on Christmas Eve," Eloise said out the side of her mouth.

Konstantin shot her a look of disbelief, then grimaced. "I didn't make clear to my assistant that I was no longer traveling with Gemma."

Lovely. He would have been perfectly happy to share a room with Ms. Tall, Blonde and Buxom, but not with her.

A quiet knock announced the arrival of the room service trolley.

"It's fine. We'll manage for tonight." Konstantin impatiently waved everyone from the room.

Once they were alone, he shrugged out of his jacket and threw it over the arm of the settee, letting out an exhale of frustration.

"It's late to call my mother, but I could try her?" Eloise offered.

"No. I don't want you going there alone. We managed to share a room last night without assault charges. I'm sure we can do it again tonight."

"I'll sleep on the sofa." Even though it was a relic with ornate wooden arms and—were these cushions actually stuffed with horsehair? She poked at one, thinking it had about as much give as a saddle.

"We can share the bed. You're so small I won't even notice you're there."

"Don't—" She clacked her teeth shut.

"Don't what?"

She crossed her arms, defensive, but always frustrated by this.

"I know I'm small, all right? People dismiss me as a child *all the time*. Mom does it." She waved her hand in exasperation. "Ilias was a big strong man so he was someone she could lean on, but I'm her little doll who she wants to dress up and gossip with and marry off so I'll have my own big strong man to protect me. I'm actually a grown-up, okay? I'd appreciate it if you'd treated me like one."

If he had been a panther, his tail would have twitched as he took in her outburst.

Her stomach knotted. She had an overwhelming sense that she'd made a horrible mistake in declaring herself an adult.

"I don't see you as a child, Eloise," he said in a quiet growl that nearly knocked her over. "I haven't for a long time."

Her heart seemed to fall right out of her body and the floor shifted beneath her. She didn't know what to do with that information. She grew so hot, so self-aware, it was painful. The room seemed to shrink and the air thinned so she couldn't draw enough of it into her lungs.

"Shall we eat?" He lifted the lid off a plate and the aroma of savory crepes under a drizzle of Dijon sauce wafted toward her.

Shakily, she joined him at the table, but it was so tiny their knees brushed when she tried to cross her legs.

"I…um… I think I'll run a bath after dinner, if that's okay?

I slept so much on the flight I'm not tired yet." And she *really* needed some distance from him, even if it was only into the bathroom.

"You were really just overtired? I can book you to see a doctor if it's more serious."

"Are you still accusing me of using drugs? If I was into them, I'd take something to help me sleep, wouldn't I? No, I barely touch alcohol since someone spiked my drink." She waved at the wine she'd only sipped. "Drugs are the last thing I'd put in my body voluntarily."

"Who did that to you?" His ability to go from bored to deadly was really something. "What happened?"

"Nothing. Thankfully." She shrank into herself, though, still bothered by the incident. "I was at a house party. Not even a wild one. I thought I knew everyone there, so I wasn't vigilant about watching my glass. All of a sudden, I felt really dopey and sluggish. My girlfriend realized I'd been dosed and helped me get home."

"When was this?"

"After Ilias, when I was trying to at least pretend I was getting on with my life. But that's another reason I wanted a fresh start in New York. I didn't trust any of the people I thought I could."

"You do need a man to look after you," he muttered, stabbing his fork into his meal.

"You need to bite me," she muttered back.

His brows shot up. "Do you want to repeat that?"

"I may not be living my life to your standards, but I've been keeping myself alive."

"Barely."

"Losing Ilias was *hard*, Konstantin. Maybe not for you, but it was for me." She hung onto her composure, but her eyes grew hot and her throat tightened.

She poked and poked at her food, but couldn't bring any to her mouth.

"It was hard. Is." His admission was so quiet she almost didn't hear it, but the words seemed to catch at her heart and draw it out of her chest, pulling it out of shape in the process.

She wanted to reach out to him, to hang onto this small link they shared, even though that grief was so acidic it hurt to touch.

"Would you—?" She sipped to clear her throat. "I know you don't like to talk about yourself, but would you tell me a memory you have of him? Something I wouldn't know?" she asked tentatively.

His brows flinched together. He attacked his plate a moment, stabbing like he needed to kill it before he could eat it. "I'm not nostalgic, Eloise. I don't look back unless I have to."

She nodded mutely. "Okay," she murmured, even though his refusal made her ache with disappointment.

The silence between them grew weighted. The sound of their cutlery was overloud in the small room.

Then he spoke abruptly, sounding aggrieved that she had demanded this of him.

"I was far behind all my classmates when I arrived at boarding school. I didn't speak English. He was the only boy I could talk to."

She lifted her gaze in surprise and found his dark eyes roiling with contained emotions that stalled her glass halfway to her mouth. She felt picked up and thrown around by those turbulent emotions. She slowly finished her sip, dampening her mouth with the cool tang of the wine, saying nothing so he could continue if he was willing to.

"Ilias was always in the top three while my grades were dead last. He tutored me for years." He jabbed at his food again. "He's the only reason I didn't flunk out within weeks of arriving. It was like that for years. Then one day in year nine, I earned a higher mark than his. It wasn't even top of the class, just one point higher than his. The culture was very competitive. Another boy would have accused me of cheating, but Ilias shook my hand and congratulated me. He was so happy for me it was embarrassing."

"Oh." She couldn't help her happy-sad chuckle, able to see her brother so clearly in that split second. He would have been grinning widely, admiring the paper, throwing his arm around his friend, building him up.

Her eyes welled and her chest ballooned with acute emotion. She sniffed.

"Don't *cry*." Konstantin's eyes widened in alarm. "I thought you would like it. You *asked* me to tell you that."

"I do like it. But I miss him so much sometimes." Her voice cracked. "And I can't talk to Mom about him because—that's another reason I haven't tried to see her. And why I didn't mind at first when Antoine was there. It's so stressful when we're together. We both want Ilias to be there, but he's not. And when we talk about h-him—" Her breaths grew jagged as she tried to push words around the sobs that were elbowing the inside of her rib cage, fighting to be released. "It's such a raw nerve, even after all this time." She used her napkin to wipe at her cheeks, but the tears kept rolling down them.

"Stop. Eloise, stop." He rose to drag her into his arms. "*I'll* be there," he said gruffly, practically smothering her face against his chest as he squeezed her in his strong arms. "It will be fine. Stop crying."

This embrace was what she had wanted from him for so long that her tears sharpened. Her stomach cramped with her effort to hold back, but she was shuddering with pent-up anxiety and despair.

"Shush," he insisted as he petted her hair. "It's going to be okay, Eloise. I'm going to make it okay. *Please* stop crying."

How was she supposed to stop when he was being so *nice*?

She gave in to impulse and wrapped her arms around his waist, clinging while trying, really trying, to stem the flow, but she was shaking and…

Wait. Was he also shaking?

She was so surprised she tilted her head back to see he was about to drop a kiss on her hair.

They both froze for several pulse beats. It was the garden after the funeral all over again. Their noses were almost touching, their lips an inch from meeting.

He drew in a sharp breath and his hand slid down her back, ironing her into him while making every cell in her body come alive.

Her toes pushed into the floor on instinct. She arched, feeling him hardening against her abdomen. As tingles of excitement raced through her blood, she offered her mouth, gaze on his parted lips, wanting—

He jerked his head up and set her back a step, exactly as he had those other times.

"Go have your bath," he said grittily. He picked up his wine and stepped onto the balcony, allowing a damp December wind to gust in.

What the hell was wrong with him? Pressing a weeping woman to his growing erection was just wrong.

He'd pushed her away and was letting the fine mist off the Mediterranean cool his ardor, but it wasn't doing a very good job. He could still feel the press of her modest breast and the curve of her lower back. He could smell her hair and—most erotic of all—had seen the way she reacted to him.

It had all percolated a rush of arousal into his groin and he shouldn't have even touched her. He wouldn't have, if she hadn't started crying. He didn't even know why he'd shared that corny memory. Absolutely everything about the past turned like knives inside him, but she had looked so entreating when she asked him to share something about Ilias. He had wanted her to know why her brother had meant so much to him and that he missed Ilias, too.

Maybe he had even thought talking about her brother would defuse the sexual tension between them and remind him why he needed to act honorably with Eloise.

He was doing a stellar job at that, wasn't he?

She had started to cry, though. He couldn't *bear* a woman's tears. It put him into a fight-or-flight response from childhood, when he had heard his mother crying. He'd felt so helpless then, trying to console her, listening to her promise she would find them a way to escape, to be safe.

It had ended in despair for both of them, every time.

Thankfully, as an adult, he rarely heard a woman cry. Once he'd come across an employee in a stairwell and once a lover had lost her dog. He'd distracted the first with a year of paid leave and the other with a generous donation to an animal rescue center.

Eloise was different. Her sorrow had gone straight under his skin, stirring up his own grief, layers and layers of it. It was disturbing enough that his first thought was to fire up his jet and head to the Maldives.

But he couldn't. He'd not only promised her that he would be with her tomorrow, but he was still furious she was living, as she called it, so far below his standards. He took it as a personal failure on his part.

He should have been looking out for her all this time. When he thought of the number of men who had tried to take advantage of her, he could hardly contain his fury. And the idea of her holing up in a dorm room, unable to get herself to class, ground like a heel against his conscience. Of course, she would have been too devastated to get on with life. He should have *known* that. He should have done something far sooner than this.

He shouldn't have left it until she was living his worst nightmare: struggling and going hungry, unable to think of the future because today was so uncertain.

She *did* need someone looking out for her.

At the same time, he understood why she would rather struggle on her own terms than be beholden to a man like Antoine. If Konstantin had been older when his grandfather had come into his life, he might have rejected him and made his own way, too. He'd resented needing to rely on the old man, especially because his grandfather's "generosity" had come with its own costs and obligations.

He didn't want Eloise to think she owed him anything for his help so he had resisted the urge to crush her mouth with his, even though the plump, soft pout of her lips had been nearly irresistible.

When his grip on the iron rail of the balcony began radiating ice up his forearms, he stepped back inside the room. He was immediately assaulted by the fragrance of whatever beads she'd poured into the tub. As he topped up his glass of wine, the water shut off. He heard the ripple of water and the squeak of her naked body against the porcelain.

His lizard brain exploded with the image of her nude form all shiny and soapy, eyelids heavy with relaxation, mouth curved into a smile of invita—

No.

He yanked the leash on his libido.

She's Ilias's little sister. She's vulnerable.

She trusted him. And he'd already lied to her. He'd told her he wouldn't notice she was in the bed beside him, but he doubted he would sleep a wink.

CHAPTER SEVEN

ELOISE WAITED IN the bed while Konstantin brushed his teeth, telling herself this was no different than sharing the flat with her roommate where she took the sofa and her roommate had the murphy bed that came down from the wall.

This was very different, though.

This is what marriage would be like.

Routine intimacy. A shared bed during the most vulnerable time: sleep.

Going to bed together after a fight.

Not that they'd fought. No, it was worse than that. She had thrown herself at him and he'd turned her down *again*. They'd spoken in stilted tones after her bath, agreeing they should get some sleep. She'd waited until he was in the bathroom to take off the robe and put on her T-shirt and underwear to sleep in, then she'd climbed into bed and was trying to fall asleep by sheer willpower, hoping to be unconscious by the time he joined her.

The door opened and the light went off. Konstantin found his way to the bed. She didn't know what he was wearing. Behind her, the covers lifted and the mattress dipped. The blankets settled and he exhaled.

She stared blindly at the paisley pattern she couldn't really see in the wallpaper, trying not to move, but how was she supposed to sleep? She used to think about sharing a bed with him *all the time*. Sharing her *body*.

What diabolical biology made her obsess over him this way? She'd had plenty of offers from men over the years, but the kisses she'd invited had been pleasant rather than moving, the caresses more ticklish than erotic. No one had ever made her react the way she did to Konstantin, even though all she had with him were fantasies. She didn't even know *how* to make love. She'd never done it outside her imagination and that had always been with the man in this bed.

She tried not to let her mind wander down those avenues, tried not to move, even though she wanted to look at the clock. She distracted herself with trying to predict what would happen tomorrow. She berated herself for not making more of an effort when she'd first gone back to university, then spent some time listing all the solves for the world's current events. Nothing made her less aware of the man beside her.

Was he asleep? Or awake like her?

She couldn't sleep. She felt ripe. She felt as though her skin were thin and sensitized, her blood flowing fast beneath it. Her erogenous zones pulsed a signal of yearning, calling out to him, inviting his touch.

Then, miraculously, his hand was between her thighs, both soothing and inciting. His hot body surrounded hers; his lips caressed her nape. He said something against her ear that she didn't catch. She was too enthralled with the way he was sliding his touch between her folds. She was soaked and throbbing with arousal. His finger slid and teased and drew her closer and closer to climax, making her moan.

"Eloise."

She snapped awake to the silver light of early morning. Konstantin loomed over her, propped on his elbow. His hand on her shoulder flattened her to the mattress.

"Are you having a nightmare?"

"No." Her voice was throaty with the lust still gripping her.

He was close enough that she saw the way his pupils exploded, swallowing up the dark chocolate of his irises with inky black. His nostrils twitched and his gaze dropped to her mouth.

She reacted purely on instinct, not sure if it was dream or reality, but she rolled her hips toward him, reaching across to find his waist—his naked rib cage and the indent of his spine, inviting him closer.

With a noise that was half agony, half aggression, he dropped his head. His mouth capturing hers the way it had in Athens so long ago, with such ferocity she should have been alarmed, but she only curved closer while his hand swept behind her, drawing her even more fully under him.

If this was a continuation of the dream, she didn't care. The feel of him was glorious. His smooth back was beneath her splayed hand. His heavy chest crushed her aching breasts. His tongue sought her own, spearing excitement through her.

When his naked leg brushed hers, she moaned in supreme pleasure and luxuriated in the feel of his leg hair against the inside of her thigh and calf. He reacted by pushing his knee with more purpose between hers, pressing the ironlike tension of his thigh firmly against her mound.

Stars of sensation shot through her. She clamped her thighs on his, rocking her hips to increase the pressure, arching and rubbing, thrilling when his hand ran to her bottom and clenched into her cheek, possessive and encouraging her to keep rolling and writhing—

Climax struck. It wouldn't have happened if she hadn't already been halfway there in her dream, but here she was, thrust into the explosive joy of orgasm. She might have scratched his back. She definitely moaned long and loudly into his mouth.

His whole body went taut. For long seconds, he held her in place, letting the waves of orgasm wash over her.

When it began to subside, he slowly, almost tenderly, lifted his mouth from her panting lips. He brushed a strand of hair off her eyelashes and asked in a lust-soaked voice, "Are you even awake?"

Reality crashed over her with such mortification she groaned, "No. I mean, yes, but—"

He was already leaving the bed, swearing as he threw back the covers and locked himself in the bathroom with a firm click of the door. The shower came on.

She rolled her face into the pillow and kicked her feet against the mattress, wishing she could run to the other side of the world.

Eloise was going to be the death of him, she really was.

Konstantin came out of a shower where he'd had to— *had to*—take himself in hand and relieve the urgency gripping him.

He found the room empty. *Damn it.* He knew he shouldn't have touched her. Even as he had kissed her, a voice in his head had been bellowing that he should stop.

That kiss, though. He'd waited six long years to taste her again, telling himself he'd imagined how incredible she was, but that had been every bit as potent as he recalled. As he'd feared. She'd rolled into him and slid her leg along his and those signals of receptiveness had short-circuited his brain. There'd been no thought in his head except to plunder the mouth that was opening to him. To drag her closer and feel more of her.

When his thigh had notched against the cotton of her underwear, the heat of her had scorched his thigh, hardening him to acute anticipation. He had palmed her pert ass while she rolled her hips and then she had just *dissolved*.

It had been exquisite and exciting as hell, but that's also

when he realized she might not be fully aware she was in bed with him.

That thought was enough of a slap to regain control of himself, if not a cold enough shock to fully douse his arousal.

Who the hell had she been dreaming of, though?

The question grated in him as he hurried to dress, only realizing as he was pocketing his phone that there was a blurred shape standing on the balcony.

He yanked open the door. "What are you doing out here?"

"Questioning my life choices." She had her coat collar turned up around her chin. Her eyes were big enough to swallow her face. "What are you doing?"

"Going down for breakfast. Do you want to come?" The moment the words emerged from his mouth, he heard the double entendre.

So had she. A fierce blush bloomed across her face.

He turned back into the room, leaving the door open for her. Normally, he dined in the privacy of his room, but they needed space and other people and the grating whine of a child who'd risen too early.

Otherwise, they would finish wrecking that damned bed.

Eloise didn't want to talk about it, but had the impending sense that they should. Not that she was willing to bring it up in a busy dining room. All she managed to say was that her mother would serve at least three courses at lunch so they should eat lightly.

Konstantin nodded a curt acknowledgment, then ordered pastries and coffee for them. She kept her eyes on a French newspaper she stole off a nearby table. Konstantin exchanged messages with someone in a battery of muted buzzes from his phone.

This was excruciating. While she pretended to read, she was hyperaware of him. Her body was alternating between the heat of embarrassment and the heat of arousal. She couldn't glance at his mouth without remembering how ravenous his kiss had been. Any small shift of his body reminded her of the imposing weight of him against her. When he absently cupped his coffee, she remembered the feel of his palm branding her bottom.

He'd been hard against her thigh, his heart slamming so hard she'd felt it against her breast. She'd been feeling sexy and desired and buttery with her receding climax when he'd asked her if she was awake.

Now he was Mr. Remote again, barely speaking to her.

"Do you need anything from the room?" he asked as they were finishing their second coffee. "My car is waiting."

"We can't go to Mom's yet. She'll still be in bed."

"You need something to wear." His tone was somewhere between patient and patronizing.

She looked down at the clothes he'd bought her in New York. They were a fast-fashion solution to an immediate problem and the few things she'd brought from the apartment were even more wrinkled and tired. She didn't want to go further into his debt, but knew he was right. She couldn't turn up like this.

"I just need my coat," she murmured.

A short time later, Konstantin walked her into a busy salon where a stylist introduced herself as Ghaliya.

"I thought I was picking out a dress, not having a full makeover," Eloise grumbled as she saw a nail tech preparing her station for her.

"You said you didn't want Antoine to know how much you've struggled," he pointed out dispassionately, eyes on the wall of nail polish arranged in bands like a rainbow.

"What sort of look are we going for today?" Ghaliya asked brightly as she returned from hanging Eloise's coat. "Are you attending a holiday event? A special occasion perhaps?"

"Return of a prodigal daughter?" Eloise asked with a facetious quirk of her mouth in Konstantin's direction. He might as well have some say, since he was paying for it.

"This isn't an apology tour. It's a triumphant return," he stated firmly, then frowned. "Are you going to cut your hair?"

She shot a protective hand to the ponytail at her nape. "A trim, maybe. Why? Should I?" She'd worn it short through her teens and early twenties, only letting it grow out lately because she hadn't had the will or funds to cut it. She had rediscovered she liked having long hair.

"With your features, a pixie or a bob would be very cute," Ghaliya said with enthusiasm.

"*No*," Konstantin said in firm refusal.

Eloise drew her brows in question, puzzled by his emphatic reaction.

"That length suits you," he stated, cheek ticking even as he looked away. "But do whatever you want."

"I used to wear it short, but I prefer it long." Eloise played her fingers against her nape, not sure what to make of his opinion.

"It sounds like you know what you want," Ghaliya said diplomatically. "Shall we get started? Did you want to make yourself comfortable, sir? We should be finished by eleven if you'd rather come back. We'll be across the street at the boutique by then."

"I'll meet you there." Konstantin held Eloise's gaze as though he was waiting for her to confirm she would be okay if he left.

She nodded jerkily, kind of touched that he was so considerate, but also worried by how dependent she was becoming on him. Maybe she had more of her mother's tendencies than she'd ever realized, because the minute he left, she felt abandoned.

On the other hand, given all that had happened since the

elevator doors had opened in that New York high-rise two days ago, she desperately needed time and space away from him to process.

Ghaliya didn't give her a chance to dwell on any of that, though. She distracted her with a thousand small decisions around hair, nails and makeup while keeping up a pleasant chatter of innocuous topics like celebrity gossip and the latest fashions.

Before Eloise knew it, she was in the boutique across the street, staring at someone who was both recognizable and a complete stranger.

Her hair had been highlighted and trimmed to create a gold frame around her face and generous waves had been pressed into it, making it look shiny and casually polished. The longer length and shape did suit her. Those old pixie cuts had made her eyes seem too big for her face, but with a subtle touch of makeup and an understated lipstick, the balance was just right.

For clothes, she chose a cashmere sweater in fern green over a wrap skirt with diagonal buttons on her hip. It left a good portion of her left leg bare, revealing her black tights and tall boots. She was trying a beret when Konstantin entered.

His imposing presence immediately soaked up all the oxygen in the exclusive shop, making the walls shrink in around her.

In an effort to move past all the awkwardness of this morning, Eloise turned and dropped her hand on her hip, throwing her weight to one side while pointing with her other hand at the hat. "Chic? Or overkill?"

The way his inscrutable gaze traveled all over her made her feel as exposed as a doe in a field, sending a small zing through her that urged her to run.

"Keep it," he said in a deep voice. "It's cold out."

Practical, she noted with a twinge of letdown.

"Let me get you some jacket options," the stylist murmured as she disappeared to another section of the small store.

Eloise turned back to the mirror and fiddled with the hat, surreptitiously glancing at Konstantin in the reflection, wondering if he was still cross with her over the way she'd behaved when they'd woken.

His gaze was caressing her butt!

A tingling sensation of his hand there had been torturing her all morning. Now a fresh rush of heat flooded into her loins as she remembered the satisfying sensation of his hard thigh pressing against the tender, throbbing flesh, tipping her into a place so delicious her mouth dried as she remembered it.

His gaze came up to meet hers in the mirror and she couldn't make herself look away, even though she was accosted by the memory of moaning into his mouth, holding onto him as her body quaked.

Making it worse, he knew exactly what was in her mind.

"Who were you dreaming about?" he asked in a voice that sounded as though it originated in the bottom of his chest.

She flinched and was finally able to drop her gaze. "I don't want to say."

"Why not? I won't be angry."

Did he really imagine it could be anyone but him? She rolled her lips together, deeply culpable as she lifted a painful glance that was so revealing it made her cheeks and throat hurt.

She heard his sharp inhale, then Ghaliya bustled back.

"This one or…? Oh. *Je m'excuse.* I'll leave you two alone," she murmured and turned away, trying to escape whatever charged air was between them.

"No. We're expected for lunch," Konstantin said. "Has my assistant given you everything you need?"

"*Oui. Merci.*" Ghaliya gave him a warm smile of appreciation. "And Mademoiselle Eloise has my card if she needs anything else. This one would be better, I think," she added to Eloise, offering the shorter jacket.

Konstantin took it to hold it for her, making her feel clumsy as she threaded her arms into the sleeves.

She waited until they were in the car to say, "Thank you for all of this." She waved from hair to shoes. She was genuinely grateful, feeling more confident and less like a petitioner begging for handouts. "Will you please send me the invoice? I know I'm a long way from paying you back, but—"

"And risk breaking your phone?" Konstantin drawled. He plucked something from the console between them and offered it. "This is for you, by the way."

It was a new phone, one that was already activated. It was even in a pretty brushed gold case that had a designer's initials etched into it.

"*Please* don't put me this far into your debt," she bemoaned, tucking her fists into her lap rather than accept it.

"You're being ridiculous. My number is in there. I expect you to use it whenever you need something." He dropped the device into her lap.

She caught it so it wouldn't slip to the floor, then found his number along with a second one for someone named *Nemo*, whoever that was. She texted Konstantin.

Please send me a copy of the invoice.

His phone dinged and he glanced at it, sighed, then sent her a flat look. "I only argue about things that matter, Eloise. This topic is closed."

"I'll ask Ghaliya, then." She opened the faux snakeskin clutch to search out the stylist's card.

"It's a *gift*. What was that twelve days of nonsense you

were doing? Consider it that." He flicked his hand as though it were inconsequential.

"Goody. Seven more days of this?" She pressed her hands to her sandwiched phone and smiled with sarcastic excitement.

"Yes. Now I don't want to hear another word about it."

Oh, this man. She bit back arguing further, though. The car was turning into the gates of her mother's villa and the butterflies in her stomach became a swarm of bees that moved into her chest. She dropped the phone into her clutch and rubbed her damp palm onto her skirt.

Konstantin's hand came across to capture hers. He frowned at how cold her fingers were.

"It will be fine. I promise."

She wanted to believe him so she nodded as though she did.

CHAPTER EIGHT

ACCORDING TO THE reports Konstantin had received from his assistant, Ilias's mother had stayed in Athens for the first year after Ilias died. Then she had begun traveling with friends, dating a number of men before attaching herself to Antoine. They had dated, became engaged, then moved to Nice once they married. They'd been here three years.

Her new husband had money, yes, but none of it had been earned through any serious effort on his part. He had inherited a modest fortune at eighteen from an aunt. He then married one of his aunt's friends, an older woman with a heart condition. She had passed within a few years, leaving Antoine a tidy sum that allowed him to penetrate higher social circles. The next time he married, it was a French pop star. She divorced him fairly quickly, granting him a shockingly large settlement on his way out the door. That suggested to Konstantin that she'd done whatever necessary to get him out of her life.

After that, he'd had a string of long-term relationships with wealthy women of an appropriate age, all well-placed in Europe's highest social circles. He was the sort of man who thought he should have been born an aristocrat and would have been the worst kind if he had.

Konstantin had asked his assistant to track down the retired trustee, Cyrus, but discreetly, so it was taking time.

The car stopped in front of a quiet fountain. A butler hurried out with an umbrella, even though the rain was barely spitting.

Konstantin came around and took it, tempted to set his hand in Eloise's lower back, but he couldn't trust himself to keep his touch bolstering rather than a caress of appreciation. He was determined to be her bodyguard right now. Her wingman. Nothing more.

But he'd always found her naturally attractive with her eyes looking green in some light and gold in others. Her features had lovely symmetry and the corners of her mouth tilted upward in an appealing way, even when she was somber, as she was now.

When he'd entered the shop a short while ago, he'd been spellbound by her. Her mood had been light, her pose cheeky. She'd been carefree and so beautiful he'd instantly been awash in want.

God did he want her. He'd spent the hours apart from her trying not to think of the way she'd reached for him this morning, only to shudder with orgasm. He'd barely touched her! It was the most erotic thing he'd ever experienced and he damned well wanted more. He'd been fighting that craving, but as they'd stood in the shop, he hadn't been able to resist asking whom she had been dreaming of.

Her look of guilt had punched straight into his groin. He'd nearly shouted to clear the store so he could take her right then and there. His desire for her had been so obvious the stylist had recognized it in an instant and tried to excuse herself.

Pay attention, he ordered himself as they entered a foyer where a curved staircase swept to the upper floor and a domed ceiling held a sparkling chandelier.

"Eloise!" Lilja rushed toward them from a door to their left. She barely glanced at him, too anxious to embrace her daughter.

Lilja was a little taller than Eloise, but not much. Her blond hair had turned to silver since Konstantin had seen her last, but otherwise she was the same classic beauty she had always been. She was slender and elegant and closed her eyes as she held onto Eloise and drew in a savoring breath.

"I've *missed* you."

"I've missed you, too, Mom. But—" Eloise rubbed her mother's back "—did you see who I brought with me?"

"Hmm? Oh, I presumed this was your driver. *Konstantin*!" Lilja laughed into her hand. "I'm so sorry. Goodness, look at you!" She set her light hands on his arms and offered her cheeks for his kiss.

"I've been called worse," he said with genuine amusement. "How are you, Lilja? When Eloise told me she was seeing you, I insisted on coming along."

"I'm so glad," she said with misty sincerity, but sent a disconcerted look toward the door she'd come through. "You'll stay for lunch, of course. Tell the kitchen we're five, please, Marcel," she said to the hovering butler before looping her arm through both of theirs. "Come say hello. Have you met my husband, Konstantin? I don't think so."

Her smile seemed forced as she escorted them into a high-ceilinged parlor where the view beyond the windows looked to the horizon of the Med.

A pair of men rose from their armchairs. One was white-haired and slightly paunchy beneath his bespoke suit. The other was closer to Konstantin's age, clean-shaven and might be called boyishly handsome. He struck Konstantin as cocksure in his trendy plaid trousers, his thick cardigan pushed up to his elbows and his button shirt open at his throat.

Both men eyed him with keen yet somewhat hostile interest.

"Antoine, you'll never guess who Eloise has brought with her today."

"I'm sure I won't since I didn't expect her to bring anyone." There was a subtle edge to Antoine's tone that Konstantin immediately disliked.

"It's nice to see you," Eloise said weakly, stepping away from Lilja and moving so her stepfather could kiss her cheeks. "This is Konstantin Galanis. He was one of Ilias's closest friends. I'm sure Mom must have mentioned him."

She stepped aside so Konstantin could shake Antoine's hand. They took each other's measure with one succinct pump.

"Edoardo Ricci is also a good friend of the family," Lilja said.

The other man stepped forward. "It's so good to see you again, Eloise." Edoardo's hands came up as though to take hold of Eloise's upper arms.

Her recoil was only slight, but Konstantin reacted reflexively. He locked his arm across her back and splayed possessive fingers on her hip, tucking her into his side.

Edoardo's expression blanked. He dropped his hands and offered Konstantin a limp shake with a weak, "*Kýrie* Galanis. I'm familiar with your name and organization. It's a pleasure to meet you."

Konstantin nodded, always willing to let silence do his talking.

For a stalled moment, there was only the crackle of the fire in the fireplace and the imagined crackle of animosity coming off Antoine toward him.

"Sit. Tell us how you came to deliver Eloise to us today," Antoine invited, then waved his empty glass at the butler. "More cognac. Mimosas for the girls."

Konstantin waited while Eloise sat on the sofa before he lowered beside her. He hitched his pant leg as he crossed his legs and extended his arm along the back of the sofa behind her, angling himself more to Lilja than his host. Deliberately.

"Are you feeling as well as you look, Lilja?" Konstantin asked.

"I am," Lilja assured him with a fluttering smile of pleasure. "Oh, thank you, Marcel."

The atmosphere grew charged again as the butler set out the fresh drinks. Edoardo's confusion was a blinking neon light while Konstantin could feel Antoine staring holes into the side of his head.

As the butler left them alone, Lilja asked, "Am I to understand... Are you two seeing each other? Has this been going on long?"

"No." Konstantin sensed Eloise stiffening beside him and reached for her hand, signaling that she should let him do the talking.

She rose and moved across the room. "Your tree looks pretty, Mom."

Trying to shift the conversation?

"I wasn't sure about the silver and blue," Lilja said reflectively, twisting slightly to continue speaking to her. "I may ask the decorator to change it to something more traditional before our party tomorrow night. You'll come, won't you?" She directed that to Konstantin. "It's nothing fancy, just a festive little soiree for whoever is in town."

"We'd love to." Konstantin took far too much pleasure in goading the other men by claiming Eloise as his date.

How Eloise felt about it was a mystery. She was trailing her hands along the polished maple of the grand piano before she lightly touched a few keys.

"Are you going to play for us, darling?" Lilja asked with coaxing warmth. "That would be nice. It's been too long."

"Marcel is looking for us to go into the dining room," Antoine said.

Konstantin turned his head to stare the man down. He had already decided he hated him before he met him, but as

Eloise sat and picked out a few notes, it occurred to him that this viper had deliberately kept her from something else she loved: music.

Eloise ignored Antoine and set her hands into unhurried chords that gradually arranged themselves into what Konstantin recognized as "I'll Be Home for Christmas."

He looked back to where she gracefully swayed to reach the keys, manifesting the gentle climb and fall of emotions in the song. Her eyes were closed, her profile glowing in the light off the tree.

Konstantin didn't know all the words, but he knew it was about homesickness and nostalgia. As yearning flowed from her hands to fill the room and vibrate in his chest, his throat ached.

The sadness might have swamped him completely, but she somehow layered in tentative hope as she reached the end.

She sang the final words very softly as she slowed the tempo even more, searching out the last chords with supreme care. A lifetime of wishes hovered in the silence before the final note ended the song.

Konstantin was utterly captivated. His body felt rusted into place, his consciousness having been stolen and transported elsewhere.

"*Brava*, darling. That was beautiful," Lilja said as she wiped tears from her cheeks, but she was smiling widely. They were happy tears and they tugged differently in his chest, making him fiercely glad he'd given her this reunion with her daughter. "That was truly the best Christmas present I could ever have," she said to Konstantin. "Thank you."

"My pleasure," he said, meaning it.

Antoine stood and bent over Lilja so he broke their eye contact. He offered his wife a handkerchief and rubbed her shoulder.

"My sensitive little love. We were at the opera a few weeks

ago and she cried her way through that, too. Didn't you? Shall we go to the table?"

They all stood and Eloise left the piano to join them.

"That was very good," Edoardo said.

"Parlor tricks," she claimed with a self-deprecating smile.

Hardly. Konstantin had never been moved by sleight of hand or the flair of a bartender. The fact he was feeling so unsettled by a dated Christmas carol was disturbing in the extreme. He much preferred numbness over this agonizing prickle that resembled a return of sensation to a limb that had fallen asleep. Typically, when something affected him, he removed himself the way he would back away from a bonfire that threatened to light his clothes on fire, but that option wasn't open to him right now, was it?

"You're the guest of honor. You can escort Lilja," Antoine said to Konstantin as though this were a royal procession. "I'll take Eloise." He crooked his arm imperiously.

Lilja gathered her composure and set her hand on Konstantin's arm.

"Actually, you go in with Edoardo. I need a word with Marcel," Antoine said, stepping back at the last second to wave the younger man toward Eloise.

Did the man think he was playing chess? And winning?

As they arrived into the dining room, and the butler transferred their drinks to the table, Konstantin saw how Antoine was continuing his puerile machinations. The seating arrangements were meant to put Edoardo between Eloise and her mother. Eloise was positioned at Antoine's left, while Konstantin was supposed to sit across from her and closer to her mother's end of the table.

As Konstantin seated Lilja, he ordered Edoardo, "Eloise can sit there. I'll sit next to her." He nodded at the chair closest to Lilja. Edoardo could visit Siberia on the other side of the table.

"Lilja prefers the proper etiquette of alternating ladies and gentleman," Antoine told him with a patronizing smile.

"The women want to catch up so we'll indulge them." Konstantin could play the doting game, too.

Antoine looked to Edoardo, perhaps seeking an ally, but Edoardo was canny enough to see he had a decision to make: whether to stick with whatever Antoine had promised him or curry favor with the much bigger fish that was Konstantin Galanis for the bank that bore his family name.

Edoardo took the chair on the far side of the table.

The meal went on forever. Konstantin participated in the expected topics of sports and politics and business, all the while listening to Eloise deflect her mother's probing inquiries about their relationship by asking after mutual acquaintances.

When Edoardo excused himself to make a call, and Lilja was busy relaying details of a play she'd seen recently, Antoine leaned toward Konstantin.

"What exactly is your intention here?" He flicked his gaze toward Eloise. "Is this a dalliance for your own entertainment? Because I have responsibilities where my wife's daughter is concerned. There are things I won't allow."

Konstantin was rarely taken aback by the levels that a man could sink to, but he was genuinely astonished that Antoine would accuse him of being a womanizer. And was casting himself as the guardian best suited to protect her. Exactly how desperate was he to marry her to Edoardo? *Why?*

The women stopped speaking, sensing the change in temperature.

Edoardo returned with a polite, "I apologize—" He cut himself off as he came up against the wall of hostility between the men.

Antoine held Konstantin's penetrating gaze and Konstantin wondered if the man was dangerously obtuse or simply too arrogant to see how far out of his league he was.

"A dalliance?" Konstantin repeated with disdain, abandoning good manners. "No. I don't use women for entertainment. I certainly wouldn't start with the sister of my best friend."

"I'm sure Antoine didn't mean to imply anything like that," Eloise murmured in a soothing undertone. Her hand found his arm, trying to stay his temper.

He flashed her a glare of outrage because he had heard what he heard.

Anxiety pinched her mouth and there was a line of tension across her cheekbones that seemed to repeat what she had asked him in New York.

What are you going to do? Shatter her beliefs and force her to suffer yet another heartbreak? She would blame me.

He shot his attention to Lilja. She was staring into her plate, blinking back tears, seeming mortified that her luncheon had gone sour.

Look after your daughter, he wanted to shout at her. But hurting Lilja would hurt Eloise, and Lilja was not the villain here. Antoine was. Ilias would expect Konstantin to protect his family from such a man, but how?

The answer arrived the way intuition struck sometimes, when Konstantin saw the way forward long before he had worked through the logistics and reasoning behind it. If Konstantin were the fanciful type, he would say Ilias whispered the solution in his ear.

"My intention is to ask for your blessing, Lilja." Konstantin was far too pleased with the choked noise that came out of Antoine. "Eloise and I are marrying."

CHAPTER NINE

"KONSTANTIN," ELOISE BREATHED, APPALLED.

"We weren't planning to announce it today." Konstantin rose and drew Eloise onto her feet and into his arms.

"No, we weren't." Her limbs didn't feel connected to her body. She pressed weakly at his chest, but it took all her control to lock her knees rather than collapse in a heap.

"But look how happy this news makes your mother."

Oh, that was just evil, stopping her protests in her throat.

"Oh, darling," her mother said weepily, eyes bright with joy.

"Mom—" She hesitated to slap that look off her mother's face with the truth, but there was no way she could lie to her about something like this.

Konstantin's arms tightened around her, pressing tingles of sensual memory through her skin and muscle and blood cells, urging her to go along.

Was he drunk?

But even as she tried to find the words to say that Konstantin was full of it, his ruse got rid of one very sticky problem.

"As I was saying, I've been called away," Edoardo blurted. "Happy news. Congratulations." With one final wild look toward Antoine, Edoardo made his escape.

Ironically, Eloise wished she could go with him. The malice she felt coming off Antoine was so thick it oozed.

Antoine rose to shake Konstantin's hand in a very perfunctory way. "Congratulations."

"Thank you. Eloise was concerned you would be upset." Konstantin held Antoine's stare in challenge.

"Antoine has only ever wanted what's best for you, darling. I hope you know that." Her mother rose to embrace each of them, but Eloise felt Antoine's malignant glare. He was more than upset. He was blistering with such fury Eloise couldn't help pressing into Konstantin's solid presence when her mother stepped back.

"No ring yet?" Her mother kept her hand, and covered it with her own, exclaiming, "Darling! You can wear my ring from Petros. It's in the safe. No." She touched her chin as she started to turn away. "The box at the bank in Athens. We'll have to make a special trip," she said to Antoine.

"In the New Year, perhaps." Antoine manufactured a lovey-dovey smile. "We're expected in Como for Christmas. Remember? You're looking forward to seeing Melissa."

"That's true, but…" Her brows drew together in consternation.

"Mom, that's not necessary," Eloise protested.
This isn't even real.

"I want you to have it," her mother insisted. "It would have gone to Ilias for his wife and it bothers me that it's locked away. Ilias would want you to wear it, especially if you're marrying Konstantin." She tilted a watery smile up at him. "You're practically family already."

Did Konstantin flinch? If he did, he masked it before Eloise had registered more than a twitch of his arm around her and the bob of his Adam's apple as he swallowed.

"That's kind of you to say, Lilja."

"Shall we sit and finish our meal?" Antoine said tersely, attempting to take control by moving to hold Lilja's chair.

"And champagne, please, Marcel," her mother instructed

as she sat. "Oh, there's so much to discuss. Have you set a date?"

"Nothing is decided yet," Eloise stressed.

Don't get attached, Mom.

Did Konstantin not understand how wrong it was to build her mother's expectations like this?

"Yes, there is much to discuss," Konstantin agreed as he held Eloise's chair. His tone was both pleasant and lethal. "Details of the prenup," he added in Antoine's direction. "I have interests to protect as well."

For once, Eloise allowed herself a huge gulp of alcohol when the champagne arrived.

"What—" she could barely keep the pitch of her voice to a level tone as the car left her mother's front steps "—the hell."

"It's the most expedient solution," Konstantin said in that same tone of finality that he'd used earlier when he'd said, *I only argue about things that matter.*

"It's a bluff and he knows it." She curled her cold fists, still shaking from Antoine's warning as they left. "He just said to me, *don't come in here with a gun that's not loaded.*"

Konstantin turned his head to give her a look that was unimpressed. "I can't decide if the man genuinely lacks intelligence or is so driven by desperation he's becoming reckless. Either way, he is the one holding the gun and he's already shot himself in the foot with it."

"How? You've made things so much worse." She propped her elbow next to the window and covered her eyes. "You heard Mom. She's already planning the wedding."

"Good. Now you have a reason to speak to her as often as you like."

"What am I supposed to do? Let her think it's real for a year, then yank the rug? I told you I don't want to hurt her."

"Tempted as I am to force Antoine to foot the bill on an

extravagant wedding that winds up canceled, we're not waiting a year." He glanced at his phone as it pinged, then touched the driver's shoulder.

"Sir?" The driver removed his ear bud.

"The jeweler has agreed to come to us. You can drop us at our hotel."

"Very good, sir." He screwed the bud back into his ear and made the turn to the Promenade des Anglais.

"What jeweler?" Eloise hissed.

"The one providing your ring. Wear anything your mother gives you if it makes you happy, but you'll wear my ring at that party tomorrow."

"For Antoine's sake? You're taking this too far," she protested. "I'm glad you put Edoardo on the run. Thank you for that. Really. But Antoine is not stupid. He knows I have nothing going for me beyond passable looks and presumed fertility. That's why he offered me to a man who wants a society wife and a vessel for his heir. He thinks it would put Edoardo in his debt. *You* don't have to settle for someone who is broke, though. Antoine knows that."

"Thank God you're here to explain patriarchy to me. I've never gotten the hang of it."

"No, you're doing it right," she assured him. "This game of chicken you've entered into with Antoine is a classic use of a woman to one-up another man. But I refuse to be part of it. This lie has gone far enough. I can't mess with my mother like that."

"Eloise." He frowned at her. "I'm not sure where the communication has broken down. Do you not realize I'm serious? We're marrying."

"What?" Her heart lurched. Maybe she was still asleep in her bed in New York and none of this had happened. She pinched her arm, half expecting to wake up on the subway, cold and hungry and miserable.

She was awake, though. This was real. Her blood was skimming so fast through her arteries her whole body vibrated. Her inner seventeen-year-old wanted to faint with excitement, but she was a sensible adult now. She knew dreams were only dreams. They never came true.

"We can divorce later," Konstantin added in a throwaway rumble. "If necessary."

And there it was. The wake-up call. He didn't really want her. Why would he? That was why Antoine wasn't taking this seriously. Her stepfather knew as well as anyone that she brought nothing to a marriage.

The car stopped at the curb and the bellman rushed to open her door, giving her the chance to mutter over her shoulder, "Romantic as your proposal is, I'd rather swim back to New York and pick up toys from the gutter."

Her exit would have been glorious if she didn't have to go back to the room they shared for her passport and other effects.

Konstantin caught up to her as she stepped into the elevator. His expression was an iron mask as he took her hand before she could touch the button for their floor. Her heart leaped, but he was only forestalling her so he could choose a different button.

"They've moved us to a bigger suite."

"I just want my things," she said stiffly, pulling her hand free and trying to put space between them in the close confines of the elevator.

When the doors opened, a starlet and her entourage were waiting, everyone gabbling gaily.

Eloise pressed a smile onto her lips and stepped out, still shaking with turbulent emotions.

Konstantin led her to a door that he unlocked before he leaned to push it open, allowing her to precede him into the room.

It was even more beautiful than the one they had shared

last night. An abundance of windows offered bright views overlooking the sea. There was a sitting room and inside one of the bedrooms, a young woman was putting away clothes. Bags and bags of them.

"What—? *Konstantin*."

"Oh! Shall I come back?" the startled young woman asked in French.

"*Oui. Merci*." Eloise was barely hanging on to her fraying temper. As the maid left, she turned on him. "You're doing exactly what Antoine did. You're telling me what's going to happen and assuming I'll go along with it."

His head went back. "That's insulting."

"Am *I* not allowed to be insulted? You proposed marriage *out of spite*." It was especially hurtful coming from him, the man she'd girlishly dreamed of marrying. "You slapped him in the face with me as the gauntlet. Excuse me while I don't fawn all over you for treating me like chattel. I'm not a tool or a weapon. I'm not—"

Oh, she was going to cry. This was so humiliating.

Locking her throat against the bubble of pressure trying to burst free, she moved into the bedroom and searched for her long coat, double-checking that her passport was still in its zipped inner pocket. It was, along with her well-worn and mostly empty wallet. She took off the jacket she was wearing, throwing it onto the bed.

"Think this through, Eloise," Konstantin said crisply. "Negotiating the prenup forces Antoine to open your mother's financial books to me. If there's malfeasance, I'll find it and put a stop to it. You want that."

She did, but—

"He can't marry you to anyone else if you're married to me, can he?"

No, but... "I don't have to marry anyone if I don't want to," she blurted, still hurt by his drive-by proposal. "Especially when it's only a ridiculous stunt. You really want to go through all of this trouble and expense, buy me clothes and a ring, stage a *wedding* and negotiate a prenup just so you can get a peek inside a few ledgers? Fake a business deal with him," she cried, waving her hand in the air. "There are thousands of ways you could sic accountants on him."

"How are you missing that marriage accomplishes so much more than that?" He clasped the top of the door where he stood. "Think of the power and influence you'll have. He thought you'd make a good society wife? Hell, yes, you will. If you are my wife, no one will dare cross you, least of all him. And if he were to somehow steal all of your mother's money—which I won't allow to happen, but if he did—you'd have the means to support her."

"How?" she cried. "You *just* said we'd divorce."

"*If* necessary," he repeated.

"How could it not be necessary? You don't *want* to marry me."

"Of course, I want to. I don't do things I don't want to do," he said pithily.

"Yes, I know that," she said heatedly. "You've pushed me away enough times to make that very obvious." She hated to bring that up. It made her stomach hurt, the rejections were so sharp, but it was the truth.

"Really?" He dropped his arm to his side. "You're upset that I didn't kiss you when you were seventeen? *You were seventeen.*"

"What about the funeral?"

"It was a *funeral*. And last night you were crying."

"I wasn't crying this morning, was I? But you still couldn't get out of bed fast enough!"

His brows shot up. After a pause that caused her heart to batter the inside of her chest like a trapped bird, he said in a low rasp, "If I'd stayed in that bed, we would be marrying anyway because I didn't have a condom. I do now, by the way."

Gulp. She tried to look away, but the man was the king of staring contests, able to put erotic visions in her head with eye contact alone and forcing her to hold that vision between them until her scalp tightened. So did her nipples.

"We don't have to marry to have sex," she mumbled, hugging herself. Then she put up a hand, even though he hadn't moved. "That wasn't an invitation. I'm just saying that insisting on marriage is an overreaction."

"No, Eloise." His voice hardened. "What I've done until now has been an *under*-reaction." He pushed off the door so he filled the whole space with his powerful presence. "I cannot believe I left you and your mother to your own devices for this long. Marrying you is a correction. A necessary one. I intend to provide for your needs for the rest of your life. I intend to look out for your mother to the best of my ability. Marriage is the most expedient way to do those things."

"And what do you get out of it? A clean conscience? Sex?"

"Yes."

"You know that's not any more romantic than marrying me out of spite, right?"

He muttered a tired curse toward the ceiling.

"Look." She hugged the coat she still held. "I'm tempted to let you take over and look after us. That's a really nice offer, but as far as making corrections goes, I want to be strong enough to help my mother myself. Using you to do it makes me feel like I'm not enough. Like I'm still a—" She cut herself off and looked at her coat, wondering what she thought she was doing. Where would she go if she walked out? To her mother and Antoine?

"Still a what?" he prompted gruffly.

She threw the coat on the bed and took a few restless paces between the bed and the open wardrobe.

"Mom never *called* me a burden. She never said she didn't want me, but she didn't intend to have me. She met my father while she was on vacation. They had a brief affair and she didn't realize she was pregnant until it was too late to make other choices. And it was all on her to raise me. Dad was never there to change a diaper or anything."

"Did *she* change a diaper?" His brow went up with skepticism.

"No. I had nannies, obviously. But paying for them came out of the fortune that Ilias's father left her. My father didn't give her anything but a responsibility she hadn't asked for."

"Has she ever said anything to make you think she regrets having you?" he asked with gentle challenge.

"Not in a mean way. More like mother–daughter advice. Like, she was always very frank telling me about sex and warning me that pregnancy and babies are harder than anyone tells you. And that once you have a baby with someone, you're connected for life so, you know, choose wisely. It was a warning not to get into her situation."

"Your father was never part of your life at all?"

"I saw him a few times a year, but I was really young. My only strong memory is a yelling match when I was five or so. Ilias was thirteen so I asked him about it years later. Dad had tried to talk Mom into letting me go on the circuit with him, but she was afraid he would forget me somewhere or I'd drown. It's kind of heartening to know he wanted more of a relationship with me, but then he died and…" She shrugged. "It really was on Mom to support me. With Ilias's money."

"Ilias would never have begrudged his inheritance going to your upbringing. It was her money when you were a child and it is again. I think you're letting Antoine's manipulations get into your head."

"But he's not *wrong*. You're right that Ilias made it seem natural that Drakos money would pay for my upkeep. I took for granted that it always would, until Antoine called me a freeloader."

"He is *not* one to talk."

"But he has a point. It's time that I looked after Mom, not the other way around."

"You can't. I'm not saying that to be cruel. It's the truth."

She bit her lip, angered by reality, but unable to refute it.

"I understand where you're coming from, Eloise. I *hated* that I needed Ilias's help. I couldn't have saved my grandfather's company without him and your allowing me to help you allows me to let go of my own sense of having fallen short."

"But you *shouldn't* feel that way," she insisted, taking a few steps toward him. "If Ilias was in this predicament, then fine. You could marry him. But—"

"Don't make jokes," he said sharply. "Ilias is one of the few people I ever trusted or cared about. I know where I would be if he hadn't stepped in when he had. It would look a lot like the ruin you've been wallowing in."

"Nice."

"True," he asserted. "And your situation is my fault. I don't claim to be anything but self-interested, but even I have my limits. Your mother called me family." His profile flexed with his effort to resist some intense emotion. "You're supposed to be able to trust your family to support you, not leave you in harm's way, which is what I did."

"She didn't say that to obligate you!"

"Because she doesn't realize the harm *she's* in. Instead, she feels—sincerely—that there's something in me worth caring about, the same way your damned brother did. That's why I'm so ashamed of letting her down. And him."

He was radiating the coiled energy of a lion with a thorn in his paw, but she was getting the sense this was about more than a twinge of disloyalty to his friend. How could he not think he was worth caring about? She cared about him. She always had.

How to make him see that, though? Without getting rejected again?

There was a knock at the outer door, startling her.

"The jeweler. At least look at what he's brought."

CHAPTER TEN

ELOISE WAS STILL distracted by that glimpse into Konstantin's psyche as she followed him out to the sitting room.

He let in the jeweler who introduced himself as Girard Pascal. He was somewhere in his thirties and very handsome in a tailored blue suit that set off the dark brown of his complexion. One of his bodyguards stayed outside the door while the other entered and swiftly checked each room before stationing himself against a wall near the door.

The reason for the precaution was obvious once Girard unlocked his case and set out his trays containing millions of euros' worth of diamond jewelry.

"Oh, my." Eloise couldn't help sinking onto the settee, dazzled by the array.

"I can make a custom piece if you don't see anything that suits," Girard offered.

"By tomorrow night?" Konstantin asked as he lowered beside her.

"That would be difficult." Girard closed one eye. "I can definitely resize any of these by tomorrow, though."

"We'll need that. Look at these piano fingers." Konstantin picked up her hand to caress her fingers, then perused the selection. He chose one and slid it onto her finger.

"What do you think?"

Her heart started to thud even before she got a proper look at it. So many long-suppressed notions were raging back to life, all as vivid and insubstantial as the flash of rainbows from the marquis-shaped stone. It had to be five carats and was surrounded by a halo of smaller diamonds. More were set down the sides of the platinum band.

Konstantin left her hand draped over his, lightly grasping her curled fingertips as he tilted their grip, allowing the ring to shoot out its sparks from all angles. It was unique and extravagant and yes, a little loose, but so beautiful, Eloise could hardly speak.

"No? Something else?" Konstantin started to release her.

Her fingers instinctually tightened to keep hold of his hand.

His dark gaze lifted to crash into hers, reaching deep into her soul and wrapping around all those deeply embedded dreams of hers.

If she went through with marrying him, she would give up every vestige of herself to him. She knew she would. She would offer her heart and he would take it and could very easily break it. So very easily.

But there was another hidden, hopeful part of her that wanted to think maybe, just maybe, this was the chance she'd always yearned for. That this could be a real marriage to the only man she'd ever wanted.

"You'll wear this one?" Konstantin prodded gently.

She knew what he was really asking. *Will you marry me?*

She nodded before she realized she was doing it, then her husky voice caught up. "I will."

Her fingers trembled as he lifted her hand to his lips and kissed her knuckles.

As he sent Girard away to size the ring, Konstantin experienced a conflicting tide of reactions. Intense satisfaction was the primary one. He had always seen marriage as an encumbrance, but the rationale for this one kept growing. Along with balancing the karmic scales, he would gain a partner who would suit him in many ways—including sexually.

Contrary to what Eloise seemed to think, he did want her. Very badly, in fact. His desire was like a panting beast inside him, ready to run her to ground if necessary.

Which gave him pause. These overly strong responses she provoked were the reason he'd avoided her. He had known since that long ago Christmas that she was far too capable of disarming him when he least expected it.

He would have to be careful, he cautioned himself, and keep a cool head. But even as he turned back to an empty sitting room, and heard a rustle from her bedroom, his libido leaped with intrigue, frying his brain cells.

No. When he arrived in the open door, he found her rifling through the bags that surrounded the bed.

"Call the maid to unpack everything," he told her.

"I'm looking for the jeans I was wearing this morning. Ghaliya said they would be returned. Good grief, Konstantin." She abandoned one bag and picked up another. "This is more damage than I ever did on a back-to-school shopping spree in Paris."

"What of this soiree of your mother's tomorrow? She said it wasn't fancy. I'll wear a suit?"

"She meant it's not white tie. You'll need a tuxedo. I'll call Ghaliya and tell her I need a gown. Are we really doing this?" she asked with distress, looking up from the bag she was searching.

"The party?"

"Marriage." She rubbed her eyebrow. "I mean, I guess the engagement will give us time to see if we actually work, but that comes with certain risks."

"Such as?"

"The ones my mother warned me about. If we…" She waved at the bed. "I don't want to be in my father's situation, where I have a baby with someone who has all the money so I get cut out."

"That will never happen." What kind of man did she think he was?

"You don't want children?" She dropped her hand to her side, seeming shocked. Disappointed?

"I meant that I can't see us being in such a bad place that I would refuse to let you see our child. I've never given much thought to having any, to be honest. Not beyond the fact I've been told that I should, as part of my succession plan."

"Who stands to inherit now?" She picked up a different bag and set it on the bed.

"I have a foundation that administers to a number of charities."

"You don't have any other relatives?" She paused. "Who's your emergency contact?"

"My assistant." It had seemed perfectly reasonable until he saw her appalled expression. "Now I'll have you." It was another point in the pro column for marriage. "Why? Where do you stand on children?"

"I've always wanted at least two." She hitched her shoulder self-consciously. "So they would be friends the way Ilias and I were."

A pang struck inside him, similar to nostalgia, but different. It was a glimpse of a future that he suddenly wanted. Which wasn't like him. He didn't *yearn*. Especially for something so nascent and fanciful. He brushed the vision aside.

"We can start on that whenever it suits you."

She had found the jeans and paused in shaking them out. She looked to the bed with consternation. The tension around her eyes denoted genuine apprehension.

His mind flooded with those things she'd said about overbearing men and spiked drinks. His gut knotted up.

"If you have concerns about having sex with me, tell me so we can address it," he said quietly.

"Oh, why do you need to know everything about me?" she asked plaintively, shaking the jeans again.

He ran his tongue over his teeth, aware he needed to proceed delicately, but that wasn't his strong suit.

"The irony isn't lost on me that I've told you flat out I don't like to talk about myself so I can't expect you to be an open book." He did, though. He had a ravenous need to know everything about her, which was strange. "For what it's worth, I've shared more with you in the last few days than I've told anyone in years."

A little choking snort noise came out of her.

He lifted a self-deprecating shoulder. "I don't like the memories that are in my head. Why would I put them in yours?"

Her brow crinkled with concern, which made the inside of his chest itch. He looked to the window so she wouldn't see more than he could stand to reveal.

"If we're going to be married, we'll have to share more with each other than we would with anyone else." That combination of intimacy and intensity already wasn't comfortable. It made his nostrils sting with a sense of threat, which was ridiculous. What was she going to do? Waterboard him into revealing his favorite color? He knew how to set boundaries and would. "But I won't force you to tell me anything you don't want to."

"You'll find out eventually, anyway," she mumbled toward the floor. "So I'll just say it." She was blushing bright red. "I'm a virgin. Okay?"

He had one of those discordant moments where his grasp of English seemed to fail him. Was there a different meaning to that word? Because it didn't compute with his assumptions about her.

"*How* old are you?"

"It's your fault," she threw at him before turning her back on him to sit on the bed and work off her boots.

That took him aback. "How?"

"By being all mysterious and good-looking! You know I had the worst case of puppy love." She kept her back to him as she stood and skimmed her legwear down from beneath her skirt. "You think boys my age held any interest for me when I had *you* on the brain?"

"I wasn't trying to encourage that."

"Yes, I know that," she said in a supremely maddened voice. She stepped into the jeans and gave a little hop. "You rejected me enough times—"

"Because—"

"I *know*." The bunched skirt was whisked away and she finished closing her fly. "It doesn't mean I didn't keep thinking about you. It's not like I wanted to have sex with anyone after Ilias, anyway," she allowed sullenly, turning to face him. "But even when I was at university…" She pinched the bridge of her nose. "When I was just this awful mess and couldn't seem to function, I thought, Konstantin would never want someone like this, and it got me out of bed."

Her words were a punch in the chest. He winced, breathing her name, but maybe it was a plea for her to stop because this hurt. It hurt to think of her struggling and thinking of him and *he hadn't been there*.

"I know that sounds stupid, but I needed something to shoot for. I needed to believe that if I got myself together, then I would see you one day and we'd be on equal footing. You'd finally see me and want a relationship with me. Something real. I wanted you to fall in love with me. Instead, it's *this*." Her hand waved aimlessly, voice cracking. "A convenient marriage for sex because I *don't* have my act together. And that sucks."

Oh, hell. Those weren't tears in her eyes. His stomach dropped.

She moved to the night table and blew her nose, taking a shaken breath.

"I'm realizing that I've been nursing a crush on a man I invented. It wasn't *you*. I don't even know you. Not really. But I do want to have sex with you. Obviously." Her expression flexed with deep vulnerability. "And I've never wanted to have sex with anyone else so…"

So she would accept his terms.

She was right. There was something very flat and disappointing in this bloodless arrangement.

"But it's happening really fast." She had her arms wrapped around her torso, supremely defensive.

"We can wait." They were the hardest words he'd ever spoken. Literally hard. He swallowed.

"Are you mad?"

"No." He could use a beat to assimilate all of this, though. He didn't have a fetish around being anyone's first. A lack of experience with sex was no different than never having jumped out of a plane before. Or eating ice cream. It was something that hadn't been tried before. That's all.

But *he* would be the one to jump out of that plane with her. To show her how it was done. And he wanted her to love it.

"No, I appreciate your honesty." He did. Even though it was making his head swim. "I need to make some calls."

We can wait.

For how long? Eloise wanted to call the question to his back. How much long*er*?

She didn't have the nerve to ask, unwilling to face yet another rejection.

She barely saw Konstantin until they were ready for her mother's party the next evening. She went back to see Ghaliya about her gown, then they dined at the restaurant where they were interrupted by someone he was loosely acquainted with. Afterward, he went to the gym to workout. She had fallen asleep before he got back.

The next morning, she had a fitting, then spent an hour on video chat with her New York roommate who was using the windfall from Konstantin to move to California. Under Eloise's direction, her roommate whittled Eloise's few possessions down to a small box that their neighbor agreed to post when Eloise had a permanent address.

Then she'd been tied up with Ghaliya again, having her hair and makeup done while Konstantin disappeared to pick up her ring.

When she met him in the sitting room, she was nervously petting the rich velvet of her dark mulberry gown.

"Wow." The flicker of his gaze from her eyebrows to the hem of her gown made her prickle all over.

"It's too much, isn't it? Between my size and the late notice, I didn't have much to choose from." She never would have picked something so sexy. The soft fabric hugged her arms and waist and hips before spilling wide around her legs. The low neckline cut over the top of one shoulder and fell off the other. It was outlined in delicate silver lace that added wintery sparkle.

"I think you look incredible. Will you come here, please?" He picked up the ring box from the table beside the sofa and opened it.

She didn't know why his grave tone made her ankles wobble on the six-inch heels as she moved toward him.

He looked incredible, too. His tuxedo jacket was ivory with a black shawl collar and accentuated his wide shoulders and the taper to his waist and long legs.

When she was eye level with his bowtie, she realized, "It matches my dress."

"I told Ghaliya to find me one that would."

Eloise was absorbing what a cute gesture that was when Konstantin stole a cushion off the sofa and dropped it to the floor. He lowered to one knee upon it.

"What—?" Her voice failed her and she clutched at her closing throat. He couldn't be doing what she thought he was doing.

He held out his hand in a request for hers. "I disappointed you yesterday. I want you to have a better story to tell, when people ask you how I proposed."

She bit her lips together, so touched she couldn't speak, only blink to keep the welling tears in her eyes.

"I've never wanted to marry anyone, Eloise. But I want to marry you. That is the truth. Will you marry me?"

He sounded so sincere, her vision blurred. "You're going to make me ruin my makeup," she said on a sniff.

"No," he chided and stood to pluck a tissue from the box he must have placed on the end table for exactly this reason. "I really can't bear tears, *glikia mou*. That is something you need to know about me." He touched her chin to tilt her face up and dabbed the tissue into the corners of her eyes, his expression very somber. "I will try not to make you cry. I promise you that. It hurts too much."

"Oh, you're making it impossible to *not*." She stole the tissue and pressed it under her nose, then fanned her eyes, blinking and fighting the press of emotion. "This was really thoughtful." She had to clear the thickness from her throat. "Thank you." In so many ways, this was her dream come true. Could she really complain if it wasn't *exactly* perfect? "I would be honored to marry you, Konstantin."

"Good." He slid the cool ring onto her finger.

It felt heavier this time. Firmer. More real. It made her heart still, but in a good way. As though it came to rest after a long, long journey.

He looped his arms behind her.

Her hands went to his lapels, still nervous, but quivering with delight at having the right to touch him.

She looked up at him, expecting him to kiss her, but he only caressed the edge of her jaw with his bent finger.

"I've just been cautioned not to ruin your makeup." He dipped his head into her throat and nuzzled his lips against her skin.

She gasped and shivered. Her nipples stung and her knees grew weak.

"I like this height." His breath pooled near her ear, fanning the arousal taking hold in her. "But I don't like these earrings."

"No? Why not?" They were oversized gold hoops that she'd chosen so they wouldn't detract from her gown or engagement ring.

"I didn't buy them for you."

"You did actually—oh."

He had another box in his hand. This one held pear-shaped yellow sapphires dangling from round diamond studs.

"Now I just feel spoiled," she admonished.

"Good. That's what I'm aiming for."

She didn't know what to make of that. Her hand shook as she changed out the earrings.

"Thank you," she murmured as she moved to the mirror and touched the weight of each one, ensuring they were secure. "They're beautiful."

"So are you."

This was surreal. Too perfect. Like a Christmas miracle.

Not that she believed in such things, but maybe, just for tonight, she could.

A hush fell over the crowd as they entered the party. The wall between the front parlor and the great room had been opened and the furniture moved to the sides, creating a ball-room. While her mother and Antoine greeted them at the entrance, everyone paused to smiled and offer a polite round of applause.

"I've shared your exciting news with our guests," her mother said cheerily. "Oh, you look beautifully festive, darling." She stepped back from pressing their cheeks to admire her gown. "And, Konstantin. You've made me the happiest woman in the world."

"I could have sworn I did that, *ma chère*," Antoine said smoothly, but Eloise heard the edge in his tone. He caught Eloise's hand, bringing it up so he could inspect the ring with a cynical curl to his lip. His gaze touched her earlobe before drilling into hers. "Buttering all sides of your bread, I see."

"I thought you'd be pleased to see me make such an advantageous match. For the family," she added with a saccharine smile and subtly tried to extricate her hand from his grip.

His hold tightened, not painful, but to show her that he would decide when to let her go, not her. After a charged second of warning, he released her and shook Konstantin's hand before turning his attention to whoever was coming in behind them.

Fresh nerves attacked when they moved into the heart of the party.

As the daughter of Lilja Drakos and the sister of Ilias Drakos, Eloise had always been accepted—maybe *tolerated* was a better word—by her mother's peers. She was illegitimate and only a half sister to the heir of the Drakos fortune, not in line for any money of her own, so she'd never deserved much attention, good or bad. Which suited her. She wasn't built for notoriety.

Konstantin was very well-known, of course. He hadn't been kidding when he had claimed she would have influence as his wife, either. Even as his just-announced intended, she had more cache than she'd ever imagined. People who would, in the past, expect her to come to them, were suddenly coming forward to congratulate them, vying for her attention and an introduction to her powerful husband.

They circulated for well over an hour, making small talk and deflecting prying questions. It was a relief when her mother and Antoine finally started the dancing, taking the attention off them.

Then Konstantin took her in his arms and Eloise was aware of only him and the music, nothing else. His hands were sure on her, his steps smooth and perfectly on tempo. The solidness of his shoulder and the brush of his thighs and the fading spice of his aftershave all put her into a spell where she let herself believe, just for a moment, that her life was turning out exactly as she had always wanted it to.

"Are you going to play?" Konstantin asked.

"Hmm?" She lifted her gaze to see he was looking toward the piano where a serious young man in wire-rimmed glasses and a suit vest over striped trousers was mastering the instrument. "No." The ensemble of five was expertly moving from background classical to waltzes and contemporary instrumentals, interspersing them with a few Christmas carols. "Having an audience was always my stumbling block. I had ten years of classical lessons so I can get through a performance if I have to, but I don't enjoy playing for crowds. I do it for me. If someone wants to sit down and listen, that's their business."

"Is that why therapy appeals? Because it's about the individual?"

"Yes, exactly!" She looked up at him, pleased to be understood. "Oh."

"What's wrong?" He pivoted her out of her small misstep.

"Nothing. Only that we were under the mistletoe—"

"Were we?" He twirled her back, forcing another couple

to make a quick turn to avoid them. When they were directly below the dangling ornament of berries in the middle of the floor, he said, "What do we do now?"

"I think you know," she said with amusement twitching her lips.

"I do," he agreed and cupped the side of her face as he dropped his head to press his mouth over hers.

From the outside, it probably looked chaste, but it was a lingering, sensual kiss that subtly claimed her, curling her toes and making her pulse trip. She let her eyelids flutter closed and melted against him.

When a ripple of amused *aahs* rose around them, he drew back, obsidian eyes filled with banked heat.

"Shall we switch?" Antoine appeared beside them with her mother. A new song started.

Konstantin's expression cooled, but he found a warmer look for Lilja.

"I would be honored." And it would be expected that her fiancé dance with his future mother-in-law while Antoine took Eloise for a spin.

The tempo was a foxtrot and Antoine was a good dancer, leading her expertly through the steps while saying with quiet malice, "You don't really expect me to believe this charade?"

She didn't bother playing dumb. "Edoardo wanted to marry me. Why wouldn't Konstantin?"

"Because I sweetened the pot for Edoardo. What could you possibly offer a man like Konstantin? That you're not already giving up," Antoine added scathingly. "Or is that how you got the ring? By holding out on him? That will only work so long, girlie. He won't go through with marrying you. What could he possibly gain?"

She didn't want be so withered by his words, but he was giving voice to the insecurity she already felt. Maybe Konstantin was only intrigued by the sex they weren't yet having. She might not be any good at it, for all she knew. And beyond that, all she offered him was a chance for him to feel he was squaring things with her dead brother. He had already mentioned divorce and turned away from her more times than she cared to count.

Not that she revealed any of that to Antoine. She kept it to a stiff, "I'm not here to prove anything to you. I just wanted to see my mother."

"You want her ring. And for her to pay for a wedding and all the parties and frills that go with it. I won't let that happen. Get what you can out of Galanis. That's no skin off my nose, but don't come crawling back here when he throws you out."

Whether it was a newfound boldness that came from knowing Konstantin was in her corner or an old spark of her former self, before life had delivered so many blows, Eloise threw back her head and said, "I haven't wanted to make my mother choose between her husband and her child, but do you honestly believe she would pick you if I did?"

"She already did," he said with a cruel tilt to his mouth.

The music stopped and Eloise was close enough to the edge of the dance floor that she melted into the crowd, but her pulse was pounding in her ears and her hair felt as though it would catch fire any second.

"What did he say to you?" Konstantin asked grimly, coming up behind her where she was accepting a glass of wine from a bartender.

"Nothing," she lied.

"You might hide how you feel about him from your mother, but not from me. What did he say?" he repeated through clenched teeth.

She glanced up and felt incredibly defenseless, not just because he read her so easily, but because of the things Antoine had said.

"He thinks I'm using our engagement to get Mom to go

back to paying for my lavish lifestyle. He said she's already chosen him over me."

"I've had it with him." Konstantin turned his head to search over the heads of the crowd. "Are you ready to leave?"

"Yes, but—" She set aside her glass and touched his arm to keep him from walking away. "You're not going to make a scene, are you?"

"No. I'm going to make a point." He took her hand and wound her through the crowd to where her mother and Antoine were speaking to another couple. "Lilja. Thank you for inviting us, but we have an early departure for Greece tomorrow. We're calling it a night. Are you sure we can't persuade you to spend Christmas with us?"

"I'm tempted. I miss Athens."

"We're going to Como for the holiday," Antoine said firmly. "Lilja has been looking forward to it."

"And we're going to Crete," Konstantin said, still speaking to her mother. "But we'll have the wedding in Athens if that's easier for you. I'll fly to Como and kidnap you myself if I have to."

"That won't be necessary. We're only staying until the second. Eloise." Lilja touched the large emerald pendant dangling from the thick gold chain around her throat. "You're *not* marrying on Christmas Day."

"No." She sent an alarmed look to Konstantin. *Were they?*

"Much to my dismay, there's a seven-day waiting period in Greece," Konstantin said. "So it will be the twenty-eighth or ninth. I'll let you know once we've finalized everything. You and I have a lot to cover before then." Konstantin finally swung his attention to Antoine who was looking like he'd been kicked in the peanuts. "Expect paperwork first thing in the morning."

"You're marrying in a *week*?"

"Konstantin. We need a year," her mother protested before she sent a startled look to Eloise. "Are you pregnant?"

"*No.*"

"Oh." Her mother pouted. "That's too bad. A grandchild would have been icing on the wedding cake, but, Konstantin—" she touched his sleeve "—I only have one daughter. I want her to have the perfect wedding."

"So do I. You and Eloise may spend as much of my money as you want, on a ceremony as extravagant as you want, on whichever day you want to have it, but I am making Eloise my wife before the year ends." He wove their fingers together. "That is nonnegotiable."

"He reminds me more and more of Petros by the minute," Lilja confided with amusement to Eloise. "I wouldn't dream of missing your big wedding day, darlings. Melissa will understand our leaving Como early. I can't wait to tell her. How exciting!" Lilja hugged them both again. "Have a lovely Christmas. We'll see you both in a few days."

CHAPTER ELEVEN

"A WEEK?" ELOISE BUSTLED ahead of him into their hotel sitting room, sounding agitated. "When did you decide that?"

"When I found out the waiting period was a week," he drawled. "It's a month here in France. Would you rather marry tomorrow? We could fly to Gibraltar." *Say yes*, he willed.

"But why are you in such a hurry?" Her skirt billowed as she whirled and face him. "To put pressure on Antoine?" She was fiddling with her ring, looking anxious, so he took a moment to consider how his words might land.

"I thought my motive was obvious." He shrugged out of his tuxedo jacket and loosened his bowtie. "When you said you're a virgin, I presumed we'd wait until our wedding night. I don't want to wait a year to make love to you. It's all I can do to wait a week."

She started to say something, hesitated, then blurted, "Do *I* have any say in that?"

"You have all the say in that. Why? Is that too fast?"

Her gaze skittered away from his, chin setting belligerently, and he was overcome by the most tender delight.

"Or is it too slow?" he asked knowingly.

"Don't make me feel embarrassed for it!" she said crossly.

"How exactly do you feel?" He padded toward her, trying not to be smug, but damn this reaction of hers was satisfying. "Are you impatient? You seemed nervous when we talked about it yesterday."

"I'm terrified," she admitted, letting her hand alight on the pleats of his shirtfront before she jerked it back as though scorched. "What if it's awful? And then we're stuck with each other? Do you really want that? To go into marriage blind?"

"Now your inexperience really is showing." He took her hand and lightly tugged an invitation to move closer. "There's no chance of it being awful. We have incredible chemistry, Eloise. That's why you melt every time I touch you."

She was doing it now, leaning into him, but fighting it. He tried to rub the tension from her shoulder blades.

"It's not the same for you, though," she mumbled into his shirt. "You don't feel this helpless. Do you?" Her brows came together crossly.

"No, I feel powerful. Like I'm holding the sun." He brought her hand to the back of his neck and trailed his touch down the velvet that covered her arm. She shivered and caught her breath. He smiled. "It's intoxicating. Exciting."

"That doesn't sound equal. It sounds like you're in control and I'm not."

"But how does it *feel*?" he chided as he shifted the velvet of her gown against her, rubbing the slippery silk lining against her skin.

He definitely liked her in high heels. When she let her head fall back, her mouth was right there for the slant of his.

The taste of her sent a sweep of heat through him, like a sip of fine scotch. He wanted to get drunk on her. To gulp her down, but therein lay the danger. He had to keep some control in this.

Still, as he made himself lift his head and say, "I'm going to shower," he couldn't resist adding, "I won't lock the door. Join me if you want to."

* * *

He left her with heat searing from her lips to the pit of her belly. With a sense of being abandoned, but of wanting to abandon herself.

Take me, she thought.

But he wanted something that was infinitely more difficult. He wanted her to give herself to him. That took bravery and trust. It might even cost her soul.

But he was already in possession of it.

Was she being a complete fool? How well did she really know him? Barely at all! Her brother had trusted him and Konstantin felt a compelling debt toward Ilias, but what did he feel for *her*? Nothing so deep as what she felt toward him.

It made the act of going to him more than just a conscious decision. It was a huge risk, but she wanted to believe that if she had the courage to take this step, she might find the deeper regard and loving relationship she was looking for.

She kicked off her shoes and walked on unsteady legs into his room, dropping her gown to the floor along the way. She came up against the cracked door where she could hear the quiet rustle of clothing. She slowly pushed it open.

He turned from hanging his trousers on a hook, naked but for the snug black underwear that outlined his erection straining the front. His gaze ate up her powder-pink strapless bra and matching lace cheekies while she admired the bronzed cast that was his chest and muscled shoulders and tense abdomen.

His attention came back to her face and he said, "I should have got the pink ones."

She touched her ear. "I should, um…" She removed her jewelry, leaving it in the empty soap dish with her hairpins. Then she used a couple of the complementary makeup removal wipes, aware of him standing so close she could feel the heat off his body, but he didn't touch her.

"You're not going to start the shower?" she asked as she dropped the little pads into the bin.

"I'm enjoying watching you. And don't be mad when I say this, but I'm surprised how short you are."

She dipped her chin in warning.

"It's because you have a very sunny personality. I saw it tonight. You make people smile and when you tell a story, people want to hear it. It makes you seem bigger than you are. I think that's why I didn't recognize you right away in New York. I genuinely remembered you taller than you really are."

"Thank you, I guess?" she said wryly.

"I mean it as a compliment. I hate parties and you made tonight bearable."

"That's another compliment? Maybe if we workshop them before delivery."

His mouth twitched. "See, like that. You're funny and engaging."

He leaned into the shower and wrenched the taps on. As the hiss of the water filled the room and the air grew so thick it was hard to breath, he very casually skimmed down his underwear and stepped out of them, then straightened to his full intimidating height. His erection jutted out, unabashed.

"Let's not waste water," he chided, and nodded at her to finish stripping.

Her stomach pitched with nerves as she reached behind herself to release her bra, letting it fall to the floor before she rolled her cheekies down her legs, too shy to look at him as she stepped out of them.

He held the door for her like a gentleman, then followed her into the cubicle.

It wasn't the spacious shower of his New York penthouse and she didn't have it all to herself. This one was big enough for two, but just barely. His body brushed hers beneath the spray and his arm grazed her breast when he reached for the soap. He rolled the bar between his hands, then he slid his soapy hands over her skin, dragging her close and planting a wet hungry kiss across her mouth.

A glorious rush pulsed through her. She gave in to her wicked, greedy urge to slick her hands over his sides and back and up to his shoulders, then rubbed her breasts against the lather in the fine hairs on his chest and welcomed his tongue with the brush of her own.

He groaned and pressed her into the cool tiles. There was a dull thud of the soap falling. His hands covered her breasts, massaging and flicking her nipples in a way that sent wires of electric heat deep between her thighs, making her writhe.

His erection was a thick insistent shape against her abdomen and she started to touch him, then hesitated.

"Go ahead," he rasped, easing back enough that she could stroke the steely shape of him.

"Show me?" she asked shyly.

He wrapped his hand over hers and crushed her fist around his girth, moving in her hand as she began to strokc him. She was fascinated and smugly pleased when he closed his eyes and bit out a ragged curse.

He leaned down to kiss her, saying against her mouth, "I can feel you smiling. Do you think I'll let you take me over the edge without you?" His hand slid down her abdomen and between her thighs, capturing her mound in a possessive cup that pooled water against her flesh, rinsing away the soap before his touch delved into her folds.

Despite the lack of lather, his fingertips slid easily against her aroused flesh. She gasped at the stark intimacy of it, the sensitivity and sparking points of pleasure.

"What if we're not good together?" he mocked and probed lightly against her entrance. "Do you want this?"

"Yes," she whispered, not even sure what to expect, only

knowing that she wanted *more*. More pleasure. More intimacy. More of him.

His long finger penetrated her. It wasn't painful, but it was strangely intense. Deeply personal, then...

"Oh..." she groaned as he played his thumb across the bundle of nerves that sent pleasure thrumming through her whole being.

"Squeeze me tight," he urged against the corner of her mouth.

She didn't know if he meant with her hand or her body, but she was nothing but tension from head to toe, making noises that echoed off the walls of the shower while he danced his touch into her body and against her clit. She gave him her tongue and moved with him, wallowing in how sexy and smutty and *good* it felt.

Then she was teetering at the pinnacle. He held her bottom lip in a gentle scrape of his teeth while his dark eyes turned midnight black.

The tension inside her released in a sudden rush of contractions. She might have been embarrassed by how quickly she'd fallen apart, but he was tilting back his head, groaning at the ceiling while the water rained down and he pulsed in her hand.

After they dried off, he left her in his bed with a lingering kiss, saying, "I need to make some calls."

"It's midnight." She felt like butter and wanted to melt herself all over his toasty form.

"Not in Australia. That's where your mother's trustee retired to." He pulled on the trousers he'd been wearing earlier in the day. "I want to speak to some of my Sydney people about locating him. I don't know if he has ties to Antoine so they need to be delicate."

"Oh." She had thought they might continue making love. Was he being chivalrous or had she done something wrong?

"Sleep. I'll join you soon." He rose and walked out.

She tried to stay awake, but all the travel and stress must have caught up to her. She was deeply asleep when she realized Konstantin was rolling away from spooning behind her, leaving the bed.

"What's wrong?" she asked drowsily, completely disoriented by the sound of him zipping into his trousers. Hadn't he done that already?

"Some genius ordered the maid to come early so she could pack up all your new clothes." His voice was graveled with sleep. "Our flight plan is filed for nine."

"Oh." She couldn't help grimacing. "Are you the genius?"

"I am the genius."

She desperately wanted to duck under the blanket and sleep longer, but as he closed the door she heard him let the maid into the sitting room. She threw off the covers and hurried into the bathroom so she could steal the robe off the back of the door.

The rest of the morning was taken up by travel. They flew straight to Crete, landing in Heraklion before they transferred into a helicopter that hopped them to Konstantin's mountaintop villa.

It was a spectacular estate, especially when viewed from above. The house sprawled in decadent white wings with pretty balconies and windows that reflected sky and sea. There was a courtyard with a pergola of vines over it and a broad terrace with a pool set into it like a jewel. The roof was covered in solar panels and the surrounding hillsides were skirted with vineyards and olive groves amid the broken walls of ancient ruins.

The path from the helicopter pad toward the house was

flanked in bougainvillea and potted citrus trees struggling to bloom in the cool temperatures of December.

A stocky young man hurried out to greet them, black curly hair cut very short, glasses slightly askew.

"*Kýrie… Kyría*," he greeted, adding in heavily accented English, "Once again, I must apologize for the confusion with the rooms in Nice."

"It's done," Konstantin dismissed. "Eloise, this is Nemo, assistant to my EA. I was expected to be on vacation, so I've been leaning heavily on him this week."

"I'm honored to meet you, *kyría*. Welcome to Greece. My number is in your phone. Please call or text me with anything I can do to make you more comfortable here."

"I was born in Athens," she said in Greek. "I'm already very comfortable here."

"You speak Greek?" Konstantin snapped his attention to her. "Why have we been speaking English?"

"I'm rusty," she excused with a shrug. "I didn't want to embarrass myself. I'll brush up now that I'm here, though."

"You certainly will," Konstantin muttered. In Greek.

Nemo looked between them, not sure if he was supposed to be amused.

"Please come meet Filomena," he decided to say. "She's the niece of the regular housekeeper who is on vacation. She has a young family so she can only come in for a few hours each morning. I've contacted an agency if you'd like someone here full-time?"

"Mornings are fine," Konstantin said to the young woman when they found her putting away groceries in the kitchen. "Thank you for coming on short notice."

"Of course." She smiled shyly at both of them.

"Oh, this is beautiful," Eloise said as they moved from the expansive kitchen out to the living area.

The decor was soothing grays and muted earth tones, picking up the colors of the marble floor and contrasting against the white walls. Beyond the abundant windows, the terrace and pool sat against a screen of endless blue sea and scudding clouds. Eloise was drawn outside to the covered dining area where she was protected from the bite of the damp wind.

Inside, she heard Konstantin say, "When can we expect the—wait. Let it be a surprise for Eloise, since it's for her. When will it arrive?"

"This afternoon," Nemo assured him. "And where... um...?" He smiled uncertainly as Eloise came back inside, drawn by curiosity. "Where would you like me to put it?"

"Here." Konstantin waved at a cozy seating area next to the fireplace, where she could imagine herself curling up to read a book and sip a glass of wine.

"Are you getting a tree?" Eloise guessed, warmed that he would indulge her like that. "You don't have to do that for me if it's not something you usually have."

"The tree will be here tonight," Nemo said, faltering in a brief way that suggested to Eloise that he was expecting more than a tree. "Filomena's husband will bring it. She looked for decorations in the storage room, but couldn't find any."

"I don't have any," Konstantin said.

"I'll pick some up later and hang them tonight. Do you have a color preference?" Nemo asked Eloise.

"You probably don't know, but I happen to be one of Santa's helpers." Eloise splayed her hand on her chest. "As such, I would love to buy decorations and hang them. It sounds like you have enough to do."

"It's no trouble for me." Nemo looked to Konstantin for guidance, seeming anxious not to step on her toes, but nor was he about to shirk his duties.

"We'll go into the village and see what we can find," Konstantin said, adding ironically, "So Santa can get his sled in here without being seen."

"Konstantin, I haven't even got you *one* gift," Eloise protested, growing anxious as she suspected something else was planned. Her finances did not run to plane fare and sapphire earrings and whatever else he was planning, either. Buying a few baubles for the tree would be a strain.

"I don't need anything," Konstantin said dismissively. "Except thirty minutes to finish speaking with Nemo. Please tell Filomena we'll find dinner while we're out. She doesn't need to prepare anything." He turned back to Nemo. "Come into my office and tell me where we are with the lawyers."

Eloise delivered her message, but Filomena wouldn't let her help in the kitchen or let her carry up the luggage that the pilot had left on a cart in the breezeway.

"Nemo and I will unpack it while you're out," she promised.

She told Eloise where to shop for decorations, but didn't have any suggestions for a gift for Konstantin. "My husband enjoys assembling model planes and fishing so I always have options in that vein."

Did Konstantin have hobbies? Eloise didn't know, which was an uncomfortable reminder that she was marrying a man who was still a mystery to her. One who had made her feel divine, then left her in the bed and walked away, not seeming nearly as affected by their interlude in the shower as she had been.

He had also delivered her back to her mother and put her stepfather on notice. She wanted to show her gratitude for that. She had to give him something and it had to be meaningful.

She picked up her phone to search *inexpensive gifts for men*, but was struck by the perfect idea before she'd unlocked her screen.

She hurried back to the kitchen to ask Filomena where she could find what she needed.

* * *

Konstantin parked the Jeep in one of the spots facing the beach, then walked around to wrap his arm around Eloise, trying to protect her from the gust of salt-scented wind.

"Do you want to get a coffee?" Eloise asked as they reached the stoop of a *kafeneio*.

"Sure." He used his free hand to reach for the door, but her words halted him.

"Good. Stay here while I nip out for something."

"What is it?" He flexed his arm, keeping her beside him. "I can go."

"Filomena told me where I could get your gift."

"No, thank you." He held onto her as she tried to slip away from him and leave the stoop.

"What do you mean *no thank you*?" She scraped at a tendril of hair that the breeze whipped across her face. "It's for Christmas."

"I told you I don't need anything. But let's get coffee. We can drink it while we shop. It won't feel so cold once we're in the alleys." He started to open the door again.

She dug in her heels. "Konstantin. You didn't ask me if I wanted three thousand gifts in four days. You just gave them to me."

"Because they're things I want you to have."

She said nothing, only stared pointedly at him.

"I don't like receiving gifts," he admitted, shifting so he was at least forming a buffer against the wind, protecting her from it.

"Why not?"

In his mind's eye, he saw a toy sailboat hit the stones of the chimney, smashing into pieces. "I just don't like it."

"So the gift you refuse to give me is the gift of giving you a gift?" she challenged.

"Yes."

The amusement in her gaze turned searching. Troubled.

"It's a lot of secrets and subterfuge. For what?" He tried to downplay it.

"It's fun. Otherwise, you would tell me what's being delivered while we're out."

He didn't want to tell her. He wanted to see her reaction when they got home and found it there.

"I'm not getting you dance lessons or an ugly tie, I swear," she cajoled. "It's just something small that I want you to have because I don't think you do. I think you'll like it."

That was the issue. If he did like it, and revealed that, it could be used against him.

She wasn't like that. He knew she wasn't. But there was still a hard wall inside him that wanted to stay firm and strong against even the possibility of cruelty.

She looked so earnest, though.

He sighed shortly. "It's really that important to you?"

"I could have bought it by now if we hadn't been arguing about it all this time."

"Go, then. Be back in ten minutes or I'm coming to look for you."

He went inside to order coffee, then he sat at one of the outdoor tables, watching up the street for her to return, irritated with himself for being so churlish with her.

He'd been feeling off-balance since their shower last night. The sex hadn't been adventurous, but it had been intimate enough and powerful enough that he'd needed some time to put himself back together afterward.

Thankfully, she'd been fast asleep when he came to bed or he would have made love with her. He wanted to. Physically, his body was craving hers the way vampires craved blood, but on a more psychic level she was churning up his equilibrium.

He kept himself closed off for a reason, trying not to ruin

lives through deliberate negligence, but otherwise he took little responsibility for how others felt. Eloise was different. Every emotion that emanated from her sifted through him in some way. If she seemed distressed, he wanted to remove the reason for it. If she smiled, he felt it like a thousand rays of sunshine bursting into life within him.

This growing attachment to her grated most of all, warning him that he was developing an Achilles' heel.

If he were honest with himself, he would admit that she'd always been one. It was only widening now that he was spending time with her, encompassing more and more of him as he allowed her to get closer.

Damn it, he'd forgotten to ask if she needed money.

He tapped his pocket to ensure he had his phone and wallet as he rose to stand, but there she was, walking toward him. If she had purchased something, it was in the shoulder bag she had brought with her.

"Cream, one sugar," he said, offering the take-out cup of coffee he'd ordered for her.

"Thank you." She sipped and closed her eyes. "Mmm… Greek coffee. My one true love."

Not me?

The whimsical words hovered on his tongue. He bit them back, but wondered where the urge to say them had come from. He wasn't jealous of coffee. Was he?

"Filomena said there's a shop with a green awning that would have decorations. I think I saw it when I passed that alley back there."

They shopped for the next hour, picking out garlands and ornaments and a centerpiece for the table, then ordered sweet and savory treats from the bakery to be delivered the next day. After leaving their purchases in the Jeep, they went into a nearby taverna where they sat by a window overlooking the wharf.

"We should walk out there after dinner. I always loved seeing the boats decorated with lights." Eloise cupped her hands around the *tsikoudia*-spiked toddy she'd ordered and smiled across the steam that rose from the mug. "Ilias would buy cookies and we'd eat them on the beach while we watched boats go by. It was one of our Christmas traditions. Thank you for today. This is the first year without him that I've felt the least bit interested in celebrating."

"You're welcome," he said, mildly amused that she was expressing more gratitude over glass ornaments and strings of lights than she had for the designer clothes or sapphire earrings he'd given her.

It had been a pleasant afternoon, though. More enjoyable that he would have expected. He put his mellow mood down to the warmed shot of raki with honey, cinnamon and clove he was nursing.

"What sorts of traditions did you have, growing up?" she asked.

"None," he dismissed and looked to the menu neither of them had read yet. "Should we have the *stifado*?" It was a rustic beef stew made with red wine and tomato. "It seems to be their specialty."

"That sounds good. Thank you." She waited while he waved over the server and ordered, then said, "I'm sorry, Konstantin. I didn't realize that you don't celebrate Christmas. I presumed you were culturally Christian if not practicing. Do you observe something else?"

"No."

"Then why...?" She frowned with puzzlement.

He came up against the contradiction where he preferred not to discuss his past, but saw that it would be more practical to make his explanation so he would never have to talk about it again. "It's nothing to do with religion. When I was very young, there wasn't any money for birthdays or Christmas. If we had a good meal on any day of the year, that was celebration enough. After my mother was gone, neither my grandfather nor I had much interest in any of the holidays so I've never observed them."

"What about when you were at school? We always had a year-end party and exchanged gifts in our dorms. You didn't do things like that?"

"The other boys did." They would buzz with talk of where their family would travel to ski or see relatives, excited by what they hoped to find under the tree. "Some would pester me to draw a name, but there were a handful of other boys who didn't celebrate for whatever reason. It was easy enough to opt out."

"Ilias never gave you any gifts?" She couldn't believe that.

"Video games," he said drily, under no illusion as to his friend's motive. "So I could be coerced into playing them with him."

"He was always sneaky like that, wasn't he?"

He was. And he would look at Konstantin with an expression like hers, too. Not pitying exactly, but earnest and fretful, wanting to pull him into the group. Wanting him to experience a high that Konstantin knew would only put him in danger of a fall.

"You don't miss what you've never had," he said in a tone of finality.

She flinched, which he regretted, but their stew arrived so it was easy enough to close the subject and move on to other things.

CHAPTER TWELVE

ELOISE WANTED TO respect Konstantin's privacy around his childhood. He had said he didn't talk about how he had come to live with his grandfather and, given the small glimpses he'd offered of his past, she suspected there was a great deal of pain and sadness along with poverty and a certain amount of neglect.

It made her heart hurt to think of it, but it helped her understand why he was so remote and unused to small gestures of kindness. She couldn't stop thinking about that remark he'd made the other day about not thinking he was worth caring about. Did he really feel that way? It made her wonder if he even believed in love or would ever offer her his heart.

What did that mean for their marriage if he was so closed off?

She was lost in introspection when they arrived back at the villa. They paused to hang their coats and put on the slippers Filomena had left for them, then moved into the great room with their purchases. Filomena had gone home and Nemo was staying in the pool house so the villa was empty. Eloise looked for the tree that—

"Oh, my God!" she cried as the Steinway piano hit her eyeballs. A giant red bow sat atop the closed lid. "You didn't? Oh, my God, Konstantin. Oh, my *God*." She wanted to *hug* it.

She spun to hug him instead, but craned her neck to stare at the piano through eyes that blurred with tears.

"You're shaking," he said with amusement as he rubbed her back. "It's okay. It's real."

"I'm just so—" She turned her face into his shirt, trying to dry her face since tears disturbed him, but they were overflowing anyway. She'd missed playing *so much*.

"You're not crying. Eloise, *no*." He sounded agonized as he cupped the side of her face and used his thumb to wipe her cheek. "This was supposed to make you happy."

"I'm ecstatic." She could hardly speak she was so overwhelmed. She ran her trembling fingers under her eyes. "I know I should say it's too much and you shouldn't have. I won't even call it mine. I'm just happy to see it and play it. I'm never going to leave here. I hope you know that. I'm going to sit right there for the rest of my life." She pointed at the bench.

"Then who will play the ones I've ordered for Athens and New York?"

"No!" she squealed, slipping into gales of laughter because there was no other way to let the joy burst out of her. She clutched her fists into his cable-knit pullover and leaned into him, so overcome she couldn't process it.

"You're being silly," he scolded as he kept her from collapsing weakly to the floor.

"*I'm* being silly?" That was even funnier. That grand piano was worth six figures and he was buying them by the dozen, like eggs. Her shoulder's hurt, she was laughing so hard.

"Are you going to play with your new toy, or not?" He was trying to sound stern, but there was a big smile on his face and *that* nearly broke her.

She'd never seen him smile, not like that. Not with his whole face so he looked carefree and star-power handsome, with a glint in his dark eyes and creases beside his mouth.

She reached up to urge him to dip his head so she could kiss him.

His arms tightened across her back, holding her as he

arched over her, making her tingle to her toes as he immediately took over the kiss, consuming her for several wild
heartbeats before he straightened and set her on her feet.

"Go," he said huskily. "The tuner was here when they set
it up. I want to know if he needs to come back."

She had a feeling he was trying to tamp down on his own
emotions, but she was torn between the dual desires to touch
the piano and touch him. She was dizzy as she moved toward the instrument, still buzzing with sensuality and now
growing anticipation and absolute delight. She flexed her
fingers as she sat, then lifted the fallboard. Her hands found
her warm-up scales and it sounded perfect.

"Don't judge my mistakes. I'm out of practice." Especially
for a masterpiece that she hadn't played since relearning it
for her audition to the therapy program earlier this year. It
suited this occasion, though.

She began picking out the first notes of Beethoven's "Ode
to Joy."

As she did, Konstantin came to stand behind her. He rested
his hands on her shoulders, sending a force down her arms
that felt electric. She flubbed a couple of notes and kept going,
feeling more alive than she ever had in her life.

Konstantin carefully drew her hair tie from her ponytail
while she cheated her way through the most complex chords,
then sifted his fingers through the length as she poured her
elation into the keys.

As the emotion built, then softened, then built again, his
light touch caressed her nape and into her throat, making
her breasts tighten.

Her shoulder brushed his fly and she realized he was hard,
but she continued to race her fingers across the keys, chasing the flights of notes.

It was like they were having sex, folding feeling onto tension, building one on the other in thicker and thicker layers.

She wanted that. She wanted sex. She wanted Konstantin. She wanted to feel this wild intensity inside her while *he* was inside her, driving her up and up and up to the heights and then…

The finale. She held that chord soaked with carnal yearning, allowing it to resonate through the room, from her body into his.

His hand slid lower to fondle her braless breast. She arched into his cupping touch, tilting her head back. He swooped to kiss her, drawing her off the bench and kneeing it aside as he pressed her against the piano. Her backside hit the keys in a discordant hum as he kissed the hell out of her.

She had wanted this for years, this hunger that was pouring out of him as though he were starved for her. It was so much more than she had imagined. Wilder. More dominating, more all-encompassing. It probably should have alarmed her, but this craving of his was everything she wanted. The love she'd always had for him was maturing as they spent these days together. It expanded further as he kissed her with unfettered passion. She didn't know how else to express her feelings except to kiss him back with the same ferocious energy.

As she looped her arms around his neck, he scooped her up and lifted her onto the piano so she was more eye to eye with him. His gleaming gaze was atavistic, his features tense and flushed with lust.

Had she done this to him? It was thrilling. She cupped the sides of his head and spoke against his mouth. "I want to make love."

"Lie back."

"I meant—"

"I know what you meant. We'll get there. But I've been thinking about this since I saw you play 'I'm Coming for Christmas.'"

"That's not what it's called."

"I know. Lie back." There was a twitch of amusement at the corner of his mouth.

"Hilarious." But she actually did think it was funny. "Careful," she added as he pulled her hips closer to the edge. "My jeans might scratch the finish."

"Then we should remove them."

A nervous quivering invaded her abdomen as she settled on her back and opened her fly. When he grabbed the waistband in his fists, she lifted her hips and let him drag them away, only realizing as the cool air hit her damp folds that he'd taken her underwear with them.

As her bare backside settled on the cool maple, his hands ran up her naked legs, claiming her thighs firmly and pushing them open.

"I—" She shyly tried to find leverage to close them, stepping on a few keys that plinked.

"Let me," he said, hot breath stirring the fine hairs on her mound, increasing the unsteadiness deep in her belly.

His fingers tickled and trailed around her outer folds, stimulating her. Teasing until heat gathered there with dampness and throbs of need. Then his touch grew more intimate, exploring and exposing her. When anticipation was coiled in her abdomen and she was biting her lip with yearning, the first lick of his tongue landed with such sensitive precision she jerked and tried to sit up.

There was no escaping what he did to her, though. He hugged her thigh and buried his mouth against her tender flesh, swirling and sweeping her into such a state of intense pleasure that she could hardly bear it.

Before she knew it, she was hooking her heel into his back, lifting to increase the pressure, seeking the culmination that was building inexorably inside her. She was filling the room with more song than the piano, moaning with pleasure and tight sobs of need.

When he eased one finger, then two inside her, it was the tipping point. Her moans turned to cries as climax shuddered through her, arching her back and twisting powerful contractions through her that sent flushes of heat chasing through her whole body.

He slowed his clever ministrations, soothing now as the rocketing pulses slowed and faded, leaving her limp and splayed before him.

"That was exquisite," he said in a rasp that abraded all her sensitized nerves in the best possible way.

She was still weak with gratification, all inhibition gone, feeling so dreamy she couldn't move except to roll her head and watch him nuzzle the crease of her thigh.

"This is the happiest day of my life."

"Ha!" He picked up his head and gave her position of abandonment a thorough, possessive study. "Mine, too." He gathered her up and turned to the stairs.

The upper floor was a his-and-hers suite with a shared sitting room and a terrace that could be accessed from all three rooms. Each bedroom had its own walk-in closet and luxurious bathroom.

Eloise had already seen her room with its pastel greens and subtle blue-and-ivory accents. Konstantin's was a stronger palette of navy and forest and silver, all of it muted by the single lamp that was burning against the shadows of night.

The bed met her back before she realized she was tipping. His weight arrived between her thighs in the same motion. He held himself on his elbows and continued to kiss her, hands bracketing her head while his tongue searched out hers, brushing and claiming and wickedly suggesting the lovemaking that was to come.

Her senses were accosted by his weight and heat and the fact her legs were scraping denim as she rubbed her thigh against his. It was erotic to be half clothed this way, making her feel vulnerable against the roughness. She was overwhelmed by his power and size, but when his hand swept under her top and claimed her breast, swooping excitement dove into her belly and heat poured through her loins.

She ran her trembling hands over him, seeking skin beneath his pullover only to come up against his tucked shirt. She bunched the fine fabric in her fist, trying to pull it free of his jeans.

He rose onto his knees and yanked up his pullover, throwing it away before tearing open the buttons of his shirt with impatience.

She sat up to help, crooking her open legs on either side of his as she clumsily slipped the button on his jeans free, then drew his fly down. It took delicate wrangling to wriggle her fingers into denim and briefs, but she managed to reveal the shape pressing so insistently for release.

When she was holding his hot, turgid flesh, she sent one glance upward and found him watching her intently. Her stomach swooped again.

Nervously, she closed her fist around the root of his shaft and bent forward. It was curiosity and desire and a need to thank him and please him and *love* him.

But she was uncertain. She licked lightly, hearing his breath hiss in, which was encouraging. His fingers combed into her hair and massaged her scalp, encouraging her to continue. She explored his shape more thoroughly, painting him with her tongue until she found the courage to close her lips around his tip to delicately suck.

His groan was tortured. His hands flexed in her hair, pulling slightly, while his flesh twitched in her hand and mouth. She saw his abdomen tighten and his whole body seemed to shake.

She would have smiled, but she wanted to keep pleasuring him. She anointed and used her tongue to search out the spots that made him curse and gasp, then bobbed her head a little, experimenting.

With a tortured noise, he used his grip on her hair to pull himself free of the suction of her lips and unsteadily petted down the back of her head, then under her jaw, forcing her to look up at him.

"Another time I'll let you finish me like that," he said in a voice that was graveled and carnal. "I'll look forward to it." His thumb scraped across her bottom lip. "But I want inside you more than I've ever wanted anything in my life."

A tiny sob of helpless arousal throbbed in her throat. She felt too weak to finish undressing, but that was okay because he was already peeling her top off before he kicked his jeans to the floor.

Seconds later, he loomed over her, pressing her onto her back again. He braced himself on an elbow, but his other hand was free and roamed her torso in a possessive claiming, sweeping to her waist and across her stomach, then up to cup her throat. He scraped his teeth against her chin.

"I want you in ways that aren't civilized. Stop me if you get scared."

"I won't." She trusted him. She always had.

His mouth twisted with a hint of cynicism, as though he knew more than she did, but he pressed his lips to her collarbone while his scorching touch went down her front again, pausing to squeeze her hip before searing the top of her thigh.

"Do you want me to wear a condom?" He caught her earlobe between his lips and gently sucked.

Did she want his baby? Her mother's cautions rang briefly through her mind. She ought to heed them, she knew. They weren't married yet, and there was that small anxious part of her that worried something would happen and he would decide he didn't want her, after all.

But when she checked in with her heart, and the part of her that yearned to be a mother, she not only wanted children, she wanted him to be their father.

"Oh…only if you want to," she said tentatively.

He lifted his head long enough to look into her eyes, doing that thing where his near-black eyes swallowed her soul, leaving her trembling.

She closed her eyes and tried to bring his mouth to hers, wanting the mindlessness again. She rolled toward him, seeking the delicious brush of his naked skin with her own, but he wanted her on her back. He pressed her flat and she let him settle between her legs. Eloise set light hands on his shoulders, wanting this, but suffering last-minute apprehension as the reality closed in on her. He was an imposing presence, tense and strong and so casual with his propriety touch. So *strong*.

He was so attuned to her, however, that he lifted his mouth from nuzzling the corner of hers and asked gruffly, "Second thoughts?"

"Nervous," she admitted, and skated her hands across the bulk of his shoulders.

"You didn't seem nervous a few minutes ago. You seemed to know exactly what you were doing."

She smiled with bashful pleasure and sifted her fingers into his hair, encouraging him to linger so they could kiss more deeply.

As they did, all the small sparks of nerves inside her began to pulse with renewed longing. She grew melty and soft and moved her legs against his, reveling in the textures and flex of his muscles.

"You're very beautiful." He only spoke Greek to her now and it felt even more intimate and sincere to hear him say these things in his native tongue. "You know that, don't you?"

She didn't. She wasn't voluptuous or stately or glamorous, but she felt very sensuous as his mouth sought under her chin. She arched her neck, luxuriating in the damp kisses he left on her throat.

"And here," he murmured, cupping her modest breast and sliding down to roll her nipple with his tongue.

"You're not disappointed that—? *Oh*." Sharp sensations lanced into her belly and lower, flooding her loins with renewed heat. With urgency.

"That you prefer to go braless? How could I be disappointed in that?"

"I didn't think you noticed."

He paused in moving from one nipple to the other. "I *always* notice, *asteri mou*. It turns me on." He closed his mouth over the tip of her other breast, curling her toes.

She writhed, fingers in his hair, body feeling not her own.

When his open-mouthed kisses trailed down her abdomen, she shifted her legs, conflicted. She wanted that. Loved it. But...

"I thought you wanted..."

To be inside me.

"What I want, *ómorfi mou*, is for you to want me as badly as I want you. Open your legs and let me remind you how good I can make you feel. Yes..." His breath hissed in pleasure while his wide shoulders nudged her thighs.

He did make her feel incredible. She didn't bother with false modesty or biting back the moans he elicited from her. She let herself sink into the hot pool of wanton sensuality, giving herself over to him completely.

But just when she was nearing the peak, when she was growing blind with need, he moved his mouth to her inner thigh.

"What—?" She picked up her head, almost frantic. Did she do something wrong?

"Now you know." His teeth scraped her thigh before he

closed his lips against her leg and applied light suction, as though drawing the juice from a peach. "This is how I've felt for years." He continued to trace his thumb against her aching flesh, keeping her on the precipice while avoiding the swollen knot of nerves that begged for the brush of his touch.

She panted, ready to cry she was so aroused. His soft kisses against the crease of her thigh and her belly were sweet pinpricks of torture. Then his mouth was at her breast again, sucking so strongly she curled her nails into his shoulders with urgency.

His kiss on her mouth stole everything from her. She had no defenses left. All of her was his for the taking. Forever and always.

Which he knew because the wide dome of his sex slid against the slippery, ready flesh between her thighs.

"Tell me to stop if it hurts." He was prodding for entry.

She tossed her head, not caring if it did. There was no tension in her now. Only need.

As the pressure increased and the stretch threatened pain, she reveled in the sensation because it was him. Because this was what she wanted more than her next breath. Because he was filling her and joining with her. His hips pulsed once, twice, then slid deep enough that his pelvis was flush against hers.

She shook under the magnitude of this moment, feeling both overwhelmed and jubilant. Taken and possessed, but accepted. She was offering herself to him and he was claiming her, but she was the one holding him deep inside herself.

He was shaking with tension, she realized, and ran her hands over him because she could. His body was iron and heat and couched power, hips pinned to hers while his sex pulsed intimately inside her.

His hand cradled the side of her face. "Mine," he claimed gruffly.

She was. She turned her face enough to open her mouth over the tip of his thumb.

His body flexed in reaction. His movement sent a small quake through her abdomen.

They both groaned and, in the next second, he shifted so he could move more freely. His flesh dragged from hers only to return with more intention. More ferocity and depth. He dropped his fist to the blanket beside her ear and she brought her knees up to bracket his ribs.

"Tell me—" He swore, teeth gritted. "Tell me if I'm too rough."

"Don't stop," she cried because the friction had shot her straight back to the pinnacle and, impossibly, she was soaring past it. Higher.

Her whole body was one raw, erotic nerve. Her senses were overloaded by their combined scent and the damp brush of skin on skin. They were both breathing raggedly, releasing tight agonized noises. The bed was shaking as he moved with more speed and power. She couldn't see. Her eyes were closed or she'd gone blind. She didn't care. Her loins burned in the most exquisite way while his movements pushed her to the absolute edge of her endurance.

Then, for one eternal second, she felt nothing. She left this earthly existence and saw the wide expanse of heaven open before her, then she slammed back into a body that was pummeled by such waves of intense sexual pleasure she clung to him and screamed.

His hips crashed into hers again and again before he held himself deep inside her, arms straight as he released his own shout of exalted defeat.

Konstantin managed to roll off her and drag her close so she wouldn't smother or chill, but that was all he had in him. His muscles were twitching as though he'd finished a marathon. He was still catching his breath and waiting for his heart rate to slow.

He couldn't even open his eyes so his brain should have flatlined into unconsciousness, but his mind was racing like he'd hit a mental iceberg.

This was what he'd been afraid of. This depth of want. This need to make an irrevocable claim.

Until this moment, he had avoided articulating to himself why Eloise seemed so dangerous to him, but now he knew. The gratification of having her in his life, in his arms, in his bed put him in that horrible state of treasuring something that could be taken from him.

Why couldn't it have just been a desire for sex? His libido was something that could be satisfied by his own fist, if necessary. Or any woman. He met willing partners all the time. He preferred to want things he could find in quantity or provide for himself. That's why he stockpiled money and houses and estates that grew food. So he would never be without those things.

He didn't allow himself to want abstract things that were impossible to truly own, like one specific woman. He didn't want to have this pulse beat inside him that said, *This one. Only this one will do.*

Nevertheless, as she shifted and a tendril of her hair slid in a tickling ribbon against his knuckle, he turned his wrist so he could play with the fine strands, smug in his right to do so.

The alarm bells continued clanging inside him. He was sexually satisfied, yes, but there was a greedier beast in him that wasn't yet calm. He had told himself he was marrying her to ease his sense of obligation to Ilias and expose Antoine, but he was marrying Eloise because he wanted to keep her in his life and protect her. He wanted to tend her like a fire, to keep her glowing bright.

He wanted to get her pregnant, apparently, because they'd

had sex without protection. He should damned well have thought that through more carefully, but in his most primal of lizard brains, he wanted to have sex again and again until he knew they were bound inextricably by a child. Children.

He couldn't even fathom what that would look like. But he wanted it. Which made it yet another thing he was deeply wary of reaching for.

With a sensuous little sound, she rolled herself half atop him and set her chin on her hand. Her breasts flattened against his ribs and her heavy eyelids blinked as though she were waking from a spell. Her lips were soft and still pouted from their kisses. Her sigh was one of supreme contentment.

"If I run a bath, will you join me?"

Retreat, he told himself.

He ought to offer to run it in her room and encourage her to sleep in her own bed, but his finger swept her hair off her cheek and tucked it behind her ear.

"I'll bring the wine."

CHAPTER THIRTEEN

NEMO WENT TO Athens to spend Christmas with his family, but Eloise and Konstantin weren't alone on Christmas Eve. Filomena asked if her children could come caroling. She had two boys and a girl and the older two each brought a friend.

Eloise eagerly welcomed them into the house and accompanied them on the piano, singing along with great enjoyment. She had prepared little bags of sweets that she handed out when they finished up. Then Konstantin made their eyes nearly pop out of their heads by giving them envelopes stuffed with a hundred euros each.

"*Kýrie*," Filomena protested, but Eloise assured her she was wasting her breath. If she had learned nothing else about Konstantin, she now knew him to be a ridiculously generous man behind that facade of stony aloofness.

Later, they attended a casual neighborhood party and came home to make love and sleep late.

On Christmas morning, Eloise woke and stretched against her fiancé's solid heat. She reveled in waking naked against him, thinking that in this moment, her life was as perfect as it could get.

Except for that tiny thread of doubt that continued to run through her, the one that said this was too perfect. Too easy.

She wanted to believe that time would prove her wrong. Eventually, she would trust in this union, but in these early days, she couldn't seem to keep from feeling quietly anxious that she was kidding herself. That this would all disappear in a blink of an eye.

Which meant she ought to embrace what she had while she had it, literally.

The brush of their skin was pure decadence, as was the right to reach across and caress his back and buttocks. She gave in to the urge to ease atop him and drape herself over his back.

"I feel the weight of expectation," he said into his pillow. "You want to go downstairs to see what's under the tree, don't you?"

"I want to see if you like my gift."

His back rose and fell beneath her in a sigh.

Why was he so resistant to gifts?

She turned her lips against his satiny skin and kissed his spine, then moved in a whole-body caress. The plane between his shoulder blades felt each side of her face as she stropped like a cat leaving its scent. She shifted higher to kiss the back of his neck. Her breasts swayed against the plane of his back and the hard curve of his backside was caressed by her stomach and the graze of her mound. She bracketed his hip with her knee and slid her arms beneath the pillow alongside his.

"If you'd rather stay in bed a few more minutes, I could be persuaded," she said.

He rolled so he was on his back and she could straddle his hips.

Afterward, they showered, then bumped their way downstairs, drunk on sex and each other.

Filomena was spending the day with her family so Eloise started the coffee and put the casserole that Filomena had prepared into the oven. It was loaded with peppers and artichoke, herbs and sun-dried tomatoes, then topped with feta cheese.

When the coffee was ready, she brought the cups into the

lounge, finding Konstantin at the windows. The pile of gifts under the tree had grown by at least a half dozen.

"What have you done?" She sifted through them, able to tell from some of the wrapping that there was at least one bottle of perfume and a designer scarf.

"Open this one first." He plucked an envelope from the tree. It was tickets to a symphony performance in New York in the spring.

She pressed the envelope to her chest. "You'll come with me?"

"Unless you want to take your mother. Or someone else?"

"Mom would enjoy it, but I'll only ask her if something comes up and you can't make it. I'd rather take you. Thank you." She kissed him. "Okay, now mine." She plucked the small flat gift from beneath the tree and curled into the corner of the sofa, holding it out to him.

His expression stiffened as he came to sit beside her.

"Does it really bother you?" She held the flat shape between her pressed palms, distressed that she was causing him more discomfort than pleasure.

His cheek ticked. "It's a childish reaction," he said, mouth curling with dismay. "I was given something when I was young. It meant a lot to me and it was destroyed deliberately, to hurt me. It ruined my pleasure in receiving gifts."

"That happened at school? Sometimes girls were spiteful that way, too."

"No." His brow flexed briefly. "Things like that happened at school, yes, but I didn't care about that. I had stopped letting myself feel any sort of sentiment by then. Things are things. I can buy them for myself if I want them. I don't..." He set his hands on his knees and looked straight ahead as though searching for the words. "I don't like the sensation of someone knowing me well enough to give me something

I'll like. It feels like a weakness. Like I'm painting a target on my chest."

She looked at the gift she held and chewed the corner of her mouth. "Now I'm worried this could hurt you. I was excited when I thought of it, certain you would like it, but…" She drew a breath that made her lungs ache and winced as she offered it. "If you don't want to open it, that's okay. Put it in a drawer and we never have to talk about this again."

"Well, now I'm curious. Is it anthrax?" He picked at the paper, in no hurry, but it became obvious very quickly that it was a framed photo.

He tore away the last scrap of paper and stilled with surprised recognition.

She watched his profile as he studied the photo of himself with Ilias. For a long moment, he said nothing, gave away nothing.

"Are you upset?" She set a concerned hand on his shoulder.

"No. You're right. I like it very much." His hand came up to cover hers while he tilted the frame as though looking for some hidden detail. "Did you use AI?"

"What? No! I took it."

"When?" He turned his head, expression astonished.

"The day you came to Ilias's apartment, when you were supposed to spend Christmas with us. See? That's the tree behind you, before I started to decorate it. You helped him carry it up. I made you two pose in front of it. It was my sly way of getting a photo of my secret platonic boyfriend. Secret because you didn't know," she explained. "And platonic because…"

"I knew," he said out of the side of his mouth, but the corners were tilting up as he studied it again.

In the photo, Konstantin still had his arm outstretched to hold the tree upright. Ilias had looped his arm beneath Konstantin's and set his hand on Konstantin's opposite shoulder.

Her brother wore his most carefree grin, always up for a photo while Konstantin had a look of patient tolerance on his face.

"He would have beheaded me if he knew what I was thinking that day. I would have deserved it," he added with dark humor. "But thank you for this. I don't let myself think of him too often. It makes me feel robbed. And I'll forever be sorry I didn't stay longer that day. Didn't spend more time with him when I had the chance."

"I feel like that, too." She looped her arms around his neck, leaning her head against his as she also looked at the photo. "But I try to remember the laughs and be grateful he was in my life at all. Without him, I wouldn't have met you so he's still bringing good things into my life, isn't he?" It was the closest she dared get to admitting how much she was growing to love him.

Konstantin set the photo on the end table and drew her into his lap. "You're like him in that way. You always see the bright side. To me, everything ends in pain and loss."

"Because you lost your mother so young? Did you lose your father at the same time?"

His expression turned stony and she felt him withdraw so completely, it was as though his body temperature dropped several degrees. "I did."

She felt the pain he was trying to stem in the tension that had invaded his embrace.

"You don't have to tell me about it if you don't want to," she assured him, cuddling into him, trying to radiate warmth and comfort through his skin, into his heart and bones. Into his soul. "But you can."

"Not today," he said after a brief hesitation. His hand roamed over her hair and down her back, as though trying to soften his refusal. "I don't want to ruin Christmas. Get the blue one." He nudged her knee.

It was a pendant to match the earrings he'd given her in Nice, dangling from an ornate Byzantine chain.

"This is too much," she scolded. "I'm going to absolutely smother you in gifts next year to make up for it. Actually, when is your birthday?"

"I'll never tell."

"Nemo will."

"Not if he wants to keep his job."

"Then I'll pick a random day and call it your birthday," she warned as she straddled his lap, pleased that her frothy skirt allowed it.

The confection of white feathers piled around her like a snowdrift and he dug his hands into the folds to bracket her hips while she affixed the chain beneath her loose hair. She centered the stone against the wine red of the top that hugged her torso.

"Thank you," she said sincerely. "It's very pretty."

"So are you."

She loved seeing his expression relaxed like this. His gaze leisurely caressed her braless breasts—yes, she had forgone a bra for him. It meant her nipples were constantly stimulated by the soft knit, standing at subtle attention and now prickling and tightening that little bit more as he admired her.

It was such a perfect moment that she almost said it. Almost admitted she loved him. It wasn't the immature crush of her teen years or infatuation with an idea of a man. It wasn't the beguilement of being showered with gifts, either.

She was beginning to know him, truly know him. He was withdrawn, yes, but beneath that hardened veneer was a man who had a chewy caramel center. He was outrageously generous—in bed and elsewhere. He kept his promises and he made her feel special and sexy and cherished. If he hadn't been able to afford a sapphire, he would have found another way to make her feel as though she was incredibly important to him, of that she had no doubt.

He was important to her. Did he know that?

Sliding her fingers into his hair, she leaned forward and set her mouth to his, trying to make him feel the love that was brimming out of her. She didn't know what the hidden sadness in him was, or what made him cynical or who had deliberately hurt him, but she wanted to heal all of that. The only way she knew to do it was to love him. To pour her feelings over him and dispel all his inner shadows with the golden light that glowed from the depths of her heart.

His breath hissed in and his fingertips bit through the downy skirt. She thought for a moment that he was going to move her off him, as though she was touching some part of him that was too raw.

Then a groan rattled deep in his chest. His hands found her breasts through the cashmere and his thumbs stroked against her nipples.

It was good, so good, but also a tiny bit painful. Not physically. It was painful to love him this much and not know how he felt about her. She wanted to tell him how she felt, but feared he would push her away if she did.

So she showed him. She burrowed her hand beneath her skirt and found his fly.

He bunched her skirt up and out of the way, then ran his finger beneath the placket of the tanga she wore. When she was stroking his steely erection, he moved the silk aside and helped her guide his tip to her entrance.

With a small shudder, she sank upon him. The anxiety of not being able to fully reach him dissipated when they were like this—not just joined physically, but connected on a deeper level. When he caressed her, he seemed to know where and how she needed it. When she pressed her mouth to his, their kiss ebbed and flowed between sweet and passionate, inciting and easing, then inflaming again.

They had made love only a couple of hours ago, much like this, so it shouldn't have felt this urgent. At first, it was simply pleasure and desire building at its own pace. They barely moved as they sought skin and ran their mouths into each other's necks and exchanged wordless praise and appreciation.

But for some reason his talk of things ending in pain and loss played in her ears like a ticking clock. She didn't want him to be right. She wanted them fused indelibly for the rest of their lives. She began to move with more purpose, as though she could forge a more permanent connection through force of will.

Her clamor seemed to ignite something similar in him. His kiss grew harder. Hungrier. His hands clamped onto her hips, urging her to take him deeper. Her breathing grew erratic and she clung to the back of the sofa as she rode him, feeling as though she raced toward a paradise that could turn out to be a mirage.

It was real, though. It had to be, because orgasm was slamming into her and his arms were folding around her, crushing her as he threw back his head and lifted his hips and shouted out her name.

Joyous pleasure cascaded through her, but so did something else. Fear.

She folded onto him and closed her eyes, suffused with bliss, but also a sense of being stalked. Of the future being uncertain and clouded and dark.

When she turned her mouth against the side of his face, his profile was grave, making her wonder if he felt that same lack of permanence, too.

They flew to Athens on the morning of the twenty-seventh. Eloise's mother had invited them to marry in her villa on the morning of the twenty-eighth. Since it was the home Eloise had grown up in, she thought it would feel as though Ilias were with them in spirit. Konstantin said he was happy to indulge her and her mother.

Lilja had been texting a lot more than normal, seeming to have reclaimed her phone for wedding plans. She was determined to make Eloise's day as special as possible and was fussing over every decision from flowers to music, from wedding breakfast to photo sitting. She even wanted Eloise's approval on her mother-of-the-bride dress.

Antoine was still managing to be a pain, though, now putting all his energy into stonewalling Konstantin.

"I haven't even asked him for the audit I want," Konstantin said with disgust. "He refuses to give my team contact info for his lawyers and accountants. Their request for a list of assets that belong to you, to include in our prenup, is being ignored altogether."

"Because there aren't any," Eloise pointed out.

"Then he should say that, shouldn't he?" Konstantin was no longer the lover she'd been pre-honeymooning with on Crete. He was crisp-voiced and hardened as he changed into a suit of charcoal armor.

"I was thinking of booking a massage after my fitting." She'd had a limited selection for wedding outfits since she was marrying so quickly, but Ghaliya had found her an elegant skirt suit that only needed a tuck and hemming. The seamstress would be here soon. "I could ask for a his-and-hers session this afternoon?"

"No. I hate people touching me."

She blinked, shocked as much by his blunt, vehement tone as the words.

He checked himself and a curl of irony arrived on the line of his stern mouth.

"I mean strangers, obviously. I'm addicted to your touch."

He came across to set a hand on her hip and drop a tender kiss on her mouth. "I have meetings with Nemo all day, anyway. Book something for yourself if you want to."

"Maybe I can talk Mom into joining me at a spa for a few hours. I don't know how else to pry Antoine away from her." He was like a lamprey.

"I'll send the car back so it's here for you if you decide to go out."

"Thank you."

Konstantin left and Eloise sighed in loss, finding this return to reality very jarring. Life was so much simpler when they made love, then made coffee. He worked off his laptop while she played piano. Maybe they walked after lunch or drove around the island before returning home to make love again. It had been bliss.

It had been impossible to have doubts about their future when she was with him all the time, drinking in his attention and affection.

She called her mother and wasn't surprised when the call was not picked up. She texted her an invitation to the spa and received a reply that had to be from Antoine.

Going to the bank today.

To get the ring from Petros? Eloise wondered. She could only imagine how that was sitting with Antoine.

Purely to let him know she wasn't fooled, she texted back.

Are you taking her or are you meeting with Konstantin?

He left her on Read, the jerk. He probably deleted it on that end, too, so her mother wouldn't see it. Eloise had lost her ability to give him the benefit of the doubt and was starting to think she would have to have a more serious chat with her mother.

What a dreadful thought. She'd wait until the wedding was out of the way, she decided. Not only would her mother have that happy memory, but Eloise would feel more secure in her own position and ability to support her.

The seamstress arrived and Eloise was tied up for the next hour. She was about to settle in for a relaxing hour of playing piano when Konstantin called to snap, "The car is waiting downstairs for you. I need you to meet me at your mother's."

"Is she okay? I thought Antoine was taking her to the bank."

"They're going to the *bank*? When? Which one?" He swore and told someone to, "Get that notice to all of those institutions. Immediately. I'm sure your mother is fine," he told Eloise, but his voice was steely and cold. "I'll find out where they're going and have the car bring you to me there. Leave as soon as you can."

"O—" he'd already hung up "—kay."

What on earth had he found out?

CHAPTER FOURTEEN

KONSTANTIN'S INNER WARRIOR was already agitated. Seeing Eloise enter the lobby of the bank only riled his inner protector more. He wanted to shout and clatter his shield in warning against anyone who might dare to threaten her.

He wanted to kill the man who had.

Despite her worried expression, Eloise was her beautiful self. Her dark hair bounced in waves that framed her face as she moved with purpose toward him, looking confident in her double-breasted coatdress over heeled boots.

She had blossomed in this short time with him, not only reverting to the cheeky young woman he'd known in the past, but growing past her into a sophisticated woman who made his insides twist with admiration and pride.

In this moment, however, all he could see was the thin ill-fitting elf suit she'd been wearing when she'd been scraping by in New York—thanks to Antoine's machinations.

"The manager put them in a VIP lounge next to the vault," Konstantin said, nodding curtly at their escort to take them there.

"What happened?" she asked in the elevator.

"I finally spoke to Cyrus. He's standing by to talk with your mother." He slid a look to the bank employee, reluctant to elaborate until they had privacy. "It won't fall to you to tell her."

"Tell her what?" Her eyes widened in alarm, but the doors

opened. They were escorted down a carpeted hall, through an open cage door, and into another anteroom where Antoine and her mother were sipping coffee.

"Darling!" Lilja stood, smiling with surprised pleasure as she stepped forward to hug Eloise. "What are you doing here? You're not putting my ring directly into your own box. No. It hasn't seen the sun in years. I want you to *wear* it."

"Actually…um… I'm not sure why we're here?" Eloise looked to Konstantin.

"Neither am I," Antoine said with cold precision, holding Konstantin's hate-filled glare with a staggering amount of audacity.

My fault, Konstantin realized with a fresh kick of guilt.

His neglect of these two women had allowed Antoine to believe he could not only get away with what he'd done, but that he still might.

"I apologize for the delay, Madame Roussea." The bank manager entered. He dismissed the other employee with a nod, then addressed Lilja. "I've had an urgent call from our head of security. He's requesting you thoroughly examine the contents of your safety deposit box while you're here to ensure the inventory is exactly as you expect it to be."

"Goodness…" Lilja touched her collar and looked at all of them in turn. "Has there been a robbery?"

"No," the manager assured with a calming smile. "Our hope is that this is a false alarm. Will you come with me, please?"

Antoine was sending daggers into Konstantin from his narrowed eyes. Eloise looked as apprehensive as her mother. The room was filled with a charged silence.

"Take your time," Konstantin said to Lilja, finding as calm a tone as he could. "We'll stay here with Antoine. I need to speak with him, anyway."

Still faltering with confusion, Lilja followed the bank manager out.

Konstantin pressed the door closed and pinned the older man with his contemptuous glare.

"I suppose you think you've gained the upper hand in some way?" Antoine sneered.

"Not me, no. My fiancée is the one with all the power here. Even more when she turns twenty-five and is entitled to become cotrustee of Lilja's fortune."

"I didn't want to believe he was that rotten." Eloise grappled for the back of the nearest chair.

Konstantin took a quick step to grasp under her elbow, bracing her.

"Until then, you only have the privilege of consultation and the right to demand a full audit if you feel there is just cause," he explained. "I would say there's more than just cause, seeing as Antoine has been withholding your living allowance and all the statements and notifications that you ought to be receiving."

"Is that why you wanted to marry me off to Edoardo?" she asked Antoine with outrage.

"Now you know why *he* wants to marry you," Antoine scoffed, pointing at Konstantin.

"Nice try," Konstantin snorted, but was aware of his hand tightening incrementally on Eloise's arm, feeling under threat at a very primeval level. "I only found out about this today. Cyrus was surprised you didn't know about these arrangements," he continued explaining to Eloise. "He sent a letter to you at your mother's home when he retired, outlining everything in detail. I'm guessing it was waylaid." Konstantin curled his lip with disgust as he looked to the reason for the letter going astray.

Antoine was stiff and watchful, mouth twitching into a snarl.

"She wasn't even coming home," Antoine said as though it was a sensible defense of his actions. "She was behaving as erratically as a drug addict. I was protecting Lilja's fortune from someone who was not responsible enough to use that money wisely. Now she's marrying *you*? How well do you think that will play in court?"

Antoine's derisive tone was a poison-tipped arrow directly into Konstantin's chest. He shouldn't have been surprised. This particular secret reared its head occasionally, but it always leaked toxins throughout his whole body, turning it to stone. He only wished he'd taken his chance when he'd had it. Eloise had asked him a few days ago, and he'd turned away from the opportunity to bare all. He hadn't wanted to ruin the day.

Instead, it would ruin her view of him.

He had the old sense of holding something he had desperately wanted and having it snatched from his grasp. Again.

"I do my homework, too." Antoine's mouth wore a smile that was nothing but a denigrating stretch of his lips. It sent a chill of premonition through Eloise's nerves, curdling her breakfast in her stomach.

"See if your mother—" Konstantin began, but Antoine spoke over him in a tone of evil satisfaction.

"His father murdered his mother. Has he told you that?"

Eloise had started to obey the nudge of Konstantin's hand.

Antoine's shocking statement was so cold and unexpected, so gratingly harsh while delivered so conversationally, she felt as though she'd been struck. Her ears buzzed and her skin turned to ice.

She turned back to see Konstantin retreating into the furthest depths of himself, presenting only a granite shell and the radiation of hatred directed toward her stepfather.

The crackle of danger between the men had her flight-

or-fight response activating, sending stinging adrenaline through her limbs.

"He died in prison. Violently." Antoine continued to turn the knife. "It was all covered up by his grandfather, but that's where he comes from. Do you really want to tie yourself to a man like that? Is that the kind of man you want to *sleep* next to?"

Konstantin's hands had been all over her for days, but that wasn't why Eloise felt so sick right now. No, it was the vileness of Antoine dragging up something so painful and leaving it like entrails in the middle of the floor.

"You think you're the first to throw that in my face?" Konstantin said with icy disdain. "Or that it gives you any leverage over me? Eloise is the one with the power right now. Cyrus has already sworn a statement. My lawyers are sending notices recommending all of Lilja's accounts be frozen until the appropriate trustee is identified. If you've been squirreling funds to other accounts, it will come to light."

"And you'll do what?" Antoine spat in her direction. "You can't charge her husband with stealing from their common property. She was of sound mind when she put me in charge. You have nothing and you'll get nothing. All you'll do is break her heart."

She would. Eloise knew from experience how awful this would become and was already sick as she absorbed that she would have to do it again. It killed her that she would have to shatter what peace and comfort her mother had managed to find these last years, but she was seeing that it was a horrible illusion, anyway.

"I'm going to tell her that you don't deserve her because you don't."

Antoine puffed up and Konstantin stepped between them.

The door opened behind them and her mother came in, still flustered.

"Everything was fine," she said with a shaken smile. "I'm not sure what the fuss was about. The manager said he would be in touch soon with more information. What, um… Is everything all right?" She flicked her gaze around the room. The worried lines in her expression etched themselves deeper.

"*Parfait*," Antoine lied smoothly. "We've come to a gentleman's agreement. I told you lawyers weren't necessary. Shall we go?"

"Not yet. I have to give Eloise the ring. Look at it." Her mother smiled mistily as she showed the platinum set diamond on her hand. "I forgot how much I loved it."

"Keep it on, Mom. I'm taking you home." Eloise's voice shook as hard as the rest of her. Everything within her wanted to run from this moment. She had hoped to never go through it again, but… "Antoine isn't coming. He's not the man you think he is."

"They're not marrying," Antoine blurted with a cruel bare of his teeth. "Once you hear why, you'll question all of this."

Eloise opened her mouth, appalled he would use Konstantin's past as a weapon.

Before she could protest that learning about Konstantin's past didn't change her view of him, Konstantin spoke.

"We don't need to marry. Not anymore. Not when Eloise has money and power of her own."

His blunt words landed straight in the middle of her heart, shattering it like glass.

"I'll keep him here," Konstantin said in her direction, without actually looking at her. "He can either give me a list of the relevant accounts and assets, or he can give them to the police. I have all the time in the world for him to make that decision."

"What on earth? Eloise, tell me that…?" Lilja looked with agonized eyes from her husband to Konstantin's grim expression to Eloise.

Regret rose to choke her voice as Eloise said, "I'm sorry, Mom. Let's go home and talk. We'll call Cyrus and he'll explain." As she nudged her mother out the door in front of her, she told Antoine, "Your suitcases will be on the stoop in an hour. Don't come into the house."

Konstantin entered the villa he'd only been in a handful of times. He and Ilias had both lived in Athens when not at school, but Konstantin wasn't a social person. He had sent regrets to all the parties Ilias had invited him to through their early years. Later, Ilias had been in the US, so they had met for the odd sporting event or a beer if Konstantin happened to be there.

No, the last time he'd been here was immediately after Ilias was laid to rest. Konstantin had stood on the periphery while people ate finger food and made small talk. Eloise had looked a lot like she did now—as though the life force had been drained out of her.

That was his fault. He didn't regret telling her the truth about Antoine, but he would always regret that she had had to hear about his parents the way she had.

"Mom's lying down," she said, hugging herself as she met him in the parlor. "She's upset, obviously. I should have told her that Antoine had left me stuck in New York, but..." She rubbed her brow. "He had her convinced that I was growing up and leaving the nest so she didn't question it too much. Cyrus has encouraged us to pursue a proper investigation, but he doubts there'll be much fallout for Antoine beyond embarrassment, since Mom was in her right mind when she gave him control."

"I should have checked on you both a lot sooner. That will always sit on my conscience."

"Don't—I don't want to be anything on your conscience, Konstantin. I would hope I'm more than a duty or obligation to you by now?" Her brow pleated as she searched his expression.

He looked away, unable to express what she was to him because he could already feel that fragile connection between them thinning and fraying.

"The wedding is off." He stated it first, because he knew it to be true. He had known it when Antoine brought up his past.

Agonized helplessness flashed across her expression, but she didn't contradict him.

"Mom's a wreck and she's literally the only person I would want there. She'll need me for a while. Then I have this Gordian knot to untangle." She waved at the imaginary mountain of paperwork. "But that doesn't mean I don't want to marry you."

"This all happened very quickly." Ten days. He hadn't even been allotted his full twelve days. That was par for the course for him so he brushed aside how cheated he felt.

"Don't." She took a few faltering steps toward him. "Don't act like I was caught up in the moment. *I love you*, Konstantin. I've always loved you. You know that. I was hoping you were starting to love me, too."

He drew a breath that felt laced with arsenic. "You told me a few days ago that you had spent years idolizing someone who doesn't exist. What you're feeling is sexual desire and nostalgia and gratitude. It's not really love, Eloise."

"That's a horrible thing to say to someone. Do you realize that?" She moved so she was in his line of sight, but not close enough to touch. Her chin set with belligerence and her fists knotted at her sides. "Have your feelings toward me been equally superficial? Were you horny and mildly entertained and now you're bored so you're cutting things short?"

She was right. They were stooping to saying horrible things.

"Our marrying is one of those things that looks like it will work, but it never would have. I know what you want, Eloise. You want me to be emotionally accessible and I'm *not*. I would hurt you in the long run so let's end it now while the damage is minimal."

"How would you hurt me? You're not…violent." She swallowed the last word.

"No." Although he'd had a moment there with Antoine when he could have happily pushed him out a window. "And I'll do my best to quash it if Antoine tries to take my story to the press. I've done it before, but the day will come when it gets out. It's not something you want to be married to. You don't want it overshadowing your mother, either."

"Was that what you didn't want to tell me at Christmas?" she asked with such gentle care that his heart contracted.

"Yes." And he didn't want to tell her now, but he would give her the bones of it. "My father was not unlike Antoine, capable of charm to hide the fact he was a monster. My mother kept seeing him even after my grandfather expressly forbade it. When she got pregnant, they married and my father moved us to an isolated farm. He had violent outbursts that grew worse over time. She tried to leave, asked my grandfather for help, but he refused. He told her she'd made her bed."

"That's awful." She rubbed her chest.

"Yes. One day, he caught us trying to leave and really went after her. I got in the way and he knocked me across the cottage. I don't remember anything afterward except waking in the hospital to the news my mother was dead. My grandfather came to get me. I never saw my father again."

"Konstantin—"

He held up a hand to ward her off. "I'm not telling you this for sympathy, Eloise. I want you to understand why… God." He pinched the bridge of his nose. "I don't want to look back or talk about it or *build new memories* because those things don't *last*. I don't want to learn to care about someone only to have him crash his damned airplane. I don't want to fall in love with someone—" he pointed accusingly at her "—and have her taken from me."

"Nobody is taking me. You're pushing me away."

"I'm taking control of the inevitable."

"You don't know it's inevitable. You're making it happen so you can prove to yourself that you're right." Her mouth quivered as she removed her ring and offered it. "But I won't force you to stay in a relationship you don't want. I've always known my love for you was unrequited. I won't keep fooling myself that you'll come around. At least I tried. I'll be able to move on now. Thank you for helping us. We'll be okay now."

Would they? He wouldn't.

"That's yours." He ignored the ring and walked out, heart on a pike. He was so nauseated he nearly threw up in the car.

CHAPTER FIFTEEN

AFTER A NIGHT where Eloise and her mother both spent hours crying out their broken hearts, Nemo turned up.

"I know the wedding is off," he said when Eloise started to cry. "No, *kyría*, I'm here with a press release. Can you review it, please?"

Konstantin had drafted a statement that the wedding had been postponed due to a family concern. Since that was followed almost immediately by a statement that Lilja was divorcing Antoine, the gossip around the canceled nuptials was minimal.

Nemo then stuck around to speak with Cyrus and assist with revoking Antoine's rights to the trust. He made phone calls and canceled bank accounts and issued notices to expel Antoine from all of Lilja's properties—including the house in Nice. Technically, they both owned that one, but it was now a contested asset in their divorce proceedings. Nemo also found her mother a good lawyer for that.

"We're monopolizing you," Eloise said when he continued to turn up even after they'd rung in the New Year. "Doesn't Konstantin need you?"

"One of my colleagues has taken over my position. Since I was familiar with your situation, I'm to assist you until you no longer need assistance. Also, because your accounts have been frozen until the audits can be conducted, *Kýrie* Galanis will cover your legal fees and any other expenses while you wait for access to your funds to be granted."

Of course, he would. She stifled a sigh of despair, angry with him for looking after them so well, but from a distance. Was he afraid to *accept* her love? Was that it? Had she smothered him? Or not given enough?

After so many years of fantasy, then having marriage to him within her grasp, she struggled to let go of the dream. She lay awake at night wishing she'd done this or that differently, but the reality was he didn't want to marry her. She had to accept that.

She only wished it didn't hurt *so much*.

"Did your tea go cold while you were speaking to your friend?" Nemo asked her mother. Lilja was making a face over the cup she'd just picked up. "Let me ask the kitchen to make you a fresh one."

"Thank you, Nemo." She handed over cup and saucer. "I have no idea how we would manage if you weren't here with us. I think poor Konstantin has lost himself an assistant."

Eloise choked on a small astonished laugh, her first shred of humor in a week. How had she and Ilias never realized their mother needed a male assistant?

Thankfully, Eloise was kept busy meeting with all the lawyers and accountants, hiring a cotrustee who would teach her the ropes of managing so much money, and realizing that she actually had a crap ton of allowance owed to her that needed investing. It was daunting, but she was glad to be distracted.

She was so distracted, in fact, that she didn't realize her period was late until she was two weeks overdue.

A visit to the doctor confirmed her pregnancy. She sat in the exam room for a good thirty minutes afterward, crying happy-sad tears. Her first instinct was to go directly to Konstantin and tell him, but she knew what would happen. He would feel obligated to marry her and she didn't want to put him in that position. She didn't want him to propose to her again for any reason except that he had fallen in love with her.

Ugh. She was still doing it: hoping.

She would have to tell him about the baby at some point, though. The prevailing advice was to wait twelve weeks before sharing this news. She didn't want him to get attached to this pregnancy, then suffer the loss if something happened—which was a very convenient rationalization for being a coward, she knew. But she didn't know if she could face him yet without falling apart. She missed him to the point that she ached from the moment she woke to the moment she slipped into unconsciousness. Then she cried in her sleep, missing him in her dreams.

She would never resist seeing him if she stayed in Athens. She'd only lasted this long because she remembered he'd had business in Singapore in January. Once he returned, the temptation to go to him would be overpowering.

"Mom, what do you think of a change in scenery?" she asked when she returned from the doctor. "I was thinking of applying to that music therapy program again."

"In New York? Well, yes, I've always wanted to spend more than a week or two there. What about Nemo? Can he accompany us?"

Nemo was delighted by the opportunity to spend an indefinite time in the Big Apple. His boyfriend was equally excited and planned to follow as soon as he worked out some wrinkles in his own professional life.

Within a week, they were in a leased Gramercy apartment with four bedrooms, a private terrace, daily housekeeping and an attached studio apartment for Nemo.

Eloise was accepted into the program, thanks to her previous audition, but more because money talked and she now had an abundance of it. Along with starting school, she quietly took her prenatal vitamins and found a midwife, still keeping her pregnancy to herself. She was dying to tell her mother, but she wanted to tell Konstantin first.

The longer she left it, the more daunting that prospect became. She wanted a full plan in place when she told him, one that allowed her to raise the baby alone, but still provided him as much access as he wanted. It would be pure torture to see him on what she suspected would be a daily basis, but somehow they would have to make it work.

The churn of anticipation and dread drove her to the piano every day where she poured out her turmoil of joy and longing, her anguish and all the love that refused to be doused.

In fact, her feelings for him grew a little more each day, just like their baby.

Konstantin tried to retreat into the skin of numbness he'd worn most of his life, but it was shredded beyond repair. His feelings for Eloise were too sharp. Too jagged and hot and extreme.

God, he missed her. How had she become such an integral part of his life in such a short time? It wasn't just the sex. That had been mind-altering, setting a bar that he doubted would ever be reached with anyone else, but he wasn't plagued by unmet carnal need. He was instead struck repeatedly by the emptiness of his days. Absence and meaninglessness hit him like an echo in a cavern, leaving him feeling as though he was lost in the dark, bouncing into rough granite walls.

He woke to a cold empty bed. He ate his meals alone, finding no enjoyment in whatever went into his mouth. The silence was worst of all. The cruel lack of music, the absence of laughter. He even missed her innocuous questions about whether he wanted chicken for lunch.

His meetings in Asia should have been a welcome distraction, but he resented them. He hated every minute of being so far from her, but on his return to Athens, he learned she'd gone to New York. That somehow tore a fresh hole in the fabric of his existence.

He *hated* this feeling. It was the one he'd been trying to avoid, this sense of something having been taken from him. Of having a great hole within him that couldn't be filled.

Work had always been a useful panacea, but it did little for him these day except provide him with a small satisfaction that he was creating an additional layer of security for Eloise and her mother. When he advised his lawyers the wedding was off, he told them to continue updating his will to make Eloise his beneficiary.

He left her number in his phone as his emergency contact because, if he wound up on death's doorstep, he wanted her face to be the last thing he saw. Her voice to be the last thing he heard.

Would she even turn up?

I've always known my love was unrequited. I won't keep fooling myself that you'll come around.

Had he killed whatever she might have felt for him? *Was* he creating the very reality he feared so he could face it and move past it, rather than have it hang over his head? Because he didn't think he'd ever get over her absence from his life.

He desperately wanted the reassurance he hadn't hurt her too badly, but Nemo refused to be much of a spy, saying only a circumspect, "Legal hiccups have been minimal. Things are progressing."

"But how are Eloise and Lilja coping?"

"As well as could be expected, under the circumstances. *Kýrie*? I'm not sure how to broach this. Lilja—she asked me to call her that. She's made me an offer of employment. It's been such an honor to work for you. I wouldn't want you to think I'm ungrateful…"

Konstantin tuned out the rest, letting the young man say

his piece before saying, "The door remains open if things change."

They ended the call and Konstantin felt as though one more thread that joined him to Eloise had been snipped. It stung like hell.

Which was why he was so surprised when Nemo contacted him a few weeks later, asking when he might be visiting New York next. Lilja wanted to have lunch with him.

Konstantin hadn't been planning anything, but booked a trip immediately, concerned.

It was a sunny February day when he met his almost mother-in-law at a restaurant located one hundred stories in the air, overlooking the city and the Hudson River.

"Lilja." He was startled to feel such an intense rush of warmth when he saw her, as though he'd missed her when, much as he liked and respected her, he didn't know her well. He didn't have any reason to feel attached to her, except through her children. "How are you?"

"I'm well. You?" Her eyes, so much like Eloise's, searched his, making him feel transparent.

"Fine," he insisted briskly. "How is Eloise?" he asked once they were seated. "I was concerned that you wanted to see me."

"She's not ill or injured, if that's what you're asking, but she is the reason I wanted to see you."

"You're worried about her?" he guessed, suffering a stab of guilt. He had hurt her. He knew he had.

"Only insofar as any mother would be worried when she realizes her daughter has stopped drinking and turns green at the smell of bacon. I couldn't stand the stuff myself when I was carrying her."

"She's pregnant?" He nearly fell out of his chair.

"I'm assuming so. Thank you." She accepted her mimosa as it was delivered.

He drained the scotch that was set in front of him. The alcohol burned all the way into the back of his skull and down into his chest.

"Why hasn't she told me?" It was the most intense rejection, the worst kick in the teeth, he could have imagined.

I'll be able to move on now, she'd said.

Apparently, she'd meant it.

"You tell me." She looked to the diamond on her hand. It was the one from the bank, now worn in place of the rings that Antoine had given her. "I thought she had with you what I had with Petros. He was the love of my life." She sighed wistfully.

Konstantin signaled for another drink, then looked out the window, wondering if she had requested this meeting specifically to torture him.

"I'm deeply sorry that Antoine brought up your parents, Konstantin. When I realized afterward that that was what he was referring to, when he threatened you at the bank, I was sickened."

His stomach heaved and a clammy sweat rose on his skin. "Eloise told you?"

"No. She only said Antoine had threatened to expose something private that you don't like to talk about, but I was living in Greece with a son your age when it happened," she reminded him gently. "Word got around and for me, it struck close to home. I came from a troubled family, too. One I don't like to revisit, either."

His second drink arrived and he ignored it in favor of reaching out to squeeze Lilja's hand, hating to think of this delicate, infinitely kind, beautiful woman being at the hands of someone cruel.

She held onto his fingers tightly while a smile touched her mouth. Then she released him to sip her mimosa, blinking and drawing a slow breath, as though gathering her composure.

"I don't know if you ever told Ilias about any of it. I never said anything to him about you, but he said to me early in your friendship that you were the only boy at school who knew what it felt like to lose a parent and not have a father. It gave me some comfort that you had each other." Her brow flexed with poignancy. "I didn't know what to do with him back then. Losing Petros was devastating for both of us, but Ilias was so determined to grow up and take his father's place. I know I leaned on him too heavily, but when I didn't ask his advice, he was annoyed. There was no winning."

"He did insist on looking after people, whether they asked for help or not," Konstantin recalled with rueful affection.

"Didn't he?" She brightened, then grew misty. "That was Petros coming out in him. I used to wish Petros had lived to meet Eloise, so he could see what a protector Ilias turned into around her. Silly, right? If Petros had lived, I wouldn't have had her. That would be a crime because she's been such a bright light in my life. Effervescent and cuddly, spilling her love and life and music all over the place. I spoiled her. I know I did. I wanted so badly to keep her…" she cupped her hands into a tiny sheltering dome "…protected. Unstruck by life. But that's not possible."

Her elbow went onto the table and she tucked her chin into her hand, looking out the window.

"It's not," he agreed gravely. "And God, Lilja. You've had so many blows yourself. How do you carry on and remain so hopeful, knowing you could lose everything at any time? When you have lost so much?"

"Do you refuse to listen to a song because you know it will come to an end?" she asked with a wry smile and sad eyes. "Even the Parthenon will eventually be nothing but dust. You have to enjoy something while you're able *because* it's temporary. And yes, sometimes you might make a mistake and fall for the wrong person." Her mouth pursed with heartbreak and consternation. "I've done more than my share of that. I want to believe the best in people. I want to feel *loved*. Eloise has borne the brunt of my poor judgment too many times. It doesn't occur to me that anyone would hurt her, though. Why would they want to?" Her brow pleated with incomprehension. "She's so easy to love."

"She is." The words vibrated from behind his sternum, more a feeling than actual words, but they refused to be kept inside him any longer.

"Then why are you hurting her, Konstantin?" she asked with distress. "Why aren't you loving her while you have the chance?"

The whole building disappeared from beneath him and he felt himself plummeting to the ground.

He didn't have an answer. In fact, he didn't know why he was hurting himself.

Eloise's assignment was to learn and perform a song for her class that expressed an emotional conflict in her life.

She didn't know whether she would go through with playing this. Her classmates seemed nice, but they were still strangers. Did she really want to bare her soul to them? It was the point to feel vulnerable, she knew, but this was still so raw.

At least for the moment, this was only for her. She was alone in Music Room Two, begging the piano keys to tell her how to mend a broken heart.

She hummed through the lyrics about stopping the sun from shining and the rain from falling, then let herself be swept into the sweet, poignant, "La, la, la, la, la, la…"

The next lyrics were too painful to sing. She slipped back into humming for the final plea for help mending her heart and learning to live again.

She ended on a wistful fade into the last soft notes.

And heard a shaken sigh behind her.

She twisted on the bench, startled yet not, because she'd conjured him, hadn't she? He was the only thing that would heal this fractured heart of hers.

He looked beautiful. He always did. Even jet-lagged, with dark circles under his eyes and that shadow coming in on his jaw, he was sexy and mesmerizing. If he'd been wearing a tie, it had since been discarded. His collar was open, his hair tousled by the wind.

"Why didn't you tell me?" he asked in a voice thickened by emotion.

"That I got into this program? I thought Nemo would. Or that it would be obvious that that's why we were here in New York." She rose and nervously gathered her sheet music into its folder, using the moment with her back to him to pull her emotions back into their compartment. Or at least try, not that it was really possible around him.

"Your mom told me you were here." He was closer.

She slid out from behind the bench and turned to face him.

He was taking her in with a gaze that ate her up from ponytail to sneakers, snagging on the sleeves of her flannel top tied around her waist, over the denim skirt and ribbed long-sleeved top.

She hugged her folder in front of her. She was only eight weeks, not showing yet, but she felt as though her belly were round and obvious.

"When did you talk to her?" she asked in a voice strained by the joy of seeing him and the panic accosting her as she tried to figure out whether she ought to tell him or—

"She invited me to lunch. She thinks you're pregnant."

"Oh." She slumped onto the keys—pretty much a capital offence—and popped off before the keys had finished resounding. Her body went hot. Her mind scattered.

The only thing she could think was, *I'm not ready for this.*

"Are you?"

"I wanted to tell you myself," she said into the folder she was still clutching.

"Then why haven't you?"

"Because you'll say we should get married."

His breath choked out as though she'd kicked him in the stomach.

"Not because…" She lifted her head and stepped forward, holding out a hand in plea. "I was planning to tell you after I've had my twelve-week scan. It's a lot less likely anything might go wrong after that so… I was trying to keep you from having to go through something painful if…" She trailed off and shrugged.

"So you would have gone through that *alone*?" He swore and ran his hand down his face. "I told you to call me if you needed anything."

"I didn't. I'm fine."

"Are you?" He raked his gaze over her again, then waved at the piano. "Because your song made me feel like my heart was being carved out with a rusty spoon."

"It's supposed to," she mumbled, not entirely displeased to hear that.

Beyond the door, laughing voices walked by.

"Let's go to my apartment so we can talk properly," he said.

She pushed her folder into her shoulder bag, but when he reached to take it, he caught her wrist and stared at the ring.

"If you don't want to marry me, why do you still wear it?"

"To keep men from hitting on me." That was true, but the least of the reasons she kept wearing it. She liked feeling connected to him.

Yes, she was still harboring those old dreams, even though he had pushed her away. She handed him the bag and pushed her hand into her pocket.

His car was outside, but they didn't talk on the short ride.

Walking into the penthouse was surreal. She'd been here for less than twenty-four hours two months ago, but it felt as though it had been years since she was here. At the same time, it was homey and familiar, as though she was returning to where she ought to be, maybe because it was stamped with his personality and everything about him felt like home.

Then she spotted the piano that hadn't been there before. *Oh, Konstantin.*

"Look." She turned to face him. "I have no intention of keeping this baby from you—"

"Only yourself?" he bit out.

"That's not fair. You didn't want me," she reminded him. "And now you do because I'm pregnant? Listen to how insulting that is. I have loved you my whole life, Konstantin. I deserve to be loved back."

"You do," he agreed. "I do love you, Eloise."

"Oh, *don't!*" she cried, hurt beyond measure that he would lie to her after everything else.

"I also deserve that skepticism," he said gravely. "Refusing to say it and walking away when we could have been together all this time wasn't fair to you. It wasn't fair to us." He ran his hand over his face and took a few restless steps across the room. "It felt too good, Eloise. Hope is not something that ever worked out for me. Things would get better with my father and I would hope. He'd get a job and I'd get a gift and I would hope. My mother would pack our things and we would try to leave and I *hoped.*"

She bit her lip, wanting to rush toward him, but his tension held her off. She stayed still and quiet and let him spill out what he needed to say.

"I went to live with my grandfather and there was food and peace and I thought that would be my life, but I was sent to a bloody boarding school where it was a different kind of

chaos. I mastered my schoolwork and thought I'd be an architect like my friend, but my grandfather had a stroke and…"
His shaken sigh spoke of untold pain. "I honestly thought I
was headed back to square one at that point. That all was
lost. Again. But Ilias stepped in. He made me believe there
were people in this life who cared about me. That *I* could
have good things. Then he *died*."

Oh, Konstantin. She swallowed his name and hurried to
brush away her tears, stifling her sobs, not wanting to distress him, but he was ripping out her heart.

"And you. All you did was look at me with hope. As
though I could make you happy. I don't know what happiness *is*. I've had a fleeting glimpse of it here and there, but it
was always gone as quickly as it arrived. I don't know *how* to
be happy. I don't trust it. I didn't trust us." He turned to face
her, expression creased with remorse. "So I threw us away."

"I never meant for you to think I expect to be happy all the
time. I know life is messy and painful. Look at this baby." She
waved at her middle. "I'm ecstatic about it, but the best-case
scenario is that it's going to hurt like hell when it arrives. I
don't expect you to make me happy, Konstantin. I just want
you to be with me when I am. To share it with me."

He closed his eyes, seeming to take a minute to absorb that.

"Do you really want that?" he asked solemnly. "Because
I want that, too. I want to be with you even when you're not
happy. I can't stand to think of you hurting and alone. I want
to be there to hold you and help you and somehow find our
way back to the good times because I've realized that even
if those happy times only last a minute, it's a minute worth
fighting for. I want those minutes, Eloise. If I miss another
one, I think it might actually kill me."

"Oh, Konstantin." Her mouth wouldn't form the smile that
wanted to bloom. Her lips were quivering because she was

too moved. "You realize this is one of those minutes right now? That I'm really, really happy just because you're *here*?"

He swept forward and gathered her up so she was eye to eye with him. She looped her arms behind his neck and their noses grazed and her legs were draped against his. He started to kiss her, then drew back. "Is this okay—?"

"It's perfect. I love you."

"I love you, too."

The press of his mouth against hers was so sweet it was painful. They held it to just that, a press, waiting for the agony to pass before the joy of reunion tangled with need and combusted into deprivation. In mutual attunement, they moaned and began to kiss hungrily. Passionately.

As he walked up the stairs with her in his arms, she peppered kisses against his throat.

She smiled when he set her on her feet in his massive bedroom. "Are you going to throw these away while I'm asleep?" she asked as she began to undress.

"Whatever it takes to keep you here for the rest of our lives." He paused in stripping his own clothes to throw back the covers.

Seconds later, they were under the sheets, naked bodies brushing and hands moving with familiarity over each other. She paused to trace his ear and study his rugged features, savoring this moment.

"I'll be gentle," he promised.

"I'm not worried, just letting myself feel it. This is my dream come true. I really, really love you, Konstantin. Don't break my heart again."

"I won't. I swear." His expression flexed with emotion. "I really love you, too. I'll spend the rest of my life proving it."

They kissed again and this time, the need to be reunited in the most basic way overtook them. They shifted and caressed. She opened her legs and he slid between them. His flesh prodded hers and found a warm, sleek welcome. They both sighed.

When he was deep inside her, he rolled, bringing her atop him and they lay like that a long time, kissing and caressing and simply reveling in the joy of being intimately connected.

All good things come to an end, though. And when they rolled apart a few minutes later, still panting and breathless, they smiled at each other because, really, it was only the beginning.

EPILOGUE

Five years later...

"KONSTANTIN," ELOISE WHISPERED and poked him in the side.

"Is Ilias up?" He yanked his head off his pillow and threw his leg toward the side of the bed. "I'll get him."

"No, shh. Look." She curled into him as she showed him the baby monitor where their four-year-old daughter, Rhea, was sneaking into Ilias's room. "Someone can't wait for Christmas."

"This one is for you." Rhea dropped a wrapped gift over the rail of the crib. "I got it for you."

"It's not even six," Konstantin said with wincing glance at the clock, but he shifted so he could get his arm more securely around Eloise while they watched their children.

Eighteen-month-old Ilias was sitting up, blinking with sleepy confusion in the glow of the night-light. His sister climbed onto the hamper and into the crib with him. Once she was inside, Ilias grinned and crawled toward her. They shared a little cuddle, something they did every morning, but it still made Eloise clasp a hand over her heart.

"God, they're magic," Konstantin whispered, even though the kids couldn't hear them. "They're the best thing you've ever given me. Except you, of course." He kissed her brow.

"Back at you, handsome." She curled her leg onto his strong thigh, sighing with bliss.

Aside from caesarian deliveries due to late term pre-eclampsia, both pregnancies had been uneventful, with the added bonus and delightful coincidence of their son being born on Konstantin's birthday. Konstantin didn't like to tempt fate, though. Much as he adored their children, he'd had a vasectomy and they'd agreed that if they wanted more children in the future, they would foster or adopt.

"You can open it," Rhea was saying to Ilias, pushing the present she'd brought him toward him. "Like this." She picked at the paper to start a tear, showing him.

Ilias tore little bits, making Rhea giggle.

"No, like this." She showed him how to get a longer strip.

There was some rustling and tussling and more giggling from both of them until the box was revealed.

"You did it!" She clapped her hands.

"Dit!" Ilias copied her, grinning and bouncing on his knees.

"Do you want to play with it? It's a *xylófono*."

"They already have one," Konstantin scolded good-naturedly.

"*Only* one. Rhea wants to play duets."

"Lucky us."

Eloise grinned, but their daughter's little fingers hadn't left the piano from the time she'd crawled over and pulled herself up on it. Ilias was equally fond of sitting with Mamá to help her play. Konstantin always listened with patient appreciation to any recital and encouraged both children when they showed any type of curiosity, musical or otherwise.

Ilias watched his sister, but Rhea set the box down in frustration.

"We need Bampá to open it," she said with a pout.

"Bampá." Ilias promptly stood against the rail and called out more imperiously, "Bampá!"

"Christmas morning is officially here," Konstantin said

wryly, rolling to send tingling sensations down her back with the sweep of his hand as he pressed her to the long stretch of his warm frame. "I was hoping we'd start the day the way we usually do, but traditions change, hmm?"

"The good news is, we can start a tradition of napping in the afternoon. We're all going to need one."

"I like the sound of that." He brushed the tip of his nose against hers, then touched a kiss to her lips. "Merry Christmas, *angele mou*. Have I told you lately that I love you?"

"Not since last night, but—"

"Bampá!"

"But you can make it up to me later," she assured him with a chuckle.

They climbed out of bed to dress and spend Christmas with their children.

* * * * *

Were you swept off your feet by
Husband for the Holidays*?*

Then don't miss these other dazzling stories
by Dani Collins!

Awakened on Her Royal Wedding Night
The Baby His Secretary Carries
The Secret of Their Billion-Dollar Baby
Her Billion-Dollar Bump
Marrying the Enemy

Available now!

COMING SOON!

We really hope you enjoyed reading this book.
If you're looking for more romance
be sure to head to the shops when
new books are available on

Thursday 21st November

To see which titles are coming soon, please visit

millsandboon.co.uk/nextmonth

MILLS & BOON

MILLS & BOON®

Coming next month

RESISTING THE BOSSY BILLIONAIRE
Michelle Smart

She stepped through the door. 'I am your employee. I have a contract that affords me rights.'

The door almost closed in his face. Almost as put-out at her failure to hold it open for him as he was by this bolshy attitude which, even by Victoria's standards, went beyond minor insubordination, Marcello decided it was time to remind her who the actual boss was and of her obligations to him.

'You cannot say you were not warned of what the job entailed when you agree to take it,' he said when he caught up with her in the living room. She was already at the door that would take her through to the reception room. 'It is why you are given such a handsome salary and generous perks.'

Instead of going through the door, she came to a stop and turned back round, folding her arms across her breasts. 'Quite honestly, Marcello, the way I'm feeling right now, I'd give the whole lot up for one lie-in. One lousy lie-in. That's all I wanted but you couldn't even afford me that, could you? I tell you what, stuff your handsome salary and generous perks – I quit.'

Continue reading
RESISTING THE BOSSY BILLIONAIRE
Michelle Smart

Available next month
millsandboon.co.uk

LET'S TALK

Romance

For exclusive extracts, competitions and special offers, find us online:

- **f** MillsandBoon
- **X** @MillsandBoon
- **◎** @MillsandBoonUK
- **♪** @MillsandBoonUK

Get in touch on 01413 063 232

For all the latest titles coming soon, visit
millsandboon.co.uk/nextmonth

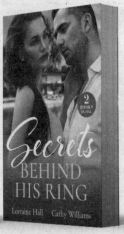